LOSING *the* MOON

LOSING *the* MOON

Patti Callahan Henry

NAL
ACCENT

NAL Accent
Published by New American Library, a division of
Penguin Group (USA) Inc., 375 Hudson Street, New York, New York 10014, U.S.A.
Penguin Group (Canada), 90 Eglinton Avenue East, Suite 700, Toronto,
Ontario M4P 2Y3, Canada (a division of Pearson Penguin Canada Inc.)
Penguin Books Ltd., 80 Strand, London WC2R 0RL, England
Penguin Ireland, 25 St. Stephen's Green, Dublin 2,
Ireland (a division of Penguin Books Ltd.)
Penguin Group (Australia), 250 Camberwell Road, Camberwell, Victoria 3124,
Australia (a division of Pearson Australia Group Pty. Ltd.)
Penguin Books India Pvt. Ltd., 11 Community Centre, Panchsheel Park,
New Delhi - 110 017, India
Penguin Group (NZ), 67 Apollo Drive, Rosedale, North Shore 0632,
New Zealand (a division of Pearson New Zealand Ltd.)
Penguin Books (South Africa) (Pty.) Ltd., 24 Sturdee Avenue,
Rosebank, Johannesburg 2196, South Africa

Penguin Books Ltd., Registered Offices: 80 Strand, London WC2R 0RL, England

First published by NAL Accent, an imprint of New American Library,
a division of Penguin Group (USA) Inc.

First Printing, May 2004
20   19   18   17   16

 REGISTERED TRADEMARK—MARCA REGISTRADA

LIBRARY OF CONGRESS CATALOGING-IN-PUBLICATION DATA:

Henry, Patti Callahan.
  Losing the moon / Patti Callahan Henry.
    p. cm.
  ISBN 978-0-451-21195-8
  1. Women college teachers—Fiction. 2. Parent and adult child—Fiction. 3. Middle aged
women—Fiction. 4. Married women—Fiction. 5. First loves—Fiction. I. Title.
  PS3608.E578L67 2004
  813'.6—dc22   2003024389

Set in Garamond Light
Designed by Eve L. Kirch

Printed in the United States of America

With immense love and admiration,
I dedicate this book
to Bonnie and George Callahan:
encouragers, prayer warriors, babysitters,
inspiration and most important—my parents.

Acknowledgments

Although a book is written in isolation, it is never written alone. My grateful appreciation spreads wide across the people in my life.

To my dearest friends who always believed and said, "Of course" (you know who you are); thank you for allowing me the space and time to fulfill my dream. Special thanks go to Sandee O, whose creative spirit is my inspiration, and to Susan Clark, whose generosity and inexhaustible service to others are amazing. I love you all.

Innumerable thanks go to some very special women in GRW—to Ann Howard White and Deborah Smith, who believed in me before I did; and gratitude to Dorene Graham, Pat Potter, Stephanie Bond and Haywood Smith.

Deep appreciation goes to my agent Kimberly Whalen. I am consistently thankful for her providential entrance into my life. I offer my gratitude for her enthusiasm and sharp sense of story. Her trust in me has allowed me to write this book from the deepest place of my heart.

I thank New American Library for their trust in me. Special thanks go to Serena Jones and to my extraordinary editor, Ellen Edwards, whose keen eye, patience and dedication to the written word have produced a novel that is deeper and more polished.

No acknowledgment would be complete without mentioning the support, love and undergirding of my family. To my sisters, Barbi and Jeannie, who believed and cried and encouraged. To Gwen and Anna, who believed. I love you.

My heart overflows with immeasurable love for my children—Meagan, Thomas and Rusk. They inspire me to want to be so much more than I am. Their towheaded beauty and fathomless love echo the God who designed them. To my husband, Pat, whose patience with his wife's dream allowed it to come true. All of you are my heart's beat.

And to my God in whom I live and move and have my being. If I write anything of worth, it is because His power flows through me. I thank Him for the gifts of story, of writing and of faith.

PART I

Here were vermin so muddled in mind, so passively responsive to environment, that it was very hard to raise them to a level of clarity and deliberateness at which mortal sin becomes possible.

—C. S. Lewis, *The Screwtape Letters*

The danger is that the soul should persuade itself that it is not hungry. It can only persuade itself of this by lying.

—Simone Weil

Part I

Chapter One

Torn pieces of sunlight whispered through aged moss, landed on a shattered log. The sea pounded on an unseen shore just steps beyond the dense maritime forest. Each crest and retreat of the waves matched Amy Reynolds' heartbeat—a beat she once believed sure and steady, a heart cleansed of Nick Lowry. But he resided in the unseen—the syncopated space between each beat, the secret she didn't hear, but knew existed.

Amy sat on the sea-aged fallen log, rested her head atop her knees and waited. She was now ready to hear what he had to say. Or she believed she was ready.

"All this time—all of it—I've been thinking of what to say to you. So many things to say to you." He touched her mouth, her bottom lip.

Her hands fluttered in the air, butterflies with nowhere to land.

He continued. "And now here you are and I can't find any of those words . . ." He closed his eyes. "Here you are, and all I want to do is touch that space below your throat."

He opened his eyes and gazed at her neck—heat flared with the memory of his touch.

Her fingers landed gently on the hollow dent between her collarbones. His hand reached to cover hers.

"There. The place your silver cross used to lie, move every time you breathed."

"I lost it," Amy whispered.

"Lost what?" He gripped her hand.

"That cross. . .you."

He moaned, bowed his head in what Amy thought might be prayer or defeat.

And all this time Amy had thought her life as neatly tucked and smooth as the vintage linen sheets on her bed; but wrinkles and folds hid beneath the surface.

The flaws of her life were covered like the thick white paint over the dirt-brown color the previous owner had painted her historic home, in the drowsy southern town where she lived with her husband and children. She'd applied another coat, and then another, until she was unknowingly suffocating in the layers of pretense.

Then Nick touched her. Then she lost the moon and crawled on her hands and knees to find it again.

Nick Lowry entered Amy Reynolds' life again on a day seductive in its ordinariness, lazy in its soft family comfort.

Late-autumn sun washed the parked sport-utility vehicles, motor homes and Coleman grills in a honeyed afternoon light. The pungent smell of barbecue and grill smoke mingled with the earth-warm aroma of crushed leaves. Every few minutes a stray leaf fell in the stagnant air, released of its own volition, not forced by any breeze from an atmosphere so still and full Amy felt as if she bathed in it rather than moved through it.

Through the afternoon Amy's limbs felt weighted and luxurious. Days like these—tepid fall days at Saxton University—brought to her heart the same impression every year: a longing—an odd misplaced sense of loss, yet also of promise. So it was a universal setup, her heart already languid and expectant.

Amy stood with her husband, Phil, on the same tailgating patch of grass they had for twenty-three years of home football games: a tradition of cheeseburgers, cold beer, potato salad, Chardonnay and old friends. Today was the day they would meet their son Jack's first serious girlfriend. Jack spoke little of this girlfriend and yet he talked much more of her than of anyone he'd dated. Amy only knew her first name—Lisbeth—and she thought the name presumptuous, uppity, as if the girl had named herself at birth.

On the two-hour drive to Saxton University from their small hometown of Darby, in south Georgia, Amy had leaned her head back on the headrest of the car, fought her never-ending battle with car sickness, held Phil's hand and mumbled, "What kind of name is Lisbeth?"

"I think it's German . . . maybe a form of Elizabeth."

"It sounds kinda snobby, don't you think?"

"Ame, let's not judge her before we meet her."

"You're right . . . you're right. I'm defensive already. Sorry. Jack is just so . . . special, so different, so much more . . . mature than other—"

"You wouldn't be a little prejudiced, now would you?" Phil squeezed her hand—playful, yet understanding her complete love for their son. It was the same way she loved her entire family, husband, son and daughter—her love a transforming filter to any average quality.

Phil pulled her hand to his mouth and kissed the back of it. "I agree with you, sweetie, but I'm also sure Jack's sound judgment of people has prevailed here. I can't wait to meet the girl who has finally stolen his heart."

Amy opened her eyes and glared at Phil. "She didn't steal anything yet."

"Ah, you didn't hear him on the phone."

Amy scrunched her nose at her husband. Phil was right. She was prejudging this girl whose last name she didn't even know. "Well, I wish we could've come last night. Her parents were here and they wanted us to go out to dinner."

"There was no way I could miss yesterday evening's meeting, Amy. We've been over this."

"I know, I know. Doesn't mean I don't wish you could've. Who works till eight o'clock on a Friday night?"

"My boss, and therefore me." Phil tightened his face the way he did when he felt she was questioning his work ethic. Raised in a strict home where work and obligation were the gods to bow to, he didn't understand her more laid-back, skip-work-for-family approach. Now was not the time to get into it.

"Well," she said, "my committee seems to be making progress. We did have one hour out on the island. An hour's better than nothing."

"That's great, honey, great." Phil flipped the AM channels; static from the radio filled the car, increasing her frustration. "I can't find the game channel. We should be able to get it by now."

Phil wasn't interested in her work the same way she wasn't interested in his job as a stockbroker, in the columns of straight numbers and ragged heartbeat lines of the stock market. But at least she listened. The island project she was working on through her teaching job at the Savannah College of Arts and Design (or SCAD) was an opportunity for her to make a difference in architectural preservation, and she felt Phil thought of it as one more little hobby—no different from the scrapbooks she constructed for the kids.

She rubbed her forehead; she wouldn't let anything ruin the day they'd meet their son's first real love.

Phil found the sports announcer's voice rattling off the football stats and predictions of the day on the AM dial. He circled the coliseum until they spotted Amy's best friend Carol Anne waving her arms and pointing to the parking spot she'd saved for them. After two hours in the car, Amy was thrilled to jump out the passenger side and hug Carol Anne.

"We're finally here." Amy stretched and inhaled the fresh air.

"I had to fight at least thirty red-faced SUV drivers to keep your parking spot. You owe me big."

Amy laughed and began to unload the packed coolers of food, grateful as her nausea shifted to a dull headache. She scanned the tailgating throng for Jack.

"Who're you looking for?" Carol Anne craned her neck above Amy's head.

"Jack. He has some new girlfriend he wants us to meet . . . and her parents."

"Ooh. Sounds serious."

Amy looked at the woman who'd been her best friend since first grade; her hair was still the color of fresh honey, her brown eyes still playful and alert—taking everything in. Today she wore a pair of jeans that Amy's seventeen-year-old daughter could fit into and an orange T-shirt with SAXTON UNIVERSITY stamped across the top in block letters.

"God, Carol Anne, you look like one of the students. Go away." Amy made a shooing gesture with her hand, laughed.

"And you don't?"

"No, I definitely do not."

Amy stood up on her toes, attempted to look above the crowd for Jack. She spotted him walking through the maze of cars, grills and tangled knots of alumni bartering for tickets to the ultimate rival football game. His arm stretched behind him as he pulled a dark-haired girl through the throng. Amy didn't call out; she didn't want to embarrass him. She waved her arms back and forth so he could spot them.

She turned to Phil, who was grabbing blankets and chairs from the backseat. "Here comes Jack."

"Great." Phil's smile widened; he placed a folding chair on the grass, and walked over to stand next to her.

Carol Anne grabbed Amy's wrist. "I'll let you say hello to your son. . . . Be right back."

Amy spoke through a pasted-on smile. "He's holding her hand."

Jack had always made time in his college social calendar to stop by with a friend or two, but never, in three years, had he arrived holding a girl's hand.

"Amy, stop." Phil patted her denim-covered bottom.

Jack arrived at her side, hugged her. The warmth and firmness of her son washed over her in tenderness. She'd never asked, but she often wondered if other mothers wanted to weep with pure joy each time they hugged their grown-up children.

"Hi, Mom." Jack kissed her on the side of her face. He always did. "I want you to meet Lisbeth."

"Hello." Amy spoke to the small girl who stared only at Jack.

"Lisbeth, this is my mom."

Lisbeth looked at Amy and smiled. Her blue eyes were so clear they seemed almost see-through. Eyes like this in a girl with pale skin and chestnut curls cascading down her shoulders startled Amy. Lisbeth looked like a picture of an Irish imp—not the German Lisbeth she'd imagined.

Lisbeth spoke with the soft shawl of Jack's arm flung over her shoulders. "Nice to meet you, ma'am." Lisbeth blinked. Amy did not. Something about Lisbeth's jaw caused Amy to feel as though she needed to reach out to touch it.

Jack turned to his father. "And this is my dad, Phil."

Phil held out his hand. "Nice to finally meet you."

"You too, sir." Lisbeth shook Phil's hand.

Amy stared at Lisbeth's face: familiar and unfamiliar, nagging. Lisbeth turned, blushed under Amy's stare. "My parents are on their way, if you don't mind. I tried to explain where you were."

"Well, you keep an eye out for them. I'm sorry we couldn't make it to dinner last night, but we'd love to meet them. We have plenty of food." Amy reached for Phil's hand. "We'll unload the car."

She turned from her son and his new love; she somehow felt young, their age. It was easy to do on a fall day with gold leaves crackling under her feet, old friends surrounding her on the university campus.

Phil carried the chairs to the other side of the lawn, and before Amy could finish unloading the cooler, Jack called to her.

"Mom, come meet Lisbeth's parents."

Amy turned. Lisbeth's father moved into her field of vision. She tried to speak, but the autumn air gripped her voice in a tight portent fist.

The man hugged Lisbeth. "Lizzy, darlin', I thought we'd never find you." He kissed the tip of her nose.

Amy stared at this man, at Lisbeth's father. He was tall, at least six foot three, tree-trunk solid with hair the color of the burnished leaves under her feet; a scar dented his lower chin. The scar: a slice of open flesh as a beer bottle slit his chin in a barroom brawl—something about whose turn it was at the pool table. Amy reached for the side of her SUV and missed.

Lisbeth giggled and Amy heard it through a long, echoing tunnel. "Daddy, come meet Mrs. Reynolds. Amy, right?"

"Yes . . . yes." Amy glanced behind Jack for Phil. He was across the lawn with his back turned.

She smelled noises, heard smells; her senses moved and crowded each other for attention, mixed up with their true function as the air wavered with an actual and measurable width. A slow tingle of recognition began as an electric pulse in her stomach, her inner thighs; memory only in body, not yet mind.

"This is my dad, Nick Lowry."

The air separated, Nick reached out his hand to Amy, as if he'd not just risen from the grave of the past, the coffin of dead promises. He looked at her. His grin broke open to the wide and recognizable face of *her* Nick Lowry. She held out her hand to greet her old lover as mind's memory met visceral memory with the internal sound of grinding bone.

His face was wider, thicker on the bottom, the jaw softened, but it was his. Those brown eyes were still like liquid copper in his face. He didn't look surprised—he must have known she'd be here.

"Well, hello, Mrs. Amy Reynolds."

"Hello" is all Amy managed to utter. She smiled, grasped Nick's outstretched hand, amazed at her good manners while the world swam sideways.

"What a coincidence this is . . . what a—"

Nick's wife interrupted as she appeared from behind a van, tucking her blond hair behind her ear. "Yoo-hoo. Well, hello there, Reynolds family. I have just heard so much about you." She stepped up to Nick and ran her hand down his bare arm, held the other hand out to Amy. "Hi, I'm Eliza Lowry."

"Oh." Amy shook Eliza's hand.

Eliza looked up at Nick, then back at Amy. "And you are Amy Reynolds? Mother of the adorable Jack Reynolds?"

"Yes. Um, yes."

"Well, nice to meet you," Eliza said.

Phil appeared at Amy's side; she reached for him, grasped him like a life preserver. Phil held out his hand and introduced himself to Nick and Eliza. Eliza gave a curtsy. The ground seemed to dissolve; Amy felt wide, rising.

Eliza wrapped Phil's hand in both of hers. "It's nice to meet you." She tilted her neck a little more to the side, her smile widening just a tad as she swung her hair behind her shoulders.

A stray yellow leaf threaded with red fell into Phil's hair. Amy plucked it from his head—ordinary motions an antidote to the unexpected.

She glanced at Jack and Lisbeth standing next to Eliza, searched for something, anything to say to Nick and his wife—but she only found a gray swirling space as her mouth opened and closed. God, this woman, Eliza, must think her a mute fool, just standing there with an open fish mouth.

"Aren't these football games fun?" Eliza said.

"Especially when they're having a winning season," Phil answered, squeezing Amy's elbow.

"Yeah, the last time Saxton won the national championship was when Nick was here." Eliza giggled. "We won't say what year that was."

Jack laughed. "Jeez, that was like, what? Thirty years ago?"

"Oh, thanks for the reminder." Eliza tickled the side of Jack's arm. Amy wanted to slap her hand away.

Amy looked up at her son. "No, more like twenty-five years ago."

Eliza then turned to her daughter, pulled her away from Jack and began to attempt to smooth down her curls while talking to her.

Phil looked at Amy with large eyes, with furrowed forehead. Everything about Phil looked eager, even when it wasn't. His smooth skin, without freckle or mole, gave the appearance of everlasting youth—soft mouth, wet eyes and rounded eyebrows creating an anticipatory look. Amy had appreciated this when he first came to her—his softness a place to finally lay her wounded self. She brushed his hair back from his eyes, his blond hair always falling in the wrong places.

"Did y'all know each other at school?" Phil said.

"Sure . . ." Nick answered.

"A long time ago," Amy said, reaching for Phil's arm.

Nick laughed and smiled at Amy. "Yes, a very long time ago."

Nick possessed the same goofy "I'm uncomfortable but aren't I hiding it great" grin that moved across his face in waves, waves she'd ridden . . . before. She smiled—certain she showed nothing of what cracked within her.

"So how have you been all these years?" She found she was speaking.

"I've been fine, just fine. And you?"

"Perfect . . . thanks," she said.

Phil tilted his head and rubbed at a spot between his eyes, at the top of his nose—something he did when he was confused.

Eliza turned her attention back to the group. "So, Reynolds family, where do y'all live?"

"Darby," Phil said. "And you?"

"We lived up north in Maine for way, way too long, but

we moved back to Garvey about eight years ago. That's where I'm from—grew up there. You know, there's just no place like home." Eliza sighed—a long, exhausted sigh as if the journey of her life had finally led her to a place of rest.

"Oh, how nice . . . how very nice . . . that you and Nick are . . . home," Amy said. *Eight years ago.* Nick Lowry had been living less than two hours away from her for eight years. As Carol Anne might have said if she were standing there, *Jesus, Mary and Joseph.*

"Of course, Nick still doesn't think of Garvey as home. But he will. He will. It does grow on one." Eliza grabbed Nick's hand.

"Like a bad fungus," Nick joked.

They all laughed, too loudly. Obviously Nick still had the gift: to alleviate tense moments with sarcasm. The memories began with his scar, then his sarcasm and Amy fell toward a well-packed storehouse of images she'd never planned on looking at again. Ever.

She excused herself and, without feeling the solid ground, walked through the tailgating crowd over to Carol Anne.

Carol Anne was not only Amy's childhood friend and college roommate, but often her source of sanity. She'd also married a hometown boy and they lived two blocks away from each other—more proof of the comfortable ease of Amy's life. She didn't want or need any change or surprise right now. She collapsed next to Carol Anne in a green canvas chair with a huge S.U. logo embroidered on its back.

She stared straight ahead and mumbled, "Oh, God."

"No, it's me, your dearest and best friend. Don't get us confused." Carol Anne touched her shoulder. "Are you okay?"

"Look over at my car."

"Okay . . . I see your cute son, Jack, your adorable husband, Phil, and some cutesy girl with her parents." She glanced at Amy. "Okay, so Jack has his first serious girl-friend. You *will* live through this."

"Look! Look at the man. Look."

Silence from Carol Anne was a rare event worthy of comment, but Amy had none. Carol Anne took a sharp breath. "Oh, God. No."

"Yes."

"I thought he . . . disappeared—you know, after Costa Rica—shit, twenty-five years ago."

"So did I."

"Who's that? Who's his wife?"

"I don't know—Eliza. I've never met her. She didn't go to school here. Says she's from Garvey."

Carol Anne snorted. "Okay . . ."

"My son—*my* son is dating *his* daughter."

"No."

"Yes."

"This can*not* be good."

"I want to go home."

Carol Anne groaned. "Me, too."

The afternoon became a slow dream sequence for Amy, no bridge between each scene—just snapshots of her son, her husband, her old lover. Everyone else seemed to move with comfort while she struggled to breathe without stops and starts, to function without twitches and flutters, to touch and kiss her husband of twenty-three years without feeling as though she were betraying her boyfriend when his back was turned.

Jack stood next to his dad, flipping cheeseburgers on the grill. He was tall and gangly, still adjusting to his height and long-limbed youth, two inches taller than the father he adored. Jack's height had come to him later in life than his friends, and at times he had seemed to trip over his own feet as though his shoes were too large. He was handsome, as expected, since his father's genes dominated in the bones, muscles and eyes. The only thing Amy could detect of herself in her son was his mouth—a wide smile that couldn't be faked. His blue eyes were softer in color than his father's, but identical in the silk-fabric appearance. He pulled Lisbeth closer.

Amy stared, shamelessly stared, at Lisbeth. She would not have been able to identify Lisbeth as any part of Eliza if she'd not been introduced. She would have expected a woman like Eliza to have a daughter who was a doll-like version of herself—a Skipper to her Barbie. Instead, Amy was stunned by the exotic beauty of a pale, dark-haired girl whose only attribute from her mother was her blue eyes snapping from a face of Nick's curves and lines. Oak- and molasses-colored ringlets fell to her shoulders; a small barrette clung to the curls—a vain attempt to restrain them. She seemed a wild and beautiful child—exotic, opposite to Eliza.

Jack and Lisbeth floated from the grill to a cluster of people without letting their hands ever leave each other—some body part in constant contact. There was no fighting for attention as was common in youthful gatherings. They were the exact same age she and Nick had been when they dated in college—when Nick had left and never returned. Unbidden images ran through her mind: tousled sheets, murmured promises, wet limbs. She pushed them to the back of her mind to examine later and turned from her son and his girlfriend.

Eliza—Amy had to fight the urge to call her Barbie—found Amy alone and sprawled in a chair, avoiding Nick.

Eliza sat down in the empty seat next to Amy, who damned Carol Anne for vacating the seat to find a bathroom in the chemistry building.

Eliza smiled, flipped her hair, and nodded toward Jack and Amy. "They seem pretty serious, huh?"

"They sure do." Amy lifted her hand, dropped it to the chair, not sure where to put any part of her—as if Eliza might know where her hands had once been.

"I never understand the hoopla around these games, but Nick and the kids sure do love them."

"Well, they're a lot of fun . . . and it's always good to see old friends and—"

Eliza raised her hand in the air. "I know—that's what Nick always says. My college didn't have a football team, so I never got into the whole tailgating thing."

"Where did you go to school?"

"I went to William-Dean—the private college about half an hour from here."

"I know William-Dean. Then you must've at least come here a lot in college—to go out or go to the games."

"Not really. . . ."

"Oh." Amy again felt as if she were floating, lost. How had Nick come to meet this woman, marry her? None of this made sense, like a picture blurred and off-kilter.

Eliza and Amy turned together in some synchronous mother-way to watch Jack and Lisbeth mingle with their friends. Eliza began to talk of her family, of her sons at home—All-State wrestling and football.

Amy turned back to Eliza and stared at her. She guessed from Eliza's matching linen pants and shirt, her forehead which didn't move or wrinkle, her diamond-stud earrings that were bigger than Amy's engagement ring, that Eliza's and Amy's paths in college would never have crossed.

Amy's group was more the "Let's go to the beach and find a place to crash—don't forget your bathing suit," while Eliza's clique seemed to be the "Let's go to my parents' condo in Hilton Head—pack your Gucci bag and don't forget the curling iron and blow-dryer."

When Eliza asked Amy what she did, Amy told her about her part-time job at SCAD and although she considered telling her about the island—about the house and land she was trying to save—she was too distracted to even try, and she wasn't sure Eliza was interested in much aside from her matching shoes and purse. So Amy smiled and cooed when appropriate and talked of her own daughter, a senior in high school and a Georgia state tennis champion in her age group.

Nick entered their sphere a few times to give his comments or opinion on talk that Amy could later never remember. She used her energy to regain her composure after he moved away. She would not allow the past to come rushing at her without warning, flaring heat inside her as she chatted with Nick's wife. It was . . . inappropriate.

"I've been thinking." Eliza looked away and then back to Amy. "Jack and Lisbeth seem so happy, so . . . I was wondering if you—you and Phil—would like to come to our lake house next weekend with the kids? I think it would be fun. We could all get acquainted while the kids hang out."

"The lake house?"

"Yes. Well, actually it's my parents', but my sister and I share it. It's at Lake Hardin—that should only be a couple hours from y'all in Darby."

Ah, yes. Amy remembered parties in college that she had never been invited to on the exclusive lake in South Carolina.

"Yes," she found herself saying. "Well, Phil has a busy schedule with work, but . . ."

"Well, that's the benefit of Nick working for Daddy—he can always make his own schedule."

For Daddy?

"That's great. I'll check with Phil. I think a trip to the lake sounds just lovely."

As soon as she agreed, as soon as she knew she would see Nick again, some ancient, hurt piece of Amy rose within her. In agreeing to go, in saying yes to the lake, the worst part of her—the part that still clung to whatever had happened with Nick Lowry—was having its say, words and actions already coming from her without her willing them.

In the clogged traffic on the drive home, Phil listened to the postgame show on the radio. Amy closed her eyes, tried to find a calming point. Her body vibrated as if it were a tuning fork humming to a new energy. She couldn't settle her mind or her limbs, and she wasn't sure she wanted to quiet herself—it had been a long time since she'd thought about or reacted to anyone like Nick Lowry.

Phil touched her leg. "Now, Ame, how did you know Nick?"

"We hung around the same crowd in college. Not a big deal."

It was a lie. She knew it was a lie. But she couldn't bear to have Phil half-listen to her, to the story of Nick, with the postgame show on the radio. It seemed these days that Phil only partially heard anything she said and the effort needed to listen to the old and painful story required much more from him than she knew was in him to give right then.

"I never knew what happened to him. He kind of disappeared after college—went to Costa Rica or something like that." Now that was the truth.

"You know, I sort of remember Nick from Hank's Pool Hall. Could you imagine if he and Eliza ended up being Jack's in-laws?" Phil laughed. "My God, Nick drunk and rambling at every gathering. It would be an entertaining way to spend holidays, wouldn't it?"

Phil laughed. A nail file rubbed against Amy's nerves.

"Drunk? I'm sure he doesn't drink like that now. And he didn't just hang out at Hank's. He actually worked there." Amy looked out the window. "He wasn't drunk today." She pushed at the bridge of her nose. Phil had already agreed in front of the Lowrys to go to the lake house. "You agreed to join them next weekend. Our children are dating and we're obviously going to have to spend some time with them. I'd like for it to be pleasant for Lizzy, Lisbeth, whatever her name is, and Jack."

Children: a great excuse. Amy felt dirty, hungover with the first lie, now the second. She leaned her head against the window.

"You're right. I'm sure this girlfriend will pass like all the others, so let's make the best of it." Phil reached out, laid his hand on Amy's knee while arguing with the announcer about the outcome of the game. She startled herself with the need to flick his hand off—which she didn't do. Instead, she told herself to pull it together, compartmentalize her emotions in as efficient a manner as her closets and drawers at home.

The drone of the radio, the vibrating hum of the car finally lulled her into a sunbaked doze as she remembered the last time she'd seen Nick Lowry.

Chapter Two

The winter quarter Nick was scheduled to spend in Costa Rica approached like a lumbering train, a hulking gray rumble in the distance. Amy heard it in her sleep and waking, during their lovemaking. She began to see the bulked shape the week before he left, smell its acrid smoke and feel the trembles of the earth as it barreled down the tracks toward them. They made the decision together, as they did all things—Nick would spend the winter quarter in a Costa Rican tropical biology conservation program where his interest in reforestation and preservation could be explored in the rain forest. She would stay at Saxton University and wait for him.

They were to reunite in three months and begin their life together after he fulfilled his internship. He would come back knowing exactly what he wanted to do, what *they* wanted to do and where. All they knew was that it would involve Amy preserving architectural gems while he saved the land and wildlife. Together, saving.

Amy stood in the airport departure lounge to say good-bye to him, consumed by a feeling of finality so complete that she couldn't catch her breath. In those days she felt everything so sharply, her skin felt peeled. Each emotion arrived strong and complete, and often Nick seemed to be her only protection against the onslaught.

During their final farewell, Amy found herself begging him to stay. He was usually the sole witness to her symptoms of emotion, yet that day the out-of-focus and sharply delineated faces of other Costa Rica–bound travelers saw her fall apart; there was the Indian woman with the dot on her forehead in the green plastic chair, the flight attendant placing white letters on the flight board while glancing behind her shoulder at Amy's tears.

The gate attendant called for the final boarding. Amy grabbed Nick's cotton shirt. She was desperate to pull him back from the bulk of the white plane outside the grease-streaked window. Her voice was raspy with fear and lack of sleep. He was so solid: his thick hair, his muscular shoulders, his dense copper eyes without variation in color. She was light, air, exposed and he held her to the earth. She clung to him.

"Don't go. Do. Not. Go."

"Amy . . ." His eyes were wet. He leaned close to her ear. "You're making this harder."

"Don't. You can't. Something bad. You won't come back. I can't breathe. Don't."

"I'll be fine. I promise. This is not an ending. It's just the beginning of our life."

"Nick, there's something . . . wrong."

"You're scared."

"Yes." He would stay now. He knew she was scared. He would stay.

"I've never left before. That's all it is, Amy."

"That's not it. Something . . . something else." She

grabbed at the silver cross that dangled from a thin chain around her neck. "Don't."

The final boarding call came through the waiting room like an executioner calling her name.

"Don't." People behind Nick stared at her: the Indian woman clutched a child, the flight attendant pursed her lips, an obese man wiped his face with a handkerchief.

"I love you." Nick kissed her lips, kissed her tears, kissed her cheeks. Then he held her face in both hands. "Close your eyes." He kissed each eyelid. "Keep your eyes shut until I'm gone."

She did. She didn't want to open them again until the gray metal door opened in three months and Nick walked out with stories of the rain forest, a three-month beard and his arms around her.

But he never walked back through the door and the last Amy Malone ever felt of Nick Lowry was his lips on her eyelids as he kissed her one more time and promised to come back to her.

Nick threw the cooler into the trunk of the Mercedes and slammed down the lid. For good measure, he kicked the tire. He glanced over his shoulder at his wife as she walked toward the car, chatting with an old friend she had run into at the football game. If she knew who Amy really was, she would probably hurl herself to the ground.

When Eliza had told him, in calm tones, whom his daughter was dating, whom he would see today, he'd done a gut-check and realized it was okay. Eliza obviously hadn't made the connection with Amy's married name. Amy and Eliza had never met and, more than twenty years later, all Amy would be to Eliza was the old girlfriend. Although he'd never tried to track her down, he knew her married name:

Amy Reynolds. He hadn't been positive it was her, but the coincidences were too many to ignore, and he was right. He'd known it was her before she turned around—the way she stood, the way her hair fell across her shoulders, the way his heart flipped inside his chest.

If he'd anticipated feeling anything when he saw Amy, he'd thought it would be pure acidic anger for her betrayal. He was wrong. The anger had somehow been replaced. The vacant feeling he'd thought he put to rest when she betrayed him, when she never came for him, rose again.

Eliza walked up to the car, threw her purse in the backseat, then hugged her friend goodbye. Nick pulled the keys out of his back pocket and climbed into the driver's seat, slammed the door. This old ache would pass, it would most definitely pass.

Eliza tucked her head into the car. "What's your problem?"

"I don't have a problem I'm aware of." Nick put the keys in the ignition, started the car. *At least not one you want to hear about.*

Eliza climbed in and sat down. "You didn't even say hello to Ansley Worthington. Don't you remember her? Her father is the CEO of Southern Energy—it wouldn't have hurt to say hello."

"Didn't realize I missed an opportunity to further my career."

"That's not what I meant, Nick. What's going on?"

"I just want to get home. The traffic only gets worse by the second. . . ."

"Well, then, let's go."

When Nick turned on the radio, Eliza leaned over, turned it down, and asked, "Did you have fun today?"

"Yeah, great game. Saxton wins again."

"That's not what I meant. Did you like Lizzie's boyfriend?"

"He seemed very nice, Eliza. Very nice."

"Yes, he did, didn't he?"

Nick reached over and turned up the radio. Amy and her family were not something he would discuss with his wife, or anyone else for that matter. He'd vowed, when Amy didn't show up in Costa Rica after the accident, never to think about it all again. Seeing her at Saxton University—their place—with her son and husband was not going to change how he felt about dredging up the painful past.

"Well, I'm glad you like him. I invited his family to the lake next weekend."

Nick turned. "What?"

"If you'd turn down this radio, you could hear me." She turned it down again. "I invited them to the lake house next weekend."

"The hell you did."

"I did. What's the big deal? We always have guests there."

"The last thing I want to do next weekend is entertain Lizzie's boyfriend's family. This latest project's been exhausting and I just want a weekend to relax. Why does everything have to be a social event?"

"It's not a social event, Nick. It's Lizzie's boyfriend. And all you have to do is tell Daddy you need more help."

Nick held up his hand. "Not now, Eliza. I don't want to discuss this now. I don't want to hit the PLAY button on this same old conversation." He patted her leg, unsure if he was trying to ease her frustration or his own.

For many years he'd done well enough with a large corporation in Maine that Harlan Sullivan had seen fit to offer him a job at his company. Nick's job with Sullivan Timber

did have its advantages—he utilized his expertise in re-
source management and wildlife preservation, and as an
added bonus, he didn't have to listen to Eliza lamenting the
perils of living up north when she longed for the South.
Surely the fact that he worked for the family company and
that she had moved back to her hometown would decrease
the whining, but no, she always wanted more—wanted him
to climb the social as well as the corporate ladder. He
couldn't care less if he made it to the first rung as long as
he could have his hands in soil, be truly involved in some
part of the work he loved.

He sighed. The landscape danced past the car window
in harmony with the tires' thump against the pavement as
they drove the two hours back to their house in Garvey.
Nick glanced over at his wife as they pulled into the driveway. She was leaning back against the headrest; her mouth
was slightly open in sleep. He looked back up to the
house—white pillars, resembling the bars of some pristine
prison, stood guard over a front porch with an all-white
wicker couch, rocking chairs and swing.

Fresh lawn-mower marks covered the front lawn; it
looked like someone had vacuumed the grass in a crisscross
pattern. The landscaping company must have come while
he and Eliza were at the game. They liked to arrive when
he wasn't home—they didn't appreciate him coming out,
telling them where to prune, cut or leave his plants alone.

As he stared at the landscape of his home, his life, an hon-
est question rose out of long-held patterns of denial—how in
the hell had he come to live in this spotless house that, eight
years later, still smelled of new carpet and wet paint, on a
manicured, construction paper–cutout lawn, when he wanted
to live in the middle of forest, tree and plant?

He closed his eyes and rubbed his eyelids.

Eliza stirred and Nick reached over and touched her cheek. She opened her eyes and turned to him, smiled.

"Hmm," she murmured.

"We're home."

"I didn't even realize how tired I was."

"Me neither," he said. And he meant it, as fatigue settled into his bones at the thought that there was no use trying to figure out might-have-beens; yet there they were, roaring at him with a fierceness he had thought squelched.

Chapter Three

The week before Amy and Phil were to go to the Lowrys' lake house, Amy felt her whole tucked-in life start to wrinkle as if left in the dryer too long. Memories and questions about Nick Lowry leaked out and she couldn't stop them. Was it menopause? Almost-empty nest? Seeing her son with a serious girlfriend? All of these were possible reasons for the disintegration of her well-being. She began to look, really look, at things that had never before bothered her.

She usually moved with ease in their home. She once loved the laundry—the small piles of neatly folded clothes representing each member of the family. She adored the evidence of family life under her feet, the sound of children running through the home, moments spent planning the next birthday, the next Easter-egg hunt. She had listened to the complaints of mothers in her children's schools and neighborhood—about their unfulfilled lives, their hatred of the minutiae, their quandaries with housekeeping, and she would wonder that she felt so grateful for all the things they found so grating.

She sought perspective now, grounding, and remembered how when her parents had been killed in a car wreck when Molly and Jack were infants, Phil had provided the only solid foundation in a world adrift. The sudden loss of her parents was filled only by the love she had with Phil, Molly and Jack. The loss of Nick's love had seemed, then, insignificant compared to the dank emptiness of soul her parents' deaths had produced. She needed to remember that—remember what was important.

She stood in the laundry room with its blue-and-white-striped walls that she and Molly had painted during an excruciating 102-degree day four summers ago, and she pulled the clothes from her daughter's tennis bag in slow motion. Her actions seemed apart from her—distinct but separate. There was a time when she was dating Phil, when her heart had begun to heal after Nick's breaking it, that Phil had asked her why she liked country music. She'd told him that she didn't know why she liked it, or why she adored the color Tiffany blue, or the smell of her grandfather's sweater or the way rain ran down bubbled antique glass. Why would she want to know why? Wouldn't analyzing it ruin the knowing of it? Just knowing what she liked was enough.

She tossed the laundry and realized this was how she felt now—she didn't want to analyze why she was anticipating this reunion. She was afraid it would ruin the expectation that she hadn't felt in . . . she couldn't remember how long. For now, the feeling was a remembrance of the days when possibility was endless and she didn't know what would happen next, when things weren't so set and understood. She compared it to the anticipation of preadolescence, knowing a change was coming, but not what it would entail.

This week her dreams had become vivid and she could

finally answer the stupid question she'd once been asked, "Do you dream in color?" Yes, she could now say—many, many colors.

On Thursday morning she awoke at two a.m. Phil was staring at her. "What?" She snuggled closer.

"You've been kicking me. Tossing, turning all night."

"Really?" A metallic guilt flooded her mouth.

"Yes, really."

"I don't know why." She was astounded at her new-found capacity for white lies.

"Are you getting sick?"

"I feel fine. Really."

"I'll get up with Molly in the morning and send her off to school. Why don't you try and sleep in? Obviously something has been keeping you up." Phil rolled over and went as softly into sleep as he entered each day. Nothing was done harshly, abruptly with Phil.

Amy tried to sleep, but couldn't. Something about the way Phil told her what he was going to do—how he would take care of it all—irritated her. He had always prided himself on how he took care of things, of her, of the kids. She was proud of him and often told him so.

Phil came from a strong line of chiseled German ancestors from whom he inherited his sense of responsibility—yet his emotions were often stashed behind a shiny armor of high ethical standards. Amy didn't focus on what he lacked because, as she often said, we're all missing something. Her emotion, she understood, was too much on the surface, yet it balanced the family. Whatever ability she lacked in taking care of things or providing, her husband filled. What he lacked in emotion, she filled. So for the kids, both existed.

But only for the kids, she thought before she could censor the betraying idea.

As the alarm went off, Phil rose quietly from the bed, and Amy kept her eyes closed while he took care of everything. She listened to the familiar sounds of her own home: the thump of the cabinet (Molly was removing a cereal bowl), the creak of the door (Phil was getting the newspaper off the front porch), the dishwasher opening and closing, the grind of the garage door, the slam of car doors, and finally the puff of the Toyota leaving the driveway. She snuggled deeper into her pillow.

Questions plagued her; she couldn't find the answers, but they existed—out there, dancing to some taunting tune of the past. Why hadn't Nick returned on the plane he was scheduled for? Why hadn't he ever contacted her? Why had he stayed in Costa Rica? When had he come back? Why hadn't she been able to find him, no matter how hard she tried? And, most of all, when had he met and married Eliza?

In those days before cell phones and e-mail, she hadn't been able to access him or ask if he'd received her letters. He was as far off as Jupiter, with its unreachable surface and toxic gas. She'd been blocked at every turn; his mother and the school had told her Nick had decided to stay in Costa Rica, and yes, they would tell him to contact her. He never did.

When she married Phil, she entombed those questions behind a solid wall. Seeing and touching Nick Lowry now was like a sledgehammer pounding on the crumbling mortar of that very wall, and the questions tumbled out.

She finally rose from bed after giving Molly and Phil time to leave the neighborhood, to let Molly notice she'd forgotten something at home and come back to retrieve it: a book report, her tennis racquet. She sat on the side of the bed and hung over her knees, groaned at her fatigue. She wanted to return to a week ago when none of this was anywhere near the surface of her life, of her thoughts. She rose to go to the kitchen. Coffee, she needed coffee.

A luminous day poured through the window over the kitchen sink. Amy moved to close the blinds, but her hand hung in the air as she watched a red-breasted robin grab a sunflower seed from the wooden bird feeder that Molly had made in fourth grade at a Home Depot workshop with her dad. Molly had proudly brought it home, and she and Amy had painted it bright apple green and blue to match the kitchen. They'd gone outside together and hung it in front of the sink's window. For eight years now, Amy had started the morning by watching which bird came to visit.

At this memory of Molly, Amy felt tenderness akin to what she had felt when leaning over her babies' cribs, knowing there was nothing she could do to force them to continue to breathe in and out. She could not start or stop what life brought to her, including Nick Lowry.

Exhaustion lay behind her eyes as a burned patch of sleeplessness. She turned to the counter and knocked her favorite brown pottery mug on its side next to a full, hot coffeepot.

"Oh, Phil. You're so sweet." She spoke out loud and lifted the front page of the *Darby Chronicle* that he'd left for her.

She filled her mug just as the phone rang, startling her. She fumbled with the pot and coffee spattered on the counter, on her white cotton nightshirt.

"Damn." She was shaky, unsure, and she hated it. She grabbed a kitchen towel and the phone at the same time.

"Hello." She wiped at the spilled coffee, preoccupied.

"Amy? It's me, Eliza."

Amy was wordless.

"Amy, are you there?" Eliza spoke with soft, drawn-out

syllables that reminded Amy of the way one would talk to a stranger's child.

"Yes, yes. Sorry. I just spilled coffee all over myself. How are you, Eliza?"

"I'm very fine, thank you. I just wanted to touch base with you about tomorrow. Give you directions and all that."

Tomorrow? Was it really tomorrow? She needed a pedicure, a new bathing suit.

"Sure. Sure. I was going to call you today." Amy looked at the rooster clock on the far wall: eight sharp. "What can I do to help?"

"Well, I've already talked to the kids and they're all set. We're all just going to have the best time." Eliza's words sounded robotic, prerecorded.

"Well, we're really looking forward to our time at the lake. And it'll be great for Molly and . . . What's your son's name who is the same age as Molly?"

"Alex."

"Well, it'll be nice for Molly and Alex to meet."

"You're bringing Molly?"

"Well, yes. She's part of the family. Aren't you bringing your boys?"

"Well, they have wrestling practice and all. I was going to leave them with my parents."

"I don't have . . ." Amy took a deep breath and Eliza filled in the gap.

"Can your daughter stay with friends this weekend?"

"I've already told her she could come."

"Well . . ." Eliza paused while Amy waited and knew what the silence was for—Amy's chance to give in, but she wouldn't. Eliza must give in or be the worst of all Southern epitaphs—a bitch.

"Molly and Alex would have a lovely time together,

I'm sure. Max has a wrestling match . . . so he can't come, but . . . I'll bring Alex," Eliza said.

"Okay . . . well, tell me what I can do to help."

Directions obtained, meals assigned, Amy hung up. Throughout the conversation, Amy had realized Eliza had assumed she and Phil went to college together. She didn't correct Eliza, didn't tell her that she hadn't dated Phil until she had discovered Nick wouldn't be returning from his trip to Costa Rica.

Phil was from their hometown, Darby, but hadn't gone to Saxton University. The people Amy had always known were his friends, too; their lives had been intertwined since they'd been delivered in the same county hospital two months apart, since they'd attended the same nursery school. They were never close friends, or even casual friends, despite knowing each other.

Phil's parents couldn't afford an out-of-state university, so he'd gone to the local community college. Studies, books and high grades had come easily to him, therefore frequent time at a university not his own hadn't caused a dent in his academic prowess. He'd had the pleasure of watching and vaguely participating in the Saxton rituals and parties without ever becoming wholly part of them. Even now if you asked an alumnus would say Phil went to school with him. Amy had always perceived him on the outskirts, part of the scenery but never the center of it. It wasn't until she'd needed the comfort of his familiarity that she had finally noticed him waiting for her. His aloofness became part of his attraction, his separateness part of his belonging.

She sat at the kitchen table after hanging up with Eliza and ran her fingernails along the grooves and marks on its surface. She followed the small numbers and letters pressed there over years of homework assignments.

"Get it together," she mumbled out loud to herself. There were things to do. Eliza had asked her to make one lunch and one breakfast this weekend. She'd use this chance to show off her homemaking expertise. No prepacked sandwiches for the Lowry lake house.

Amy pulled down a set of cookbooks from the kitchen shelf. If she focused, some thick cement of obligation would obstruct thoughts of Nick.

But she couldn't find the magic recipe—or the will—to stop the escalating memories of the night she met Nick Lowry.

Chapter Four

The congested room reeked of stale beer and the sweet-rotten smell of human contact. Sweat trickled down the back of Amy Malone's neck. Her skin felt thick under her blouse and she wished she hadn't worn long sleeves. The frigid air outside had fooled her into believing that she wouldn't sweat in the airless, windowless cinder-block basement of the Kappa Alpha house. She'd lost her roommate, Carol Anne, the minute they walked in the door and she didn't know a soul in the room.

She glanced around; there was a boy with a cleft lip smiling at her, a boy with a pledge pin on his Izod shirt being convinced to drink beer through a long plastic tube: funneling. A frightened look clouded his face, and she imagined that he wished he were home in his adolescent bedroom dreaming of college, not facing the reality. She turned from him, walked toward the bar, hoping for ice water and a glimpse of Carol Anne.

A slime-thin mixture of substances she would rather not think about coated the floor, and she realized she was ruining her JCPenney shoes.

"Excuse me. Sorry." She bumped her way to a slab of plywood on top of old kegs—a makeshift bar. Fraternity pledges stood dutifully dispensing beer from a silver keg into red plastic cups for girls they could never hope to lay a hand on that year. They would wait for their time on the other side of the bar.

"Water," Amy yelled across the plywood.

"Water?" a boy with a pimply face asked.

She couldn't look at him; his blemishes made her feel soft inside, sorry for him. "Yes, water. I am dying here. A big water."

"What?" He obviously couldn't hear a word she said over the thumping Rolling Stones screaming about finding satisfaction.

"Water. Water. Water," she screamed as the vibrating bodies of the crowd swayed in an animalistic grind to the music. Everyone in the room moved to the same universal rhythm, while she stood rigid and unaffected.

The pimpled pledge searched for water and finally held out a lukewarm cup. Amy took it, chugged its contents, and nausea plowed through her. She pushed her shoulder up against a side door: escape. The door opened and she fell ungracefully on her Levi's into the yard of the imitation antebellum mansion. She looked toward the sloping front lawn, through the magnolia trees frozen in their winter waiting, to the white pillars anchoring the roof to the front verandah. The architecture mixed two separate Southern historical periods. She scoffed at the sloppy counterfeit.

"There would never be a party like this at a real Southern home," she whispered to herself, lifting her face to the cool air. The smell of night-blooming jasmine cleansed the stench of the party from her head.

"Excuse me." A hand reached down and touched her

shoulder as she sat on the hard, cold earth. She started, but the air fanned out to allow room for this voice. She didn't hesitate when she reached for the hand belonging to the disembodied sound, allowed it to lift her from the ground.

Amy stumbled to her feet. "Huh?"

"Are you, my darlin', implying that we, the KAs of the South, are not truly Southern?"

"You heard me?"

"Ah . . ."

Amy laughed, decided to join in the playful banter. "Well, sugah . . . are you a true Southern gentleman?" She found herself answering this boy as if she knew him, and in an odd way, she felt she did. The full moon lit one side of his face, his jawline a shadow across his neck, his eyelashes casting a feather on his brow. His hair corkscrewed around his right ear and a thin layer of stubble covered his chin. It wasn't any single attribute, but the combination that caused her insides to quiver—something broke loose, leaving part of her exposed.

He laughed. "Am I a true Southern gentleman? Ashley Wilkes, maybe?"

"No, you seem more the Rhett Butler type." Her body began to shift to the rhythm that the others inside siphoned from the Rolling Stones.

He stepped from the shadows into the moth-diffused ring of light from the bulb over the back door; she stared at him. His shadow swallowed hers, overcame it, and she couldn't find her own outline on the yard underneath his bulked shape. A shiver trailed down her legs.

His brown hair fell to the side—curly, hiding his left eye. She wanted to brush the curl aside so that she could see where the black of his pupil ended and the deep copper color began. His stance was wide—his legs apart as if he were leaning back against an invisible wall. His jeans were ripped at the knee and he wore a wrinkled white button-down shirt, a jean jacket.

A moth flew into his hair and she reached to shoo it away. He didn't move.

"Well," she said when she felt she could speak again. "I don't believe real Southern gentlemen lurk outside back doors."

"They do if they're protecting the innocent girls inside. I was instructed that no true Southern belle leaves un-escorted. It is my assigned duty." He bowed, revealing the hair at the back of his neck. She almost reached to touch it—discover what it felt like, if it was bristly or fine.

"You mean making sure they don't escape."

"You." He lifted her chin so she directly faced the light. "I won't let you escape."

Her blood ran thicker, warmer, in the instant his finger touched her face. The cloying warmth of the basement party seemed to return. She pulled her face away from him. "I guess you'll just have to tell the troops that you failed in your mission. I'm leaving."

She walked away from him, feeling she was escaping some potential danger; a parachute jump where the chute wouldn't have opened.

He called after her. "Don't go without telling me your name."

She kept walking, digging the car keys out of her purse.

"Ah, but tomorrow is another day," he called after her, repeating the final line of *Gone with the Wind.*

How unoriginal, she thought—just another frat boy try-ing to get laid. "That's my line," she called back, without turning around.

His laugh carried over the night air—grainy, deep and as

"too much" as his body and eyes. She began to jog to her car. She wanted to be in her VW with Billy Joel's latest eight-track turned up as loud as it would go, with the car's cloth seats absorbing this vibration she knew as her body's signal of danger. At that moment, she couldn't have been more thankful to her mother for winning the fight with her daddy about having a car in college. Her mother had finally convinced him that it was actually safer for Amy to have her own transportation than to be at the mercy of other students. So her daddy had given in, but he had bought her the cheapest stick-shift station wagon he could find in Darby, Georgia. She was allowed to have a car, but she wasn't allowed to be a show-off about it.

The cool air began to seep down her neck, drying the sweat. Although she knew she shouldn't leave Carol Anne unescorted at the party, she longed only for what she thought of as the me-filled dorm room. Carol Anne was the one who got her invited to this party, Carol Anne could find a way home—this would not be a difficult task for her.

Amy wanted to bury her head in the pillow that smelled like mother's laundry at home—an aroma Amy hadn't been able to duplicate in the dorm quad's clanging laundry even when she used the same detergent. Now she brought the sheets home every other week. She thought of it as the magic smell of home—a potion Mother wouldn't give her the recipe for, as it kept her returning with her overflowing pink laundry basket.

Her parents lived only two hours away and Amy had the freedom to escape when college life overwhelmed her. Of course, she would never admit to the need for escape; she was only coming home to get her laundry done. She felt sad for the girls from farther away, the ones who were relegated to holiday visits with family. Their muffled cries of homesickness and the whispered calls on the hall phone to parents they pretended were boyfriends saddened her, made her appreciate how lucky she was.

The dorm room she shared with Carol Anne was just like the other rooms that ran up and down the hall, up and down a thousand buildings like it on campuses across the kudzu-covered South. Brick buildings holding rooms with posters taped crooked and tattered on the walls, filled with bedspreads and pillows bought with parents the weeks before school started, in a frenzy to claim one's own space in a mass of uniformity. Gaudy colors and crisp sheets filled the rooms the first day. Framed pictures of family and friends sat on gunmetal desks and bedside tables in an attempt to conjure up their love and presence in a chaotic world of books and competition.

Amy's bedspread was blue and green plaid. She'd chosen it from the Sears catalog and had thought it grown-up and classy. When she'd first smoothed the quilt across her dorm-room bed and lain on top of it, she'd realized with a twist of sadness that she was no different than any other freshman putting her quilt on her bed.

Now, curling beneath the covers, she felt somehow that in meeting the boy with no name, in touching his hand, in allowing him to touch her face, she had become a tiny bit of an individual; maybe she could claim something different than the sameness surrounding her. She tried to sleep, but found herself in a spiral, never quite reaching its end. She would begin to fall asleep, then startle to the touch of the boy's hand on her chin, to the flash of his jaw. She tossed against the sheets as she heard his gravely drawl thicken her sleepless fatigue.

Carol Anne's drunken attempts to navigate the minefield

of their dorm room—full of books, laundry and clothing they'd tried on but discarded that night before going out—thoroughly woke Amy. In the full dark, Carol Anne cursed each shoe and book she tripped on.

"You can turn the light on, Carol Anne."

"Oh, you're awake. My loyal roommate is awake." Carol Anne flicked on the overhead light and Amy buried her head under the pillow.

"I believe the bedside lamp would have done just fine."

"Oh, but you deserve it. Leaving me all alone at the KA house. My, my, what would our dorm mother say if she knew the sainted Amy left her roommate at a fraternity keg party?"

"I couldn't find you anywhere. I looked."

"So you just left."

"Hmm."

Carol Anne giggled, hiccuped. "I'm glad you did. I got a ride home with the evening's designated protector of innocent young ladies." Carol Anne sat on the side of the bed, pulled a cigarette from beneath the mattress and lit it.

"Don't, Carol Anne. You're going to get us expelled from the dorm. Go outside."

"Don't you want to hear about this delicious boy?"

"I'm glad you found a ride home. Now go to bed and sleep it off. I have a study group at eight a.m. I'm gonna be a wreck."

"Who in the living passion has a study group on a Saturday morning?"

Carol Anne was always doing this: sounding as if she was going to say "who in the living hell" and then replacing the word "hell" with some other word that struck her fancy. And never the same word twice. Passion, Amy thought, was a good choice for the evening.

"I have a chemistry midterm on Monday," Amy said.

"Oh, yeah, that's why I don't take chemistry. That would be your fault for having an architecture major . . . not mine."

"I'm finding a new roommate first thing in the morning."

"Oh, no, you're not. You adore me, and where would you find such a complementary and perfectly opposite companion to complete your soul?" Carol Anne took one more drag of her cigarette and stubbed it out on top of her history book.

"Carol Anne, you should be a drama major. Now leave me alone."

Carol Anne turned off the light, stumbled into the bathroom they shared with their suite-mates. The sink gurgled its ancient song down rusted pipes—a song heard by hundreds of other freshman girls.

Amy fastened her mind to this—to the water, to the dorm, and to the chemistry midterm. She began to picture the neat rows of numbers and their conclusions: only one answer for each row, no maybes. She saw the white test paper in front of her. Then a hand landed on the paper, large enough to lift her chin to a muted overhead light and copper eyes.

Damn. She opened her eyes to the morphed shapes of her dorm room. She would imagine her home in Darby; her bed, her room. She envisioned her childhood room in sequential order, used it as a sedative to assuage the body-humming thoughts of the boy at the back door. She began to fall into a misted gray oblivion.

Carol Anne banged back into the room; she had more to tell.

"Ooh, Ame. You should've seen the adorable boy who brought me home. I'm going to find him again. He was absolutely edible."

Amy considered telling Carol Anne about the boy she had met at the door, then she decided she wouldn't speak of him. She lacked the words to describe him; it was as if she needed another language to explain how he made her feel—a language she wasn't sure she was ready to learn.

"If I know you . . . you at least got a taste of how edible he actually was."

"Well, thanks for your confidence, Ame, but he was a perfect gentleman. Nick Lowry. Even his name is cool. I *am* going to find him. Ask him to the formal next weekend."

"You already asked Cameron."

"I did, didn't I? Guess I'll have to come up with something extremely creative."

"You're the worst."

"I think you're mixing up the word 'worst' with the word 'amazing.' 'You're the most amazing' is what I think you meant to say. Someday in your old age you'll appreciate me."

"Not tonight, Carol Anne. Not tonight."

Carol Anne laughed, then abruptly fell asleep. Amy listened to her soft, rhythmic breathing—a lullaby for Amy as she finally fell into a blank-slate sleep without copper eyes and large hands.

Chapter Five

Nick stood in the back hall, the hum of the air conditioner the only noise he heard except for the vague thumping sound of the boys, obviously wrestling each other, in the upstairs hall. Only four days had passed since Nick had seen Amy, and the reality of her, of her son dating his daughter, had only begun to sink into his consciousness. He walked into the kitchen, set his briefcase on the kitchen floor and lifted the mail from the counter. He did the same thing every damn day—walked in the house, dropped his scarred leather briefcase in the same spot on the floor, sifted through the mail. Any second now, Eliza would come in and kiss him on the cheek and ask him about his day—and he would tell her it was fine, just fine. How had he settled into these routines?

Questions, way too many of them, had begun to bubble to the surface since he'd seen Amy. He wasn't quite sure how to squelch the wondering of what had happened to her, so he allowed the thoughts to pass through. There was one thing he had decided—he was not going to the lake house and pretending for an entire weekend that he didn't care about Amy and what had happened between them, that there weren't decayed years of betrayal between them.

He kicked at his briefcase, pushed it away from the spot on the hardwood floor where he always laid it, as if this would change something, *anything*.

Eliza walked into the kitchen, as he knew she would, and kissed him on the cheek. "How was work today?"

"It totally sucked."

She spun on her heels. "What?"

"Nothing—it was fine, honey."

"What are you working on right now?" The all-white, all-straight smile was back on her face.

"Candler Enterprises wants to develop that tract of land over by the plantation. We own the timber. I'm evaluating the land." This would be enough to stop the questions; anything having to do with a prestigious company or enterprise would change the subject.

"Oh, that's great, honey. Hopefully you can still get off early on Friday to head for the lake. I'd like to get there before the Reynoldses and clean up."

Nick looked back down at the mail, opened a letter. "I don't think I can get away this weekend. Y'all have a great time."

"No way. You're not getting out of this. I can't entertain their entire family for the weekend without you. You know I can't handle the boat and all that stuff. You *are* going. Remember, this is why you work for the family company. So you can get away when you want." She reached over and rubbed his arm.

"That is not why I work for the family company. And I just can't go this weekend. Too much to—"

"Do?" She lifted her palms up, raised her eyebrows. "You can do it on Monday."

He slammed the mail on the counter. "I don't want to go this weekend. Can't that just be enough?"

"No, it can't. What is your problem? You met these people for one afternoon—they couldn't have made you mad in such a short time. Come on."

He hadn't thought this far ahead. Excuses—he needed them and he didn't have them. At least not any she'd want to hear.

"Answer me. Is it the Reynoldses? I have never, ever seen you not want to go to the lake house—it's your favorite place."

"Drop it. Please. I can't go this weekend. I'm buried."

"Then bring your work with you."

"Damn! Don't you ever give up?"

"God, what did these people do to you? Date your precious daughter? What did you think—that she'd never fall in love?"

"Jack seems like a very nice guy."

"Do you know something about him that I don't?"

He picked up his briefcase, then turned to walk out of the kitchen. "What're the dinner plans? The boys home?"

"Can't you hear them?"

He glanced up to the ceiling. "Yeah—just wondered if they were staying for dinner."

"Don't you dare change the subject on me. Reynolds, Reynolds—I'm trying to place their name, figure out what they've done to you to make you not want to go to your favorite place."

Nick continued walking.

"Phil Reynolds. Hmm . . . never heard of him. Jack Reynolds . . . did he get into some kind of trouble? Amy Reynolds . . . I only know one other Amy."

He froze, but didn't turn. *Stop*, he begged inside his

head. *Stop now.* But she never did. Eliza was relentless in all she did; this single-mindedness was one of the many complex reasons he was here—carrying a briefcase down a polished pine-paneled hallway to his tray-ceilinged bedroom with the floral wallpaper.

A hand gripped his shoulder. He turned and realized he hadn't taken another step—waiting for the revelation. There was a certain dull-edged fear in the approaching subject of why he didn't want to go to the lake. The air was full of some magnolia-like smell not found in nature, and it was making him nauseous: some arrangement sprayed with fragrance in the foyer. "Those flowers stink." Nick pointed to the silk flowers. *Please change the subject. Please.*

"Please tell me this is not *the* Amy. No."

He closed his eyes.

"You would've told me—that day, right? You wouldn't have waited until I figured it out for myself. There is no way *my* daughter is dating *her* son. God, no."

He nodded.

Eliza dropped her face into her hands. "This is like having a recurring bad dream that you think has stopped and then—bam—there it is again." She turned away from him, her shoulders dropped—her precursor to crying.

"Eliza, don't start."

When he reached out to touch her back, she looked at him. Her face changed immediately from brittle with threatening tears to stone-hard determination. "Okay—here's the deal. We'll go to the lake, have a good time, show her that we're fine and leave. We will *not* discuss Costa Rica, or what happened, or where we've been and why. The end."

Eliza, God bless her soul, had written the end of the story before he'd even found the beginning.

"Did you hear me?" She punctuated her question with her hands thrust forward.

"Yes, but it doesn't matter. I'm not going."

"Oh, yes, you are. You're showing her that we *are* fine. If you don't go—she'll think she still has some . . . power over you."

"I'm not going."

He walked toward the bedroom. She grabbed his arm. "Yes, *we* are."

"Stop this."

Now the tears came, and the guilt surrounding his inadequacy to stop them—and his responsibility for them—passed over him.

"You have to go. And you should've told me, Nick. You should've told me it was *her.* I would have never invited her to the lake."

He walked through the French doors to the bedroom, then sat on the edge of the bed. "Listen, I didn't say anything because there was no need to dredge it all up. And I figured this guy would go by the wayside like all Lizzie's boyfriends. I didn't know you'd invite them to the lake."

"God, and I really liked them."

"Of course you did. They seem like nice people. But I see no reason to spend an entire weekend with them."

"You're not going because you still care . . . that she never . . ." She swiped at the betraying tears.

He touched her face and wiped a tear from her chin. "I'm not going because I don't care, and I don't want to spend the weekend with them."

What he spoke wasn't the complete truth, but there was no reason to hurt Eliza with an explanation of the hunger pangs just beginning inside him that he hadn't felt in years—the need for something beyond what he had now.

He couldn't name it anyway—this want, this desire for who he used to be, for what he'd dreamed, for what he'd meant to do, and of course, for who he was supposed to be with. All that was stolen in Costa Rica, and looking at the past— and feeling the emotions of that loss—had little use in his present life.

"Then go for me, Nick. If you don't care about them, at least go for me. I can't take back the invitation," Eliza pleaded.

Nick grasped her hand. "I don't know. I really am buried with work and—"

She turned her back on him, mumbled to herself as she walked into the bathroom. He couldn't understand what she said—something about *paying*. But he didn't know who was paying—him, Eliza, or Amy—or what they were paying for. And he definitely didn't want to ask.

Chapter Six

Trees flew past the car window like toothpick replicas of pines in one of Amy's kids' school projects. The sky was so blue, an aqua more appropriate to summer than to late fall. The drive to the Lowry lake house passed in silence—not a normal state for the family that thrived on chatter, interruption and debate. Nothing this week had seemed normal, and Amy longed for just one moment of feeling like she had the morning she'd packed the SUV for the football game, the morning before Nick reappeared.

Molly pouted because this lake trip was causing her to miss a huge "seniors only" party that she'd been invited to. Amy had been tempted to let Molly stay home until she remembered the position she'd assumed with Eliza on the benefits of family togetherness. Phil drove the SUV immersed in his own thoughts of "something at work." He was so preoccupied with it these days, on the cusp of earning the promotion he'd been striving toward for years, and Amy didn't want to interrupt him. For once his distraction meant more than being ignored; it allowed her to wallow in her own thoughts without interference.

Phil turned the SUV down a long dirt road, with too-cute signs pointing the way to "Lowry Lake House." Each sign had a fish, a hook, a fishing pole or some other lake accent etched in pine—no need for the printed directions lying on the console.

"What adorable signs," Amy said, breaking the silence with the acidic tone of sarcasm.

"They bother you?"

She turned to see if Phil was picking a fight, if he was serious. But only the normal preoccupied sweet smile that let her know he was on her side—even when not fully there—lay on his face. Since she had no real answer, nothing to defend herself with, she only poked at his side and turned to see what Molly thought.

Molly was in the backseat, her head cocked to the left, her mouth slack in innocent sleep. The image of her as a toddler, propped in the car seat with her pacifier and stuffed Winnie-the-Pooh, brought a flash of tears to Amy's eyes. Her beautiful family. How could she let images of Nick intrude on this? She pushed the small black button to roll down the car window, scrubbed at her eyes.

She pushed her head out the window, like their old dog, Duke, and let the pure mountain air clean her face, her eyes, her mind. Duke—what a faithful and sweet dog he'd been. Why had they never bought another? Oh yeah, Phil had said there was enough to do around the house without training another dog.

A burst of anger at Phil surprised her. It was unwarranted: an uncontrolled flash. She pushed the emotion down. She'd agreed—no more dogs. She almost always agreed with Phil. She was the one who'd given the kids the lecture about how few years they had left at home, and who would be the one to take care of the dog after that?

She hadn't been angry about it then. Or had she? Her emotions confused her, the years melding; what had she felt then? Now?

She inhaled the wet and cleansing mountain air that was thinner up here; it was weightless compared to the cloying air of the city, of the beach, of home, yet carried in it so much more. They'd discussed this once, the character of the air—why it was different and how it made them feel. She pulled her head back inside the car, pushed her hair from her mouth.

Phil looked at her. "You trying to knock yourself out on a pine tree to avoid the weekend?"

"Very funny. I'm just feeling a little carsick. Phil, do you remember when we talked about the air? How light it is in the mountains, but at the same time it carries so much more in it . . . weighty but not . . ." She looked out the window. "I'm trying to remember what we were saying . . . why."

Phil looked straight at her; she felt his eyes on her and turned to him. She had his full attention, so she tried to string together an explanation—words that would only have made sense if one had been there for the original discussion. She wanted, desperately wanted, him to remember. It had been an amazing day. She felt it without seeing it. Cool autumn air, a tent, dew in her hair, cold noses, sleeping bags. No . . . it was one sleeping bag.

Nick. Shit, *shit.* It was Nick.

"What're you talking about?" Phil turned back to the windshield.

"Nothing . . . nothing. It's colder up here, isn't it? I hope I brought enough sweaters, sweatshirts. I packed for the weather at home . . . not here." She was talking too fast.

"Ame, are you okay?"

She grasped the directions from the console and used

them as an anchor to the present, yanking herself away from the memory. "Phil, whoa, stop. There it is. The house on the left." She held up the detailed directions, the paper the most important thing now. "Turn there. It's that house, there on the left."

Phil stopped the car, stared at her.

"We don't have to go, Ame. We can call and tell them Molly's sick. Anything. We don't have to go."

"We don't?" She laughed, pointed to Eliza in her jeans and white cotton blouse waving them down. "She's making sure we're punctual."

Eliza looked light enough to be blown off the porch by the slight wind shivering the trees, sending the last of the reddened leaves to the ground.

Molly awoke in the backseat. "Mom, Dad . . . hello. That lady is waving at you."

"We know, baby. Back up, Phil."

Nick appeared on the porch in a pair of jeans standing with his legs spread wide as if he were straddling something. A beer bottle dangled from his left hand as he attempted to button a flannel shirt and hold the beer at the same time. He looked like a frat boy at a party after the alumnae had left. He closed the last button of his shirt and waved, but not before Amy noticed the cleft of his chest that had once been her pillow.

Phil backed up, then pulled into the driveway. Three cars stood parked in the pine straw: a Dodge pickup splattered in mud and leaves, a white Mercedes without even a pinecone to mar its surface, and Jack's red Jeep off to the side under a shedding oak. Amy had no problem guessing which car was Nick's and which was Eliza's.

She waved to Nick and Eliza on the porch through the protection of her car window. Eliza pushed Nick's beer down and gestured for Amy and Phil to come up to the porch. Nick wouldn't tolerate Eliza pushing down his beer, would he? Amy waited for him to dump the beer on Eliza, to entangle the barley and hops in her pencil-sketched ponytail; but of course he didn't.

Phil turned and smiled at her. "And the weekend begins."

She grabbed Phil's hand. "It's only two days. Come on. At least we can spend the weekend with Jack. Let's have fun."

Phil leaned across the console and kissed her—a totem, she hoped, against evil.

Molly opened the car door. "Gross . . . *Dad*. Let's go."

Amy turned and smiled at Molly. Parental affection was high on the disgusting factor for her, but Amy knew it made Molly feel protected and part of a family.

The Lowry house curled to the left and right in cedar-shake nooks and dormers on a lot nestled at the end of a cove, a coveted spot on the lake. The porch wrapped around the house from front to back, the sides screened in for the mosquito-laden summer afternoons. Phil, Amy and Molly climbed the steps to the front porch, then appropriately greeted and hugged everybody, curt embraces of uncomfortable unfamiliarity. Amy did not look directly at Nick—at all.

The men descended the steps to retrieve the bags and Eliza walked Amy through the house, giving her a tour.

Amy stopped in the living room with the hand-hewn beams running across the vaulted ceiling. "Eliza, this house is just gorgeous, but I've got to get some fresh air—those winding roads kill me. I get so carsick."

Eliza held her hand over her stomach. "Oh, I'm so sorry—I don't get motion sickness, but I hear it's a lot like morning sickness, which I had with all three of Nick's and my children."

"Oh." Amy's nausea increased.

Eliza pointed to the French doors that ran along the back of the living room. "You can go out to the deck—walk down to the lake if you want. I'll show you the rest of the house later."

"Thanks, Eliza. I'll be right back." She walked past Eliza and out to the back deck, down the stairs to stand on an elaborate dock system that stretched across the water—a sprawling monstrosity that loomed over the cove with a slide, a diving board, Jet Ski and boat notches.

She lifted her face to the sun, let its warmth ease her receding headache. Nick appeared on the upper deck of the back porch; he stared down at her, his beer poised on the edge of the cut-log railing, his smile aimed at her.

"What?" she said, suddenly self-conscious, girlish. She almost giggled, wondering where all the anger she once felt toward him had gone.

"I knew you'd love it here. You love the mountains." He descended the stairs to the lower deck. She heard the unspoken, *I know what you like. I know you.* His bark-colored hair was too long and it rode the waves of the breeze as he came near her. It sent shivers of more than the coming wind down her legs. Her body moved, swayed to the old rhythm: the dance begun without the touch. She looked for Phil, for Eliza—for some hope of being saved from this uncontrollable movement.

"Where are the kids?" she asked. "And where is my beer?" Step one, move two in the dance.

Nick laughed, full, head back. Amy's stomach rolled with the familiar sound of joy.

"The kids are out on the lake and . . . voilà." He pulled an Amstel Light from the pocket of his flannel shirt. "Yours."

"Thank you, sir." She smiled; her lips shook.

"Hmm. You don't look like you mean that."

Amy damned her quivering smile.

"I'm fine. I just got a little carsick on the way here . . . need some fresh air."

"I'm sure you do, darlin'."

"I'm sure I do."

She was lost . . . then found as she began to move in the familiar cadence of their words and speech patterns.

"It really is good to see you, Amy. I'm glad you came this weekend."

"Me, too." She meant it. Right then, right there, she meant it. All the years filled with wondering, and the anguish of not knowing what happened to him, momentarily disappeared. Silence rolled between them and it was all right. There was time to say whatever waited out there.

They stared out at the lake. A lone sailboat dipped and swayed in a beautiful water-waltz. Then it dipped too far, flipped over, tipping two kids in life jackets into the lake. Laughter spilled and echoed across the lake, bounced up against the pilings of the dock.

"Cute kids," Amy said.

"They're ours."

"Ours?" She was dizzy.

"Jack and Lizzy."

She squeezed her eyes shut. "Of course. Yes . . ."

"You okay?"

"Oh, yes."

Nick reached to touch the side of her face, lift her chin so she looked directly in his eyes. "Amy . . ."

Whatever he wanted to say was cut short by the shrill staccato of Eliza's call from the top deck.

"Amy, honey. Which of these grocery bags needs to go in the fridge?"

Her voice, sharp with quills at Amy's inadequacy, slid down the stairs. The beer was gone and its warmth in Amy's blood sent an uncommon smart-ass comment to her mouth.

"Oh, *hon.* I'll get it." The sarcasm came without forethought and her regret moved rapidly to her gut. She laughed—always a good cover—and bounced up the back steps to Eliza's side. "I'll do it. I just got carried away admiring your beautiful home and grounds. This is such an amazing place. It's so peaceful I actually forgot there were things to do. Forgive me. I'll be the consummate guest from this moment on and help with everything."

"You don't have to help with everything. I just needed to know what groceries to put up." Eliza took the empty beer bottle from Amy's hand.

Amy followed Eliza's straight back into the house as she held the empty beer bottle out in front of her, as if it would bite. She tossed it in the kitchen garbage and wiped her hands on a dishrag.

Eliza turned to Amy. "Another?"

"No, thank you. I'll put up the groceries."

"When you're done, your room is the second on the right down the hall. I believe your husband is in there unpacking." Emphasis on the word "husband."

"Good. I was wondering where he went. Where's Molly?"

"She's on the front porch, reading, I think."

"Thank you, Eliza. For everything. For inviting us . . ."

"You're welcome, Amy. It'll be fun."

Amy unloaded the weekend's worth of planned meals into Eliza's labeled and precise kitchen. She needed to lie down with the acidic taste of an empty stomach and the buzz of a full beer in her head.

With the last loaf of bread plopped into the labeled breadbasket, Amy walked down the hall filled with twig-framed pictures of vintage hunting-magazine covers. She pushed open a bedroom door. "Phil, you in here?"

Phil stood next to the bed, unpacking with familiar movements; he laid piles at the end of the bed, identical to the ones he'd made in the suitcase. He had his own system: shirts in a pile, briefs in a pile, shorts combined with bathing suits. These heaps would be reviewed for depth and width before he decided which drawer to plant them in.

He turned to Amy. "There you are."

She leaned against the doorframe desperately wishing she'd eaten. She glanced around the room, squinting against the sun filtering through oak-stained shutters onto a twig bed, a plaid quilt, carved bear lamps.

"Such original decorating, huh? A lot of creative thought went into this," she said.

"I detect some sarcasm, honey."

"I should cut poor Eliza a break. She didn't decorate a square inch of this place. She inherited the house, the decorator and the plaid quilts from the same place she inherited her stick-straight still-blond hair and crystal blue eyes—from good genes, great money."

"Ame, sit down. What's your problem?" He patted the bed.

"Where, exactly, am I to sit with all your perfect little piles?"

He threw his hands up, then picked up his toiletries kit, walked toward what Amy assumed was the bathroom, intelligently avoiding a fight.

She called after him. "I'm sorry. I think I'm a little carsick."

"Move my stuff and lie down. Do you want me to unpack your suitcase?" he called from the bathroom.

Amy didn't move anything, but sank into a Blackwatch plaid easy chair and leaned back, closed her eyes.

Phil came back from the bathroom and the sound of him moving things around, opening and shutting drawers, caused Amy to open her eyes. He stood next to the bed pulling clothes out of her suitcase.

"Where is the gerbil cage?" she asked.

"What?"

"It smells like a gerbil cage."

Phil sat at the edge of the bed and laughed. "It's a cedar bathroom."

He shifted to point down the hall and a pile of her clothes fell off the bed.

She stood, bent to pick up her clothes, turned to the hewn-log dresser and opened a thin drawer, laid her shorts and shirts neatly in it, then squished them down to close the drawer.

"They would fit easier one drawer down," Phil said.

She began to tell him she knew how to take care of herself, that she didn't need to be told what to do. And then she wondered, really wondered, if she actually did know how to take care of herself.

She looked up at him in the mirror over the dresser, glanced away then back at herself, the way her eyes squinted, the green dull and muddy compared to Eliza's bright eyes. The neat and pulled ponytail she'd made at home sprang loose, not in sweet curls or straight pieces of golden sun like Eliza's, but in frizzy tufts, dust balls. She smoothed her hair—a futile attempt.

It was a colossal mistake coming here. Things could only get worse, a downward spiral. She wanted to go home.

She turned to the bed then flopped facedown, half on

the pile of neatly stacked clothes courtesy of Phil, and buried her face in the pillows—pure down pillows.

"Down," she mumbled through the plaid.

"Did you bring your allergy pills?"

"I hope so."

"I'm sure I have some."

She turned her head. "Always taking care of me."

He tousled the back of her already puffed hair and went to the bathroom to look for the lifesaving antihistamine that would ward off the effects of mold, mildew and down. If only it could ward off memories.

She wanted to go home. She wanted to unload the dishwasher, tidy the living room, read the paper, go grocery shopping, fold the laundry, work on her class lesson plans. The sleepless nights of the week joined with the one beer and she began to doze off, float above the room.

"Ame . . . here's some water, your allergy medicine." Phil rubbed the back of her neck.

"I want to go home."

"Too late. I offered the option earlier. They're waiting for us, and Jack and Lisbeth are here."

"I'll be out in a minute." She looked at him with one eye open, the other squished against the plaid pillow sham.

He walked across the hardwood floors, kicked at the corner of a kilim rug that had folded over—fixing it, righting things as he always did.

"Take your time." He walked into the hall and casually closed the door with his foot; it shut with a soft click into its frame. The doors in their historic home swelled and shrank without reason and never moved with the smooth slide just witnessed. Phil opened the bedroom door again, as if to praise its actions; he appreciated efficiency and never understood her love of old and inefficient houses.

"This is a very nicely built house," he said before closing the door again.

"For a gerbil." Amy swung her feet off the bed and bent over her knees before she walked to the bathroom, rubbing her eyes.

She washed her face in the soapstone sink, scrubbed it to pink with the washcloth laid in perfect hotel folds on the side of the counter. Embroidered on the cotton towel were the initials MSH; Amy took some perverse satisfaction in the fact that these were Eliza's mother's initials, not Eliza's.

"Pull it together," she told the woman in the mirror.

She stroked mascara on the lashes of her puffy eyes and dabbed concealer over the translucent blue skin; the improvement was miniscule. She smoothed her hair and wrapped a few tufts of fuzz around her finger, attempting to go for the "few loose curls" effect. It wasn't working. She turned away from the mirror—it was time to face everyone else.

She walked into the kitchen and found her son, wet and laughing, with his arm coiled around Lisbeth's waist. His hair dripped lake water on the front of her T-shirt, over her breasts. Even as they stood and laughed, it appeared that they were in a slow dance, slightly bending as if there was a gentle wind blowing just for them. Amy's legs felt weak, unhinged at the joints.

She was jealous of them, how they held themselves in the middle of the kitchen regaling the others with their tale of the tipped sailboat. They didn't even notice her. The awkward parents were the free-floating planets, the kids the sun.

Eliza turned to Amy. "You okay?"

Molly, Jack and Phil turned to Amy as she ignored Eliza

and hugged Jack. "I saw you flip the sailboat. Smooth move, Romeo."

He laughed and shook his hair on her. "It was all for your entertainment, Mom."

Phil answered Eliza. "She's fine. She just has allergies."

Amy glared at Phil, then smiled at Eliza. "I'm totally fine."

"Oh, poor thing," Eliza said. "Carsick and allergic."

It wasn't as if she was dying of a down allergy. "I *am* fine. Should we get dinner started, or stand here talking about my swollen eyes and puffy face?"

The thin ice of pure crystalline silence covered the kitchen. Amy's children and husband stared at her with gaping mouths. Amy, the mom of love and laughter, did not freeze rooms with sarcasm and unpleasant words.

Nick stepped into the kitchen and broke the awkward standoff, melted the disbelief with his smooth voice. "Nope, Ame, it's too early for dinner. Cocktail hour here. Let's go for a boat ride. I'll show y'all some of the lake." He bent over to grab a cooler off the hardwood floor; he winked at her as he stood.

Amy was grateful for Nick just then—only grateful. Yet she also wanted to hug him, run her hand down his back and find the mole she knew rested at the base of his spine.

Chapter Seven

A my stood on the Lowrys' dock and, from a safe distance, watched the sun catch Nick's curls poking from beneath his baseball cap as he walked into a boathouse at the side of the cove. She'd believed the boathouse was someone else's cabin. She looked away when Molly called from the upper deck.

"Mom, Mr. Lowry said it's okay to double up on the Jet Skis and follow you in the boat. I'll ride with Alex. You don't mind, do you?"

"No . . . go ahead. Wear a life jacket, honey."

"Duh, Mom."

Molly ran off to follow Alex; they ran down a dirt path toward the shingled boathouse. The shafted light of an evening sun parted to allow them through the trees. Amy sighed as she watched them; Phil came to her side.

"She'll be fine."

"I know, I know. Jet Skis just freak me out a little."

"She won't be driving. We'll be with them the whole time."

Amy glanced out at the lake, its surface unbroken by the wake of the boat still pulling out from the boathouse. "It's beautiful here."

"Amy, you'll probably want to grab a sweater or fleece."

"You're right."

"I'll go get your pullover. You want the gray fleece?"

"That and a glass of wine."

"At your service, ma'am." Phil bowed, then walked back to the house.

The grind of the boat engine came closer and Amy turned to see the white and black Cobalt lurch from the boathouse and fill the satin lake with waves and white froth. Nick drove the boat, spinning in a 360-degree turn, showing off, lifting his baseball hat off his head. He pulled the boat into the notch and shouted up to her, "Come on. Jump in."

He threw a rope to her; she caught it and wrapped it around a cleat.

"Jump in," he hollered again, over the roar of the engine.

Waves banged against the wood pilings; she wanted to wait until the water calmed before she jumped. Nick broke the calm of the water, broke the calm of her mind. Debris rose to the surface: a Coke can, a bottle cap, memories—but she listened to him and jumped with the waves still returning to bang the boat against its slip. She mistimed the waves, and she and the waves hit the hull of the boat simultaneously. She flew into the air; Nick grabbed her arm and used his body to steady her—to keep her from plunging between the dock and the boat. He held her tight against his chest, his arms wrapped around her waist.

She knew where to rest her hands, her mouth; she knew what to hold and when. His hand pushed on the small of her back and she understood where to bend and push at the same time. But of course, she didn't.

She laughed. "That was graceful of me."

He didn't laugh. Pain passed over his face—a look she recognized with acute awareness. "Did I hurt you?" she asked.

"No, you didn't."

"Thanks for catching me. It's not your fault I decided to hit the boat like a whale." Her lips shivered as her smile shook—he'd notice.

He touched her bottom lip; she pulled away.

"You still leave me weak, Amy Malone."

"Reynolds. It's Reynolds. Stop." She held up her hand.

"Nicky . . . is the cooler already in the boat?" Eliza called from the top deck. Amy turned.

"Yes, got it," Nick called up.

Amy laughed out loud. "Nicky?"

"Not funny, Ame."

"Yes, very funny, Nicky."

Eliza's drawl and domestic familiarity broke the reverie as Phil walked down the wooden planks leading to the dock. He appeared, Amy thought with shame, smaller, dimmer against Nick's magnitude and energy. She reached out her hand for Phil as he climbed into the boat balancing a glass of wine and a fleece.

Jet Skis roared up behind the boat; Molly sat behind Alex, who bore the genetic kiss of Eliza in his high cheekbones and thin face, his flashing hair falling over his eyes. Molly arms grasped Alex's waist. She leaned forward, yelled out, "Come on, let's rock."

"Whoa . . . " Phil said. "Slow down, Mol."

"Whatever, Dad."

Alex yelled over the engine, "Which cove do you want to head to, Dad? I'll meet you there."

"Son, wait for us." Nick leaned across the boat and pulled in a rope.

Jack and Lisbeth pulled up next to them on another Jet Ski. Lisbeth's legs were wrapped around Jack's'; her hands were clasped in front of his chest as she melded to his body. Amy turned from their physical contact, her limbs lazy as though she herself sat on the back of the vibrating Jet Ski.

Eliza climbed into the boat, bearing towels and plastic tumblers and Amy felt amiss with her real glass of red wine. Maybe bringing glass on board was against the rules.

Eliza dropped her load on a white seat and turned to her husband. "Honey, why don't we head over to the large cove. We can see the sunset better and the kids can drive the Jet Skis there."

Nick backed the boat from the dock, popped open a Heineken and steered the boat with his knees. He turned and asked Phil if he wanted a beverage.

"I got it, Nick. You just drive."

Amy scooted to the back of the boat and sat to watch the children race each other. She pulled her hair to the back of her neck and fastened it with the rubber band in her pocket. She smiled and waved at the kids. Hers. Nick's. Impossible, but not. A hand came to rest on her shoulder. She looked up at Eliza's plastic tumbler of white wine and flawless white smile.

"You have everything you need?" Eliza asked.

"Absolutely. Look how much fun the kids are having. Thank you so much for inviting us."

"I'm glad you brought Molly."

Amy felt warm, sure of herself. She took another sip of wine. "Y'all are so lucky to have this place. Do you come often?"

The two women leaned into each other to talk.

"Not as much as Nick would like to. He thinks we can come anytime he wants. He doesn't know how much trouble it is to clean it, pack. You know . . . all the stuff you have to do to open and close a lake house."

No, Amy didn't know, but she nodded.

After looking out at the water, then back at Nick, Eliza lowered her voice. "They just don't understand. They throw in a toothbrush and underwear and they're ready to go."

"I know . . . I know. They have no idea," Amy said, although this was not true of Phil. Particulars were irrelevant when searching for a way to talk to Nick's wife. "They think the groceries and kids' stuff are magically packed for family getaways."

Eliza sighed, and it sounded very much like *It's good to have someone understand.* So Amy continued. "They arrive at their destination, pop a beer and the vacation begins for them."

Eliza exhaled. "Yes."

None of the things Amy described were actually characteristic of Phil; he would pack, then unpack and she couldn't remember the last time he had actually popped a beer. He would uncork a fine bottle of Merlot, but only after the contents of the bags were neatly arranged in drawers. She was pretending to be Nick's wife. She was trying it on, a hand-me-down dress, seeing how it fit, where it would be too loose, too tight, too fancy.

The boat slapped over the wake of a pontoon boat and the red wine splashed onto Amy's jeans.

Eliza giggled. "That's why we drink white instead of red on the boat."

"Good thinking." Amy smiled at Eliza, feeling they'd found common ground—sinking, but common.

Eliza's straight hair flew around her face in a halo of caramel gold. Her skin was free of makeup and her clear blue eyes held no malice. They were, if anything, empty and waiting for approval: a child looking for a compliment.

The wind picked up, and the kids jumped the wake of

the boat. Amy waved at Jack and he gave her a thumbs-up. She looked at Molly, her hair splayed around her face, her legs in a wide squat behind Alex, her head back in laughter. The Jet Ski came sideways over the wake and leaned precariously; Molly sailed off the back—a beautiful raven in flight. She landed sideways in the water as the Jet Ski turned in on itself. Alex shut the motor off when Molly's body went underwater with a sickening *thud* as some part of her made contact with the Jet Ski. She popped to the surface; her head lolled back on the headrest of the life jacket.

Amy didn't react; she sat on the seat at the back of the boat with her wine in hand, and watched Molly, who looked so peaceful resting on her back, rocking to the motion of the water. Before the next millisecond came and realization set in, Amy actually smiled at her daughter bobbing in the water, admiring her beauty and poise. Alex, Jack and Lisbeth on Jet Skis resembled hazy images of people in the background of a snapshot.

Nick shut off the boat and flew to the back, dove in the water before Amy even moved. As he pulled Molly to the side of the boat, Amy stood and screamed. Phil jumped in, pulled his daughter from Nick as they simultaneously reached the boat.

Molly shouted, "My arm! Dad, let go of my arm. It's broken . . . or something. God, it hurts so bad." Molly scrunched up her face.

Nick hoisted himself onto the back running board of the boat and lifted Molly under her arms. Phil pushed her from behind until she landed on the back of the boat. Amy saw Molly's face—pain and tears were evident. Nausea rolled over Amy and she dropped her wine; the glass shattered on the fiberglass basin and no one noticed.

Nick sat down next to Molly. "I'm going to take your arm now."

"No!" Molly's voice was strangled, an animal's wail.

"Don't touch her." Phil climbed onto the running board. "It's broken." He reached for Nick's arm.

Nick did not look at or answer Phil. He grabbed Molly's chin, lifted her face. "Look at me. I'm going to check your arm."

Amy felt her body swell as she stood in the center of splattered wine and broken glass. She froze watching Nick's hands on her daughter's face.

Nick positioned his hand under Molly's elbow and moved it around, asked her to flex and rotate her arm. Phil lurched toward Nick, and for a second Amy thought Phil was going to punch him, wrestle him to the ground. But Phil only reached for his daughter, wrapped Molly in his arms as Nick backed away from them and jumped into the basin of the boat.

Molly lifted her arm as if she couldn't believe it was attached. She looked at Nick.

"Is it okay?"

"It's fine, just bruised. You have full range of motion and you can move it on your own. You'll have a nasty bruise there."

Eliza stepped forward now, boat keys dangling in her hand. "It's one advantage to Nick's time in the forest. He knows a lot of first aid."

Phil looked up at Nick, nodded at him, then looked over to his wife. "Amy, you okay?"

They all looked at her now. Even she'd forgotten she was there.

"I'm just fine. Don't you think we should take her to the hospital or something . . . a doctor?"

"No, she's fine." Nick's voice was soft, low—the sound he had once used when he was explaining something to Amy when they were alone. "If there was a break or fracture she wouldn't have been able to move it like she just did. It might be sore later . . . nothing a little Tylenol won't cure."

"Okay . . ." Amy looked at the mess at her feet. She waved her hand over it. "I'm sorry, really sorry."

Eliza glanced down at the wine and shattered glass, then threw a towel over it and smiled. "We'll deal with that later. Let's just get home and eat."

"Good idea." Nick grabbed the keys from Eliza and started the motor.

The boat bobbed in the wake until Amy realized everyone was staring at her.

"What?"

"Darlin'," Nick said, "you need to sit down before we can go."

"Sure. Sure."

Amy sat, motioned for Molly to sit next to her. Phil's arms were still wrapped around her as he brought her over to Amy as if holding fragile porcelain. Molly and Phil sat down and Phil put an arm around Amy, leaned down, whispered in her ear, "You okay?"

Amy whispered in return, "Sure. Molly flew off the Jet Ski. I broke Eliza's crystal. No biggie."

Phil squeezed her shoulder. "Don't worry about Molly. She's fine. Just fine."

Amy decided not to tell him that it wasn't Molly she was actually worried about.

Dinner appeared on the hewn-log dining table as though prepared by magic while Amy took a long, hot cedar-scented shower. She wasn't sure when the dinner had been cooked or how it ended up on the table. Eliza was the perfect hostess and Amy felt she was the slack guest as she appeared from the back hall, clean and dressed in a pair of old jeans and a white T-shirt—her official at-home apparel. She glanced around the table. Everyone except Nick was there, staring at her, obviously waiting. She was fully clothed, yet felt completely naked.

"Oh, my. Dinner is ready. I would've helped." She reached up to the base of her neck.

Eliza motioned for her to come to the table. "You feeling okay, Amy?"

"Great, just great. Sorry if I kept you waiting."

"Not at all." Nick appeared from the kitchen. "I believe they're waiting for me—late as usual."

Amy wanted to hug him. She walked toward the table and stood where Eliza pointed: between her children, across from Phil. Nick and Eliza stood at the head and foot of the table; bowls of steaming food were scattered across like pebbles. Large, slate-colored plates sat next to silverware decorated with deer antler handles; burning bark-covered candles looked as though they had been carved from small tree trunks. Black-eyed Susans filled a blue vase in the center of the table.

Amy sighed. "This is all so nice. The food looks delicious. I really am sorry I didn't help."

Eliza reached her hand behind Jack, touched Amy's arm. "We wanted to give you some time to . . . we were worried you might be a little shaken up."

"Well, I was fine," she said.

Eliza tucked a strand of hair into her ponytail. She was "dressed" for dinner: gray cotton slacks with a pale blue linen blouse that closed down the front with small pearl buttons. Amy fingered the bottom of her T-shirt, tried to smile. She was disoriented.

Phil added to the humiliation. "You still look a little pale."

"Why, thanks, honey. I was hoping I looked pale." Amy glanced around the table; seven sets of eyes stared at her. Her skin prickled with the peeled-off feeling Nick used to give her.

"Look, I just got scared for a minute there. It's my daughter. I'm not used to Jet Skis and—"

Nick spoke up, turned the faces from her to him. "Let's eat. Can't let all this good-looking food go to waste now."

Molly grabbed Amy's hand. "Mom, I'm so fine. Really." She placed her elbow in Amy's hand, moved it back and forth. "See?"

"Yes, I see." She kissed her daughter's elbow, kissed her cheek. "Let's eat. I'm starving," she lied.

Chairs scraped across the pine floors as the group sat in unison—orchestrated seating. Amy thought now would be a good time to scream; instead she sat and smiled.

Eliza looked around the table. "Phil, you're our guest. Would you please bless the food?"

Amy glanced at Phil; he didn't like doing this in public. Praying at home, at their scarred table, was great, but he considered it an act of showmanship elsewhere. Still, he bowed his head and offered a simple prayer of thanks for family, friends and food.

Eliza lifted her head. "Thank you, Phil. Let's move the food clockwise."

Amy suppressed a "Yes, ma'am," and lifted the bowl of okra in front of her. The evening began to unfold as conversation swirled and laughter began to fill the cracks of unease. The red wine Amy drank came from a crystal goblet that never seemed to empty as the kids told stories about their friends, about escapades in college.

Jack told the story of his friend Billy, who'd jumped off the ledge at the rock quarry into the water below and broke his wrist.

Eliza interrupted. "He's lucky that's all he broke."

"Yes, ma'am, he is. But guys jump off that rock all the time and don't get hurt. It depends on how you hold your hand or your arms," Jack said, demonstrating with his arms held straight down at his sides.

Eliza held her fork, full of pork tenderloin, in the air. "How high is it?" She placed her fork down on the plate.

"I'm not exactly sure." Jack turned to Lisbeth. "Do you know?"

"Forty-five, fifty feet, something like that."

Eliza looked at her daughter with a glance that would have shriveled Amy's own soul, but Lisbeth must have been used to it, because she didn't flinch at her mother's question.

"You've never jumped off it, have you, honey?" Eliza said.

"I'm a scaredy-cat, but Jack did." Lisbeth touched Jack's shoulder.

Jack gave Lisbeth a playful punch on the arm. "Thanks, babe."

"You jumped off that, young man?" Eliza's tone held obvious concern for her daughter's future.

"Yes, ma'am, once."

"He was perfectly safe, Mother. Really. He knew what he was doing."

"People break their backs, or their necks, jumping off that thing." Eliza looked at Nick. "I remember reading about some guy at Saxton when I was in college—he jumped and broke his back or something terrible like that."

"That was Jim Foley," Nick said. "But he was—what? One guy in thirty years? He was a great guy. He just over-estimated his ability—tried some crazy stunt off the highest rock."

"Well, I do not want *our* children jumping off that thing."

Alex rolled his eyes, popped okra in his mouth with a flick of his finger.

"Use your fork," Eliza said, without looking up or changing her expression. Did she even know she'd said it?

"Dad." Alex swallowed and leaned down the table toward Nick. "I bet you jumped off it when you were at school, didn't ya?"

"Alex, my boy." Nick's voice took on the tone he had once used to break up fights at Hank's Pool Hall—a tone that simultaneously held strength and playfulness, and could reduce even the most testosterone-fueled aggression. "I don't think that is your mother's point. I do believe she was trying to tell Lisbeth not to—"

"Oh, please," Lisbeth interrupted. "I already jumped, okay? Okay?" She reached for Jack's hand. "We jumped holding hands. It was not a big deal. We jumped off the lowest rock. Just drop it, Mom."

Eliza took a deep breath. "Dear God, Lisbeth." She looked to Amy as if it were her fault that Lisbeth, the dearest one, had jumped.

"I jumped in college."

Amy turned to see who had just confessed such a sin when she realized she herself was speaking. "I still remember the way my stomach tingled like it was too heavy and didn't want to jump with me, like it would stay up on the rock while I jumped. I remember." She turned the antler fork around in her hand. "My friends were down below, floating on black inner tubes that seconds before had seemed huge and safe, but now looked like black doughnuts with open mouths. They were screaming, 'You can do it. You can do it.' Carol Anne had on a neon bikini we'd bought together at JCPenney. My throat had a little flutter at the bottom. Then I jumped into the water. My breath was sucked out of me." Amy paused, took a breath. "Then I popped out of the water. I only did it that one time. Just once."

Amy dropped her fork on the white linen napkin, looked up to see silverware paused in midair, wide eyes unblinking. She closed her fist in her lap, the thing she did when attempting to stop a flow of unwanted words. It usually worked.

She hadn't said the worst part out loud, had she? That she'd jumped with Nick, that it was how love felt—then. Not solid and grounded as it did now. Then, love was like flying—fearful flying without breath—through the air, weightless.

"Very cool." Lisbeth spoke low, a whisper across the silent table.

"Yeah, Mom. How come you never told me?" Jack asked.

"You never asked." Amy smiled at her son and didn't dare look at Nick. "You think you're the only one who had fun in college?"

"Obviously not." Jack turned to Nick. "Did you ever jump, sir?"

"Well, since I can't seem to avoid the question—yes, I believe I did."

"I'm sure you did," Amy said, her clenched fist not doing its job.

"And, Amy, do you remember such an event?" Eliza asked.

Amy placed a forkful of mashed potatoes into her mouth; the food tasted like the inside of a dried apple. She held up her hand to show she had food in her mouth, couldn't talk. They were all patient, willing to wait for her answer while she chewed and swallowed. Eliza held her head straight, not a single hair out of place. Jack lifted his eyebrows; Phil leaned back against his chair, his soft jawline now set.

Nick finally spoke. "That was all before Jim broke his back." He turned to his daughter. "Your mother is right, Lisbeth. You shouldn't—"

"Whatever." Lisbeth waved him off. "Let's change this stupid subject."

"Let's," Nick said.

"So." Eliza coughed, took a long swig of her wine and looked at Phil. "So tell us a little about yourselves. How did you two meet—you went to college together?"

"Actually, we didn't," Phil said. "We're from the same hometown."

"Oh." Eliza pursed her lips, looked at Nick.

Amy smiled. "I went home for a college break and well—"

"The rest is history?" Eliza smiled.

"History," Amy said. "Yes, history."

"Now how did you two meet?" Phil asked Eliza.

Eliza pushed away the plate containing her barely touched food with her forefinger. "We met on a state-sponsored trip to Costa Rica—it counted for an entire semester of school credit, for an internship on reforestation."

Phil rubbed the back of his neck. "And you?" He motioned with his hand toward Eliza. "You were in reforestation . . . whatever that is? Sorry if I'm having a hard time picturing this." He smiled at her.

Eliza laughed. "I know, I know. Hard to see, isn't it? The truth is that my major was business. But my daddy said if I wanted to come work for his company, I had to have some practical experience—prove to the board I was worthy." Eliza rolled her eyes. "And so I looked at all the internships and picked the one with a beach—Costa Rica." She laughed and Amy wanted to roll her own eyes, but instead she closed them, wished herself at home.

"Granddad made you go to Costa Rica?" Lisbeth leaned into the table. "I never knew that."

"No, he didn't exactly make me. I picked the trip, but I wanted to prove I could work for him when I graduated. And because it's a publicly held company I had to prove it to more than just him."

Amy opened her eyes. Ah, the magic words: "publicly held company." Phil would be drooling now.

"Which company would that be?" Phil asked.

"Sullivan Timber. It's—"

"The largest timber company in the southeast," Phil said.

"Yes. How did you know that?"

"I'm a stockbroker. We manage that account for quite a few clients. It's done well. How long have you worked for them?"

"Well, that's the funny part. I never even went to work for them. I met Nick on the trip to Costa Rica and we fell madly in love and"—she glanced at Amy—"as you said, the rest is history. So the trip was worth it."

Amy couldn't help it: she wanted to avoid Nick, but she looked directly at him. He stared at the table; then instead of turning to his wife, he looked across the table at Amy. Her blood was warm as it filled her cheeks and neck.

"What did you do after Costa Rica?" Phil asked Nick.

"Well . . ." Eliza began for him. She covered her mouth with her hand. "Sorry," she said from behind her palm, "bad habit."

"I did—still do land-use planning, protected-area development, wildlife utilization and other boring things," Nick said.

"That's not boring," Amy said. "It sounds—"

"Interesting." Phil finished for her. "Did you stay in Costa Rica?"

"No." Nick turned to his son. "You kids wanna clear the table for us?"

"Sure, Dad." Alex stood. "Thanks, Mom. It was great."

The four kids loaded up their arms with dishes and empty serving bowls, then walked to the kitchen, talking about a Scrabble game in which they'd beat their parents by a million points.

"Where did you go after Costa Rica?" Amy asked, before she could decide whether she really wanted to know.

She could have said what she'd once known—what Nick had wanted to do, what they had wanted to do—but she had no idea of the valid answer now. She wanted to stand up, walk away, but how could she when her legs were made of nothing more than the blue-black air outside the French doors? She had as much command over her body as she did over the wind and water of the lake. She wanted to hear his answer and she wanted to scream against it.

Nick looked down the table at her. "We moved to Maine."

"Oh." She shifted her eyes away from his copper stare.

He stood, began to walk away. She was embarrassed to ask again—where in Maine? Why?

"Men, I swear they give only as much information as the CIA," Eliza said. "We moved to Maine because Nick got a job with one of the most prestigious timber firms in the U.S. and he was in charge of all their—"

"Eliza." Nick turned around. "They do not want to hear about this."

"Sure we do," Phil said with the strained voice he used

after he'd been sick and was trying to pretend he was already well.

"So," Eliza said, "anyone want coffee?" She leaned across the table. Her eyes looked uneven, like a child had stuck Mrs. Potato Head with two different eyes. But maybe it was just an effect of the wine.

"I'd love some," Amy said.

And once again the evening took on the cadence and rhythm it had before the reminder that Nick defined, for Amy, everything to do with college and jumping and young love, before the still-unanswered question was raised: what happened in Costa Rica?

Chapter Eight

The Scrabble board and jumbled letters covered the oak coffee table with deer-antler legs. The wineglasses scattered across the table looked like red and white jewels that had tumbled off a bracelet; wineglass identifiers with various charms circled the stems. There were a bear, a moose (when was the last time anyone had seen a moose at Lake Hardin?) and other emblems of the woodsy lake house. A pine tree dangled from Amy's glass and she thought how she would have preferred the canoe, to take her far, far away from here.

The conversation about family and school swirled around her in disjointed sentences. She smiled when appropriate and attempted to concentrate on the wavering letters in front of her. She found words in her head, but couldn't spell them from the small tiled letters—she'd drunk too much and needed to go to bed, or home for that matter. But she dared not be any ruder than she already felt she'd been.

The conversation—as she'd prayed it would not—turned to her. Eliza had just finished listing the nineteen hundred causes she worked for, including her volunteer work with the Junior League and the Botanical Society.

What was Amy to do? Tell them all she worked part-time at the college and took care of the family and home? It was what she did, but to sum it up that way suddenly seemed feeble. She began to tell Eliza about the island with the Colonial-era house that she was desperate to save.

She just wanted to talk about what she did, about what was important to her. This small thing—this justification of her existence beyond her home and job—began a series of events that she would never have been able to predict; a sense of inevitability took over. Phil had heard her story often enough and never really listened; she always felt her words fell hard and unheard. Here she felt the others were ready and willing to hear all about it.

"Tell me about it," Eliza said, blinked in an almost flirtatious way.

"It's a small island called Oystertip Island and a very wealthy, and anonymous, man wants to buy it—develop it into a personal playground," Amy said.

"A neighborhood—a development?" Nick put down his letter tiles and leaned across the coffee table, his eyes wide.

She stumbled over her hurried words as she attempted to tell him about it—as if she'd been waiting for someone besides the committee to care.

"It's only about one hundred twenty-five acres. This man wants to build his own private retreat—you know: a house, pool, guesthouse, dock. We haven't seen the full plans and we don't know who he is. There's a crumbling Colonial-Palladian house at the center of the island that the original owners built before the Civil War—it's one of the very last of its type. Anyway, the developer wants to tear it down, build a replica on another part of the island."

"And the land—what about the land?" Nick said.

"I got roped into this committee—the Oystertip Wilderness Protectors, OWP—by default. The others are botanists and naturalists and they're the experts on the land. They're doing everything they can to save it. They only came to me for my expertise with period-style houses. And I just can't stand to see them tear it down. It makes me nauseous to think about it."

"Who started this group—who's in it?" Nick leaned closer and so did Amy.

He had to speak above everyone else as the kids, Phil, and Eliza began their own discussion—something about whether "skitter" was a real word and was there a dictionary in the house.

She glanced around the room and realized it was only Nick who was listening, who cared; she wanted to tell him all about it.

"The OWP is a group of students who believe there are enough endangered species on this island to get a protective grant from a Heritage Trust. They worked on this project for at least a year before I came on board. They've discovered that one of the things the Trust program protects is architectural gems—so that's how I got involved."

"They're looking for a wildlife-refuge grant from Georgia?"

"No, and actually the island is in South Carolina—right over the Georgia border into the ACE Basin, where the Ashapoo, Combahee and Edisto rivers meet. The Heritage Preserve inventories, evaluates and then protects the most outstanding representatives of the state through the Trust. The OWP feels they have a good chance of the island becoming a Heritage Preserve. But we have to prove the island is both worthy and that the need is urgent because money is tight—there are about fifty million dollars' worth of projects that deserve to be protected and only about two million dollars in the Trust right now."

"Wood stork, osprey, peregrine, brown pelican, loggerhead are a few of the endangered ACE Basin species," Nick said.

Eliza tuned back in, shivered and laughed. "Yeah, those and water moccasins."

"Eliza, water moccasins are not endangered," Nick said.

"Well, I wish they were extinct." Eliza faked a shudder.

Amy looked at Nick and he smiled at her.

She placed her elbows on the coffee table. "I'm trying to stay out of that part—I'm just trying to prove that this house should be saved."

"Have you seen it? Been in it?"

"I've been to the island, but not in the house. The Eldrin clan that owns it are the great-great-grandchildren of the original owners, who were slave merchants and indigo farmers. Now this family has some bankrupt business and they need to sell the land—and they don't care to whom. They fiercely protect the island and house from nosy naturalists like the OWP. It's amazing how they don't care, how they just want the money."

"Which island is this, Amy?"

"It's off the coast from Savannah, next to Osprey-head Island."

"I know exactly where that is."

"You do?"

Phil poked at Amy's ribs. "It's your turn, darlin'."

Amy returned to the couch, her head swimming and tiles jumbled. She looked at Phil. "I was in the middle of telling Nick about the island."

"It's your turn," he repeated.

She looked down at her letters—all consonants. "I can't spell anything."

Nick leaned farther across the coffee table, tiles scattered. "Phil, it's pretty cool that she's involved in this. She could save another island from the damnation of bulldozers and paved roads."

"Island? She's always trying to save one house or another. She does a good job of it. Which house are you talking about, honey?"

"The one *on* the island, the one I've been telling you about."

Phil tilted his head as if she'd just spoken Gaelic to him, as if she hadn't been blabbering for months on end about this project, as if she'd just grown another damn head.

"Which island?" Phil asked.

"Phil, there's only one island. You know, the Oystertip Island project. The small island with the historic house."

"Yeah, yeah. That one."

And she saw, as she was sure everyone else did, that he had no idea what she was talking about. Irritation nestled below, far below, but embarrassment became her primary concern.

"Yeah, that one. The one with the committee I'm on and the meetings and the endangered species."

Eliza put down four letters and looked up. "Nick's always trying to save things, too—trees, animals. You know, nature takes care of itself." She shrugged. "Sometimes I just don't get it."

Amy's mouth opened, then closed. *Just don't get it.* Nick was married to a woman who just didn't get the one thing he was most passionate about. Amy had so many things to say about that, but she couldn't find a thing to say.

"Neither do I."

Amy looked up to see who said that. Who else didn't get it?

Phil.

She fought hard against the intruding thought that she was married to a man who just didn't get one of the things she cared about the most—but the idea came as unbidden as the movements she'd felt in the boat with Nick.

No, that was not true. Phil did get it. How could he possibly be married to her, love her, take care of her the way he did if he didn't get it? *Because he never listens to you— that's why.* Dizziness enveloped her.

Jack stood up and stretched. "I'm out of here. I'm wiped. Mom—you do a great job saving all those old houses." He leaned down and kissed Amy on the cheek. "Good night, everyone."

A chorus of "Good night, Jack" rang across thoughts that had never before risen to Amy's consciousness. The other three kids found their excuses to leave and wandered off.

Amy stood. "I'm right behind the kids. Good night, y'all. And thank you for dinner, Eliza."

"Amy?" Nick said.

"Yes?" She looked down at him. He stood.

"I'd love to help you with this project. This is my specialty, you know. I know the barrier islands pretty well. My buddy Reese runs the Eco-Tours on the islands and—"

"That's how we got out there the one time we went," she said. "But we can't seem to get permission to go back. The owners are freaking out that we're going to mess up their big-time sale."

Nick's smile moved in shifting sand patterns of other islands, other smiles. "I'll take care of it," he said.

Phil stood up and coiled his arm around Amy's shoulder. "Her committee—what did you say it was called, honey?"

Nick answered, "The Oystertip Wilderness Protectors."

"Yeah, that, they're doing a great job. I'm sure they have all the help they need."

Eliza chimed in. "Yes, I'm sure Amy knows exactly what she's doing."

From far away came a voice that said exactly what Amy wanted to say: "We'd love your help." A subterranean shift moved below these spoken words, and she avoided all eye contact as she worked her way down the hall to the bedroom.

Chapter Nine

Nick Lowry sensed the rest of the house sleeping. He always could; the sleep felt like a dark, crouching figure, and even without checking he could tell if anyone in the house was up. If they were awake, the dark figure representing sleep would be alert and waiting for him to execute another mistake.

The smooth leather of the couch, the only piece of furniture in the lake house that he had picked out, wrapped around him as he dropped into the cushions. There was no way sleep would visit him tonight. His mind consisted of nothing but twisting thoughts of Amy that seemed to circle around a metal-grated drain, but never go down the hole, never disappear. For the past twenty-five years he'd avoided the barbed pain of finding out why Amy never came for him, why she'd turned away.

"Shit." He stood from the couch, restless.

He wanted to be angry with her for screwing him over the way she did. But today he had only seen her gentle face, the hair soft around her eyes. She had always tried to tame that hair, pull it into place, but he most loved her when she let it go, when she let herself go.

In college she'd been the type of person who drew others, not only because of her inherent beauty, of which she was completely unaware, but also because of something in her, around her, that turned her into what others wanted or needed from her. Strangers and friends were constantly coming up and telling her: "You look like my sister," "You look like Farrah Fawcett," "You look just like a girl I dated in high school."

She would smile and, just for a second, be that person for them. She had always told him that with him she was only and rightly Amy, Nick's Amy. His beloved. She could morph and change for the others, but for him she let her real self surface. Who was she now for this man, these children? He was sure she was exactly what they needed, loved, wanted her to be. Because she could be.

Nick walked over to the French doors that led to the back deck. He leaned his head against the dark doorframe and stared out at the rock-black lake melding with the pine-lined gray horizon.

Something moved, flickered against the dock: a flash of silver? It was the first thing he had noticed the second time he met Amy—her silver cross and how it rested at the base of her throat.

He had stood at the front desk of Dorm B, waiting for the girl, Carol Anne, who had asked him to a sorority formal. Kappa Alpha pledges were instructed to go to any formal they were invited to—it was part of the pledge process. He began, then, to see that maybe he wasn't so sure he wanted to be part of the whole pledge thing, belonging to a fraternity just because his dad had. It had seemed so necessary when he arrived at college, but now it seemed juvenile and insulting. Either way, he had a date.

He picked up the black rotary phone to call Carol Anne's room—no boys allowed past the gray metal door to the back halls. Her roommate said she would be right down. But when he spun on his heel at the sound of his name, the world spun with him; he blinked at the quick flash of a silver cross around her neck.

It was the girl from under the light, the girl who fell out the back door of the KA house, then ran to her car without telling him her name—the girl who made him talk like some stupid wimp from *Gone with the Wind*. He knew he'd made a fool of himself and now he had a second chance.

"Well, now, tomorrow *is* another day, isn't it?" he said. Well, there went his second chance.

A blush spread across the freckles on her cheeks. He felt the heat of it in the curve of his own neck. She reached for the cross that hung on a thin silver chain and looked like it would break under the strain of her finger.

"Carol Anne, my roommate . . . she sent me down to tell you that she's running a little late. A curling-iron catastrophe."

"Hmm, what exactly is a curling-iron catastrophe?"

"You know, when you're curling your hair and you touch your neck by accident and it looks like you have a hickey and you really don't. She's trying to borrow a turtleneck to wear." She blushed deeper, pulled harder on her chain.

"Well, thank you for the information. But I don't believe I can properly thank you until I know your name."

"Amy . . . Amy Malone."

"Beloved."

"Excuse me?" She backed a few steps from him; he reached across the space between them.

"Amy. It means 'beloved.' I learned that in French class."

"Oh."

"It should mean 'beautiful.' "

Amy turned around, moved toward the door he couldn't go through. "I'll go check on Carol Anne for you."

"I'd prefer if you just waited with me." He moved toward her and touched her hair, just the back of it.

She turned and smiled, but her smile shook—so beautiful, the way it shook. "I believe it would be better if I checked on your date."

He saw his time was running out. "I've been looking for you. You know, around the school. I even looked in the sorority composites, but I couldn't find you."

"Looking for me?"

"Yes. Well, now I found you."

"Yes, on your way to a date with my roommate. My best friend, coincidentally."

"She asked me."

"Yes, she did. You said yes."

"It's a Kappa Alpha rule."

"Nice rule. Very . . . gentlemanly and all that." He knew, right then, that he would quit Kappa Alpha.

The metal door banged, but neither of them turned. Every detail appeared magnified: her eyelashes were lighter on the top than the bottom, tendrils of hair had pulled from the ponytail high on her head. He'd never had trouble with girls. Teachers maybe, parents always . . . girls never. But this one seemed immune to his charm, staunch against his now witless comments.

The more he spoke, the stupider he sounded. She was disarming him, one weapon at a time. He reached within himself for one last piece of ammunition: direct eye contact, assurance.

"Tomorrow night I work at Hank's Pool Hall. I get off at ten."

"And?"

"You'll go out with me tomorrow night. Please."

She opened her mouth to speak, but another voice said the words: "Nice beginning to my formal. Perfect. Just perfect."

Amy turned. "Carol Anne."

"Nice turtleneck," Nick told Carol Anne, who wore a black sweater with ostrich feathers around the neck and a long silver skirt; it was all he noticed about her.

Carol Anne glared at him, but he felt no heat from it. None. "What in the living sorority formal are you doing asking my roommate out?"

"Please forgive me. I met—"

"He was joking with me. Nothing big, Carol Anne. I met him at that party when I couldn't find you. We were joking about movies, stuff like that."

"You didn't tell me about him."

"No, you were too busy telling me about him." Amy laughed and walked away, not even looking back as she said, "Have a great time tonight."

And the metal door slammed.

This memory was a brick on his neck—aching. He must be seeing things outside on the dock. Amy didn't even wear that cross anymore. He didn't often visit these memories where each detail, if probed, was still as sharp as the needle that had sewed their relationship together. She had a quote, an old quote she used to say about their relationship . . . something about being sewn together. He would ask her. He would ask her a lot of things. Nothing else mattered except this second chance he was now being offered—even if it was through his daughter's boyfriend.

Eliza had talked him into coming to the lake house this weekend, her tears and pleading accomplishing the intended job. Or maybe he hadn't really needed to be talked into it. Either way, now he just wanted to know Amy again, the spaces of her: the dents between each vertebra, the soft spot below her anklebone, the curve of her earlobe. And now another desire rose—to find out why she had never come, to find out what had caused her to abandon their promised life together.

By the time he'd been released from the hellhole they called a jail, he had sufficiently buried all the good of Amy and had only found, when probed, fury at her broken promises.

He glanced out to the lake—there it was again, a flash. *Amy.* Now she was here—all her goodness lucent and evident again. He couldn't fool himself into bitterness and hatred when she was present.

Amy awoke to the pinprick pain of numb legs. She opened her eyes to a pure black void; she was afraid to move. She curled her legs up to her body until she could remember where she was and why. It came back to her in short bursts: Nick's lake house, red wine, dinner, a dizzy sleeplessness that had sent her out to the lake and the large deck chairs, away from her snoring husband. She leaned back on the teak steamer chair—no plastic lounge chairs at the Lowry house.

The night was an erased chalkboard: starless, moonless. She strained backward, gazed to the right and left in the dark, looking for the moon. Her heart rolled as she realized she'd lost all sense of direction, lost the moon.

Where was it? There was always a moon.

Was she facing east, west? She didn't move, fearful she would fall in the lake. Then she placed one foot on the dock, pushed on the wood, placed her other foot down and stood.

Footsteps echoed through the night, vibrated across the dock. She grasped the arm of the chair, not caring who walked toward her as a need to find the scarred face of the moon consumed her. If she didn't find the moon in that pitch dark, she would be lost forever, bobbing in this new great divide between the present and the past, between the seen and unseen. She would disappear into the white noise of water, a world without directional markers—vaporous, weightless as she now was.

She scanned the sky.

"Ame, you okay, darlin'?"

Nick.

She rotated her head, careful not to shift her body.

He moved down the dock toward her in the dark, a shape more than an outline. He appeared at her side, apparitional; she reached for him.

"Where's the moon?" Her fingers curved and grabbed a handful of his shirt as she pitched forward. He caught her and she leaned against his shirt, inhaled his smell of fresh-cut wood and soil—a part of all the land he tried to preserve. She laid her head on his chest, a resting place.

Words came through the vibration in his upper body. "The moon?" His fingers wrapped in her hair and she heard a slight moan. Was it his or hers?

"I can't find the moon," she said.

"Well, Ame, the house is facing east. It's two in the morning, so . . ." He turned her body and lifted her chin, pointed to a faint glow. "There's a massive cloud cover, but the moon is under there. Right there." He took her hand and lifted her arm and index finger, wrapped his hand around hers and pointed.

She stared at the diffuse and rounded filtering of a moon with no light of its own.

"Thanks." She felt her feet on the wood, her hand curled in his denim shirt. "Is it really two in the morning?"

"Yes, darlin'. You must've fallen asleep out here. The rest of the house is asleep."

"Not you." She backed away from him.

"No, not me. I don't sleep well. You know that."

Yes, she knew that. Even in sleep he had always seemed to wrestle some imaginary force of life.

She released an involuntary whisper. "Hmm." It was a sound easily heard in bed, asleep, half-asleep.

He pulled her back toward him. "God, Amy, I've missed you. I never thought I would see you again, but I've never stopped missing you—not once. Shit, you still make me lose my breath."

"Nick, don't."

"I wanted to hate you when you didn't come."

His voice came low, raspy, and the whirling darkness that she was afraid would encompass her now rolled over her.

Her voice came from the other side of the lake. "Didn't come where?"

"For me."

A star fell—a flash between the clouds.

"What?"

"When you didn't answer the telegram, I understood. I did. I was *not* the man you thought . . ."

Her body fell into him. She'd placed her desire for him in a honeycombed labyrinth, so deep below her life that she shook with its rising force. Below her breast, inside the V-shaped convex of her ribs grew a widening shakiness, a quiver that expanded, without possible escape. With the growing feeling also came a serrated pain that had grown and changed while hidden in the dark; it now appeared as anger.

The anger and desire braided together, fighting each other, leaving her without strength to push him away. Nick slid his hand where the cotton of her T-shirt billowed away, forming an air pocket between the vertebrae of her spine—warmth spread as evenly and firmly through her body as her mind. The small groan came from the bodily memory of him.

His body pressed against hers. She closed her eyes to overlapping images behind her lids: his wide hand splayed across a white pillow, his sandals on a hardwood floor, granules of sand encrusted in the sole of a shoe lying on its side, the smooth white porcelain of a tub, his hand reaching above it, pulling her down.

His lips found hers in the dark; she responded with visceral memory as a shock of anger broke from the woven pattern. She pushed him away.

"No." She made an unconvincing strangled sound. *A telegram, he'd said something about a telegram.* "What telegram?"

"The one I sent."

"I never . . . got a telegram."

He released her, sank to a lounge chair and groaned. "Oh, God, no."

In the silence between them, something undefined began to move toward her, growing exponentially. She shivered, backed away from him. His bent body punched the dark like an old bruise. Panic rose from a well within her pelvis. Whatever he had to say—she couldn't hear it. Now sure of the dock and where to step, she ran.

She slammed the door as she entered the house and a

phrase from a poem she'd written in her journal the day she had fully given herself to him, a phrase she'd long ago repeated to him, rose from the released memories: *We are bound at the edges, sewn firm down the center: one.*

She fled now, step by step, to her husband and children, to those she was now bound to and would never, ever betray.

Chapter Ten

Eliza ran a baby blue dishrag under the faucet, squirted pine-scented soap on it, then ran it up and down the kitchen's speckled black-and-taupe granite counters. She was precise, never wasting a movement. Nick wanted to grab the dishrag from her, tell her to pull her hair out of her damn ponytail and go outside: swim, splash in the lake, run naked down the dock—anything but clean and pack and act as if this were a normal day, as if they were just leaving the lake after another weekend of entertaining.

But how could he despise the same qualities in her that had saved his life, that had made it possible for him to be standing here with children, with a lake house, with a life? Her methodical way of living, along with her family status and influence, were to be praised, not ridiculed.

He wanted something other than his own altered heartbeat to prove that none of this weekend qualified as normal. He reached across the counter and grabbed the dishrag from Eliza's hand, flung it across the room. It landed with a squashed-slug sound against the far wall.

The kitchen clock ticked one second, then another.

She clenched her teeth; he saw it in her jawline as she spoke. "What are you doing?"

"I am going outside to say goodbye to our guests. What are you doing?"

"Cleaning the kitchen. Not anything you would know about." She turned and glared at him. "You were right. You shouldn't have come."

He lifted his hands in the air. "A no-win situation there, Eliza. It was wrong for me to stay home and wrong for me to come."

"No, I was wrong. You shouldn't have come." She turned away.

He'd hurt her; he hadn't meant to, as his pain now entered the space they occupied together.

"Go say goodbye to our guests," she said.

He walked out the door, timing each step to the clock he'd never noticed before. She mumbled, but he couldn't hear what she said. He shut the screen door on her words, on the clock, but he couldn't shut out the hunger that rose inside him.

He'd waited, watched all day yesterday for a chance to talk to Amy, his need consuming all else, but never fulfilled. Family, skiing, boats, meals and late-night Scrabble never allowed contact with her. She was a master at making sure someone was by her side all day. The need to talk to her had sat like an unwanted and wakeful companion through the night.

He stood on the back porch and leaned over the railing. There she was: alone. She stood behind the car, bent over, pushing a suitcase into the back. Her jeans hugged the parts of her he had once touched as easily as his own skin. Now he couldn't even look directly at her; she was as untouchable as if a solid but transparent wall lay between them.

She stood, then turned to him, smiled. A wind visited from the back of the house and lifted her hair, raised it to the sky. A bird flew from the branch above her. Her white blouse billowed from her chest as she waved. "Are you gonna stand there and watch, or help me?"

He walked down the steps, sensing the wind and the way it must feel as it whispered through her blouse. "Need a big strong man to do your work?"

"Oh, forget it. I got it."

He stood next to her, touched her arm and bent to look in the back of her SUV for a sign—anything to show him who she was now. Sunglasses lay lopsided on the dashboard, an Anita Shreve novel was open facedown on the console, a hair clip was attached, clawlike, to the visor. He made quick mental calculations: she was not a neat freak; she still loved reading; she still tried, in vain, to contain her hair.

He knew he must say what he had to say—fast.

"Will you please meet me, not anything really, just a cup of coffee, something? You can tell me about the island project. We can talk."

She looked around. Up, down, to the left and right. He had forgotten to do that, to check that no one else could hear, as if the two of them still existed alone.

She spoke low; his skin remembered her other whispers.

"Well, um, I'd love to tell you about Oystertip and—"

"I want to talk . . . tell you . . . ask you what happened."

"What good would that do?" She brushed a leaf off the bumper, looked away from him.

He lifted her chin so she would have to face him.

"Stop doing that. I can't . . ." She backed away from him.

"Have you slept at all?"

"Stop. Please," she said.

"I can't sleep. I can't breathe. Please say you'll see me."

"No."

He pulled a scrap of paper from his back pocket. "This is my cell phone number. I'll wait. Just to talk. *Talk.*"

She took it, stuffed it in the back pocket of her jeans. She looked up toward the porch, and waved at Molly. "All packed, except your bag," she called in a voice he didn't know, in a voice of family. He felt a stab below his ribs—her family.

"Look at me," he tried again.

"No."

"Look at me."

She slammed down the hatch and looked at him. Her brown eyes were hard, boulder and dirt, for a moment before they turned fluid and full.

"Nick. Stop."

"Please."

She turned from him and waved to her daughter coming down the steps.

"Please." He mouthed to himself, to the universe that had returned her to him.

Chapter Eleven

The dusty scent of familiarity surrounded Amy as she pushed open the door from the garage to her home. Phil unloaded the trunk while she walked to the answering machine to check messages. She was anxious to know if there was any news about the island project from the OWP. Among the multiple reminders of Molly's tennis match (change of location), meeting for the art fundraiser, and a cocktail party at the neighbors' house that night, there was a message from Carol Anne about her husband, Joe.

"Amy, I talked to Joe about the island project. He believes he can find out who the buyer is. He's gonna ask the private eye his old law firm uses."

Amy let out a whoop and crossed the kitchen, walked down the hall to bounce into their bedroom, where Phil was unpacking the suitcases. He looked up at her.

"Any messages for me?" he asked.

"Just a reminder about the party at the McCanns' tonight. But guess what."

He glanced down at the pile he'd sorted into clean and

dirty. "I'm not in the mood for a party tonight. Can you call and bow out?"

"Didn't you hear me? I said, 'Guess what.' "

"What?" He stopped and looked up from his task.

"Carol Anne called."

"And?"

"She said she thinks Joe can do some digging and find out who the anonymous buyer is."

"Honey." He stopped unpacking and touched her arm. "You don't need to get everyone we know involved."

"Everyone we know? It's just Carol Anne and she offered."

"And your college buddy Nick."

"What?" She shook her head, took two steps back. "He offered, too. I'm not trying to—"

"How can they help but offer? It's all you talk about."

"It is not."

"Forget it. . . . Do you think we can get out of this party tonight? I have a ton of work to do before my seven a.m. meeting tomorrow."

Amy sat down on her vanity chair and stared up at him. Being ignored came in various forms with Phil—this time it came in a bailout for a party obligation. She inhaled deeply and rubbed the bridge of her nose.

"No, we backed out last time."

He grabbed a pile of dirty laundry and threw it into the closet hamper. "I can't go tonight, Amy. You'll have to find an excuse or go without me. I have a ton of work to do and I probably shouldn't have gone to the lake."

She agreed internally—she, too, probably shouldn't have gone to the lake.

Her brief bubble of elation over Carol Anne's news deflated. She stood, fingered the back pocket of her jeans, slid her finger inside and rubbed the scrap of paper. She yanked her hand away.

"We'll skip tonight," she told her husband. "I have papers to grade, anyway."

There was no use getting into an argument; he was preoccupied, and it would be a fruitless discussion leading to her inevitable frustration. She turned and headed for her office, her papers and the distraction of her work.

Molly flipped her tennis racquet back and forth between her legs in the passenger seat. The radio spurted forth a thumping beat from a song Amy had never heard before and didn't care to hear now. Her head was dense, full with dreams, thoughts and frustrations—with an overwhelming need to know, just know, what telegram Nick was talking about.

She reached over and switched off the radio, rolled down her window. Molly glanced at her but didn't speak, rolled down her own window and stuck her head out. Molly laid her head on the windowsill and looked behind the car, her hair wafting up, the end of her ponytail slashing in the wind. She pulled her head back in and looked at her mother.

"Are you staying for my match, Mom?"

"Of course I am. Why do you ask?"

Molly shrugged.

"I know I've seemed busy. The school semester is winding down and the art fund-raiser is in a couple weeks. But I'd never miss a final match . . . not yours."

"Okay." Molly looked out the windshield, stood her racquet straight up and leaned against the dashboard on top of it. "Mom? Is Dad coming?"

"No, babe. He's got some big meeting with Mr. Stevenson. I think this promotion might finally come through."

"Okay. You know, he's never missed a final match."

"And I'm sure he won't miss many more. This was really important."

"I know, I know. Hey, Mom?"

"Yes?"

"Where do you think time goes?"

Amy took in a slow breath. Molly had been asking questions like this since she could speak: "Who sees the sun first when it leaves our side of the earth?" "Why do dolphins live in the water when they can't breathe in the water?" "Why don't dogs have tears?" These were questions that required much more of Amy than the usual distracted answers. Molly's intense curiosity had never bothered her before, but now, here, she felt like slamming on the brakes of the SUV and dropping her head on the steering wheel in defeat.

Instead, Amy took a deep breath, smiled. "Oh, honey, it just goes so fast, doesn't it? You were born, it seems like, a week ago."

I dated Nick just yesterday.

She maneuvered the car around a slow red minivan in front of them and glanced at her daughter.

"That's not what I mean at all, Mom. I mean really, where does it go? Like that last minute—where did it go? Is there a place it goes, like a recycle bin, or is it just gone?"

Molly's question carried with it a great somber note and as with all her daughter's questions, Amy wanted to answer well, and yet she had to admit that she hadn't, in any way, ever thought about where time went. Maybe that's what children were for—to make us think about the hard questions . . . and answers.

Molly laid her cheek on the tennis racquet.

Amy turned from her daughter, from the unanswerable question, to the familiar landscape of the city. Oak and spruce trees planted by the original founders of Darby still lined the streets, forced their roots up through sidewalks and streets. Even her hometown was a testament to rooted familiarity and consistency. She knew the name, origin and turn of every street she drove. Mr. Steele still ran the five-and-dime, Mr. Henderson still pushed down a little too hard on the scales when he cut meat at the butcher counter, and the movie theater still had its original marquee with the green lightbulbs.

The road she drove to the tennis complex took her down her childhood street. As she drove past her old home, she slowed at the front lawn. The house still resided in a neighborhood where young families lived with rectangular lawns, metal swing sets and red tricycles. She stared at the top window on the right (her pink childhood bedroom with the Eagles posters) and remembered the countless hours she had spent staring out at the front lawn, at this very street—wondering what had happened to Nick Lowry.

She shook her head and turned to her daughter. "Time . . . maybe it goes behind us, just like this road."

"No, Mom, I can see the road behind me. And we'll drive on it tomorrow. It's still there."

"We can look back at time. It's in . . . memory." Ah, she'd found the answer.

"But we can't do the time—or whatever we were doing in that time—again. Exactly again." Molly waved her hands in the air, rolled her eyes. "Oh, forget it, Mom. You don't understand what I'm asking. You don't understand—"

"Don't say it, Moll. Don't say I don't understand *you*."

"Well, you don't."

Amy took a deep breath. Here they went again—why

couldn't little girls stay five years old and still love and believe their mommies? "Well, I do understand the question. It's actually a very profound question, and it will come as no surprise to you, but your mother knows nothing. I don't know where time goes. I don't have any idea whatsoever. What made you think about it?"

Molly chewed on the side of her thumbnail. "I don't think that you don't know *anything*. I was only wondering. There are so many things I don't want to forget, but I bet I will."

Amy smiled at her daughter, hoping the love she was about to express would come through as love instead of "smothering." It was a toss of the dice every day. She knew mothers who, for now, refrained from their deepest expressions of love for their teenage daughters in fear of the retaliation and accusations, the slammed doors and scrunched faces. She would never stop telling Molly she loved her.

"I love you, Molly, and that is a very, very good question. The only answer I can think of is in our memories, in what we leave behind: life, I guess."

"Oh."

The discussion ended and Molly pushed the button on the radio and closed her eyes, thumped her head back and forth against the headrest to the beat of the music.

A tall girl in a matching Nike ensemble slammed the ball across the net toward another player. Amy sat alone in the crowded stands waiting for Molly's turn on the court. She watched the girl's muscles, taut and trained to win, and she realized that she *did* know where time went, but she wouldn't tell her daughter. Time was stored in her body in such a way that the first mention or shiver of the past called it forth; memories were not just hidden in her brain for her to gaze at in sweet reverie as a moving picture of life. Past time was attached to her body's response—muscle-gripping and emotional washes—hiding in her cells. Memory came how and when it pleased. Time grew and expanded and saved its face for dreams and moments when she least wanted or needed to see it.

Carol Anne appeared and waved her hand in front of Amy's face. Lost in thought, Amy started.

"Are you there? Hello?" Carol Anne asked.

"Hey . . ." Amy rubbed at her eyes as if Carol Anne had just turned on the lights.

"Where are you?"

"Here . . . what do you mean?"

"You look lost."

Amy leaned back against the bleacher. "I'm tired . . . just tired."

"You haven't returned my phone calls in a week, my dearest friend. Is there something you're mad at me about? Maybe that I'm funnier, cuter and smarter than you—has the envy finally overcome you?"

Amy laughed. It felt good. "I'm sorry. Really. I've been crazy busy with—"

"Yeah, yeah, I know."

"You doing okay?" Amy turned her full attention to her friend.

"I'm fine, luckily, since I could've been dying of a terminal illness and you wouldn't have known. I'm just so sick of Farley I could puke."

A woman with too-red lipstick turned and put her finger to her lips, made a hushing sound. Amy scrunched her nose at the woman, leaned in to whisper to Carol Anne, "Let's go outside. Molly won't play for another half hour. This match is in overtime."

They walked out into sunlight that looked faded and tired, as though someone had run it through the washing machine too many times. Amy turned to her friend, then leaned against the concrete wall of the tennis complex.

She was as frustrated with Carol Anne's boss as if he were her own. Mr. Farley was the epitome of the small-town businessman who used his family name in such a manner that his ancestors probably crawled deeper into their Darby graves. He was a vast and flamboyant man and he also owned the largest interior design firm in the city—and the only one, because of undue influence from his uncle, the mayor, who would not allow commercial space to be rented to a competitor.

"Carol Anne, just leave."

"I already told you I can't. We can't afford it until Joe's law firm gets more established, whatever that vague concept means. You just wouldn't believe what Farley had me do this time." Carol Anne groaned and looked up to the sky. "He had me decorate an entire house from the paint chip of the customer's antique Rolls-Royce. I had to match the paint, wallpaper, fabric to a damn car paint chip. Lord Almighty. Now, get this—*Southern Decorating* is doing a piece on the house and I don't even get a bit of credit. Nothing."

"If you're that miserable, leave."

"It's not that simple. There are a lot of things to put on the scale."

"I know, I know: Joe, the money, no clients, no work— yeah, you told me. Have you talked to Joe about it?"

"No."

"Talk to him. I bet he'll be on your side with this one. At least *your* husband listens to you."

"What's that supposed to mean?"

"Nothing, nothing." Amy waved her hand toward the parking lot.

"Well, enough Farley melodrama. Tell me everything."

"About what?"

"The lake."

"Oh, that."

"Yeah, that."

"It was fine. . . ." Amy dug the tips of her boots into the pavement, looked away from Carol Anne. "Hey, where do you think time goes?"

"What in the living tennis ball are you talking about?"

"Nothing. Nothing."

"Okay . . . Amy, you're worrying me now. And you haven't told me anything about your weekend at the lake. I know you need to tell me. And I know *I* need to hear it."

"It was fun. Molly fell off the Jet Ski and scared me to death, but we had fun."

"Fun. Okay . . . that's all I'm gonna get from you? You spent a weekend with the same stud who broke your heart and all you can tell me is 'fun.' "

"Not a big deal. There's no reason to worry about a man who ditched me almost thirty years ago—never came back, never called, never contacted me, and now has a daughter who's dating my son."

"Life is weird."

"Yes, it is. But we're all married now with kids, family."

"I wish I could've been there."

"Be careful what you wish for."

"Yeah, look at you, darlin'. Always wishing you knew what happened to Nick Lowry. Here you go."

It felt as though someone were sitting on her chest; she wanted to tell Carol Anne about the mysterious telegram she never received, about her dreams and distraction, yet she couldn't figure out how to string together an explanation.

"By the way, what are you doing here?" Amy asked.

"I called the house this morning looking for you. Phil told me where you'd be. I knew you needed me."

Amy looked at the woman she had known for almost her entire life. "Thanks for having Joe check on the buyer for Oystertip. It's truly great. Maybe the committee will actually think I'm worth something if I get the name of the buyer."

"Obviously they think you're worth something if they have you on the committee."

"Yeah, but only for the house, not for the big stuff. They really want to find out who the developer is so we can confront him—get the media all over the issue, maybe convince him not to develop the land. But he's hiding behind numbered accounts and the Eldrin clan, who own the island."

"Well, no guarantees, but Joe will definitely try."

"I think Phil was mad. I told him Joe was helping, and he got a little pissy. Said I shouldn't involve everyone I know."

"Did you tell him we offered?"

"Yes. I'm so irritated about the whole thing I don't even think I can talk about it. He just doesn't seem to care about this stuff like I do."

Carol Anne grabbed Amy's hand and laughed.

"What's so funny?"

"Has it ever been any different? He's never really been into all this historic stuff like you. Remember how you had to beg to live in that old house while he wanted to live in the new subdivision they were building in Mr. Harbor's cotton field?"

"I know, I know."

"Well, why is it bothering you so much now?"

"I don't know. But it definitely is. He could at least be glad I have some help from Joe and Nick."

"Oh, God, what are you talking about? What kind of help from Nick? No wonder Phil's pissy."

"He said he knew someone who could get us out to the island. You know, it's Nick's specialty and all that—land preservation."

"Yeah, I know what his specialty is."

"This is different. He knows a ton about the barrier islands—has contacts."

"Yeah, I'm sure he has contacts."

"There's something else. . . ."

"What did you do?"

"I didn't *do* anything, Carol Anne. He told me something . . . something about how he didn't leave me . . . then."

"What did he say?"

"Asked me about some telegram I never received. I ran . . . away. I don't want to talk about it. I'm exhausted from it."

"You have to talk about it, or—"

Amy pointed at the tennis complex. "Not here. Not now."

"Okay, but don't do anything until we can talk. Promise?"

Amy nodded.

Carol Anne hugged her. "I knew he was trouble from the day he asked you out when he was supposed to be going out with the more fabulous, more fun me." She hugged Amy again. "Damn him. Damn that Nick Lowry for showing up now."

*   *   *

Busyness became what kept the memories and wondering at low tide, not controlled by the moon that Amy had lost that evening on the dock, but by the ebb of her own memories. After watching Molly win her tennis match, Amy wandered the aisles of the grocery store, knowing that only the sharpest focus would hold back the recollections of Nick.

The tomatoes were too soft, the lettuce wilted. *Focus on the details.* She lifted the asparagus; the thick tops looked like the trunks of the palmetto trees on the beach. Which beach was that? A nature preserve? A public beach?

Nick.

She and Nick had walked, lazy, smooth. Oyster shells had cracked under their sandals. Sand granules clung between her toes. The sun was high, too bright, beating, the air viscous, blood-thick. A seagull hung in the sky, neither flying nor sinking, as if the dense air held it in midflight. A sailboat tipped; sun glinted off its hull, winking in shattered-glass fragments. The whipped-cream waves stood out from the molten navy sea. Her skin prickled with the sunburn she knew would show up that evening in red slashes.

The muscles in Nick's back rose and crested with the waves that seeped across the sand toward her toes: one force. He picked up half of a gray clamshell run through with slashes of milk and slate. He ran his finger across the top, his thumb curved along the bottom, rubbing it, and reached for her hand. A shrimp boat sounded its echoing horn across the sea. His thumb was larger than the inside of the shell, caressing its center.

"Here, feel this. Look." His voice was deep.

"It's beautiful. Really beautiful." She wanted to touch his hand, not the shell.

"The other half is lost." He placed her index finger on the edge of the shell where the lost half had broken off.

She ran the toes of her right foot through a pile of shells, many halves and shattered pieces. "All of these have lost the other half."

"But this one is so . . . perfect."

She looked up at him, away from the sand line she'd exposed between the sea's broken dishes. She touched his face, the rough growth of beard that appeared two hours after he shaved. Her legs were liquid and moving as the ocean itself.

"This shell is still whole, with no match," he said.

A blurred fin flashed in her peripheral vision, and she turned to the sea. "Look, a dolphin." A smaller fin broke through the waves and dipped back down as if pulled by an unseen force. "And a baby, too. Look."

Her lover of nature did not glance toward the sea. He was the one who had taught her about noticing each nuance, each gift of nature. He stared at the shell.

"It has a match somewhere. It could be anywhere—another ocean, another sound, crushed to sand, or even worse . . . at the bottom of the deepest part of the sea, in the dark, while this one made it to the surface."

She felt the arrow of aloneness that she'd often felt before he'd entered her life, before his copper eyes had looked down at her.

"See." He looked at her now and the isolation she'd felt before him faded, but was still palpable below her exposed skin. He touched her. "See how lucky we are. One of us could still be searching, looking, lost . . . crushed. But we're not, we're connected here—" He took her hand and placed it on the cuticle-hard joint of the clam.

"Yes."

He ran the shell across the top of her bikini, ran his finger inside, rolled his thumb inside her bathing suit. The shell fell to the ground and she moaned, glanced out to the sea, to the mother and baby dolphin dancing to a universal rhythm she now understood. She didn't, yet, look in his eyes. Sometimes when she looked, she would absolutely know that there was no way she could ever fill those eyes; other times she looked and knew that she, only she, could actually fill him, and she would.

Her legs gave way underneath her, now made of sea and sinew, no bone or muscle to obey the commands to stand; she understood the release of the mother and baby dolphins' water dance of joy as she worshiped the puffed blue sky, Nick's eyes, the conch shell that dug below her spine.

Then he rose above her and flipped her with one movement of his arm; she saw the crushed shells void of their other half, the lonely ones left to the sea's discretion. She rolled to her side and looked away from the shells and into his eyes.

She curled into the sand next to him and he pulled her to him until the connection at the shell's edge fused them. Her face burned from the searing sand, rough chin. Only if he moved could she. He rose up on his elbow, rested his head in his hand, looked down at her. "The connection breaks so easily: one storm, one wave, one rock. . . ."

"Not ours. Not ours," she said.

Chapter Twelve

A my utilized her jobs as teacher and OWP member as she never had before—as more than things she did because she loved them. She used them now, like the other chores of her life, to preoccupy her mind in an attempt to fill the crevices Nick crept into without permission. The island became more than a project; it was now a place that desperately needed her full attention. She scribbled across her lesson plan, sharpening her pencil every few minutes in the electric pencil sharpener on her mahogany desk.

This week, she would take her class on a field trip to the oldest house in Savannah, the Cherry Mansion, teach them about the vernacular intricacies that were best learned by touch and sight. As field trips were first thing in the morning after the previous day's class, they required that she spend the night in the art dorm, which was really a historic house turned residence hall. She loved the deep smell of plaster a hundred years old, the mumble of college students above and below her, the whispered rumors of the marble-playing ghost boy and the wandering ghost woman, who died as she fell down the steps looking for her husband, who was in the bathroom (perpetually, apparently) with another woman.

Amy reached for her tea, took comfort in the mug she drank from: a brown-speckled mug Jack made at camp years ago. The objects of home, the important things, she reminded herself—even as she fingered the edges of the scrap of paper she'd been keeping in the pocket of whatever she'd worn for the past two weeks. Touched it—that was all she did.

The phone's ring startled her and she grabbed it before the second ring. Carol Anne, reminding her of the fundraising meeting in an hour.

"You do not have to remind me." Lies seemed to flow so much easier now. "I'll be there."

"I do have to remind you. You've been a little . . . gone lately. You missed the meeting last week and we can't do much without the chairperson. You have all the paperwork and schedules."

Irritation swelled. Amy placed her head against her palm. "I'll be there in an hour. I was working on my lesson plans for this week. We have a field trip."

"Amy, you've been using the same lesson plans for five years. What's up now?"

"Nothing. Really. I'll see you in an hour."

She hung on to the phone long enough to hear a rapid-squeal signal. Her lesson plan was done, the art-auction paperwork was in perfect order and she did have the phone in her hand. Ah, the rationalizations. She held the receiver in one hand and reached inside the pocket of her wool pants, keeping her eyes closed as though she couldn't watch herself. She fingered the piece of paper as if she could read Nick's phone number through her skin.

She laid the paper on the desk, the phone still in hand,

and opened her eyes; the paper remained folded. She stared at it as the phone screamed its off-the-hook warning. She opened the paper with one finger and stared at the number. She reached across the desk and pushed the button to reconnect to a regular dial tone. The paper flopped closed when she lifted her finger.

She began to rest the phone back on the hook. This was not a good idea. But didn't she have a right to know what had really happened? It was part of her life, *her life*, and she wanted, deserved to know why he had never come back, what telegram he was talking about, what she possibly could have done that made him believe he couldn't come home. Also he'd said he could help with Oystertip, and the committee could definitely use him. She'd told the others on the island project about him and they knew Nick Lowry, knew his reputation, and couldn't believe that she could get him to help.

She opened the paper and pressed each number slowly, deliberately.

By the fourth ring, relief spread through her as Nick didn't answer. She would have to see him again; Jack and Lisbeth were talking true love—there would be time to find out what had happened to him, to know. She didn't need to call him.

"Hello, darlin'," his voice came on the phone.

Her stomach clenched. "Oh . . . it's me, Amy."

"I know. I have caller ID—I've been waiting."

The sound of loud motors or screeching chains filled the background. "What's that noise? Do you want me to call you back?"

"I'm out on-site. Makin' sure they are environmentally safe as they rip down another acre of pine to build a golf course."

"Oh. Well . . . okay."

"Where would you like to meet?"

She closed her eyes. "What?"

"Ame, where do you want to meet?"

"I'm not really sure I want to. I was just calling about the island and—"

"To see me."

"No."

"Yes. And for my help. But we need to talk first."

"Can't we talk on the phone?"

"No."

Something other than her will, something of her cracked internal impulses answered. "I have to teach at two o'clock in Savannah on Thursday and then I have to take the class downtown Friday morning—"

He interrupted. "I'm in Beaufort, less than hour from the college. I'll meet you Thursday. I'll arrange to have Reese, my buddy with Eco-Tours, take your committee to the island. Would that work for you?"

"Yes."

"Really? I'll meet you at—where do you stay?"

"At Porter Hall. I'll meet you there a little after three."

"Perfect. Then we can meet your committee down at Carter's Marina before four. Think they could do that?"

"Sure. Yeah, sure."

"Ame?"

"Yes?"

"Thank you." His voice, she was positive, cracked a little. The man who wavered between assured and sarcastic was still broken in the hidden places only she could touch.

Part II

I like to think that the moon is there even if I am not looking at it.

—Albert Einstein

Chapter Thirteen

Nick opened the refrigerator, lifted the orange juice carton and popped the top off, then took a swig. He glanced around his familiar kitchen; although nothing was out of place, it appeared skewed, as if someone had slanted the picture, placed something there that he couldn't identify. All of this was real: his wife, his children, his job, the photos on the shelf, the mail on the counter. Yet simultaneously Amy and the truth, destiny and second chances, were even more genuine.

It all came down to this—to today; he would tell Amy what had really happened, where he'd really been. The air felt lighter on his skin, darkness of any kind lifted with the mere knowledge that she would hear the truth. He wanted all the misunderstanding and confusion that had blighted those years since he'd last seen her to clear as fog lifting after the rising sun. It wasn't betrayal that kept her from him, it was absence of knowledge—all else faded in the bright light of this fact.

Eliza walked into the kitchen and looked him up and down. "What are you wearing?"

"Um . . . it looks like khaki shorts, a T-shirt and hiking boots. Is there a problem?" She wore silk pants with a floral-sequinned pattern down the legs and a pale blue blouse. Her satin hair and lip liner were in place and he remembered—the party, the anniversary or birthday of someone important.

"Oh, God, Eliza. I'm sorry. I forgot."

"I reminded you last night and this morning on your voice mail."

"I've been in the field all day—I didn't . . . I'm so sorry." He closed his eyes.

"Well, just go change. I'll wait."

"I can't. I committed to go to . . . on-site."

She groaned. "I told you it's an early-evening dinner—I thought that's why you were home—it's a surprise party."

"I'm already late, Eliza. I'm sorry. Please give my regrets to—who was it?"

"Oh, come on. This is Dick Foreman's sixtieth birthday party at the Club. You cannot miss it."

"Why not?"

"Don't you realize he is the CEO of Southern Timber? They were just bought out by—"

"I know who they were bought by. I keep up with all of it—trust me. I'm busy enough with my own job not to worry about somebody else's." He leaned in and kissed her on the cheek. "Case in point: I have to go."

"Can't this wait—what project can't wait?"

Nick grabbed his keys from the desk. "The Oystertip Island project."

"Not the same one that Amy Reynolds works on, right?"

"One and the same."

"Nick . . ." She turned away. "No."

"This is about an island, not an old girlfriend."

"Bullshit."

He laughed at the unfamiliar sound of his wife's prissy voice cursing.

"It's not funny. You're only doing this because of her."

"Even you don't believe that. This is what I do. How many projects like this have I worked on—or at least volunteered for?"

"That's the point. Greenpeace, National Wildlife Federation, CARE, now some OWP thing. How about you support the Lowry family?"

"What the hell is that supposed to mean?"

"It's not supposed to mean anything, except I wish you'd go to this party and I wish you were home more."

"I'm home all the time. What are you talking about?"

"I don't know. Just don't go today. This is just an excuse, isn't it? Just an excuse to see her again."

"Don't get on my back about this now."

"On your back? You're headed out to some deserted island with your ex-girlfriend and I'm on your back?"

"I'm not getting in a fight with you today. I'm not. And I'm late."

"If you go there and skip this party . . ."

"What?"

He knew what came next: something about everything she'd done for him, how he must go to this party with her. But the litany didn't come; she just turned away. Instead of going after her, Nick turned and walked toward the door to the garage.

He'd almost made it out the door when he heard her. "I do everything for you and the kids. Everything. And you can't skip this—this one thing."

He knew if he turned to this tune, he'd be singing it for the next few hours when he wanted to be thinking of something else entirely, someone else entirely.

"Answer me. You can't just walk away," she said.

"Yes, I can," he said without turning. Then he opened the door to the garage, hesitated as the other part of him—the part that lived in this house with this family—prodded him to turn. He looked over his shoulder.

"It's a project, not a reflection of all you do for me. I'll be home tonight."

Her face looked swollen, out of proportion from holding back a temper tantrum or tears. "Isn't it funny?"

"No, I really am not seeing humor here."

"Funny how things come back around, making us pay again just when we thought they were completely paid for." Her voice sounded robotic, and a shiver crawled through his gut.

"What am I paying for?"

"Oh, not you, Nick. Not you."

This time she turned away, and her motions seemed as automatic as her voice. The picture of his life now slanted even more than a few moments ago. His curiosity about who was paying for what could not match the pull of finding out Amy's reaction to what he had to tell her.

Amy plopped down on the marble bench that sank into the soft soil, slanted down on the left. She dropped her black leather teachers' planner and notebook beside her. She'd brought class work with her to distract her from the true purpose in sitting on a marble bench in a deserted courtyard behind the college dorm where she would stay tonight. She'd come here a thousand other times to grade papers, enjoy the beauty of the Porter Hall courtyard and gardens, brainstorm about the best way to teach her students about Greek-revival architecture, or the influence of the English on Georgian-style homes—something, anything that would remove the slack-mouthed stares that accompanied her students' boredom.

But as she fingered the top of her planner, no distraction lay within its pages. The facts and figures blurred and her mind wandered. Just as they had in her bed the last few weeks, her thoughts tossed and turned without logical sequence. The memories of times with Nick were just disjointed images; she couldn't delve below the surface of vague to the depth of specific.

How could he have been living within hours of her, saving trees, land and animals without her knowledge of his existence? How could she not have felt or known or heard of him? Was this how buried she'd become in her own life, in the whitewashed preservation of her own existence, in the life she'd built, brick by board, friend by friend—that she hadn't seen or known Nick was near? But she'd buried all thoughts of Nick Lowry, so that she hadn't even known him when she saw him—until he spoke.

She leaned her head back on the bench and took a deep breath. Nick would like meeting the island project group.

Nick had once told her the land possessed a power that very few people were aware of; that it had the strength to create and bring to it what it needed. She'd nodded and believed and still did. Maybe it was not her that Nick was here for, but the land itself.

Someone touched her shoulder.

Her eyes snapped open as her head jerked up, and she knocked the back of her skull against the marble—an electric flash of pain shot down her neck. "Ow."

Nick laughed, then sat down next to her. "Sorry. Didn't mean to scare you." He rubbed the back of her neck and she allowed this, stunned again by his overpowering beauty.

"You're early," she said. "Did they give you a hard time at the front desk?"

"Nope. Told me exactly where you were."

"Well, the OWP sure is excited to meet you. Seems you have quite the reputation."

"Oh, well, what type of reputation would that be?"

"I hadn't realized that you'd been around for quite a while, that you'd been"—she laughed—"saving things."

"Well, now you know."

"Not really. What exactly do you do?"

"Ah, what I *do*! I work for Sullivan Timber, advise them on land use—on the impact to the habitat and ecosystem, on the best way to develop the land without harming it more than they would otherwise."

"Oh."

"Not what you wanted to hear?"

"No. No, not at all. I just thought you'd wanted to do more research and education. I didn't realize you worked with corporations."

"Not impressed with the job?" He poked at her arm.

"That's not what I meant. I just—"

"You just remembered what I said I'd do, right? What I meant to do." He made a groaning noise in the back of his throat and she had to turn away from him, from the sound.

"That was a long time ago. Sorry. I didn't mean to imply you weren't—" she said.

"No, it's true. You're right. I'm not doing what I said I would. But if it helps anything—I do a lot of volunteer work."

"That's how you know the Eco-Tours guy taking us out today?"

"You got it."

She needed to stay on the subject—she couldn't discuss

broken plans, past promises. "I'm thrilled you're able to help us. Seems you've showed up at the perfect time."

Nick leaned in, placed his hand on her knee. She felt it as skin to skin although her jeans separated them.

"Amy, we have to talk at some point today. There are some things I need to tell you."

"Well, right now the OWP is probably pacing the dock waiting for us and we'll be on the island until tonight . . . maybe another time would be better."

Despite how much she'd wanted to know what had happened to him, she now felt that what he had to say could wait—that it would ruin the calm joy of just having him around, just knowing he was here, alive, well.

He stood and reached out his hand. "Well, then, let's go."

She took his hand and stood, felt the ground sway as if the unseen moved beneath her.

"This island is beautiful. You'll love it. And because of you, OWP now accepts me as a real part of their group, not just the housewife from Darby."

"Ah, that's because they didn't know you before you were the housewife from Darby and the beach, well, did certain things to you."

She felt a wide opening beneath her—the unseen now a gaping hole.

"Nick."

He touched her face and she turned away.

"Come on. They're waiting," she said.

Chapter Fourteen

A ragged trawler bobbed on the calm surface of the Sound, tied to a splintered wooden dock at the marina. The OWP committee, two men and one woman, stood on the dock in a scattered group dressed in khaki shorts and sun-faded T-shirts. Revvy, the leader, stepped forward and waved. Rubber bands bound his long blond ponytail every inch; his face was ruddy from outdoor life, and a camera hung around his neck and bounced against his chest as he walked toward Nick and Amy.

He thrust his hand out to Nick as he reached them at the dock's edge. "Dude, it's so great that you're here."

Revvy didn't even look at Amy as she spoke. "Revvy, this is Nick Lowry."

"Yeah, yeah, I know. So cool that you can help. We're gonna stop this, you know. Stop this guy from building on the island. You're the clincher, man. Totally. They'll listen to us now. I've heard about you from my buddy in Beaufort—how you helped save that osprey nest where they're building the new resort."

Revvy stopped and looked at Amy. "Hi, Mrs. Reynolds. How are you today?"

"Great, Revvy, great. Let's go."

Irritation rose without reason. And she always had a reason—for everything.

The OWP group carried backpacks with cameras and specimen containers, and for once, Amy didn't feel like the escort on a school field trip. Nick walked with her; the rest of the group waved enthusiastically from the dock.

In Nick's truck on the way to the marina, she'd explained the history of each member of the group. This litany not only filled the warm cab with innocuous information, but protected her from discussing the past—something she was not yet ready to do.

She'd explained that Norah, the dark-haired law student, was in charge of gathering and correctly cataloging the information to submit for a Heritage Preserve Trust. She'd never seen a hint of makeup on Norah's face, yet she was one of the most beautiful girls Amy had ever known: quiet in her passion, inexhaustible in her efforts. Amy often wondered if Norah ever slept.

Brenton was the naturalist of the group, a botany student who hoped to find a rare species of plant or animal on the island that would qualify it for the Trust. He lived in a tent on the beach in one of the national parks; he considered the stars the only roof he could tolerate. He was calm and intense, his brown hair falling to his shoulders in a wavy mass that most girls envied. She'd once heard him tell Norah that his parents quit supporting him when he dropped out of the Citadel. His father would not tolerate his son dropping out of his alma mater, considering it a chromosomal error and therefore that Brenton was a man not good enough to be his son. Brenton hadn't cut his hair since then or slept on any bed, not even a cot.

Amy and Nick reached the group and she introduced them one by one as she explained what each one did. Revvy was the leader and specialist in sea turtles and their endangered eggs.

Nick greeted each one as if they were old friends—pumping their hands, offering words of encouragement. They glanced sideways at her and she imagined she saw a newfound respect in their eyes; Nick changed her in their perception and, as before, changed her in her own.

It shouldn't be this way—that another person could change her image of who and what she was and could do; but it was always that way with Nick.

Nick introduced them all to Reese, the owner of Eco-Tours who had finagled permission for a ride out to the island—never letting the owners know it was the OWP that would be going.

Reese pulled on the bill of a baseball cap over blond curls. He looked younger than Jack, although Amy knew he wasn't. Nick had told her all about him—a corporate dropout from Atlanta who couldn't stand one more day of traffic, cell phones and beepers. When he'd arrived home to find his wife waiting for him at the front door with her suitcases packed—she'd decided she was in love with their marriage counselor—he'd taken one bag of his stuff and never looked back.

The mismatched group climbed into the boat—proof that a cause can bring largely different individuals together.

The boat sliced through the waves, and reverence for the Sound brought silence. Norah and Brenton leaned over the bow and allowed the water to splash them. Revvy, on the backseat, lifted his face to the late-afternoon sun. Reese stood at the bow and steered the boat with one hand while singing to himself.

Amy's body trembled and she blamed the humming motor of the boat; she wished she could be as still and immersed as the rest of the group. She sat next to Nick on a vinyl bench at the back of the boat—he flung his arm atop the seat behind her and she resisted leaning into it and closing her eyes as physical memory became stronger than present reality.

The sea spread before them in a blue stretch of peace, separating in V-shaped waves from the bow of the boat, allowing them to pass through the water. Amy sat straight, her hands in her lap, her satchel at her feet.

Nick pulled at the ends of her hair. "Whatcha thinkin'?"

"What a beautiful evening this is. We're lucky. The last time we came it was overcast, choppy. I got a little seasick. A representative of the Eldrin clan escorted us. They only gave us one hour to view the island. We thought we wouldn't be able to get back here unless we broke the law—trespassed. I know they were ready to do it." She waved at the disjointed group. "But jail time did not seem in my best interest."

"I'd like to take the credit, but it was all Reese."

"Well, Reese or you—or both. Thank you, Nick."

"You know, the owners can't find out about this—Reese could lose his job."

"No problem. I've already told all of these guys to keep it quiet." The boat slowed and Amy stood.

Oystertip Island grew until the curved pale beach appeared before them as a welcome mat. The oyster beds clumped together like mounds of broken china—sharp and beautiful in their clinging mass. The briny smell of marsh, earth and unseen marine life mixed with the wind. A wood stork glided over the treetops and disappeared into the thick of the marsh's cordgrass. Revvy pointed, but no one spoke.

To the left the beach faded into jagged lines of clumped grass which then merged with the maritime forest at the center of the island. Reese pulled the boat close to shore and threw out the anchor.

Amy looked at Nick. "How are we supposed to get to shore?"

"Walk."

"On water?"

He laughed. She shivered at the sound.

"No, you can touch bottom here. You might get a little wet, but you can walk in."

"Great." Amy looked down at her jeans while Norah, Brenton and Revvy took off their shoes, threw their gear over their backs, then jumped in and began to wade to shore. The water hit the bottom of their knees, and they waved at her and Nick to come on.

Nick reached down and flipped off his boat shoes, then threw Amy's satchel over his back. He hoisted himself over the side of the boat and looked up at her. "Come on, I'll carry you on my back."

"Really?"

For one moment she imagined herself riding on his back, her legs around him; then she jumped in the water. Jeans wet below the knee were nothing compared to the danger of wrapping her legs around Nick Lowry.

Norah, Revvy and Brenton stood onshore waiting for them. Brenton paced the beach, running his toes through the sand while he pulled out his notebooks.

They agreed to scatter and gather specimens and pictures, search different areas for the one thing that might save the island. Nick and Amy walked toward the interior where the house stood like a layer cake with whipped-cream icing left out in the rain.

Norah followed Brenton, while Revvy took off for the oyster-encrusted tip of the island, where he hoped to find a significant loggerhead nesting area.

Nick followed Amy as she kicked her way along the crushed-shell path toward the home. "We can't get in, but I can show you the house," she said.

"Hmm." Nick picked up a fallen leaf, held it up to the sun. "I think this leaf is from a wild orchid—only a few left in the state."

"Oh."

He smiled. "Keep telling me about the house—I'm listening."

I'm listening. Such sweet words.

"The house was built in the early 1700s by the Eldrin family, who were slave merchants and indigo farmers. It was their 'country life' house—used for holidays, parties, hunting. It is one of the few extant mansions in the Palladian style. Most Colonial-style homes were burned in Savannah's fire of 1796." She sighed. "I'm boring you."

"Absolutely not. Go on."

"I can't really explain what it is to destroy a house like this. Architecture is like a picture or a journal of lost time. You can't just tear homes down because they're inconvenient."

"I know, Amy."

While she talked, he gathered specimens and placed them in plastic bags, labeling each one. He lifted plants to the sun, rubbed them between his fingers, studied them with a concentration he'd once shown toward her. She had once seen the promise of this man, but she'd been deprived of the full blossoming. She had once listened to him talk of doing exactly this; she'd seen him learn, and now she experienced the fruition of his dream. In the subtle island sun, in the dense maritime forest thick with endangered barrier-island creatures and memories of their own past, she watched him.

He turned to her and touched her arm. "Look at us."

"What?"

His smile was full and warm. The shadow of a palmetto branch licked the side of his face like smudged charcoal and she tightened her fist to stop herself from touching him.

"We're doing what we always said we would," he answered. "Working together."

She swayed as the wind murmured through the palmetto tree, moving the shadow across his face. She reached for his arm and he pulled her to him and held her. His body was a fortress of strength, stronger than she remembered, yet diminished in what it meant to her. There were other arms now, other strength.

She pushed him away. "Don't, Nick. This can't be about . . . that. It's about the island and the—"

"I know, the house. But something we said then— something we said we'd do—it didn't go away because, look, here we are doing it."

"Weird coincidence."

"No such thing as coincidences. There are so many things I need to tell you, things you don't know."

"Not now."

She turned away and walked up the weed-clogged path. Nature's cacophony blended with his words and confused her. She didn't know what to believe, why he was here, why she was here. She'd been content to watch him pick up the plants, laugh with the others, his hair riding the wind. But there was more, and she felt it as cumbersome as any incoming storm system.

She pulled the camera from her satchel, then snapped pictures of the house. Nick came to her side and they climbed the stairs to the rotting front porch.

He pushed at a sagging board over a window. "Amy, it wouldn't be that hard to get in."

"If they found out we went in the house, they would press charges. I want to save this house, but I do *not* want to lose my job and force my family to bail me out of the Chatham County jail."

"No, that wouldn't be a good idea." He threw back his head and laughed. "But I don't think they'd know. You could get in and out through a window."

"Oh, they'd know. They would definitely know. They're watching us like hawks, trying to find any excuse to get us off their—"

"Asses."

"I was going to say 'backs.' "

"I'm sure you were."

He laughed and tousled her hair, rested his hand on her cheek.

Revvy rounded the corner to the house. "Found another dead loggerhead." He shook his head.

Nick jerked his hand away from Amy's face. "Show us."

They followed Revvy to the thin stretch of east-side beach that faced the sea. Waves beat upon the sand with the hypnotic voice of the incoming tide. White foam coated the end of each wave, coming to rest on the sand as a reminder—a wispy memory of what just reached the shore, then retreated. *Just like Nick,* she told herself. *Let this wave pass.*

Nick followed Revvy to what Amy thought was a large rock, but it was a barnacle-encrusted turtle shell, large enough to be a tabletop.

Nick bent down and picked up the turtle's head, pulled it back to expose its craw. Revvy pulled a hunting knife from his back pocket and sliced open the gullet. Sand, gray shrimp and a long piece of string fell to the sand. Amy turned her head and attempted not to gag in front of these two naturalists, who considered this study as routine as building a sand castle.

Revvy and Nick flipped the great turtle over.

"I don't see any signs of disease," Revvy said. "It's hard to tell without a full autopsy—but nothing obvious."

"Probably got caught in a shrimper's net," Nick said.

Revvy groaned. "When will the shrimpers ever believe us?"

Nick and Revvy dragged the turtle carcass to the sea and let it catch a wave to its original home. Amy wanted to help, but she only watched this man, this man who used his hands to study nature and marine life as easily as he tousled her hair and touched her cheek. She knew the danger in thinking about him like this, but like an echoing refrain from a sad song one can't help but listen to, she watched and felt him.

As the turtle shell bobbed like a floating rock, then sank to the unseen ocean floor, she asked, "Aren't they on the endangered list? Something that could get the island a Heritage Trust?"

"No. Loggerheads cover the ACE basin," Revvy said. "We would have to find a substantial nesting area, but I haven't so far." He squatted down in the sand, traced a shape of the island, looked up at Nick. "They want to build the house here." He drew an X as on a treasure map. "But the area is so dense with live oak, palmetto, yaupon holly and shrubbery that we can't get back in there unless we have some real equipment and a lot more time. I understand your buddy can't leave us here too long without jeopardizing his career and all that, but I don't think we can prove anything yet."

Nick glanced off to the horizon where the sun hung, bloated. "We have maybe an hour or more before dark."

"Find whatever you can and meet back at the main beach at sunset." Revvy stood.

Nick rinsed his hands in the ocean, also stood. "No problem. We'll meet you there."

As Revvy rounded the corner to the maritime forest, Nick looked at Amy. "Come on, follow me while I get a few more samples." He began to walk away, then turned around. "If you're done with your pictures."

"Not much more I can get without going inside."

"Then let's go. We can talk while we walk."

But they didn't; silence surrounded them like an old companion, and neither of them wanted to interrupt it. Bird calls, crunching shells and crackling leaves were the only sounds they heard. They followed a path to a dense area of live oak where branches and roots had so blended with each other that she couldn't tell which branch belonged to which tree.

She touched a mangled limb. "Is this what the rain forest looked like—felt like? So thick?"

It was as close as she'd come to asking where he was in Costa Rica, why he'd stayed. It was closer than she meant to venture into that obscure land of questions.

"Yes and no. It's completely different, but has the same dense life. You know, I wasn't in the forest the entire time."

"Oh?"

"Do you want to hear this?"

She looked up to the thick drape of moss, to the camouflaged island. Yes, now she wanted to hear it. She sat down on a fallen live oak trunk and curled her knees up to her chest.

"Okay, Nick. Tell me."

"Where did you think I went? What did you think happened to me?" He sat next to her.

"I didn't know. I went to meet your plane, just like we planned. I stood outside the door and watched every single person walk out. I had a flight attendant double-check the plane. I made her look up the manifest—did you know you were still listed?" She pushed her fingers against her closed eyes. "No. This doesn't matter. You said you had something to tell me."

"What did you do after that? After I wasn't on the plane? Run and marry Phil?"

"That's not *fair,* Nick. Not fair at all. You don't want to hear what I did after that. If you wanted to hear, or know, you would have called—or come back. If you wanted to know what I did after you didn't come out of that door, you should have tried to find out then . . . not now." The anger rose, still braided with the old want, and she desperately wished they would separate themselves so she could be purely angry.

He laid his hand on top of her knee. "I couldn't find out. I was—"

"What? A little preoccupied with Eliza . . . with the rain forest, with maybe a little tequila and—"

"In jail."

His words were a string attached to her lungs: he pulled the air from her chest. She bent toward him. "What?" she thought she said, but wasn't sure if she actually spoke aloud—the world adjusting to a new rotation after the assumption that it had spun the other way.

"What for? What happened? Why—why didn't you tell me? Call me?"

The ancient oaks were larger, the birds louder, the bark rougher, the heat heavier.

"Do you want to hear the story?"

Her answer was a hinge on a doorframe that opened the way to what came before and after his explanation, yet she had no choice. Her phone call to him a week ago had been the decision, the rest a river of knowing she couldn't stop.

"Yes." The word felt familiar, rich wine on her tongue.

He grasped her face in his hands, pulled her toward him. He moaned and ran his finger down her cheek, across her bottom lip. She closed her eyes and saw a dolphin fin streaking across the crevice of memory that he had opened with his touch.

A pool of yearning settled in the bottom of her stomach.

Torn pieces of sunlight whispered through aged moss, landed on the shattered log. The sea pounded on an unseen shore just steps beyond the dense forest. Each crest and retreat of the waves matched her heartbeat—a beat she once believed was sure and steady, a heart cleansed of Nick. But he resided in the unseen—the syncopated space between each beat; the secret she didn't hear, but knew existed.

She rested her head atop her knees and waited. She was now ready to hear what he had to say. Or she believed she was ready.

"All this time—all of it—I've been thinking of what to say to you. So many things to say to you." He touched her mouth.

Her hands fluttered in the air, butterflies with nowhere to land.

He continued. "And now here you are, and I can't find any of those words." He closed his eyes. "Here you are, and all I want to do is touch that space . . ." He opened his eyes and gazed at her neck—heat flared with the memory of his touch.

Her fingers landed gently on the hollow between her collarbones. His hand reached to cover hers.

"There. The place your silver cross used to lie, move every time you breathed."

"I lost it," Amy whispered.

"Lost what?" He gripped her hand.

"That cross . . . you."

He moaned, bowed his head in what Amy thought might be prayer, or defeat.

Tenderness welled up. She touched his leg and felt his muscles, taut. "I can't stand for you to look so . . ."

"Sad?"

"No, I was going to say 'defeated.' "

"That, too," he said.

Chapter Fifteen

"**B**ound together at the edges, sewn firmly down the center," Nick whispered close to her ear.

Now it was her turn to moan, a soft sound he'd dreamed of, used for comfort all these years. He was pleased he'd remembered it correctly, the exact pitch, tone and yearning.

She pulled away from him; he was sorry he'd spoken. She touched his chin, the scar he knew was there although he couldn't feel it.

"You remembered that . . . you remembered it," she said.

"Yes." He hadn't realized he knew the exact words until he said them. "It's true."

He saw a change, an instant shift in her eyes as she returned to the present, to who she was now. She turned away from him and plucked a leaf from the moss spilling from a live oak beside them.

"Tell me the story," she said, and this time she bowed her head in surrender.

Nick closed his eyes and attempted to see the night that had changed everything. He wanted Amy to know it, to feel it, to understand it without any gaps. He wanted her to be there.

"It was late—the middle of the night, almost early morning—humid as hell. It had rained all day and the fog was thick. It was our last night and we were celebrating. We'd survived the rain forest, the poisonous frogs, the local water, the assignments we thought we'd never finish. I was driving. I always was. I seemed to be the only one who knew how to maneuver the beat-up Range Rover they gave us for transportation. There were seven of us . . . remember?"

"Seven students?"

"Yes. And we were piled in one truck."

"What happened?" Amy whispered.

"A woman. She was crossing the street. It was late . . . and she wasn't looking."

He closed his eyes and forced himself to see the one moment he avoided, the crash he saw in horrid dreams with vivid blended colors and screeching sounds.

"I looked up and there she was . . . like an apparition of the Virgin Mary or something. Long black hair, long skirt. Her mouth was open as if she wanted to scream, say something, but she didn't. She had a shawl over her head. She looked at me from over her shoulder. I jerked the Range Rover, but it responded in its own time—it was stubborn. We skidded and I heard it, felt it like a ride on the whirly thing at a carnival. All six voices in the truck were screaming or yelling instructions. It was a moment that lasted maybe five, ten seconds, but really lasted days—hell . . . it still lasts. I don't remember anything after that. I woke up on a metal cot with a piece of foam that was supposed to be a mattress. I had a broken leg, cracked ribs and shooting pain every time I took a breath. Everything I know about the time between the accident and carcel—jail—came from Eliza and the lawyer."

"Eliza." Amy's face paled, moved too far away, fading,

and Nick wanted to pull her back. He was losing her. Panic welled up inside him—the same panic as the night he'd awakened in the jail infirmary.

"Listen, please."

"I am. I'm not going anywhere. I'm listening. What happened to the rest of the students. To Eliza?"

"Sam, another student, broke his arm, and the others had some minor cuts and bruises. Eliza had some cracked ribs. But they all—all except Eliza and the student advisor, Mr. Rivera—went home the next day as planned."

"I don't get it. Why were you in jail? Why did Eliza stay?"

Nick looked away, weighing now what to say, how much to tell her, as if his life dangled from the very rope of his words. He hadn't planned this speech well—or dared to hope she would really listen to him—and he hadn't decided what to tell her and what not to tell her.

So what he said—the partial truth—became the full truth for her, and now, for him.

"The woman . . . she died."

"What do you mean?" Amy looked as though she would stand, move, leave. The feeling of abandonment rose again in Nick—the unspoken disapproval when she never came to him. It was true . . . she would *not* accept this sin of his.

"The woman crossing the street, the one I swerved to miss—I hit her. I have no memory of it—the roll bar of the Range Rover knocked me out, or at least that's what they told me."

"Oh, God."

"We later discovered that she was drunk, and staggering home in the middle of the road, but that was later—a year later. And extradition did not come easy in Costa Rica in the seventies. There was very little communication with the outside world and—"

"And Eliza?"

"She had—*has*—a lot of connections. Her parents are good friends with the guvnah and all that." Nick affected his mother-in-law's pattern of speech, the way in which she spoke of her intimate relationship with the governor of Georgia. "Eliza contacted people at home. They hired lawyers, bigwigs—hell, anyone to get me out of the mess I was in. They sent down a lawyer."

"And in all this . . . mess, you never thought to contact me?"

"Amy . . ." He reached across the fallen tree they sat on; somehow she'd slipped to the end of the log, farther away. His hand found empty space and his fingers closed in on his palm. He sighed and looked down at the moss growing in the split cracks of the rotting wood.

"You're the only one I thought about contacting. It worked like this: I was allowed one phone call to the American Embassy, which then contacted my mother. Eliza called her parents and they sent a native Costa Rican, who was an American lawyer, to be responsible for all my legal stuff and communication. Mr. Rivera, the student advisor, told the University of the 'situation.' Then he returned home and legal assistance was . . . secured. I asked this lawyer—God, what in the hell was his name?" Nick closed his eyes. "Mr. Miguel Carreira—I couldn't even pronounce his name, but he was friendly with the locals, knew his way around. He said he couldn't reach you at your dorm. He said they even tried your house. He was supposed to send you a telegram right away, with a phone number. God, what I would've given for e-mail, cell phones—anything but a telegram."

"I didn't . . . get one." Amy closed her eyes.

"Nothing?"

"Nothing. Finish the story. Finish."

"I sent another, then another."

"No, not the telegrams. What happened to you?"

"It took a full year, a little longer, to prove it wasn't my fault—vehicular homicide, don't ya know?"

"You were in jail for an entire year?"

"Yes." This time when he reached to touch her, he found her. She buried her head in his chest and he wound his fingers in her hair, pulled her closer. There were so many things he wanted to say to her. So many. In his sleepless nights he'd practiced entire speeches.

She lifted her head and looked at him, her eyes wet. "Was it horrible . . . just horrible?"

The sun began its descent below the oak and moss-rimmed horizon; the others would be waiting for them on the beach. But he wasn't done telling her the story and nothing seemed of more importance than this—than telling Amy.

"Yes. I was convicted of homicide—of a local, for God's sake. I was not the most well-liked man in jail. Seems everyone knew her . . . and loved her. It did get me my own jail cell, for safety reasons. Mr. Carreira visited me in jail. Eliza wasn't allowed in. I would ask him about you and he would give me the most pitiful grimace. It was horrible. And then he'd say, in that Spanish accent of his, 'No, no, nothing from her yet. Let's just give her a little while to absorb the information. I'm sure she'll call us.' "

"I'm sorry—so sorry."

Nick held up his hand. "I do not want to talk about the jail, ever. It took a full year of research, getting to know and live with the locals, before Eliza and Miguel Carreira finally found the man the woman was with that night. They received a signed confession from him that proved she was blitzed, stumbling home through the streets. Eliza and

Miguel got the man to testify at what, in Costa Rica, counts as a hearing. Seems the woman was from some big influential family and they didn't want her name defamed. They dropped the charges."

"Eliza helped the lawyer? She stayed and did all that to get you out? She loved you."

"No . . . it was after I got out."

"No. That's not possible. She stayed. She didn't return to school, or family, or her faux-antebellum mansion in Garvey. She stayed in some foreign city for an entire year, or more, to get you out of jail. She loved you then."

Nick glanced at the ground.

"That was sacrifice. That was . . . love," Amy said.

"This is not what I want to talk about. Us. That's what I came here for; us—how this possibly could have happened." The anger he usually squelched with the preoccupations of his job, of his friends, of the forest and wilderness he loved, or with a good beer or three with his buddies, rose now. He stood with the force of his own rage, kicked the base of the stump, bark scattering at his feet. "This is bullshit. All these wasted years. All this wasted time. And you didn't even know."

"No. But I tried to find out. I called the school, your mother, your friends."

"What did they tell you?" He sat down next to her again.

She stared off, up toward the gnarled oak branches. "Your mother wouldn't talk to me. She just kept telling me you decided to stay on to help with the preservation program. The school gave me the same information—like a broken record: 'He has decided to stay, he has decided to stay,' over and over. It was all I could get from anybody. I wrote letters to the student P.O. box you gave me—they were returned. I went to your mother's house—one time,

Nick. Imagine the embarrassment. I drove all the way to Gunter, knocked on the door. She told me that, if you decided to stay and not contact me, I should grant you the right to get on with your life. She shut the door on me."

Tears now fell in a single stream down her right cheek. He placed his lips on the tears that should never have dropped for him. The sky filled with strips of sunset; they needed to walk toward the beach before the light disappeared with the final crest of the sun. It'd be easy to get lost on the island, with its maze of marsh that circled back on itself, and he didn't have a flashlight or matches. He hurried through the rest of his explanation.

"A year later, when I got out of jail, the first thing I did, my very first call, was . . . to you. I called your house . . . your mother answered."

"She never told me."

"I was angry when I called. More than anything I wanted to know why you never came or even sent a telegram back, sent a message . . . nothing."

"You must have hated me."

Hated her? All he'd ever done was want her . . . just want her.

"I never hated you. I wanted to, but I couldn't. Your mother answered the phone, but I don't think she knew it was me. It was a bad connection, and I'd been sick with the flu the last month in that hellhole, so my voice was scratchy. Your mother told me you weren't there, that you'd gone out. I told her I was a college friend and she told me you were out, with your fiancé."

"Phil." She exhaled his name.

"And then . . . back then, I thought I knew why you'd never contacted me. I found the reason. All I wanted then was to know why . . . and the fiancé was why."

"But that wasn't why."

"And Eliza was there waiting. In every sense of the word, waiting. And you . . . you had gone on. My misery was more than I can possibly explain to you. My grief was . . . nauseating. So I tried to forget. But, of course, there was no forgetting. I have tried."

"But now here we are. With different lives, different families—and there is nothing we can do about it."

"How can you say that?"

"There isn't. There just isn't. I see no way . . ." Another tear, a blessed tear that let him know she cared, ran down her cheek.

"You still love me," he said.

"Nick, don't say that. You don't know that. I love my family—my husband, my children."

"Yes, I know. But I know you still love me."

Her voice rose; she lifted her hands. "Do you want to tell me how you could possibly know that?"

"Because I still love you. I always have. Other things in my life have been . . . uncertain. Not this. Don't you see now?"

"See what?"

"Our vows are still there, never broken. They were . . . covered by other vows. But ours were never broken. You didn't leave me. I didn't leave you. They——our promises—are still there."

Amy groaned. "I've made other vows since then, Nick." She bowed her head. "I've always wondered what happened . . . and I wanted to find out, finally, where you were. And I'm so sorry that you had to go through all that. But you married a wonderful woman. I married an amazing man. We have lives, children, other vows. I don't, can't see any way around this . . . fact."

"It's more than that."

Amy pointed to the horizon. "We have to get back to the beach. I don't want to talk about this again. I'm sorry you went through that hell. I am. There's nothing I can do to turn back time and fix it."

"Well, I'm here now."

"Let's leave this alone. It's dangerous and ancient ground." She grabbed his hand. For that he was grateful. "This is so hard." She let go, then turned and walked toward the beach, staring straight ahead.

He stood, dizzy, to follow her. He shook his head, taking one step to every two of hers. Leaves disintegrated with a whisper under his feet as he walked behind Amy, wanting to say something, anything intelligent. But all he could find inside his head were begging words and the abysmal breach between the man he'd meant to be when he was with her in college and who he was now.

He reached to touch the back of her hair; she whipped around. Something reflected on her face in the last crest of light—ah, tears. She turned from him and continued walking; but now he knew that she, too, felt the sting of what they'd lost.

Amy attempted to stay her tears as Nick walked behind her. If she turned and reached out, he would be hers. Once that was all she'd ever wanted; now it was impossible. She kept looking straight ahead until they broke through the low palmettos and marsh grass to the beach.

Brenton sat behind Norah and she leaned into his bent knees while he stroked her hair; her eyes were closed. Reese bent over a pile of driftwood and dry leaves, lighting a match for a fire. Revvy squatted at the sea's edge, lifting handfuls of sand, then letting it dribble from his fingers.

He looked up at them first as they returned—the same people, but different. All previous assumptions were now false, and the ground Amy had once based her other decisions on shifted beneath her.

"Hey, dude, where've you two been?" Reese called out.

"Sorry, Reese. We got turned around and I thought I found a tiny-leaved buckthorn . . . time just got away from us," Nick said.

Time just got away from me, Amy thought.

They gathered around a campfire built with Reese's adept hands, and conversation turned to life stories, as it tends to do when the sun has set, the waves are slapping and the fire lights faces as magical as they were originally meant to be.

Revvy tossed a ghost-crab backbone that looked like a snakeskin necklace into the fire and they watched it crackle. "Man, what's your story, Nick? How do you know Mrs. Reynolds?"

Amy was sure she wanted to hear his answer more than they did.

"We went to college together."

"And?" Revvy asked.

"And our children are dating now. Amy told me about this island and what you were trying to do—and I thought I could help."

"Your kids are dating? Like each other?" Revvy asked.

"Like each other—yeah," Nick said.

"Okay. Well, whatever brought you here, I'm psyched you showed up. We could use one more person—Brenton over there is the blooming botanist, but we could definitely use an expert."

"Revvy, you been to any more of the islands around here?" Nick asked him—adroitly changing the subject.

"Totally. I camp out on Otter Island all the time, and kayaking through the rivers and Sound is my main escape."

As Revvy and Nick talked of islands and wildlife and escape, the last pulled-taffy strands of sunset faded. Amy leaned back on her elbows into the sand, lifted her face to the sky. The stars were clearer out here—like scattered embers.

"I can't just sit on the beach all night," she finally said into the peaceful silence.

"Yes, you can," Nick said.

He was right, but she was too comfortable—it was a scary, loose-jointed feeling and she'd felt it before. She needed to get back to her dorm room, her real job.

"I have a ton of papers to grade tonight."

"We'll get you home before class," Reese said, and everyone laughed.

Someone, she thought it was Revvy, started singing a song by the Doors and everyone joined in. By the last verse she'd lifted her voice with the rest of them to the wild rising moon, to the endangered species, to the decaying home at the center of the island and to the ghosts of all time past. While singing, she stashed away everything Nick had told her; she would stare at it when she was alone. There wasn't a safe way to ponder the newfound information while sitting on the beach with Nick in the firelight.

Reese put out the fire and they loaded up the boat to return home. The tide had risen and the slapping waves reached to Amy's waist. The others laughed and splashed and climbed into the boat. She slithered onto the back, knowing she looked every year her age—teacher, housewife, middle-aged woman. But they laughed and gave her high fives, and she rode home on the incoming tide with the hope that one of them might have enough information to save the small island from a tacky home, inground pool and putting green.

Amy dreaded the drive back alone in Nick's warm pickup truck, and felt saved by Reese's request for a ride. Although it was out of the way, Nick dropped him off at a beachside shanty that looked like it was about ready to return to the sea.

"Reese." Amy grabbed his hand as he jumped out of the truck. "Thank you so much."

"I believe y'all are gonna save it. I really do. You've got the big guns now." Reese nodded to Nick.

"Yes, we do." Amy laughed and crawled out of the back-seat, slipped into the front. As soon as they left the gravel drive, Nick grabbed her hand. She pulled away.

"Don't do that."

"Can't help it, darlin'."

"Thank you for coming tonight. I think everyone is thrilled to have you and . . ." She was running out of things to say.

Nick pulled up in front of the dorm, then walked around and opened her door. It was late; she was suddenly exhausted.

"Wow, I'm wiped," she said.

He grabbed her hand and helped her out of the truck, leading her not to the front door of the dorm, but around to the side of the building. He eased her up against the wall where the garden lamp's light did not reach. The suffused silver of the moon's glow scattered on the ground. He placed both hands on her shoulders; his right hand slipped, landed on the crumbled mortar of the ancient building.

"Can you leave with me for just a little while?"

"No, I can't," she thought she said.

He leaned in to close the gap between them. His mouth found her neck, and he kissed it, down, down until he found the small crest between her collarbones. Her body softened, became giving and malleable.

Her fingers trembled, rested in his hair. He reached his left hand up to her face, ran his finger across her lips.

Metal slammed against wood as the side door opened and closed, sending a shock of awareness to their dark hiding place. She gasped, pulled away from him. He tried to pull her back; she slipped around the corner, shoved open the door, escaped inside. She closed the door and leaned up against it, took a deep breath and closed her eyes.

"You okay?" the redheaded desk attendant asked.

"Fine. I'm fine." Amy smiled and waved at her, then walked up the back stairs to her room, where she would call her family and say good night.

"I'm just fine," she told the gray concrete walls, herself and all the ghosts residing in Porter Hall.

Chapter Sixteen

The weeks following Amy's visit to the island with Nick were like an extended moment before fully waking, a brief, immeasurable instant when time and location were meaningless, where possibility was endless, where *kairos*— a mystical timeless interval—seemed accessible. All was well, and although morning and wakefulness were approaching, her heart knew what was right and true and remained languid in its half-slumber.

During the day, Amy felt unable to shake this lethargic, off-kilter feeling of functioning in a half-sleep. Her limbs moved slowly; her thoughts remained hazy.

It was now the week before Thanksgiving, and she pulled the Christmas boxes out early. She didn't want to wait for Phil to return from his business trip in Dallas; she carried the boxes up from the basement one by one, as Christmas music blared from the stereo. Her soul slipped back and forth, back and forth between the present and the past, between the needed and the wanted.

She sat cross-legged on the oyster Berber carpet on the living room floor, lifting ornaments, then placing them back in the box. The tree was not up yet; she was killing time as she stared at the ornaments and thought about what they represented about each family member. She set the ornaments aside and opened a second bin labeled "handmade gifts." This box was crammed full of the gifts the children had made in school through the years: the pinecone Christmas tree, the juice-can pencil holder, the gold-painted walnut candlestick. She lifted them out, set them on the antique-trunk coffee table. Family tradition dictated where she would place each treasure: on the side table, on the kitchen counter, on the coffee table.

With each memento she pulled from the box, with each memory she unearthed, she became more certain that Nick's claim of their unbroken vows was bullshit. Through the years she and Phil had built an incredible life together—it was not to be discarded for some college memories.

She lifted the last object from the plastic bin: a bound and laminated five-page book constructed by Molly in third grade. She remembered how excited Molly had been about this book, about the time and effort she had put into it. As Amy had tucked her into bed Christmas Eve, Molly had pulled it out from under her mattress.

"What's this?" Amy asked, hugging her daughter.

"Look, Mommy, look what I made for you." Molly's body trembled beneath Amy's hands as she waved the book in the air.

Amy's eyes filled with tears as she took the book from Molly, asked her what it was. Molly began to bounce up and down on the bed. "Open it, open it."

Beneath the crumpled and crookedly taped Christmas paper lay a handmade book emblazoned in hot-pink crayon, THE WORLD'S BEST MOTHER, with a hand-drawn picture of Molly's rendition of her mother: a small, round face with too-big eyes, yellow hair that curled and waved around the remainder of the page. The mouth opened in a smile full of all-white, all-straight teeth. The nose was just two black circles in the center of her face.

Amy told Molly it was the most beautiful thing she'd ever seen, and she meant it. Molly asked her if she liked the hair. "Don't you think it looks just like you?"

Together they read the book. Then Amy lay down with her daughter until Molly fell asleep, secure and warm.

Now Amy curled against the back of the couch, opened the book. In zigzagging black crayon it spoke of all the "world's greatest" things about her. Of course it didn't mention her work in preservation, or her degree in architectural history, or her affinity for keeping the house in order, or her skill in assembling scrapbooks and baby books. Molly had only written of Amy's love for the family.

When asked what Amy's sports were, Molly had listed: laundry, taking me to tennis, shopping for my clothes, driving my field trips, giving me really good parties for my birthday.

Amy tossed the book on the coffee table and rubbed at her forehead, her eyes. She leaned her head back on the green toile couch with the mismatched vintage fabric pillows. Tears began as sleep crawled upon her. She reached for a couch pillow, curled up and laid her head down on it as sleep took her in slow-moving circles. She bobbed with an outgoing tide—free-floating. Warm water caressed naked skin, oyster shells tinkled—glass against goblet, toasting her with wine, celebrating her. The sand scraped her cheek, but it didn't hurt. She floated, sank, lifted. The shells became louder, insistent in their praise.

Louder the shells sang until they became a ringing bell.

She jumped to a sitting position. Her doorbell rang—the scraping sand was only the couch where she'd slipped from the pillows. She rubbed at her tear-salted face, believing for one moment it was the salt of the sea. She stood, unsure of place and time.

She walked down the hall to the front door. Carol Anne's face peeked through the cut glass from outside. Even through the distorted view, etched lines of concern on her friend's face were evident.

Amy waved at Carol Anne and reached above the doorframe for the key, moving in slow motion. She opened the door, smiled.

"Okay, that is the worst fake smile you've ever manufactured." Carol Anne hugged her.

"Well, thank you."

Carol Anne looked past Amy into the house. "Are you going to make me stand outside or let me in? You hiding something in there?"

"I'm sorry. Come in. Not that you need me to tell you to."

"Okay, what exactly is your problem?" Carol Anne leaned against the huntboard table in the main hall.

Amy noticed a gaping seam in the antique wallpaper; she licked her finger, pushed the paper to the wall. "Oh, look. The wallpaper is peeling there."

"Your whole house is peeling, Amy. You love that." A crease of unease formed between Carol Anne's eyes. "You're out of it. What's going on?"

Amy looked at Carol Anne. "Not that I'm not glad to see you and all that, but why are you here?"

"You *are* out of it. We have plans to go Christmas shopping, remember? It is Saturday, two o'clock, right?"

Amy looked up at the grandfather clock, leaning precariously as it had done for eighteen years since she'd bought it at an art auction with Phil. She'd wanted that clock too, right? She'd agreed with Phil, hadn't she?

Yes, it was two o'clock, and suddenly her dream of the sea and the oyster shells felt far more vivid, authentic, than Carol Anne standing in her hall, reminding her it was time to go and do.

She wanted to return to the dream, to the floating and celebration. She wanted to know where the dream, the sea would carry her.

"I don't feel like it today. I'm tired."

"Well, you *are* going. I can't stand you like this."

"No. I really don't want to. I can finish my Christmas shopping on the Web. Really. I'm sorry I forgot . . . maybe I'm catching that winter flu going around."

"You aren't catchin' anything but a sickness of the heart. I won't allow this to happen again. No way."

"What are you talking about?"

Carol Anne tilted her head to the right and left, then whispered, "I know you, Ame. It's Nick. Don't think I don't know these symptoms of yours. I saw them almost kill you one time. He knows, somehow knows, how to *do* this to you."

"What?" Amy looked away from her friend, her con-science screaming her own stupidity.

"You saw him, didn't you?"

"Yes, Carol Anne. But not why you think. He's helping the OWP. Nothing more. Nothing less."

"Great."

"He could really make a difference—"

"Well, you're coming with me now."

"I'm busy . . . unpacking Christmas stuff." Amy shuffled into the living room. Carol Anne followed. "See all this stuff? I can't just leave it out like this. Phil will come home and put it in all the wrong places, wonder why I didn't finish my job."

Carol Anne leaned down, picked up the "World's Best Mother" book, leafed through it.

"Isn't it weird how they see us?" Amy asked.

"Who?"

"Our children. They have this vision of us, of how we are, and it revolves only and solely around them. I mean, look at this book—it doesn't describe me, you know—me—at all. It just describes what I *do* for her—for the house, for the family."

"That *is* you . . . to her."

"But it isn't *me*."

"What do you mean?"

"It isn't me at all. She forgot to mention that I have a degree in architectural history, that I love preserving the past, that . . . I am me." Amy sighed. She wasn't lying to Carol Anne about being tired.

"Preserving the past . . . you nailed it."

God, she wished Carol Anne would leave. She'd never wanted this before, and the need to be away from her best friend shocked her. "I'm talking about buildings, architecture."

"I'm just repeating what you said, that's all." Carol Anne picked up a red ornament, rolled it in her hand.

Amy groaned. "Can we do this another day? Maybe after Thanksgiving?"

"No."

"You are being a major pain in the ass."

"That is what I intend to be, because I love you. Now come on."

"I'll drive separate in case I need . . . to come home first."

Amy walked through the living room into the kitchen.

She folded a towel left crumpled on the counter by either Phil or Molly, then placed the towel neatly over the sink. She picked up the discarded junk mail no one else threw away and tossed it in the trash can. Did she have to do absolutely everything? It irritated her, the never-ending chores and the continuous picking up and the truth that only she did it all.

She grabbed her car keys from the hook on the wall and walked into the garage, kicking the door shut behind her. A loud thump instead of the scraping sound of the warped door shutting came from behind her. She turned as if to reprimand the door for not obeying.

Carol Anne stood holding it open. "I'm driving with you. I'll leave my car here and I promise you can go home when you want."

"I want to go home now."

"Get in the car."

"Okay, okay."

As they drove the familiar streets of Darby, the company of her best friend and the tree-lined lanes of her hometown soothed Amy. Carol Anne rambled on about an artist who had backed out of the art show when he didn't receive a front-row spot in the display. "Ego, ego," Carol Anne said, then she stopped, touched Amy's shoulder.

"What in the world is that sound?"

"What sound?"

"That eternal dinging noise."

"Oh, that. I think it's supposed to warn me when I'm almost out of gas."

"Well, what does it mean this time?"

Amy glanced down at the dashboard. "Shit, I'm on empty." She whipped the car into the Texaco station on their right. "I need gas."

"You need something, all right."

Amy scrunched her nose at her friend and parked in front of the gas pump. She never let her car get below half a tank. It was a safety rule she taught her kids—one she kept herself with regularity.

Amy stuck the nozzle of the gas pump into the side of the car and noticed for the first time the phallic symbolism of the gas pump filling the car to make it go. *What is wrong with me?*

She watched the numbers go by and counted with the pump's *click, click, click* until it finished.

She paid and climbed back in the car, looking at Carol Anne. "All solved. Let's go spend money on beautiful and meaningful gifts for our families."

"Now that sounds like my best friend."

"Where do you want to go first?"

"Let's hit the Antique Emporium and go from there—I know I want to buy my adorable husband an antique golf bag for his collection." Carol Anne pulled a list from her purse. "Got a lot of stuff here to cross off."

Amy pulled the car out into the street and reached to push the ON button to the stereo to block out the loud thumping noise that seemed to be following the car.

"Now what is that noise?" Carol Anne tilted her head.

"I don't know. Something at the gas station, I guess."

Amy turned right onto Magnolia Avenue and punched the gas as a loud, long honk emitted from the Volvo she passed. Her car bumped, jolted to the right. She jerked the wheel to stop the car from sliding off the road.

"Damn, did I just run over something?" She looked at Carol Anne, then shrugged her shoulders, looked in the rearview mirror. A Jeep full of teenagers pulled up along-side them, honked, pointed to the back of the car.

"What the . . . ?" Carol Anne rolled down her window,

shoved her head out into the wind. She pulled her head back in. "Stop the car, Amy. Pull over."

"Why?"

"Just do it."

Amy rolled her eyes, pulled into the parking lot of Rosie's Cut Cabin, shifted into PARK and looked at Carol Anne. "What is it now?"

Carol Anne opened her mouth as if to talk, but laughter poured out. "You forgot to . . ." Carol Anne bent over in another spasm of laughter. "You left the gas hose in the car."

Amy didn't understand. "What gas hose?"

Carol Anne opened her car door. "Get out. Look."

Amy opened the door, stepped around to the passenger side of the car and there, sticking out like the deformed tail of roadkill possum, was the black tubing of the gas pump. She sank onto the cold, damp pavement and buried her head in her knees, not caring about her gray wool slacks, or her cashmere sweater, or the old ladies at Rosie's getting their hair set for the week and staring out the window at her. She brought her knees up to her chest and told Carol Anne the story of Nick and the jail while she tried not to cry, tried not to stare at the hose jutting out of her car, gas dribbling from its severed end like some vulgar representation of her life.

Chapter Seventeen

Amy wanted to scream, draw a deep breath and scream again. But she didn't. She rinsed the dishes and leaned up against the edge of the sink—an old soapstone farmhouse sink she'd rescued from destruction. Two round stains, rust and brown, sat on the bottom and would not be removed. She often made up stories about how they'd come to be there, what and who had caused them. She would never know. There had been things in her life she thought she'd never know . . . and now she did; she wanted to scream loud and long.

The fact that Nick had been in jail and had never truly left her didn't fit into the crammed facts of what her life had become. She'd repeated the story to herself a hundred times, trying to find the settling point of the story, the bottom line. Yet all she heard was his summary of it: *Our vows are still there, never broken*—a sentence that ran over her tongue, as rich and seductive as melted butter.

This constant playback of Nick's words reminded her of the days when she'd play Led Zeppelin's "Stairway to Heaven" over and over again on her eight-track, thinking the repetition would allow her to understand the significance of the song and she could then apply this meaning to her life. It hadn't worked then, either.

She leaned up against the sink and stared out the bubbled glass window, which offered her a wavy view of the backyard. The evening sun came through in one strip against the sill, lighting it as if a child had painted a gold stripe, uneven and slanted on the vanilla-shaded paint. An Adirondack chair faced the old tire swing that hung as a reminder of Molly's and Jack's childhood; she couldn't bear to pull it down, though no one had sat on it in years.

She sighed and picked up the last plate, rinsed it off without looking and placed it in the dishwasher. A slice of pain shot through her forefinger. She drew her hand back and looked down. A paring knife stuck out from the bottom rack of the dishwasher at a menacing slant for anyone not paying attention. Who had placed it sticking up? Hadn't she taught everyone to put the knives upside down in the rack? Blood ran down her finger in a single stream, mixing with the soapy dishwater in a washed-out pink flow.

"Damn. *Damn.*" She grabbed a paper towel from the rack and wrapped it around her finger. She'd just added to her scars: the one from slicing a bagel for Jack, the one from the scissors when sewing Molly's Cinderella Halloween costume. Even her finger was a testimonial to family life; even her scars revealed her commitments.

Our vows are still there, never broken.

She slammed the dishwasher shut with her foot. Where were Molly and Phil? Eat and run, off to what was important to them while she bled over the sink and was tired enough to curl up on the kitchen floor and sleep until next week. Thanksgiving and Christmas were around the corner, and even the thought of the energy and focus the holidays would require of her made her want to let the blood run from her finger. The thought of the boxes and decorations and parties and gifts and family obligations, of the school . . .

Our vows are still there, never broken.

The kitchen ceiling thrummed with the intensity of Molly's boom box in her bedroom. She did her homework on her pencil-scarred desk while listening to this music, and Amy didn't understand how. She closed her eyes and leaned over the counter, placed her forehead on the cool granite that she'd installed after the original countertop had cracked under a heavy spaghetti pot.

She jumped as Phil touched her shoulder. "You okay?" He hugged her from behind, kissed the side of her neck.

"I cut myself." She held up her finger for him to see. "Look. Where were you and Molly? Someone stuck a knife right-side-up in the dishwasher."

"Ow." He kissed her finger. "I was taking the trash out to the curb, bagging the recycling."

She sighed, still not looking up at her husband. Something subterranean began to shift and she made a choice between irritation and guilt; she allowed the irritation to rise like cream: thick, rich, avoiding the guilt that lay directly below it.

Our vows are still there, never broken.

She pushed back from the counter, turned to Phil and yanked her hand from him. He stepped back and she saw him as a sketch that she could erase, smudge the edges of his body into the faux finished walls.

He wrinkled his nose and tilted his head, furrowed his mouth in the concerned expression he saved for illnesses, wrecked cars, bounced checks. "Amy, what is wrong?"

"I told you, I cut my finger." She held it up for him to

see again. Blood leaked through the paper towel. She pulled off the paper towel and threw it in the trash, allowed the blood to drip onto the hardwood floor. "Hello, can't you see that?"

He reached for her hand and kissed the bloodstained finger, then opened the cabinet above her head and pulled down a Band-Aid, some Neosporin. "Here, hon, give me your finger. I'll fix it."

She began to cry.

"Does it hurt that bad? Maybe it needs stitches," Phil said.

"No, it doesn't need stitches." She wiped at her face with her free hand. "I'm fine . . . fine."

"Really?"

"I'm just . . . tired."

"Why don't you go to bed early tonight?"

"I have papers to grade, laundry to fold. I have to print the lineup for the Art Festival. I have to—"

"Stop it, Ame. Don't run yourself into the ground. Damn, the holidays haven't even started yet." Phil wrapped the Band-Aid tightly around her finger, stayed the bleeding.

"Thank you, Phil."

"At your service." He kissed her and tousled her hair.

The touch of his mouth on the inside of her bottom lip evoked the pressing, desperate need of Nick leaning her against the brick wall. Once again, she chose irritation and turned her back on Phil.

Something flashed pink in her peripheral vision, sent a weakness down her inner thighs—a pink folded paper on the kitchen counter. She didn't turn to it, but pulled on her Band-Aid.

Phil lifted the paper. "Oh, I almost forgot, with your near finger-severing . . ." He waved the scrap of paper. "I was taking out the trash, and this was on the floor of your study. I didn't know if you were aiming for the trash or if it fell off your desk. Do you need it?"

She felt naked, exposed, like she was going to throw up. "One of my students gave me her number . . . but now I forget who. You can throw it away. If she needs me bad enough, she'll give it to me again, or call the school office."

"Okay." Phil threw the scrap of paper in the white trash can. Amy turned from watching and poured Cascade in the eye-socket holes of the dishwasher, slammed the door shut and pushed the appropriate black buttons to begin the hum of the machine.

Phil leaned up against the counter and smiled at her.

"What?" she asked.

"I got a funny call today from Bill's wife. Said she was getting her hair done and saw you pull into the parking lot with a gas hose stuck in the car—that you sat down in the middle of the parking lot and laughed."

She leaned against the same counter, needing its support. So his boss's wife had seen her and thought the tears were laughter.

"It was pretty funny, actually. Carol Anne and I were so involved in our discussion I actually left the gas hose in the car."

"What did the gas station do? Do we have to pay for it?"

"No. Believe it or not they say it happens more frequently than you'd imagine."

"Where was your head?"

"I don't know. I was talking and—"

"Probably about that project of yours."

"What do you mean, 'project of mine'?"

"Well, you do seem to be obsessed with it lately."

"And you're not with your job?"

"That's different."

"Why, Phil? Because it's yours? Because it isn't my job?"

"No, honey. This is your . . . project. And I'm glad you're doing something you love."

"You are?"

"Yes, I am. How's it going?" He took a deep inhale, as if listening to her required a sustaining breath.

"I went back out there a couple weeks ago. Nick found an endangered plant that could change everything. Brenton is pretty sure it's a tiny-leaved buckthorn, a very rare shrub. Norah is taking it to the Heritage Preserve with all the other information Reese and Revvy have about the wildlife."

"That's nice, honey. Really. I hope it works out for you."

"I'm gonna try to grade some papers."

"Okay." He kissed her again, moved toward the living room.

She waited, then watched to see him slump on the couch, humming, reading his *Wall Street Journal*—preoccupied once again with stock prices. Only then did she go back into the kitchen, lift the top of the trash can, pick out the small pink paper and tuck it safely into the back pocket of her pants.

She rounded the corner from the kitchen to the living room and watched Phil leaf through his *Journal.* He was a dedicated stockbroker, unappreciated by his boss at Stevenson and Sons, eager for a promotion. He loved analyzing straight rows of numbers and diagnosing monetary ills. She walked up behind him. Why could he not, for just one minute, pretend to care about her project? He'd flunked what she considered a listening test—if he was really paying attention, he would have heard Nick's name.

She walked to her sunroom office with its rolltop desk. Eighteen years before, when the moving truck had pulled into the driveway of the house—a home she'd been watching and admiring—she'd placed the box labeled AMY'S OFFICE in the sunroom before anyone else could claim it, before a box labeled LIVING ROOM or MOLLY'S NURSERY or JACK'S TOYS landed on the antique brick floor. The minute the real estate agent had ushered her into the house, she'd gravitated to the sunroom she'd stared at for months, knowing she belonged in it.

The house had never had a FOR SALE sign in the front yard. Before they'd moved in, they'd lived in a quiet town house on the other end of Magnolia Avenue, the main street trimmed down sides and center with trees. Every day she'd take a walk down that street, first pregnant, then with a stroller, then with a double stroller, and stop in front of the 1800s house with the glazed and peeling iron gate, the brick with its crumbling mortar, the tilted front porch, yearning for something unnamed surrounding the house. There was a separate longing that accompanied the desire for the house—a longing for a home, a real home with creaking floors and marks of the kids' heights on the kitchen doorframe, with scraping screen doors that didn't close properly and probably never would.

One day on her walk, while Molly screamed (as she had through the first seven months of her life), Amy picked her up out of the stroller and stared again at the house—imagined herself in the sunroom: typing, writing, drawing, reading . . . God, even sleeping, which it felt like she hadn't done in months.

As she cooed ineffective words of solace into Molly's ear, a silver Cadillac pulled up to the curb next to her, increasing Molly's head-thrown-back screaming. Amy reached down and touched the top of Jack's sleeping head in the stroller and pulled Molly closer. A woman in a navy blue suit—

obviously well rested, with her coiffed hair and carefully applied makeup—popped from the car looking much too happy for Amy's frame of mind. The woman reached into the backseat and pulled out a briefcase. She looked up, and Amy was embarrassed to be still standing, staring, her own hair not brushed since the day before, her mascara at least two days old and surely creased below eyes that had not closed for more than three hours at a time in the past week.

"Well, hello there." The woman's perky voice matched her skipping step.

"Hello," Amy answered. This was her hometown; one must never be rude. You might actually be related to the person on some branch of the family tree. She laid the still-screaming Molly back in the double stroller.

The woman curled her mouth in a sympathetic smile. "Oh, I do remember those days. But honestly, you live through them. You really do."

"That's what I hear."

"One morning you'll wake up and realize you slept through the night . . . at least until they drive."

"When is that? Next century?"

"It feels that way, I know. But Lordy, all mine are grown and gone. I babysit now for their kids. But don't tell my clients"—she gestured toward the house and bent to whisper—"that I'm a grandma."

"Well, you don't look like a grandma, that's for sure."

"I'm a"—the woman laughed and stood straighter—"a real estate agent."

A slow tingle began below Amy's breast and she wasn't sure if the sensation came from Molly's time to nurse, or the words "real estate agent" right in front of her dream house.

Amy whispered, "Are you selling?" She gestured toward the house. "Are they selling this house?"

The woman formed another sympathetic smile. "Unfortunately, the sweet woman who lived here . . . well, she died."

In her blurred fatigue, above Molly's now dwindling screams, Amy found the words she wanted to say but normally would have swallowed. "This is my house."

"What?"

"This is my favorite house . . . on the street, in town." She swept her hand through the air.

"Well"—the woman seemed to hesitate now, her perkiness fading—"it is rather . . . expensive, you know, being on Magnolia, and it's a Historic Preservation home, protected by the city, and—"

"I know. I know."

Amy and Phil's arguments about buying the house were sedate, but genuine. She always understood Phil gave in not because he loved the house, but because he loved her. His interest was remote at best, nonexistent at worst. If there was any work or renovation to be done to the house, it was her domain. He never said it, but she read it in his eyes: *You wanted this house. You take care of it.* And she did.

The day they moved in, they made love on the sunroom floor, a threadbare cotton blanket with a picture of the state of Georgia beneath them, while Molly and Jack napped in Pack 'N Plays in the foyer amid boxes blocking the way upstairs. Never once, in their eighteen years of living there, had Phil questioned why she claimed the best room in the house—why her dried flowers, torn photographs, trinkets, papers and books resided in the room with the best view of both the sunset and the side yard with its prolific rose garden and iron fence.

She now stood in the doorway and nibbled on her

Band-Aid. When was the last time she and Phil had made love? She couldn't think about it now. There were papers to grade.

When was the last time she and *Nick* had made love? She closed her eyes and remembered: the night before he left, in the musty third-floor apartment where he lived his senior year.

A Saxton University banner hung by a thumbtack on the left wall, a clap-activated lamp crouched on a discarded beer keg turned nightstand, next to the mattress on the floor. Why waste money on a bed frame or a real table when they could use the money for another camping trip to a national forest they hadn't yet explored? The vague scent of soap mixed with toothpaste and a warm spot on the pillow attempted to seduce her to sleep even as she wanted to stay up all night, trace his face, his shoulder blades, the curve of his back. That night was to last three months. As it ended up, that night needed to last forever.

Our vows are still there, never broken.

She shook her head, shrugging off the memory. She walked to her desk, realigned her thoughts to the present, to the essays on the field trip. She sat down and leafed through the papers, then lifted and fingered the pink paper with the phone number that Phil had thrown away. She felt like an alcoholic digging a half-empty bottle from the trash, but told herself she would only use this number to ask Nick about the OWP project and the leaf he'd found.

Our vows are still there, never broken.

Enough about the damn vows, already.

She stuffed the paper in the top drawer of her desk, underneath old phone bills she'd meant to claim as teacher's expenses.

She started to grade the essays, but found she needed to

close her eyes for just one minute. She collapsed into the chaise longue covered in faded pink and yellow chintz, that she'd found at a flea market.

She awoke with Phil's lips on her forehead. "Honey, it's midnight. You need to come to bed."

She opened her eyes and looked around the room. "Oh, hell, Phil. I'll never go back to sleep now. You know I can't sleep after I wake up." She rubbed her face.

"I couldn't let you sleep here all night. You'll get cold."

"You could've just thrown a blanket on me."

"Amy, come to bed."

"I can't. I didn't finish the laundry . . . the papers."

"Class isn't for three more days. Come to bed."

She looked up at Phil, at his eyes, and she lifted up her hands, allowed him to pull her to her feet. She fell onto his chest and rested there, knowing for a moment her place.

Chapter Eighteen

The building—constructed of brick and tabby, the Low-country combination of lime, whole oyster shells and burned, crushed shells—squatted in front of Nick. The sun sank below the tips of the wrought-iron fencing across the top of the building and caused the iron to blaze. Nick looked down to the front door of the building he was not allowed into without a pass. He waited for a student, even one, to exit the dorm so he could walk in as she walked out.

He'd wrestled all afternoon with the thought versus the reality of coming to Amy's dorm. He'd imagined her angry at him for coming without telling her, then relieved when he told her what he'd found. Only a few weeks had passed since he'd last seen her, yet another twenty-five years seemed to have dissolved in her absence, as if the recent contact with her elongated both time and pain—again.

He opened the truck door and stepped out, walked slowly toward the front of the dorm. A young girl, her ponytail swishing to her flicking head movements as she talked to her friends, opened the door, bringing laughter and the exposed midriffs of undergrads going out for the evening. Nick smiled, nodded and propped the door open for them. They smiled back at him, probably believing he was visiting his daughter. He entered the foyer. The sun setting behind the building glared through the back windows, exposed streaks and handprints on the glass. Nick squinted and turned to the front desk. Everything in the room appeared harsh, overlit by the setting sun.

He had prepared a speech for whoever sat sentinel at the front desk, but it was empty, a small soundless TV flickering a rerun of *Seinfeld*. He laughed and glanced around the empty room. A scratched thick wooden door to the left of the desk was propped open half an inch, enough to allow him to see the sunlit grass, a concrete stoop: the courtyard. He sidled toward the door and opened it, walked outside.

The courtyard seemed empty save for a large blue jay splashing in the birdbath, looking over its shoulder at him, concluding he was of little concern. The corner where he had sat with Amy just a few weeks before was shrouded in shadow, just as he remembered it. He began to walk toward where he knew the bench was, behind the tree, tilted to the left where it sank in moss-soft soil. He'd sit and wait; he had something to tell her and a sleep-depriving need to see her, touch her.

He walked closer; someone occupied his seat. Behind the curtain of Spanish moss a figure leaned against the armrest, feet on top of the bench, head bent over folded legs. A twig snapped under Nick's foot. The figure's head shot up and looked directly at him.

"Sorry. Sorry." He stopped, began to turn, then laughed. Amy sat before him, staring at him, her head tipped on top of her knees. He couldn't see her whole face, but he knew her body, the tilt of her head.

"Nick?"

He walked under the moss. "Yep."

"How . . . ?"

"I have my ways." He laughed. She didn't.

"You can't just come here."

"Why not? You were waiting for me."

"No, I wasn't. I always come out here . . . to read, grade papers."

Nick swept his hand over the empty bench. "Did you forget your work today?"

She moaned and dropped her head back down on her knees.

"I wanted to tell you before I told the OWP. I had the plant analyzed and it is definitely a buckthorn. Norah can take it to the Heritage Preserve," Nick said.

"I thought Brenton was doing that."

"Well, I had a lab that could get to it faster—owed me a favor."

"Nick, that is awesome news, but you could've called me."

"I know. I tried not to come—" He leaned down and looked directly in her eyes. "It's terrible, you know, fucking terrible to need to see someone as much as I need to see you."

She looked up now. "You smell like whiskey."

"I told you . . . I tried not to come. I stopped at McNalley's for a few with the guys after work, but I couldn't sit still—couldn't find anything to talk about—and I knew you were thirty minutes away. Thirty minutes. Christ, for the past twenty-five years you've been on another planet, and today you were thirty minutes away. How could I not come?"

"Nick."

He couldn't read what she meant in that one word, but the sound of his name on her tongue, in her mouth, was worth the embarrassment of showing up at her school looking like he was stalking her.

"I really can't believe I'm sitting here looking at you," he said.

"It's like some weird half-dream," she agreed without looking up. "Or nightmare."

He laughed. "You know, I used to dream about seeing you. I don't anymore. I wish I would, but I can't . . . they don't come to me. I used to have them all the time—bizarre dreams where I couldn't get to you."

"What do you mean?" She sat up now, swung her feet to the ground.

"You'd be in a restaurant, in a crowd, across a room . . . and I would try to touch you, but the closer I got, the farther away you'd go. You never saw me in those dreams. I only had two dreams where you saw me. One time was when I saw you across a restaurant at a bar that looked like it was made completely of glass and silver. You were holding a bottle of tequila."

"I don't drink tequila."

"I don't think that was the point of the dream." He pinched her nose.

"What was the point?"

"You saw me. Noticed me. You waved and walked over. But you never said a word and we walked outside, drove off in my truck."

"Okay . . ."

"I carried that dream around for years. You saw me. You left with me. Then I had my last dream about you . . . it was years ago. You were floating on top of the ocean, on your back. You'd look at me once in a while, wave, then tuck your head back on the waves. I yelled at you to return to shore—there were sharks. I tried to swim after you, but in that weird dream way when you can't swim or walk or run, I couldn't get to you. I screamed, I tried to swim, I crawled through the sand, but you just floated and floated. You couldn't see what I saw: the sharks."

Amy lifted her head. "I had a dream recently about floating in the ocean. Well, it wasn't really a dream—it lasted ten seconds before Carol Anne rang the living hell out of the doorbell."

"Always count on Carol Anne to ruin a good time."

"Carol Anne is the best friend I've ever had."

Nick took a deep breath. "Have you told her about . . . all this?"

"Yes. Yes, I have. Well, a little. I kept some . . . specifics to myself."

"What did you tell her?"

"What really happened to you, where you were—the jail."

"What did she say?"

"You don't want to know." Amy smiled.

God, he loved it when she really smiled, a God-save-his-soul smile. "Oh, but sure I want to know what our friend Carol Anne had to say."

"She said that she thought you were down in Costa Rica the entire time getting more ass than a toilet seat." Amy's smile widened. Then she laughed.

"She is such a delicate Southern flower."

"The funny part is, she is. She is kind and sensitive and wise."

"Well, did she have any advice?"

"Do you mean before or after I drove off with the hose from the gas pump still in my car and sat on the pavement in front of half the old biddies in town getting their hair done?"

"What?"

She amused him with the tale of the gas pump, and Nick felt such a release of laughter and joy at her storytelling, at her obvious preoccupation with him.

"It's not that funny. I'm a mess."

"So, really, after all that, what did Carol Anne have to say, advice-wise? I'd *love* to hear it."

"To stay as far away from you as Costa Rica. Farther."

"Ah, she's still jealous."

"No, just protective of me."

"I'm obviously joking about the jealous part, but you don't need to be protected from anything . . . or anyone. I believe you know how to take care of yourself."

"No, I'm not sure I do anymore."

"Don't you dare let that happen to you—you were always able to be whatever someone wanted of you—the small-town good-girl syndrome. But you've always known what you wanted—always taken care of yourself."

Amy stared at him. He reached out his hand for hers. She shook her head. "Did you come here to tell me your version of who I am, or just to tell me your dreams?"

"I came to tell you about the plant, to hear your voice, even if you were mad at me. I came to see you, to touch your face, to hear you tell me what you've been thinking."

"I don't want to talk about it."

He lifted her chin, ran his finger down her neck and let it rest at her throat. "It's me. Talk to me. You don't have to make any sense, just talk to me."

"I've been sleepwalking. How does that make you feel? Better? I can't be this way. I can't. I'm burying myself in chores and—"

"It doesn't work, does it?"

"No, it doesn't." She folded her hands over her face.

"What are we going to do?"

She looked out from her hands. "Nothing. We aren't going to *do* anything. If you want to talk or . . . but we're not going to do anything."

"We're going to take a walk. That's what we're going to do. Walk down to the river, get some fresh air, a glass of wine, maybe some oysters. Come on."

She hesitated, then answered, "That sounds really nice, but—"

"But nothing. Hell, we'll call Revvy and the gang—tell them what I've found."

"Nick . . ."

"Just let me hear your voice, walk with you. That's all."

"Okay, okay. I haven't eaten in a while."

"Me neither. Come on." He stood, held out his hand for her. She grabbed it and stood. Dusk surrounded them, just as when he'd said goodbye to her last week, when she'd run from him and left him alone.

This time she was leaving with him. After she punched a code into the keypad, she opened the gate and he held it for her, bowed, allowed her out first.

"Mrs. Reynolds. Mrs. Reynolds." A shrill voice came from the front porch of the dorm.

Nick looked at Amy. "You know her?"

"A student. Give me a sec here."

Amy moved toward the small freckled girl, but the girl was quicker, reaching them first. "You forgot to grade my essay. You gave it back without a grade or marks or anything."

"Oh, Sarah, I'm so sorry. It must have stuck to the bottom or . . . I'm so sorry. Just slip it under my door inside the dorm. I promise to have it back to you by tomorrow morning's house tour—extra credit for my carelessness."

"Bonus!" The girl giggled and glanced at Nick. "Is this your husband you always talk about?"

Amy blushed—it began at her hairline and descend to the V of her pearl gray sweater. "No, this is an old college friend in town on business. He's working on the Oystertip Island project also."

"Oh . . . sorry."

"No, don't be. Mr. Reynolds loves coming to Savannah. I'll bring him to class sometime, introduce him."

"Whatever . . . cool. I'll see you in the morning." Sarah disappeared through the front door.

Amy turned back to Nick. "This is a very, very bad idea," she said.

Nick felt a rising panic; she would change her mind. "It's fine. You're being paranoid. We're not doing anything wrong . . . taking a walk, talking. I haven't even heard how your family is, what you're doing. All we talked about was my damn jail term and the OWP project. Catch me up."

Amy ambled across the cobblestone sidewalk; Nick didn't speed up for fear of her turning back. She watched the ground while she walked, looked to the left, the right, never at him. She wrapped her arms around her chest and rubbed her upper arms.

"Are you cold?"

"No. I'm fine, really. So tell me about your family—your brother, your mom, your dad," she said.

"Dad died fifteen years ago."

"I'm so sorry. How?"

"Cirrhosis. Let's talk about something else." He waved his hand through the air. His dad had made the final descent into the alcoholic's death. Nick did not want to talk about his dad at all. He had nothing in common with him, never had; the subject of his father embarrassed him.

"Okay, how about your mom?"

"Well, Mom's still in Garvey, her life revolving around her bridge club, her bingo night. But she is actually better than I've seen her since . . . well, she's slowly come out of her shell."

"Good for her. Is she still in the old house?"

He had a mental flash of the house he grew up in, the old rural clapboard house that backed up to a rambling forest. He'd loved the house and the land. Three years after he returned from Costa Rica, a strip mall replaced the woods and his mother was offered a beautiful new view of black concrete and screaming children and their mothers off on a family shopping day.

"Mama moved after they built a strip mall behind the house. She never loved that house anyway. It had been Dad's throne, not hers. She lives in a retirement community where she has her own little place, a nice view of a lake and a porch for reading. She's . . . happy."

They walked and talked, catching up on family—who lived where, what had happened over the past twenty-five years. Amy told Nick about her parents' deaths in a car crash on I-85 on a trip to Atlanta, when the driver of an eighteen-wheeler fell asleep. She told him of the grief and panic that had overtaken her, and how living in her hometown had eased some of the pain—how her children never knew her parents since they were both babies when it happened.

In broad strokes they began to paint the pictures of each other's lives—fragmented images meant to convey larger murals.

Amy took a deep breath; she looked like she was girding herself for the next question. "So what did you do after Costa Rica?"

He stopped when she asked this; the glow from the gaslight above them licked her hair. He wanted, needed to touch her.

"I left Costa Rica the instant I could. I don't think I slept there again—that's how fast I left."

Amy laughed, punched his arm. "You don't sleep much anywhere."

"True. But I left as soon as I could get my papers together—and Eliza was pretty damn organized."

"Then what?"

"It's a long story. Essentially Eliza's dad had arranged for me to get a job with one of his subsidiary companies in Maine, doing reforestation and corporate development plans. We stayed there for fifteen years."

"But . . ." She looked away.

He turned her face with his hand. "But what?"

"That's not what you wanted to do."

"And isn't that the hell of all this? Just seeing you reminds me of that. I don't need you to tell me."

"I'm sorry. I just meant—I was just curious how you changed goals."

"I didn't change my goals, Amy. The circumstances changed my goals."

"Oh," she whispered.

He placed his palm on the side of her face. "There are so many things I lost back then. And the worst of it is that I'd almost forgotten what I wanted to forget . . . and then there you were." She pulled away and stumbled on the cobblestone sidewalk. He grabbed her arm. "I lost you. I lost most of the purpose in my job. The only things I gained were nightmares of women jumping in front of my car and cockroaches under the bed."

"I'm so, so sorry. I wish . . . I wish . . ."

"I wish, too. But it doesn't do a damn bit of good—trust me on that." He drew a deep breath. "I was lucky Eliza's dad arranged a job for me. No one knew anything about the 'incident' in Costa Rica. If I'd tried to get my own job, or do it on my own terms, they would've found out."

"So no one ever found out."

"Nope. Never. It's not even discussed."

"That doesn't make it go away."

"It did for a while. It definitely did for a while."

"How did you end up back here?"

"Eliza wanted to come back to the South, badly. After Lisbeth turned ten, Eliza's need to return to the South overwhelmed her. And her dad, ole Harlan Sullivan, finally deemed me worthy to work for the family company."

"Did you decide that research and education weren't what you really wanted?"

With that question a doubled-over kind of realization knocked him in the gut—he was still not doing what he wanted, and he'd run out of excuses. His voice came choked, as if his desires were stuck in his throat. "I'd forgotten—really forgotten—until I saw you, what I wanted . . ."

"What?"

He leaned into her, grabbed both her shoulders—*she must understand this.* "Haven't you ever thought you weren't hungry, then all of a sudden you smelled something or tasted something you love and you realized that you were starving? Absolutely starving?"

"Yes," she said, but he could barely hear her as much as read her lips: *Yes, yes.*

"Well, that's how it is now. I'm starving for all that—for all those things I once wanted."

A couple walked past them, bumped them. Amy looked up and down the street. "Come on, let's walk."

"Do you understand?"

She stopped and turned; she was away from the light

now and her face was in shadow, the whites of her eyes shining. "Yes, I understand, but I can't fix it. It kills me, but I can't. Maybe then I could have—I don't even know that. But how can I fill all that . . . hunger in you? It's always been that way with you."

"But you did fill it."

"I can't now. I can't." She walked faster and he jogged up behind her.

"Amy."

"Please, stop. Please."

He closed his eyes. "Okay."

She turned now and reached into her purse, pasted one of those shaky smiles on her face. "Here, call Revvy. Tell him what you found." She pulled out a cell phone. "Go ahead. You do it. You're the hero here."

"Do you know his number?"

"I have it back at the dorm. Call information."

Two minutes later, the good news had been conveyed, and Revvy said he would call Norah and Brenton and arrange a meeting for the following week.

They arrived at the edge of the Savannah River on a walkway overlooking the water. The sound of clinking glasses, laughter and humming conversation spilled from a café behind them.

"Let's sit out here." He motioned toward the café. "Get that glass of wine and oysters."

He touched her sweater-covered arm, steered her through the café's wrought-iron gate and pointed to an empty table in the far corner.

"I'll get us drinks. Be right back."

Amy maneuvered her way through the crowd, sat at the round iron table. Nick turned from her to the bar, ordered two glasses of Merlot.

He carried the wine to the table. "I forgot to ask you what you wanted. Is Merlot okay?"

"Perfect."

"Tell me about Phil, about meeting him . . . about marrying him." He sat down and pulled his chair closer to her; their knees brushed.

"You don't want to hear all this."

"Oh, yes, I do." He clinked his glass with hers. "Go for it."

"Well, the semester you didn't return . . . I dropped out of school. I was failing anyway—never attended class. Mom maneuvered a doctor's slip . . . family doc and all that. So I was able to take a semester off without any effect on my oh-so-perfect grade point average."

"Wouldn't want to mess that up now, would we?"

"No, Mom and Dad were insistent about that. Anyway, Phil and I were friends with all the same people—you know, in school and at home. He was at the local community college, working full-time for an accountant and . . . well, he was there the semester I came home, which also happened to be spring quarter. So then it was summer break and . . . and six months into being home. . . ."

She took a long, slow swallow of her wine and looked out at the river. A barge slid by exuding a long black cloud of smoke. A couple strolled by, leaning on each other's shoulders and murmuring. Amy stared at them, tucked her hair behind her ears, twisted it behind her head; it all sprang loose before she even rested her hands at her sides.

She spoke without looking at him. "I was miserable. He wasn't. I was on an emotional roller coaster. He was stable. I was tired. He was alive, funny, awake."

"So you used him."

Her head whipped around. "That is not fair. You're not

giving Phil credit for who and what he is to me. He took—
he takes such good care of me. He loves me."

"Yeah, you already said he takes care of you. I didn't realize you needed someone to take care of you. Was it that
easy, in a year, to fall in love again?"

"Do *not* do that—act like I left you and fell in love. I
thought you were gone, really gone. I thought you'd left
me. Until my parents died, it was the most horrible thing
that I'd ever been through—thinking I'd been abandoned. And Phil wasn't the most horrible anything. He
was kind."

"And simple."

"Don't confuse simple with kind." Her lips were a tight
thin line.

"I'm sorry." The warmth of the wine filled his chest, so
he could tolerate Amy's confession of love for another man.

"Nick, there really is no reason to rehash this. To—"

"I want to know. I want to fill in all those blank spaces
where I imagined what you were doing."

"And you . . . what you were doing?"

"I was in jail, Amy."

"No, after that. You married Eliza. You chose that. I
wasn't married yet."

"I was so livid, Amy." He slammed his glass on the
table. Red wine splashed over the rim. "I thought you ignored my telegrams, ran off with some new guy. I was
not gonna come flying back to the States to have you tell
me in person what a schmuck I was, how I screwed up
by killing someone, how you were in love with someone
else."

"So there you go. You found your comfort in Eliza. You
married her."

"She did so much . . ."

Amy held up her hand, swallowed the remainder of her wine. "I don't want to talk about this anymore."

He leaned back in his chair. "Do you want to get something to eat? Oysters?"

"No, I'm really not hungry now. I need to go back to the dorm. I have an early field trip . . . papers to grade. It's getting late."

"Amy, I'm going to try to find the lawyer . . . ask him why he never sent the telegrams . . . never got through to you."

"Don't go there. It won't make any difference."

He leaned across the table. "Don't you want to know why? Make some sense of this?"

Amy closed her eyes. He wanted to lean forward and kiss the same eyelids he had once kissed goodbye in an airport.

She opened her eyes. "I really do have to go."

"I'll walk you back."

"Okay, yes, that'd be okay."

They walked in silence under waved cones of gaslight, through darker places where he reached for her back, to steady her, touch her. The click of her shoes echoed over cobblestones and concrete as they wove their way through the streets.

Nick searched for something to say that was not desperate, begging. One more word, touch, promise. With each step he told himself just to be content that she was present, there, alive.

They walked up the front steps of the dorm. The smell of jasmine overflowed the front porch of the dorm as a solid substance he imagined he could see. He inhaled. "Mmm."

"Jasmine," she said and closed her eyes, leaned against

a pillar. Now was not the time to reach for her. She opened her eyes and under the porch light he saw her face from twenty-five years ago: eager, pliable.

"Thanks for coming tonight, Nick. I do feel better that we can talk—be friends. But you can't just show up." She turned to walk in the door.

"I'll see you next week, at the meeting?" He sounded desperate—as desperate as the night he had asked her out when he had a date with her roommate.

She turned with the door open, light falling in a triangle across the floor. "I don't know. They don't really need me if this buckthorn thing works out." She waved at him and looked like she might say something else, but she turned and went inside, shut the door.

Nick walked to his truck, found the cooler from his morning fishing trip and dug out a lukewarm Heinekin. He popped the top and swallowed the warm amber fluid that he hoped would drown the fresh pain. The scars built over years and years of healing—or denial, he wasn't sure which—were now open.

Chapter Nineteen

Amy held two pieces of good news close to her heart. She wanted to savor them and wait for the right moment to share them with her family. First was the discovery of the buckthorn and its possible island-saving import; second was the phone call from Carol Anne, who had said her husband had found out something about the buyer. Jack was home from college for the weekend, and tonight she would tell the entire family—include them, so they could all band together in celebration.

She'd prepared the family's favorite dinner—homemade fried chicken, mashed potatoes, greens and peach pie for dessert. A bottle of red wine sat sentinel in the middle of the table.

Phil, Jack and Molly appeared at the table, preoccupied with their own thoughts of what the day had held, with their own activities and desires, so they didn't notice the family's traditional meal for birthdays, victorious tennis matches, anniversaries or excellent report cards. They all sat down at the table and Amy was warm, surrounded. Talk circled about school and tennis, of Phil's work and their

Christmas schedule. No one had yet noticed the obvious celebratory hint of the dinner.

"Mom." Jack put his elbows on the table and leaned toward her. "You know the Christmas open house you have every year?"

"Yep. Invitations already printed. Why?"

"Lisbeth . . . well, Lisbeth and I were wondering if you could invite her parents. She really wants them there and, well, they could take the place of the Stevensons, who never show up."

He was referring to Phil's boss, and Phil disagreed this time. "No, buddy, this year they'll come."

"Good." Jack looked at his mother. "Can the Lowrys come, too?"

"Sure," she said, picking up the wine bottle and wanting to drink the entire contents at the thought. "No problem." She was anxious to change the subject, to tell them her news.

Molly punched her brother on the side of the arm. "Are these gonna be our in-laws?'"

"Not yet." Jack smiled and shoved a pile of mashed potatoes in his mouth.

"Well, then." Molly swept her hands over the table. "This dinner must be because *you're* here."

Ah, so Molly had noticed.

"No," Amy said. "Well, a little. I'm celebrating Jack being home for the weekend, but I also have some good news." She looked at Phil; he scooted his chair closer to the table. She wanted him to ask, just ask.

"What is it?" Phil asked.

She poured wine into his glass and leaned back, savoring the suspense. "Well, it seems that we may have found an endangered plant on the island that can possibly get us a Heritage Trust—and even better, I heard from Joe today that there's a way to find out the name of the buyer."

Phil leaned back in his seat and folded his arms over his chest. She should've felt the trembles of regret already rolling toward her—and she might have if she weren't so prepared to have Phil join her in celebration, if she hadn't been so geared up for the expectation of his joy and willingness to help her.

She plowed on. "If we can get the name of the buyer, we can go to him, put the heat on through media and—" Phil held up his hand; she stopped, and her heart sank— he didn't want to hear her news.

"Amy." He closed his eyes.

"Listen—the best part is that you can help me. We can do this together. Joe found out that the wealthy buyer has a numbered account through Stevenson and Sons—his funds are through *your* company."

"I know." He opened his eyes and looked across the table at the wall, not at her.

"You know what?"

"That he has his funding through *my* company."

The table tilted.

Molly cut her steak. "Wow, Dad, now you can tell us who it is."

"No, I can't."

"How long have you known about the buyer?" Amy whispered, her disappointment becoming nausea.

"Since the beginning. It's client privilege. There is no way I could give you his name, even if I knew it, which I don't."

"You could find out. I know you could find out."

"Yes, I could, but I won't. Didn't you hear me? It's client privilege. There's a reason he has a number and not a name."

"Yeah, so he can ruin a natural treasure." She stood up.

"No, it's so he doesn't have TV crews at his door, his name smeared for wanting to build a vacation home. That's why."

"If he knew—if we could tell him how precious the island and house are, then maybe he'd stop."

"I just can't."

She turned away. "What am I going to tell the OWP and Nick? I already told them you'd help—I was sure you would. . . ."

"What does Nick have to do with it?"

"Remember I told you he's helping us—he went with us out to the island. He's the one who found the endangered plant."

"No, you did not tell me that."

"Yes, I did. I told you after I cut my finger. I told you all about the trip and—"

"I remember the trip. I don't remember Nick."

"That's because you never listen to me."

Molly and Jack looked at each other and quietly got up from the table. Amy couldn't remember if she and Phil had ever had a disagreement in front of the kids.

"Okay, that would be an exaggeration. Let's be rational here."

She did not want to be rational. "What do you want me to tell them? That my husband won't help us?"

"Why don't you tell them that I won't sacrifice client privilege? Honey, you understand, don't you? You agree, right?"

She had always carefully padded her words with Phil to avoid fighting—but now she spoke exactly what she meant to say. "No, I do not agree."

She couldn't look at him when she said it. She stood and

began to walk out of the room, but turned as she reached the door. She spoke to the back of his head. "I thought there was a way for us to . . . do this together. For you to help. For us to—"

Phil turned around and stared at her. "I don't ask you to help me with my job."

"What?" An uncharacteristic yelp came from the well of her disappointment. "Ask me to help you with your job? No, you just ask me to do everything else, so you can do your job. This . . . this I wanted us to do together."

"Amy, calm down. Don't I take care of everything for you?"

"It's not just about taking care of everything, Phil. This time it's about caring about what I care about."

She pushed the swinging door and marched into the living room. She wasn't sure where to go, other than her office. She'd told the OWP the good news already—how she'd found out where the buyer's accounts were, how she'd deliver the precious information. Now she had to call them and tell them—tell Nick that her husband was unwilling to help.

She sat down at her desk and dropped her head onto the mahogany. Her heart ached with the once-rising hope that plummeted, too quickly, to discontent.

Chapter Twenty

The house smelled of pine and cedar. Green boughs hung from the banister, the fireplace, each doorway. Ribbons Amy had made for the art festival, then bought back, hung from every available knob or bend in the home. Candlelight flickered in uneven patterns on the walls. A nativity scene was on the hall table, surrounded by real hay. Because baby Jesus had gone missing at least four Christmases ago, a peanut with eyes and a nose in black marker lay in the cradle. Only two of the three wise men had surfaced this year; they both bowed to the peanut.

Extravagant Christmas decorations filled the halls and rooms of Amy's home for the annual open house. She'd found a beautiful pattern for Christmas stockings and pulled out her sewing machine to copy them. She'd made too many—there were enough stockings for eleven children and some pets hung around the house. She would offer them as party favors tonight to those who brought gifts.

She checked the house one more time. God, she loved it. She pushed open the swinging door to the kitchen and almost knocked over white-aproned Celia, the maid who came once a month and also assisted with entertaining.

Amy hugged Celia. "We all set?"

"Yes, ma'am."

"Okay, I'm going to get dressed. I'll be out shortly to check on things." Nervous energy thrummed through her body. Thanksgiving had gone smoothly, as long as she didn't talk about Oystertip and as long as she stayed away in both word and deed from the subject of Nick Lowry. But now the Christmas party was here and certain things couldn't be avoided.

She walked toward her room, then bent to pick up a fallen ivy leaf from the candle display and slide it back on the table. Phil vacuumed the sitting room—one last sweep before the guests arrived. She tried not to think about the guests—the Lowry guests specifically.

Well, she would just think about which dress to wear. She'd bought two gowns, right after Jack had informed her of the added guests—right after Phil had informed her he would do nothing to help her find out the name of the buyer. One dress was black, cutting in a V between her breasts without being cut too low, then tapering down to thin, sheer panels at the bottom. It was slit up the side, and she'd bought black strappy sandals, a little higher than she usually wore, to go with it.

The other dress was silver: silk, long, demure. There was nothing sheer about it, yet there might as well have been, the way it hugged her body from top to ankle.

She decided to check on the kids before she began the slow and painful process of makeup and hair. It didn't matter what she did to her hair; it would wave around her shoulders by midevening.

At the top of the stairs she stopped; she'd forgotten to turn on the music. She turned on her slippered feet, stepped down the creaking stairs to choose CDs for the stereo before she checked on Jack's and Molly's progress in getting ready for the party. She hoped they'd at least taken showers. Murmurs came from Molly's bedroom at the top of the landing; Amy paused.

The warmth of her children's voices, of having them both home, felt like a lit ember in her middle. She stopped just to listen, to know they were near. They were talking about Lisbeth; Jack was complaining—something about Lisbeth's clinginess, her overwhelming need to know where he was all the time.

Amy smiled and crept up one more step. Molly was giving her high school advice.

"Ooh, don't you hate that? Calling on the cell phone every five minutes because they can't find you?"

"Yeah, and then you have to pretend you were out-of-area or that your cell phone went dead, you know?" Jack answered.

Molly laughed. Amy frowned. Jack and Lisbeth were having problems.

The conversation reached a lull and Amy moved to enter Molly's room. Jack's voice caused her to freeze; she crouched down.

"Hey, Molly, did you know Mom and Nick, Lisbeth's dad, used to date in college?"

"No. That's kinda weird."

"Yeah, a little. If I tell you something, will you promise not to get all freaked out on me?"

"What? You think I'm gonna freak out that Mom once dated someone besides Dad? Give me a break—"

"No, not that, snot breath."

Amy smiled at Jack's loving, yet disgusting nickname for Molly. He had called her that since she was four years old and had a runny nose for a solid week.

"Lisbeth's best friend, Sarah, is in Mom's class at SCAD."

"And?"

"Well, Lisbeth brought Sarah home to stay at their house over Thanksgiving. I guess this girl's family moved or something. Anyway, she came to spend Thanksgiving with the Lowrys. After she met Mr. Lowry, she told Lisbeth that a man who looks just like him was at SCAD one night—with her teacher."

"And . . . ? I guess I'm missing the point here."

"Do you think Mom was *with* Mr. Lowry?"

"Oh, gross, Jack. No way. You heard Mom tell Dad that he's helping with the island thing. That's all. She would never . . . that is just not in her to *do*. That is so . . . beneath her. No way." Molly's voice was firm, loud.

"All kids want to think their parents would never—"

"Well, Mom wouldn't. It's just not . . . in her to do."

"You're right. I mean, I didn't see anything weird about them at the lake or anything, did you?"

"Absolutely not. Mom is like totally in love with Dad. Who wouldn't be?"

"Well, they're coming tonight and I just didn't want it to be weird or anything."

"If you're so sick of Lisbeth, why did you invite her whole family? You gonna ask for her hand or something?"

Amy heard the loud thwack of a pillow.

"Ow," Molly yelled. They both came running out of the bedroom, Molly with a pillow in hand, Jack with his arms over his head—an expanded, stretched-out version of them when they were two and four years old, wrestling and screaming, but not really wanting any help. They stopped short when they saw Amy squatting on the top step. They looked at each other, then at her.

"What're you doing, Mom?" Jack asked.

"Picking up the fallen needles from the pine garland." She lifted a handful of needles, proving her point, then stepped to the landing at the top of the stairs.

"Mom, please, it's just a Christmas party, not a visit from the president."

"Ah, you never know who'll show up at an open house."

"You better not let anyone upstairs in my room," Molly said.

"You know how people sneak around," Amy said. "You better at least make sure your bed is made."

"I'm locking my door." Jack walked toward his room.

"So you and Lisbeth can go at it without anybody seeing you?" Molly threw the pillow at him and ran back to her room, Jack chasing her.

Amy sighed, dropped the pine needles to the carpet and strolled slowly down the steps; her legs felt like yarn unraveling. How had she thought that no one, absolutely no one, would notice what she was going through? How could she have assumed this mess with Nick could occur in a bubble, that backlash would not shake her world?

She had considered the ancient desire that was rumbling deep within her to be her own personal struggle. But as though she were tied to her family by more than blood, by an invisible sinew as well, they, too, sensed that struggle. Jack and Lisbeth were quarreling. Jack thought his mother . . .

She walked into the bedroom and found Phil waiting for her.

"Do you like this shirt or this one?" He held up what looked like two identical shirts.

"They're the same, Phil."

"No, one is navy and one is dark blue."

"They are the same."

"Which one, of the same shirt, do you like better?"

She rolled her eyes. "The one on the right."

"The dark blue it is."

"I thought that was the navy one."

"It might be." He leaned across the space between them and kissed her. "Thanks for the fashion advice. What're you wearing tonight?"

"I bought a new dress."

"Can't wait to see you in it." He walked toward the bathroom, humming "Jingle Bells" as he moved.

The music—it's what she'd meant to do before she heard her children—the music and now a much-needed glass of wine.

She went downstairs and pulled the Christmas CDs from their labeled box. She laid them across the floor and picked her ten favorites and arranged them in the CD changer. She pushed the RANDOM button and started the stereo, then checked that each speaker button was pushed to ON for each room in the house, from the dining room to the kitchen. Garth Brooks began to sing about the most wonderful time of the year . . . caroling out in the snow . . . and Amy walked to the kitchen to grab a glass of wine.

Celia looked up and squinted. "Hello, Mrs. Reynolds."

"Something wrong?"

"I thought you were going to get dressed."

Amy looked down at her robe, her fuzzy red Santa-hat slippers. "Whoops, I was." She looked up at Celia. "You don't think this is a very nice outfit?"

"If you want it to be a well talked-about party, why yes, I do."

"No, I just need a glass of wine—white—then I'm finally off to dress."

What she really wanted was for her legs to tighten beneath her; she couldn't walk around all night with the sturdiness of a tumbling toddler.

She picked up the glass of wine and walked back to her bedroom, placed the wine on the bedside table next to their wedding photo in its silver frame. In her closet, she pulled both dresses from the rack and laid them on the bed and stared at them, decided instantly that the silver dress was the more appropriate: sexier in its simplicity.

She sat on the bed and untied her robe, looked down at her flattened stomach. She really had lost a lot of weight these past few weeks; food held little appeal. Sleep was what she craved, yet she couldn't find much of that either.

Phil came into the room and stood in front of her. "Whatcha thinkin'?"

She looked up at her husband. "Can't decide what to wear."

"Well, I know how to take your mind off it."

"Oh, you do?"

He looked down at her; she grasped her opened robe. He smiled, and pushed the robe off her shoulders. It fell to the bed, covering the black dress. He pushed her, gently, onto her back. She rested on top of the robe and whispered, "Will you put that silver dress over my vanity chair?"

Phil reached for the dress without ever looking away from her. He placed the dress on the chair behind him and bent to kiss her. She closed her eyes and tasted the familiar kiss of her husband, of comfort. She reached behind his neck and pulled him closer. She mumbled, "Did you lock the door?"

"Yes." He slid his hand down to open the robe at the bottom, then pulled it away from her body.

"Hmm," she whispered into his neck. She buried her head in his shoulder, let him transport her where he wanted to go. She was the willing and pliable one underneath. No effort on her part was needed this time, and she floated in their lovemaking, letting his hands and mouth wander where they pleased while she basked in the comfort of familiar intimacy.

He snapped at her white silk underwear and she lifted her hips, the most motion she'd made since he touched her, then let him slip them off, let them slide to the floor. She wrapped her legs around him, let his feet, still on the floor, steady both of them.

She reached in her wandering mind, far below, for some sort of reaction, something beyond comfort, something that moved toward strength and desire, but found only an odd wondering if she'd laid out all the silver for Celia to polish, or if she could return the black dress she was now lying on top of, or if the red roses would open before the guests arrived.

As Phil shuddered, she unwrapped her legs and he rolled, then collapsed next to her.

She turned to her side, stared at his face. A slow guilt passed over her in the form of a deep sadness. She reached over and traced his chin, his unshaven cheeks.

"I'm sorry you don't understand why I can't help you with your project," he said.

She looked away. "I don't."

"I know. And I'm sorry, but I love you."

"I love you, too. And, no, I don't understand why you can't help, but I don't understand a lot of things right now." He wouldn't pursue this subject; he probably hadn't even heard her.

He brushed the hair from her forehead. "Well, we have a party to give, guests coming." He stood and stretched.

"Yes," Amy said. "Guests coming." She sat up and shivered.

Chapter Twenty-one

Nick stood in the closet doorway, where he could see Eliza's reflection in her vanity mirror. She leaned forward, wiped below her eyes, brushed upward against her eyebrows, then lifted tweezers from her flowered makeup bag to pluck one stray hair from the outside line of her perfectly arched brows. Can't have anything out of place now, can we? Eliza was a beautiful woman, not much different from the beautiful girl he'd married. She was what people called "well-preserved," as she should be, considering all the time and money she spent on herself.

She did draw attention—she and her family. He was lucky, men told him. Watching her was almost like observing a stranger. Then, as if a fist had been shoved into his stomach, he realized he really didn't know her at all. He bent over with the force of this knowledge, with the intensity of wondering to whom he was married. She had loved him well these years, loved him in spite of himself, taken care of their life, their children; but he didn't know her, and he wasn't sure he loved her.

This thought, this truth, came so clearly to him, he wondered why the words had never formed in his mind even before Amy had reentered his life. Amy had been a force beneath everything he felt, but had not been fully present until now.

He and Eliza had never discussed Amy after he left the jail. The day he was released, he'd asked Mr. Carreira, one more time, if he had heard from Amy. "Nick," the lawyer said, "I think you need to let this go."

"No," Nick had replied, knowing Amy was coming, still coming.

The damn lawyer had looked up, staring everywhere but at Nick. "Eliza did a little research, found out she is engaged to some hometown boy."

The anguish that had entered him then had been more cutting than the broken ribs and horrific nights spent listening to cockroaches crawl around in his bed. Right there, in the dank jail cell, he'd turned the grief and longing into rage and decided he would never speak to or think about Amy Malone again. He would hate her for the rest of his life for betraying him when he needed her most.

The day he'd walked out into the blazing sun, into the heat of freedom, Eliza had been standing under a banana tree, her blond hair reflecting the light. She'd been a mirage of the American beach girl. She was waiting only for him.

Eliza's joy at seeing him was so complete that she had cried the minute he touched her. He had only seen her once in the year he was in jail: the morning of his so-called arraignment. Yet he knew she'd been working behind the scenes all along, that she was the reason he now stood free. The school had left him to what they considered his due. His mother was too damaged by his drunken father to tolerate even the slightest problem. Over his years of drinking and verbal abuse, always followed by repentance, his father had robbed her of all her inner strength. Despite her love for Nick, she could never have helped him.

His mother was as grateful to Eliza and her family as he was. Remembering now what Eliza had done for him, what she had sacrificed, sent a tendril of tenderness through him.

He leaned against the closet door and stared at their bedroom, painted bland oatmeal and decorated with pastel accents, as if nothing could be allowed to break into color, into anything inappropriate. Eliza leaned closer to the mirror and applied liner to her lips. Focused on this task, she still hadn't noticed him watching her. She looked no different than the woman who'd once leaned against the tree, her arms, mouth and body waiting for him. She looked up now and saw him; she smiled.

"What?" she asked. "Don't you like the gown?"

She was dressed for the Reynoldses Christmas party. They'd been invited through the children, and since they only lived an hour and a half away, Eliza hadn't thought it proper to decline. Somehow in the last few months they'd been able to avoid all contact with the couple, yet this time Lisbeth had formed tears in her eyes, which always made Nick and Eliza say yes. Lisbeth said it was important, *very* important that they come. So here they were getting ready to go to the Reynoldses—as a family. Nick couldn't get over the small thrill of being able to see where Amy lived, how she lived, what her house looked like, the part of her that had become a mother and wife.

Eliza repeated her question. "You don't like it, do you?"

"Yes. Yes, I do. I'm sorry. I'm off somewhere else. . . . This job in Beaufort is exhausting. They—"

"I know." She stood from the dressing table. "And you're helping with that island thing, aren't you?"

"Yeah, but that was just one trip."

"With Amy."

"Yes, Eliza, it's her committee.

"Are you sure you want to go to this party?" She slid toward him, then touched his face. "We don't have to go." She wore a silver silk taffeta gown, lace covering the skirt like frosting.

"Lisbeth said it was important."

"God, I hope they don't announce an engagement, or pinning, or something god-awful like that."

"I hadn't thought of that."

Eliza tilted her head. "You hadn't?" She dropped her hand from his face.

"No."

"Well, I have. And I hope it's not true. Lisbeth is only a junior. She has so much more to see . . . do. She has to finish school and—"

"Ah, how quickly we forget. You married me when you were still finishing college."

"That was different. Extenuating circumstances, should we say? Plus, I finished all my credits and graduated." She laughed and kissed his cheek, ran her finger across the stubble on his chin. "Aren't you going to shave tonight?"

He rubbed his hand across his cheek. "No, I'm not shaving. Why was it so different for us? What if Lisbeth is really in love?"

"Don't defend this. You know why it was different. I was . . . it was true love with us—not what they have. Not some college infatuation and toss in the sheets. We were in a situation that made us grow up very, very fast. It was different and you know it."

"You think what they have is infatuation, a toss in the sheets?"

"Dear God, I hope it's not a toss in the sheets."

"Then who's in the sheets?"

"I just meant that . . . it . . . you and I weren't that. We passed through fire to get to the other side." She kissed him, opened her mouth against his as a peace offering.

He closed his eyes. He knew who she was talking about, mixing and melding Lisbeth and Jack with him and Amy; she was implying that he and Amy were a college infatuation, *a toss in the sheets*. It was the first time in many years that they had even come close to discussing what had happened in Costa Rica, to what had brought them together. He grasped at the chance.

"Do you remember the lawyer from then?" he asked.

"Mr. Carreira?"

"See, you could always say his name. I could never even pronounce it."

Eliza smiled. "Yes, he told me that."

"Do you know what ever happened to him?"

"I have no idea. And I don't care. He let you walk out the door to me, and that is *all* I care about. Why do you want to know?"

Her face closed in. He wanted to stop; he didn't want to bring this subject into the room, into their life, but there was a rising force stronger than he was, and he had to know.

"There were . . . some telegrams I asked him to send that he never sent. I was just curious. I wanted to ask him about them."

His previous brittle attempts at controlling the subject of Amy caused Eliza to give way; she seemed to actually cave in upon herself as she sat on the edge of the bed. Her dress fell around her like a thick taffeta accordion.

"No."

"What?"

She didn't look up. "Twenty-five years later."

He could not see her face, but he knew from the shake of her shoulders, her back, that she was crying.

"What do you mean?" he asked.

"Twenty-five years later I thought it was safe. I thought you wouldn't know . . . or at least if you did know, that you wouldn't care."

"What are you talking about?"

"How . . . ?" She looked up with a thin line between her eyebrows hardened as when she was fully concentrating on a puzzle or family problem. "How do you know these specific telegrams were not delivered?"

He saw his mistake now; the casual question had just brought Amy into the room. How could he have believed he could wonder about this, could ask this question about the lawyer and telegrams, without repercussions? But he'd gone this far; he needed to know the answer.

He sat down next to his wife, folded his hand over hers. "Okay. I asked Amy why she never responded to some telegrams I sent her. She said she never got them. I was wondering—curious, that's all—why she never received them, or why he never sent them."

"When did you find the time to ask her this?" Eliza pulled her hand away, stood up and stepped aside to glare at him. "At the lake, on some island? Just a casual question over a game of Scrabble, or in the middle of trying to save an old house?" She turned her back to him, then seemed to change her mind. She turned as tears ran through her freshly applied face powder.

"You've never let this go. I prayed and prayed that somehow you'd let this go. That you'd given up wondering, that the anger and impatience I've seen grow in you all these years had nothing to do with her not coming . . . nothing to do with *her* at all, but that it was all about what you went through there, in jail. Twenty-five years later I'd actually convinced myself this was true. When I figured out who she was, I thought it was a test from God. I thought it was a sign to prove to us that it was over, that we'd survived her memory, her perfect almighty memory."

Nick lurched toward her to stop her words, her pain. She held up her hand and he remained still as she continued. "I fell in love with you in Costa Rica, and have never stopped—not once—loving you the same way, and you still want to know about her, about what *she* thought then." Spittle landed on her lip. "I loved you even when you came out of jail an angrier man. I loved you then, love you now."

She wiped below her eyes with a rapid movement, as if the tears betrayed her in the same way he did.

"When you asked her if she received the telegrams, did you tell her everything? About jail, the accident?"

"Yes."

"I know you didn't tell her everything. You wouldn't want her to know all of it."

"Eliza . . . stop."

"You asked her. You actually asked her about the telegrams."

"Yes." His voice seemed to come from the other side of the room, the other side of his life.

"Haven't you had a good enough life to stop wondering? But you know, this is a betrayal I deserve." Eliza stomped toward the door.

"What do you mean?" he called after her.

She didn't answer as her dress swished in silver folds down the hallway. He thought of Carol Anne and the skirt she wore to the formal when he met Amy again; every thought these days was a link in a chain that ended with Amy. There was nothing he could do to stop returning to her—not that he tried very hard.

He heard a slam, wood against wood. He jumped up and ran to the hall, where muffled rap music emanated from Alex's room. The attic ladder fell from the gaped opening of the attic and landed on the cream carpet; pink insulation tumbled out to mar the vacuumed surface.

"What the hell are you doing?" He grabbed the end of Eliza's dress as she stepped onto the ladder.

"Let go of me. I'm going to finally end this wondering of yours, this endless fascination with what ever happened to the adorable Amy."

"Stop." All of a sudden he didn't want to know; having Amy around right now was enough.

Eliza pulled at the waistline of her dress and Nick found himself with a handful of silver lace. She didn't even notice the ripped dress—that alone set off an alarm in his head. He needed to stop this—now.

He stepped on the bottom rung behind her; she kicked backward. "Get away."

He jumped to the carpet, stood at the bottom of the ladder; she disappeared into the vacant space of the attic.

Alex opened his bedroom door; the rap music's volume increased. He stuck his head out into the hall. "Hey, Dad." Alex nodded toward the attic. "What's up with Mom?"

"I guess she forgot something in the attic." Nick glanced at his son's jeans hanging low enough on his hips to show his boxers. "Are you going with us to the Christmas party in that?"

"No way, Dad. I'm not getting dressed up and driving an hour and a half to hang out with Lizzy's stupid boyfriend, who she'll chase off in a week or two anyway. Plus, I have a wrestling match in the morning. You'll be there, right?"

Nick cut a punch to Alex's shoulder. "Wouldn't miss it."

"You missed one a few Thursdays ago—first time, Dad."

Nick smiled shakily. The night he drove to the school—to Amy. "Won't happen again, son."

Alex shut the door behind him, and the music, improbably, went up a notch.

Nick stared at the scrap of lace in his hand, then up into the black space of the attic. The light flicked on and boxes scraped across the floor, sounding like squirrels had invaded the attic. What could she be looking for? She had already decorated the house for the holidays—this was always done, no matter where they lived, the day after Thanksgiving. It was a routine as dependable as roasted turkey and pecan stuffing—the taking down of the Christmas boxes the morning after Thanksgiving. It wasn't even discussed anymore, just as January second marked the return of the boxes to the attic.

Eliza spent days on end perfecting the house for the five-week period the decorations would hang. She took pictures of certain arrangements so she would know where to set them the next year. She added to the knickknacks, china and Santa paraphernalia every year. She required Nick to string the multicolored lights and he waited to be told where to hang them.

He couldn't figure out why her anger sent her to the attic now. He'd retrieved every single box two weeks ago. The only things that remained up there were storage boxes from her youth: old horseback-riding trophies, faded swim-team ribbons and yellowed yearbooks from her privileged childhood.

He turned away, dropped the remnant of her dress on the floor. Let her be angry; he'd pushed it one step too far by bringing up the telegrams. He should've tried to find and contact the lawyer himself, not asked his wife. She tolerated enough, but the single moment of tenderness he felt for her had allowed him to believe there was enough in her to bear another question, another wondering about Amy; as if what was important to him could not hurt her.

"Fool," he mumbled to himself and walked to the bedroom. She was probably retrieving a present for the Reynoldses; she wouldn't show up without a hostess gift. She was doing what she did best in the face of conflict: avoiding it.

In the bedroom he entered his closet—they had his and hers, another way to keep conflict to a minimum. She never opened his closet, except to put away his clothes. Years ago she'd stopped complaining about the way he scattered his clothes. He pushed aside the suits, wondering if he should wear a suit or just khakis and a button-down shirt. He hated suits. If he'd wanted to wear one, he wouldn't have gone into land preservation. He pulled a pair of khakis from the bottom rack, pressed by Eliza. He leafed through the top rack of shirts and chose a Tommy Bahama shirt with red and green palm leaves—a gift from Eliza's mother, and as Christmassy as he could get tonight. He was severely lacking in holiday spirit.

His mind was not on Christmas, on its meaning, on family. All this—all of what he was surrounded by now—was somehow transparent gauze compared to the solid existence of Amy. Sometimes he looked at his house, at his bedroom, at his wife and wondered how things so vaporous could appear so solid.

He started to the slam of the attic door, forgetting for a moment where Eliza was. In his boxers, he walked into the bedroom carrying his clothes. He dropped his pants and shirt on the bed and looked at Eliza . . . but not Eliza. The woman who stood at the foot of the bed, her outstretched hand holding wrinkled papers, was some façade of the woman he'd married. She was blanched, her face pinched in on itself. Her cheeks were splotched; makeup ran in grotesque furrows.

Something was drastically wrong; the world seemed to tilt, disorienting him. Routine Eliza behavior broken and panic rising—that was all he knew.

"You want to know so bad? To know what happened to your precious Amy, why she didn't show up? Because *I* . . . *I* . . . *I* never sent the telegrams. That is why." Eliza held out her hand and opened her palm. Crumpled yellowed papers fluttered to the floor.

His own strangled reply was as incoherent as his understanding. "What . . . ?"

"What part of this don't you understand?" She kicked at the papers. "I didn't send them. Miguel gave me all the grunt work to do . . . all the communication, letters, phone calls, filing, telegrams, all of it. He thought I sent them, thought I called her dorm and home. I was the one who told him I couldn't find her. I thought by now you'd understand why, that you'd see it was for the best, that I gave you a life she never could have given you. Hell, I gave you a life, period. You would have rotted in that jail for who knows how long if I hadn't." She turned from him, sank to her knees in a puddle of silver fabric.

He leaned down and lifted the papers from the floor, stared at the words he'd written almost twenty-five years ago, words he still remembered . . . begging words.

"No . . ."

Eliza lifted her head. "Yes. You can't stand it, can you? Now you have your reason to hate me. You've been looking for one for years. Now you have it."

He should tell her he did *not* hate her, but he couldn't.

He could only ask the one question that bubbled its way to the surface of his disbelief. "Why?"

"Why?" she shrieked. He recoiled at the intensity. "Because I loved you. I saw that I was the one who really loved you, that what you had with Amy was . . . obsession and infatuation. I saw no other way to make you see that I was the best one for you. I spent the entire trip, that whole three months, trying to make you see . . . really see me. But you wouldn't. Amy this, Amy that . . . go home to Amy. You couldn't even enjoy the trip, what was right in front of you. When the accident happened, I saw it as a sign—a way to save you in more ways than one."

"You decided . . . what was best for me?"

"I knew—I know what is best for you."

"Why now? Why tell me now, after almost twenty-five years? Why now when I can't do a thing about it?" He moved toward her.

She held her hands up as if to ward him off. "I had actually convinced myself that you were over it . . . over her. I decided I would never tell you what I did—that it would give you all the reason you needed to hate me. But you can't let go of her, and whether I tell you or not, she . . . she has a hold on you, or you on her, that I'll never be able to break. God, I just wanted to believe . . ." She stood now, wiped her face with her hands. "I know this is the moment when I should apologize, offer you my sincerest repentance for what I did wrong. But I can't. Because I still believe I did what was right for you. She could never, ever have loved you like I have, like I do. She could never have put up with your moods and your habits. She couldn't have given you the life I have. I prayed so hard that you would be over this by now, that it was the purpose in Jack and Lisbeth dating. But as usual, I was wrong."

"Dear God, Eliza. Why would you pray when you act like a god—a god who can control others' lives?" In a trance, as his flimsy life became even more transparent, Nick slowly dressed himself in the clothing he'd laid out for the party.

"I didn't believe I was God, Nick. I just loved you . . . love you like no one else can, or ever will. Can't you see that? What I did was for *us.*"

"No. I see a woman I don't know—at all. A woman who is capable of . . ." He zipped his pants and went to the bedroom door, his steps careful. He felt as if the very floor might crumble beneath him.

"Where are you going?" Her voice rang with uncontrolled desperation.

He turned and lifted the scraps of paper from the floor. "I don't know."

"We have a party to go to. We're going to be late."

"What?" She used duty to stay the panic; he'd seen it a thousand times with the kids. They would come to her with a problem, a bad grade, trouble with a coach, and she'd move them to the next task and the next, never truly addressing the problem, but preoccupying them.

"We have a party and we're going to be late." She sounded like a broken record.

"You are cracked, Eliza. You want to just wipe your face and go? You have lost it."

"We have to show up for the kids."

He shook his head in disbelief, neatly folded the papers, then placed them in his pocket and turned away.

"Don't go," she said.

He turned back to her. "Your dress is ripped."

She looked down at the hemline, picked it up and stared at it. By the time she looked up, he was gone.

Chapter Twenty-two

Amy sat in her robe on the faded blue vanity chair and slid open the makeup drawer. She was never one for wearing much makeup, but a Christmas party required a little bit more care. She began to rub the foundation across her face. The lady at Saks had said it would smooth her complexion, but all she saw was how the spiderweb lines around her eyes caught the beige cream in clumps of obvious age. She leaned closer to the mirror, stared into her own eyes. She flicked on the milk-glass lamp with the lacy shade, looked closer. Yes, there was another line in her forehead, and the age spot next to her eye—it looked like a melted freckle—had grown larger.

The eyelash curler stuck on her lashes, and she cursed the entire beauty routine. When she was done applying makeup, she stepped back from the mirror, satisfied she'd done all she could with her face, then walked to the bed where her dress lay. She picked it up and shook it out, slipped it over her head, then walked to the full-length mirror in the armoire in front of the bed. She pulled her hair up and let it fall. Down, she would wear it down. She shook her head, vaguely satisfied with her final appearance.

She walked into the foyer as the doorbell rang, its chime muffled by the excessive Christmas decorations. She glanced up at the grandfather clock: five after seven—someone was early. The red-and-green-plaid engraved invitation had said seven thirty, not seven. She glanced around the foyer for Phil, but didn't see him. She wanted him to answer the door; she wasn't yet in the mood to entertain. She just needed twenty-five more minutes.

But there was no ignoring the face that peered through the door—staring at her in cut-glass octagons of eyes and facial features. Damn.

Amy pasted on a teeth-baring smile and opened the door.

Eliza, in all her glamorous glory, stood on the front porch. Her full-length red coat fell to the ground, her hair spilling over the crimson shoulders in a platinum waterfall.

"Oh, Eliza, it's so good to see you. You're early."

"I thought it would take longer by car. You live a little . . . closer than I thought. I'm sorry I'm so early. It was too cold to sit in the car."

"Oh, that'd be crazy. Come in. Come in." Amy stepped aside and swept her hand across the foyer in what she hoped was a welcoming motion.

Eliza stepped in and stomped her feet, as if there were snow on her pale gray pumps.

"Let me take your coat." Amy held out her hand.

"Thank you." Eliza attempted to unbutton her coat and her hands shook, unable to maneuver the large fastenings.

Amy leaned over the banister, called up, "Jack, Molly . . . come on down." They were responsible for the coats, putting them in the guest room, hanging them in the closet. She turned back to Eliza, who was still struggling with the buttons.

"My fingers are really cold," Eliza said.

"Let me go get you a cup of hot tea. Would you like that?"

"Actually a glass of white wine would be even better."

"Well," Amy turned to the kitchen, "I was just headed that way for one myself. I'll grab two. Make yourself at home. I'll be right back."

Amy walked as fast as she could without looking rushed through the parlor to the kitchen. She pushed the door open and exhaled with a grunt.

Celia looked up from a silver tray, where she was placing toasts with cream cheese and salmon in an artful display. "You okay, ma'am?"

"Argh, I have a guest who's early. I can't find Phil, and I desperately need another Chardonnay."

Celia laughed. "Coming right up." She wiped her hands on her apron and reached for the wineglasses. "Ma'am, you look absolutely beautiful tonight."

"It's amazing what a shower and some makeup will do." Amy smiled, shooed her hand at Celia to move aside. "Celia, I can pour my own glass. But now I need two." She began to walk toward the lined-up bottles of wine, soldiers ready for the battle of the Christmas party.

The golden liquid poured into the crystal glasses, Amy walked backward out of the kitchen, opening the swinging door with her hip. She returned to the foyer holding out a glass of wine while sipping her own. "Here, Eliza."

Eliza stood in the middle of the foyer, her coat draped over her arm, scanning the surroundings. "You have a beautiful home. Very sweet . . . it must be what? A hundred years old?"

"Yes, I'm glad you like it. We love it. It has a great history and a lot of charm. Molly thinks it's haunted—by good ghosts, of course."

"How . . . nice."

"Oh, look, you're still holding your coat." Amy leaned again over the banister and called louder for her children.

"We're coming, we're coming," came a chorus of voices and pounding feet as they appeared in the foyer, Jack in front.

"Oh, Mrs. Lowry . . . hi." Jack held out his hand for her coat. Molly mumbled hello behind him, rolling her eyes at Amy.

Eliza handed Jack her coat. "Hello, Jack. Where's Lisbeth?"

"She said she was coming with you."

"She did?" Eliza looked at Amy, then back at Jack. "Well, she wasn't at the house when I left and I thought . . . I thought she drove separately earlier today."

"No." Jack shifted the coat in his arms and stepped down onto the landing. "She told me she was gonna shop for a dress, then come with you. Did you leave early?"

"I did. Yeah, I did. I drove around a little, got gas . . . you know, and I wanted to make sure I was on time, with it getting dark so early and me not knowing where I was going. Oh dear, I better call the house." She turned to Amy. "Do you have a phone I can use?"

"Of course." Amy pointed into the parlor. "Right there on the side table. It's portable if you want some privacy."

Eliza looked at her, glanced up then down. "That is a beautiful dress you're wearing. It's silver."

"Yes . . . thank you."

"I had on a silver dress tonight—it even had silver lace, but it ripped right before I left."

"Well, the dress you have on is gorgeous." Amy glanced at Eliza's full-length black dress and surmised it probably cost more than Amy's first car.

"Thank you . . . this old thing." Eliza walked toward the parlor while looking down at herself, as if trying to remember what she had on. "Well, I just need to find out where Lisbeth is." Eliza looked at Jack again. "Have you heard from her?"

Jack glanced at his sister, then turned and smiled the all-fake smile his mother recognized. "I'll go check my cell phone, see if she's tried to call." He started up the stairs, handing his sister Mrs. Lowry's coat. "Will you hang that up for me, sis?"

"Sure, bro." Molly stepped down to the foyer and leaned in to whisper to Amy as Eliza headed for the parlor, "She seems a little out of it." Molly rolled her eyes toward Eliza as she hung up the coat. "Just like her daughter."

Amy grabbed Molly's hand and pulled her into the back hall. "You don't like Lisbeth?"

"Don't you think she seems a little prissy, kinda, I don't know . . . spoiled and needy?"

"Molly, you don't even know her."

"No, I don't. Whatever. By the way, Mom, you look gorgeous."

"Well, thank you. I need to find your father and see if he thinks so."

Molly twisted away, then turned back, bit her lower lip and asked, "Where's Mr. Lowry?"

"I have no idea." Amy averted her eyes from Molly and glanced at the pine-bough-covered hall console, picked up a miniature skater, and rearranged the grouped display on its tinfoil surface. "I like your dress, too. Good choice tonight."

Molly ran her hand down the front of her red mesh dress; a black slip-dress peeked from behind the holes of the mesh and fell to the ground in soft folds. "I borrowed it from Lindsey. You like it?"

"I do. And I bet you look a hundred times better in it than she does."

"Yeah, right, Mom. She's like the homecoming queen."

"You look like a queen to me."

Jack came up from behind Molly. "Queen Molly does the Christmas party. Sounds like a porno flick."

"Oh, gross, Jack. You are just so disgusting." Molly stuck her tongue out at him.

Amy twisted her son's ear; she had to reach up to do this now. "Jack Reynolds, what are you learning in college?"

Molly leaned over and straightened her brother's tie. A flood of love filled Amy's belly, overflowed to her throat, where she stopped the tears that would embarrass her children.

She placed her hand on Jack's arm. "Did you find Lisbeth?"

"Yeah, well, sorta. I found her twenty messages on my cell phone. I tried to call her, but she's probably on the way and she's not answering her cell."

Molly laughed. "What, exactly, would one say in twenty messages?"

"Obviously I'm exaggerating a little, but not much. She was really upset. I actually feel pretty bad. I guess her mom didn't wait for her and she didn't want to drive by herself in the dark and . . . she couldn't find me."

Molly snorted. "She's a grown girl. Surely, she can drive an hour and a half without help."

"She just didn't know where anyone was . . . I don't know. She sounded like she was crying pretty hard."

"Great. Nothing like a little girlfriend drama to start the party." Molly slapped her brother on his shoulder.

Eliza called from the parlor. "Amy?"

"We're back here . . . come on back." Amy stepped into the light and motioned for Eliza to join them.

Eliza stepped into the back hall, took a long sip of her wine and stared at the family as they all looked at each other. Amy spoke first, overlapping Jack.

"Did you find Lisbeth?"

"Did you reach Lisbeth?"

Eliza looked to Amy, ignored Jack. "Yes, she's on her way. She's almost here—maybe fifteen minutes."

"Good." Jack exhaled. "I tried her cell phone, but she didn't answer."

"She's very upset. She said Jack didn't answer his phone all day and she wanted him to come pick her up."

"I'm sorry, ma'am. I didn't realize it was turned off. I was Christmas shopping all day, then working in the yard with my dad to help get ready for the party."

Eliza looked at Jack now, and if ice could fly from her blue eyes, it would have happened right there, landing on the miniature ice-skaters, slicing them to ribbons. "Well, you can just tell *her* you're sorry when she gets here."

"I will, ma'am. But what she sounded upset about on my phone messages was that you left without her."

The plummeting feeling in Amy's stomach made her want to yelp, *"No, Jack."* She loved him for his truthfulness, but at twenty years old he still had not learned when honesty was not the best policy. Confrontation was definitely not how she wanted to begin the Christmas party.

"Where's her dad?" Jack continued. "Where's Mr. Lowry? Isn't he coming? Could he have given her a ride?"

"He got caught up at work. I don't even know if he's coming."

Silence fell as cold as the ice Amy imagined in Eliza's eyes. Amy held up her hands and turned to Jack. "Okay, okay, guests will be here any minute. Where's your father?"

Where's Mr. Lowry?

Molly pointed out the side door. "He went to find out why the side lights weren't on."

"Excuse me, please." Amy sidled to the side door, away from the clot of tension, opened the door and let the frigid air chill her.

Where's Mr. Lowry?

She took a deep breath just as she heard the doorbell ring. *Let the fun begin.*

The crowd filled the house in a swarming body of warmth and Christmas memories. Friends old and new, relatives separated by three or four aunts and uncles, relatives who weren't really relatives at all, but had somehow become aunt and uncle to Jack and Molly, all filled the house. Amy returned to the stereo to turn up the music being drowned out by laughter and the clank of dishes.

Guests handed her bottles of wine in shimmering wine bags and Christmas ornaments wrapped in crinkled tissue, as offerings of gratitude. Friends arrived rubbing their hands up and down their arms and hugging, kissing. At an early hour, Amy had given out all the stockings she'd made; making them hadn't just been an aimless adventure in busyness—everything would work out just fine.

This year Phil's boss, Mr. Stevenson, and his wife actually showed up at the front door, bearing a magnum of champagne and overwrought smiles; his smile was large by sheer volume, hers by collagen. Phil escorted them in and showed them through the house and the Stevensons mingled, talked and laughed for more than the three minutes Amy had expected them to stay. Yes, things were going beautifully.

Fragile and puffy-faced, Lisbeth arrived before most of

the guests and quickly disappeared upstairs on Jack's arm. True to his word, Jack's door stayed locked, but it was not the sounds his sister had predicted that emanated from his room. Amy only poked her head up once to hear sobs and muffled words coming from under the door.

She knocked. Jack called out that he would be down shortly. When Amy informed him that it was rude to hide in his room during a Christmas party, she heard fresh wails from Lisbeth. She left them alone, so she could return to the warm throb of people below.

Eliza appeared, misty and apparitional, throughout the evening. Whenever Amy found her at her elbow, she introduced Eliza to other guests, depositing Eliza with at least three separate groups, only to have her appear once again at Amy's side.

Reese, Revvy, Norah and Brenton spilled laughing into Amy's home as wild and disarrayed as the cordgrass on Oystertip Island. Of course she'd invited them, but she hadn't expected them to show up.

"We just had to come and see where you live." Revvy slapped her back.

Brenton stood behind Norah, who was dressed in a long velvet broom skirt and white lace shirt; she was brilliant—a candle among their khakis and wrinkled attempts at dress shirts.

"Well, thanks for coming. Make yourselves at home. The bar is in the drawing room." Amy laughed, thinking how formal this must sound to them considering Brenton's tent and Reese's shack. "Oh, just come in," she said.

Revvy stepped forward. "Is Nick here yet?"

Where's Mr. Lowry?

"Well, if he's coming, he's not here yet. His wife"—Amy pointed into the den—"is in there if you want to meet her."

"No, thanks," said Reese. "Heard enough about her to not particularly want to meet her."

Norah pushed at his back. "That is not very polite, Reese."

Amy pretended she hadn't heard him. "Norah, is there any news about the Heritage Trust?"

"Well, they're shut down until after the holidays, so we'll just have to wait and see. They intimated that one plant might not be enough—so we're still trying. Have you found anything new about the house?"

"No, I've got to get into it to prove there's something worth saving."

"We'll do it," Norah told Amy, touching her arm.

Revvy chatted with Molly in the corner of the hall, and she giggled and blushed. Amy turned and the door opened again.

Carol Anne entered, all light and good cheer in a bright red knee-length vintage dress, looking like a mirage deposited from a 1940s movie. She swirled in the front parlor. "Don't I look fabulous?"

"Absolutely."

She leaned over and kissed Amy on the cheek. Joe reached around Carol Anne and hugged her. "You look beautiful, Amy. Really."

"Thanks, Joe. I'm glad you guys made it, even if you're an hour late."

"There is no late in 'open house,' Amy." Carol Anne took her coat off and opened the hall closet.

"There is when I need you," Amy said.

Joe extracted himself from them with the excuse of finding Phil and a nice gin and tonic.

Carol Anne looked around the foyer, peeked into the parlor. "Did he come?"

"Who?"

"Don't play coy with me, young lady. Is he here?"

"No. But she is."

"Who?"

"Don't play coy with me." Amy poked at Carol Anne. "Eliza and Lisbeth are both here."

"Well, where the hell is he?"

"I don't know. I really don't. So stop looking at me like that."

"He didn't tell you if he was coming?"

Amy looked around, then whispered, "I don't talk to him, Carol Anne. Stop."

She held up her hands. "Okay, okay. But what in the living Christmas carols are his wife and daughter doing here without him?"

"Well, his wife is getting sloshed in my parlor, when she's not following me around. His daughter is upstairs having some kind of emotional breakdown because Jack didn't answer his cell phone all day and she ended up having to drive here by herself."

"Oh, poor little princess."

"My thoughts exactly. Now let's mingle. The Stevensons showed up this year."

"That's a good sign for Phil, isn't it?"

Where's Mr. Lowry?

"I guess so."

"How are you?" Amy asked.

"Trying to get over Mr. Farley's Christmas bonus."

"Which was?"

"Nothing."

"What?"

"Zip. He said we didn't make enough this year. Nutcase."

"I'm sorry."

"Yeah, me too. I haven't even told Joe."

"He'll be fine with it . . . just talk to him."

"I will. I will." Carol Anne looped her arm through Amy's and they grabbed glasses from Celia, who slid by with a platter of full champagne flutes. They clinked glasses and smiled. Ah, all was well, it really was.

Bill and Mrs. Stevenson—damn Amy couldn't remember the woman's first name—came and grabbed her elbow. "Thank you for having us to your party. You have a lovely home."

"Well, thank you for coming. I'm glad you're enjoying yourselves."

Revvy appeared at Amy's side, leaned across her and spoke to Mr. Stevenson. "You in charge of Stevenson and Sons?"

Mr. Stevenson lifted his head like a peacock just asked to show his feathers. "Yes, young man, I am."

"Well, did you know you have a client who is trying to ruin a national treasure, a nature preserve full of endangered plants and animals, not to mention a historic pre–Civil War home?"

The floor seemed to shift beneath Amy—if only it would open up and take her.

"Revvy, not here." Amy grasped his hand, pulled him away from the Stevensons and into the parlor.

"What? You don't care about it now in front of all your highfalutin friends?"

"Revvy," she whispered. "They know how I feel but that is my husband's boss. You can't just get in his face like that."

"Why not?"

She looked over her shoulder at the Stevensons standing

in the same spot, watching her like disapproving parents. The mixing of her two worlds was not going well.

"Revvy, let me talk to them."

"Whatever you say, Mrs. Reynolds. It's your house."

Disappointment filled his voice, the letdown that she was not quite as cool as he'd thought when she'd brought Nick Lowry on board.

She walked back to the Stevensons and apologized for Revvy.

"No problem, sweetie," Mrs. Stevenson said. "Young people are just very passionate about their causes and they don't always know all the facts."

Amy squelched her speech about how they did know all the facts and it was not simply a cause, but an actual island. "Well, I hope you're having a good time," she said instead.

"I met your sweet daughter at the front door, but I have not yet met your son. Is he around? I see his pictures," Mrs. Stevenson said.

"Oh, he's upstairs. He'll be down shortly. I'll introduce you to him." Complete frustration rose within her, and she directed the feeling toward Lisbeth. What was she doing keeping Jack up there all night?

Amy excused herself and climbed the stairs, determined to end this stupid fight and bring her son down to the crowd.

She knocked on the door. "Jack? Are you still in there?"

"Yes, Mom."

"Hon, you need to come down and help your sister with the coats, mingle. . . . Mrs. Stevenson wants to meet you." Amy leaned her forehead on the door frame as she spoke.

"I'm coming." Then there was something she didn't understand as Lisbeth's sniffles and nose blowing camouflaged Jack's words.

"What?" Amy called through the door.

"I'm coming . . . in a minute, Mom."

"Now, Nick, now."

The door flew open. Jack stood with his tie undone, brow furrowed. "What did you just say?"

"I said to come now. This is rude." She didn't care what Lisbeth thought of her intrusion. This was ridiculous.

"No, what did you just call me?"

"I didn't call you anything. I told you to come down now."

"No, you called me Nick."

"I did not."

Lisbeth appeared in the door, her face still beautiful beneath the red eyes and swollen nose. Her blue eyes, even liquid with tears, were extraordinary.

Lisbeth spoke through a tissue. "You did. You called him Nick—my dad."

"Jack, Nick, they must sound the same. I did not. Now come on down to the party." She couldn't have said that—was her internal confusion turning external? *Please, no.* She softened her voice, lowered her eyes in what she hoped was a demure look of pleading, not the bitch mom.

Lisbeth spoke. "Is my dad here yet?"

"Not that I know of." She turned from them. "But your mom is still here. Y'all come on and join the party."

Amy didn't turn to see if they'd obeyed her. She didn't want to look at Lisbeth's face, or Jack's accusing eyes. *Nick.* Had she really said that? She wasn't even sure. No, she couldn't have.

Their footsteps followed her down the stairs—good.

As she reached the bottom step, Eliza appeared from the side door to the sunroom, Amy's office. Amy had shut the door before the party, even tied a red satin ribbon across the glass doorknobs to prevent anyone from entering. It was an off-limits room during a party.

"You lost?" Amy asked.

Eliza glanced up, started at the sight of Jack, Lisbeth and Amy on the stairs.

"No, no. . . just looking for a bathroom."

"Down the hall to the left." Amy swept her hand down the banister as she came to the foyer.

Eliza looked up at Lisbeth. "You all right, sweetie?"

"Sure." She reached for Jack's hand. "We came down to . . . what was it, mingle?"

Amy turned to say something to Lisbeth, something she was sure she would later regret, but Mr. Winters from next door stood waving goodbye at the front door.

"Excuse me, please." Amy walked to her neighbor and thanked him for coming, retrieved his coat, then opened the front door. She walked out with him and stood under the porch light away from Lisbeth and her endless tears, away from the party and guests. She waved goodbye; a few of the candles, in red tin buckets with Christmas tree cutouts, had blown out. She closed the door behind her and reached under the porch swing for the matches. She lit a match and began to ignite the three candles as the frigid air cut through any white wine, champagne haze that might have had a chance to settle over her mind.

She glanced up at the sound of a passing car. A white Dodge pickup truck turned the corner. *No. Stop.* She shook her head and turned back to the house. The din of the party sounded like a muffled recording. The cold sliced through her bare arms like small needles. A flare of fire hit her finger, the same damn finger with the Band-Aid on it from the knife cut.

"Damn, damn, damn." She dropped the match, stomped on it. "Damn you, Nick Lowry. Damn you and your telegrams and forest preservation and damn your neurotic, whiny daughter." She stepped on the match one more unneeded time and looked around. Had anyone heard her? Had she said all that out loud?

She began to sit down on the swing before she remembered her silk dress and the distinct possibility of bird doo or some other treat of nature that might be on the swing. She kicked at the screen door and opened it.

Phil stood on the other side of the door. "Amy, come in the house. What're you doing?"

"Some of the candles blew out."

He ran his hand up and down her arm. "You should've told me. I would've done it."

"Phil, for God's sake, I can light a few candles."

"Yes, Amy, you can. Now go drink a glass of champagne with Carol Anne and have a good time."

"I am having a good time. Did you talk to the Stevensons?"

"Yeah, seems your friends got ahold of Bill about the island. Could you please tell them there are better places than our Christmas party to accost Mr. Stevenson?"

"They didn't accost him, Phil. It was Revvy, and he just asked him a question. I already told him to drop it."

"I didn't even know you invited them."

She took a deep breath. "I told you I did."

"Oh." He looked away and waved at someone she couldn't see. "I wish you hadn't told them about the buyer at my company. That was information they just didn't need."

"I'm sorry, Phil. I told them before you told me about the client privilege. I'm sorry. Now go have fun."

"I am having fun," he said, but his mouth was straight and his chin set.

She kissed her husband on the cheek, then turned to take his advice: find Carol Anne and have another glass of champagne.

Chapter Twenty-three

C andles flickered in buckets on the railing of Amy's front porch. Cars lined the street on both sides and a few people arrived while other guests trickled out. Icicle lights hung from the eaves. A small holly bush at the bottom of the stairs flashed with colored bulbs; oversize Christmas balls hung from the branches.

Each time Nick drove by the house, he noticed these details one by one. He held one hand on the wheel, the other on the disintegrating notes of legal paper he'd once scribbled on for Mr. Carreira to translate into telegrams. Mr. Lawyer had obviously given this menial task to the cute college girl helping him free Nick Lowry. Eliza had then apparently used her manipulative powers of persuasion to convince both Mr. Carreira and Nick that she was the perfect one, the helpful one, the goddess of freedom from jail; she would take care of everything.

He found he now felt an underlying disrespect for his wife. No, he didn't hate her. But he'd never understood the below-the-belly anger he felt for her; the best he'd been able to do was admit rage's presence and ignore it. What

had once been subtle, under the radar, was now obvious—
he was now able to identify what caused his anger: her manipulation.

He, independent and strong Nick Lowry, had allowed
his life to be controlled by guilt and obligation, always believing he owed Eliza something: his life, his job, his children, his home. But in reality he'd kept one thing—his
heart. He hadn't realized it, but he'd been saving it for Amy.

Now it was too late. Look at her house, her family. She
had forged a life from the raw materials of love, not obligation. The unsent, scribbled and desperate telegrams
might change that, but . . . only maybe.

Nick circled the block again, then slowed in front of the
house. His daughter and his wife were in the candlelit
home. A woman in a silver dress came out the front door,
hugged someone and began to light candles drowned by
the wind. She stomped her feet on the porch floor: Amy.
He recognized her temper, which came as a slow quiet boil,
rising unnoticed, then spilling out in a quick spurt before
disappearing.

He turned the corner. Had she seen his truck? It wasn't
until he had passed the quaint DARBY LIMITS sign on the two-
lane road that he'd decided to come. He still wasn't sure he
would go into the party. There were better places to see
her, easier places to show her, to tell her about the
telegrams his wife had hidden.

His heart raced. He felt nauseous, not in control of his
own emotions, unsure of his place in the world. Why
couldn't he run in and tell her he loved her, touch her face,
carry her to the kitchen countertop and make love to her?
Because of binding vows, propriety, rules and laws. What
about desire and connection and destiny? What about those
damn things?

Nick waged an internal war as he circled Amy's block. So vows were made, families were formed. Could they be mistakes? Hell, they couldn't be mistakes. Not if all of them were here, alive, breathing inside Amy's home. Kids, lives—not mistakes. Did circumstances converge only to show him what he was missing, to make him laugh at his mistakes, then tell him to walk away—once again reminded of all he ever wanted?

He fingered the telegrams. Damn, damn, damn to hell all those other vows and promises offered under false pretenses, based on wrong assumptions. What was it his father used to say, through slurred words? Don't assume: it makes an *ass* of *you* and *me*. That's exactly what he was: an ass.

Once again, he played the "if only" game with himself. If only he had insisted on talking with Amy when her mother said she was out with her fiancé. If only he had come home before her wedding, instead of moving to Maine. But he'd drowned these instincts in his rage at Amy's betrayal, and in Eliza's soothing clucks of comfort and ease.

Now he was in another nightmare in which he saw Amy but she didn't see or acknowledge him.

He parked the car on a side street, around the corner from the quaint house with the flickering lights, the coat-draped guests, the glassed-in sunroom and his wife's car parked out front—the car her mother bought her, because the Volvo he gave her wasn't good enough. Only a Mercedes would do for a daughter of the Sullivans, thank you very much.

He threw the gearshift into DRIVE and made another turn—he didn't know how many total now—around the block. A slick black Lexus pulled out from a parking spot and left a lost-tooth gap next to the curb. He slid his truck into the space and looked up at the house; Amy opened the door, hugged a guest goodbye.

There she was: touchable and untouchable, present and lost, his and another's.

Reese's battered Jeep sat parked at the curb. Nick was surprised Reese had made the trip. He hoped the entire OWP group was inside. He smiled; so many things were bringing him and Amy together—it was inevitable.

He glanced down at his clothes. He'd been interrupted in the middle of dressing and had neglected to bring a coat. He stepped from the pickup truck and began to walk toward the house, stuffing the notes in his back pocket. It was freezing, the air a knife of wind where his shirt flapped out and exposed his waist. He stopped, tucked in his shirt and smoothed his hair back with his fingers. A couple emerged from the front door and leaned against each other, murmuring something he couldn't hear. The woman laughed, threw back her head. They didn't notice him and almost walked into him. He stepped aside, but the woman's purse brushed his arm.

"Excuse me," Nick said.

The woman looked up and stopped, released the man's arm. She wore a long black coat, gloves, and a lipstick red scarf was wrapped around her neck and pulled over her head. She tilted her head: Carol Anne. He'd seen her at the tailgate party, but he hadn't spoken to her. He almost told her that in an odd, ass-backward way he'd always been grateful to her: if she hadn't asked him to the formal, he might not have found Amy again, or if he had, the moment might have passed, the destiny disintegrated.

"Carol Anne?" He held out his hand, which dangled in the air, purposeless, as she stared at him without reaching out her own.

"Nick."

"Yes, yes. It's good to see you." He put his hand down.

"Oh, I wish I could say the same."

"Wow. What Christmas cheer . . ." His warm feelings for her vanished in a surging flood of animosity.

"Nick . . . I'm sorry. You don't need to go in there."

The man whose hand she was holding stepped forward. "Do you know this man, honey?"

Carol Anne turned to the man, who was also in a long black coat. "This is Nick Lowry. I knew him in college. Old boyfriend of Amy's." She turned back to Nick. "This is my husband, Joe."

Nick held out his hand and this time the other person was polite enough to grab it. "Nice to meet you, man."

"Same at ya," Nick answered. He wrapped his arms around himself. "Well, I'm freezing and my family is waiting inside, so I'd better go. Good to see you, Carol Anne."

She opened her mouth as if to speak, then closed it, glanced at her husband. "You know what, honey? I forgot my purse. Do you mind going back in with me?"

Joe flicked at the purse hanging off her shoulder. "It's right here, babe."

"Well, I have to go to the bathroom. Do you want to wait in the cold, or come back in with me?"

Her husband rolled his eyes at Nick, as if to say, *Women,* and Nick laughed. But he knew why Carol Anne had the sudden urge to powder her upturned nose. She considered herself Amy's protector, the shield between her and some shattered morality.

As Nick walked up to the front porch, his pulse in his throat quickened. He rang the doorbell and Molly opened the door with a hostess smile on her face. He was struck by how much she looked like Amy—as if someone had drawn Amy's outline and then replaced the nose, mouth and eyes from a different cutout pattern.

"Hi, Molly."

"Hello, sir." Her smile lifted to show straight white teeth. She was a cute girl—Amy's girl. "Mrs. Lowry is looking for you."

Carol Anne and Joe came up behind him, politely waiting for the conversation to end as Nick walked into the house.

"Aunt Carol Anne, did you forget something?" Molly asked.

"No, sweetie, just need to use the ladies' room before I leave." Carol Anne and her husband stepped into the foyer.

Molly shut the door. "It's freezing out. Feels like it's gonna snow or something. Argh. It never snows on a school day, just the holidays." Molly turned back to Nick. "I think Mrs. Lowry and Lisbeth are in the living room. That's where I last saw them."

"Thanks, darlin'. Which way is the living room?" Nick glanced around the house; he wanted to be alone in the house, absorb it in small sips, not in one big gulp while others watched. He wanted to taste the details of her surroundings, going down warm and full of her.

Molly pointed down the hall. "In there."

Nick followed the hall that opened into the living room, weaving his way through a thin crowd. He didn't see any of the other people; they were faceless suits and dresses blocking the path to his destination.

He stood at the entryway to the living room, glancing around at the old plaster walls, framed landscapes hanging from immaculate hooks on the crown molding. "One does not puncture plaster walls with nails," Amy had once told him. The fireplace, big enough to hold half a cord of wood, roared with fire, heat.

Over the fireplace hung a twenty-by-twenty painting of

Amy's two children——toddlers on the beach bending over a shell or a wave; one could not see what the children were looking at, as they were the focus of the picture.

The furniture was spread into what his wife called "conversation triangles" and he wondered if the living room was usually set up this way, or had been rearranged for the party. Small silver trays lay around the room with spaces where food had been removed. Napkins with wet rings or crumpled with leftover cocktail sauce were scattered haphazardly on tables.

The windows reflected the candles and minimal lamplight like an abstract painting of stars, warped and misplaced on a grid of windowpanes. He scanned the crowd.

Someone touched his elbow. He turned.

"Daddy." Lisbeth threw her arms around his neck.

"Honey, I'm sorry I'm late. Work and all."

"I'm so glad you're here. Mom looks kinda lost, wandering around the party without anyone to talk to."

Nick looked at his beautiful daughter, whose face was chiseled with the finest features of her aristocratic Sullivan ancestors. Her cheeks were red, not from heat or cold, but from what he affectionately called her "cry spots." He knew the signs in his daughter, had witnessed them since she was two years old—a crying jag of immeasurable length had ensued and he, thank God, had missed it. He loved her, but the endless tears drove him insane.

"What happened, darlin'?"

"Nothing . . . why?"

"Don't give me that baloney. I know all the signs. . . . What happened? Did your mother say something, do something?"

"Oh, Daddy, it was all just a huge mix-up. I'm fine,

really. I thought Mom was driving me to the party. She thought Jack was. Jack thought she was. I couldn't find either of them, or you . . . and I just sorta freaked out a little. It's okay now. Really."

"Well, you look beautiful. Is your mom around anywhere?"

"Wandering . . . Does she know you don't have a tie on?"

Nick looked down. "Didn't know it was so formal."

"Jeez, Daddy, Mom has on a formal full-length thing."

A squat woman in a white uniform walked by with a tray full of champagne glasses, which she held above her shoulder. The tray reached to Nick's chest. He grabbed two flutes; his daughter held out her hand.

"Ah, you're not old enough yet," he said.

"Dad, give me a break. I will be in one week."

He glanced around the room and handed the drink to his daughter. "Don't tell your mom."

Lisbeth pouted out her lower lip. "Not that she'd notice. She's grabbed one too many of these herself."

"Great. Just great," Nick mumbled as he looked toward the swinging door that obviously led to the kitchen, the door fluttering like a defective heart valve. He guzzled his champagne.

He had resumed his search when Revvy caught him by the arm. "Hey, Nick. We've been lookin' for ya."

"Hey, man. Did all of you come—waste all that gas to drive from Savannah?"

Revvy laughed. "Yeah, thought we owed it to Mrs. Reynolds to show up—seein' that she's done so much for us—you know, bringing you and all."

"Where's everyone else?"

"Well, Brenton and Norah snuck off somewhere. I'm sure Mrs. Reynolds does not want to know where. And

Revvy is off flirting with her daughter. Sure she doesn't wanna know about that, either."

"No, I'm sure she doesn't." Nick laughed. "Have you seen Mrs. Reynolds?"

"Yeah, she's around here somewhere, all dressed up, serving food and stuff. Wouldn't have recognized her at school all dolled up like that."

Nick punched the side of Revvy's arm. "I wouldn't be ogling the teacher now."

"No ogling. Just an observation. I did meet your wife, though. Think she might have been a little confused by how I knew you—or else she's a little sloshed."

Nick groaned. "I hope she's just confused."

"Hey, man, I really think this buckthorn thing will save the island."

"We'll see. It's always a toss of the dice. I wish we had just one more thing—"

"Maybe we can get Reese to take us out there again."

"Yeah, let's see what happens with this. Then we'll ask."

Revvy grabbed Nick's arm and pointed to a stout man in a shiny suit with a red tie. "See that dude?"

"Yeah."

"That's the owner, or CEO or whatever, of Stevenson and Sons. The guy who Mr. Reynolds works for—"

"Stay away from him, Rev."

"Well, I think I might have goofed up a little, pissed Mrs. Reynolds off."

"You didn't say anything to him, did you?"

"Just told him his client is ruining a national treasure."

"Man, there's a place for that."

"Yeah, that's what Mrs. Reynolds said."

"Rev, go have a good time. Get a free beer."

Nick caught a flash of silver out of the corner of his right eye. He turned as Amy backed out of the kitchen, her hands underneath a tray of something he thought was called pigs-in-a-blanket—the ever-present party food.

He absorbed her beauty in the few moments he was permitted to stare unobserved. Her hair fell on bare shoulders, save for the thin straps that somehow held up the remainder of what looked to him like a luxurious nightgown, an outfit she should only wear in private. His legs felt loose, as though his knees had somehow dissolved, leaving him without the ability to move. "Want." He couldn't find another word, much less a coherent sentence, as she turned and saw him.

She froze; the closing door flapped again and smacked her on the bottom. She fumbled the tray, dropped it. Food flew onto her blue-and-yellow flowered carpet. He still couldn't move. What a fool he must look like standing there, with his champagne glass in midair, his mouth open while the hostess spilled her food all over the carpet.

There were quick movements from guests on couches and chairs, cursing from the maid who came out of the kitchen, and laughter from Amy—all of which covered his complete and utter stupidity in standing like a frozen statue.

He recovered and placed his empty champagne glass on a table. He reached the scattered food in time to pick up only one squashed sausage, the job already accomplished by Amy and much faster, obviously more agile guests.

As he crouched down on the carpet, he found himself staring at her face-to-face.

"Hi, Nick."

"Hey, Ame."

"I'm smooth, aren't I? The perfect Christmas hostess." She picked up the last piece of food and stood, looked down at him.

He stood up and held out the crumpled appetizer. "I don't like these things, anyway."

She smiled. Thank God, she smiled. "Neither do I. I always wonder who actually eats them, but they're always gone."

He held up his hands. "I know it was *not* me."

She looked around the room. "I think Eliza and Lisbeth are looking for you. Plus the entire OWP, who are only here to see you."

"I'm sorry I'm so late. . . . I need to talk to you."

She smiled, but it was not a smile as much as a nervous shake of her lower lip against her teeth. "Shoot," she said.

Nick looked around the room, which had resumed its previous rhythm. "Not here, outside maybe—is there somewhere?"

"If this is about Oystertip, I can't discuss it tonight. Rev already embarrassed the hell out of me with Phil's boss, Phil is pissed and I'm not in the mood to talk about it."

"No, this is about us."

"No way, Nick. Please don't do this. This is my house, my Christmas party."

He leaned closer, used all his willpower not to touch her.

"It's about the telegrams."

Amy glanced around the room, waved at someone he didn't turn to see, as it didn't matter at all to him who else was there.

"Please just mingle, Nick. Have a glass of wine. Come meet my friends." She spoke through clenched teeth.

The door behind them opened. He wanted to carry her to another room, outside, another house—damn—another state where he could pull the papers from his pocket; someplace where a door did not open.

Carol Anne, like the ghost of Christmas protection, appeared in the doorway. "Oh, Ame, there you are. I've been looking all over for you." She glared at Nick.

Amy reached up, touched her throat. "I thought you left, late for Joe's company party."

"Yeah, he's gonna kill me, but I just couldn't tear myself away." She looped her arm in Amy's and began to guide her down the hall.

Nick followed them into the parlor. His wife sat in a chair in the corner, alone, sipping oh so quaintly from a glass of white wine.

Carol Anne turned to him. "Oh, look, there's your wife. Weren't you looking for her?"

Nick hoped his piercing glare at Carol Anne communicated the signal he intended: *Go away.*

Eliza spotted him, but seemed to register him in slow motion. She stood and grabbed the side of the chair, smiled and swayed more than walked toward them.

They were in a corner, up against the open French doors that led into the room. Eliza wobbled over and stood in front of them.

"Hi, honey." Nick leaned in and kissed her cheek.

Eliza waved a fluttering, unsteady hand at Amy. "Isn't that a beautiful dress she's wearing, all silver and sparkly?" She looked at Carol Anne. "I had a silver dress on tonight. It ripped."

Nick felt sheer panic; his wife was drunk as hell. He'd seen her drunk only once before, at a family reunion attended by an uncle she hated for various offenses. The awful things she had said, and didn't remember afterward, were still part of Sullivan family legend.

Nick grabbed Eliza's elbow and attempted to steer her out of the room. She resisted, falling back into a semicircle with Amy and Carol Anne. Carol Anne reached her hand up to steady Eliza, then looked at Amy.

"Honey," Nick said, "let's go find Lisbeth and head home."

"You're so late. Did you finally come to show her . . . ?" Eliza shook her hand, thumb and forefinger together as if holding a piece of paper.

"Eliza, come with me." Nick held out his hand to his wife. Her face was pale, her makeup now appearing in stark contrast to her skin, like a child who had broken into her mother's cosmetic case and rubbed on all the wrong colors, in all the wrong places.

"No . . . I don't think so, Nick. If you want to tell her, tell her with me here. I would just love to see her reaction to my dastardly deed. You're not the one who gets to have all the fun, you know."

Amy backed up, banged into the wall.

Carol Anne reached for her. "Come on, Ame. Let's help Celia pick up some of this trash. She doesn't seem to be able to keep up with it."

Eliza's hand shot out in the space between them, patted Nick's butt, felt the front of his pants.

Nick backed away from her. "What are you doing?"

"I know you have them on you. You must. You'll never give them up."

"Eliza, stop." But he was trapped in a corner and Eliza slipped her hand into his back pocket, jerked the papers from it. "Voilà." She waved them in the air. Nick grabbed at the papers and missed.

Eliza attempted to hand them to Amy. Amy held her hands up as a sign that she did not want them.

"Here. Here. They're yours." Eliza shoved the papers at Amy.

"What?" Amy held up her hands.

Eliza threw the papers at Amy's feet; they fluttered to the ground. Nick grabbed at his wife's arm, hauled her through the French doors to the foyer. Escorting her was not a difficult task as Eliza was unsteady.

Revvy met them at the front door. "Hey, man, guess she was more sloshed than confused."

"Yeah, I guess so, Rev. Now move."

Nick opened the front door and half-carried, half-thrust his wife onto the front porch. He closed the door behind them and leaned into her face. "What do you think you're doing?"

"The same thing you were gonna do . . . show her the notes. I've waited all night for you to get here, knowing that if you did, it was only to see her. I was just beginning to hope that you weren't coming. But it's the same me, the same stupid me who thinks maybe, just maybe you're over her. I was wrong about that, and about you coming here. I'm so stupid, stupid, stupid." She wept bent over, shaking.

"You are not stupid, just drunk. Climb in my truck. I'll take you home."

"Why? Why would you take me home when it's not me you want to take home at all?"

Chapter Twenty-four

The background noise of the dwindling party had served as a cloak to the bizarre discussion with Nick and Eliza. Now they were gone into the frigid night and Revvy stood in the foyer staring at Amy, shrugging his shoulders.

She had considered each part in her life—family, friends, Nick, the OWP—as separate and distinct; now her worlds had collided in a grinding mess.

She turned to Carol Anne, whispered, "What the hell was that?"

Carol Anne pointed to the papers on the parlor floor. "What the hell are those?"

Amy picked up the papers, held them to the light; they were yellowed at the edges with a brownish tea color in the middle and a round coffee stain on the lower right corner. The paper was lined but the writing slanted across it, not following the lines. The note was written in all capital letters, as if screaming the smudged message.

She began to read the words, then looked up at Carol Anne. "No . . ."

Carol Anne grabbed the papers, but Amy's tight grip caused them to rip in half. She stood still as she held half of Nick's ancient pleas and Carol Anne held the other half.

"Sorry . . . whoops." Carol Anne handed her the torn paper.

Amy dropped her half on the floor, stared straight ahead. She didn't want the notes; she didn't want to hold them, read them, know them. If she hadn't been able to see them twenty-five years ago, now was not the time. Sitting in her dorm room, waiting, wondering, praying—that would have been the time to read the telegrams, not here in her parlor, in her home, at her Christmas party, with her son walking toward her with Nick's daughter on his arm.

She glanced, frantic, around the room. Molly's fourth-grade teacher, Ms. Raven, waved, moved toward Amy. Ms. Raven, whose divorce was final six months earlier, wore a dress cut low enough to reveal her divorce settlement—a brand-new pair of upright breasts.

Ms. Raven hugged Amy. "Oh, what a beautiful party. Thanks for inviting me."

Amy smiled, she wasn't sure how, as Carol Anne reached down and picked the scraps of paper off the floor.

"Oh, Ms. Raven, it sure is good to see you. I'm glad you came."

"Listen, Amy, I am dying to know who is that very yummy man who you were just talking to. I've been watching him. . . ." She leaned in and whispered, "Is he single?"

Jack and Lisbeth joined them just as Ms. Raven finished her summation of Nick Lowry.

"That man is my dad," Lisbeth said. "And the woman with him is my mother."

"Sorry." Ms. Raven held up her hands in surrender. "Just

asking—no harm in asking." She placed her hands on her curved décolletage and backed away from the group.

"Thanks for coming." Amy patted Ms. Raven's arm and turned to Jack and Lisbeth.

"Mom, where is Mr. Lowry?"

Where is Mr. Lowry?

"He and Eliza just, well, just left," Amy stuttered.

Carol Anne shoved the torn papers in her purse, looked at Lisbeth. "If you run out there now, you can probably catch them."

Lisbeth turned toward the door, then back at Amy. "What happened?"

Amy tilted her head in question.

"What happened? Did you say something to make them leave?" Lisbeth leaned closer.

Carol Anne stepped forward. "Lisbeth, I think maybe you'd better go find your parents, get a ride home with them."

"Nothing happened, Lisbeth. Your mother needed to go home," Amy said.

Jack clasped Lisbeth's hand. "Come on, babe. I'll take you home."

Amy grabbed her son's arm. "No, Jack. I don't want you driving both ways this late. She can stay here . . . in the guest room, of course."

"I don't want to stay here." Lisbeth's tears started again.

"God, you have been crying *all* night. Aren't you sick of crying?" Amy looked around the room, shocked to discover she'd spoken aloud.

"Mom . . ." Jack exhaled, flashed his mother a furrowed-brow look of disgust. Newly manufactured tears poured down Lisbeth's cheeks.

Amy meant to find an apology but came up empty of remorse, of anything but disgust. "Lisbeth, I don't want you driving home this late by yourself. Your parents have left. So unless you can catch them outside right now, the guest room is your only option."

Lisbeth looked to Jack, who by now seemed to also be weary of the tears; his expression of sympathy had decreased in voltage.

Jack draped his arm around Lisbeth's shoulder. "Come on . . . it'll be fine to stay here."

"Why can't you come home with me and stay at my house?"

Amy stepped closer to Lisbeth. "I guess you did not hear me say I don't want you two driving that far this late."

"I heard you, ma'am."

"Good."

Carol Anne lifted Lisbeth's hand, patted it. "Honey, you'll be just fine here with sweet Jack. Now you two run along."

Jack looked at his mother. "You okay?"

"Just great, hon. Just great. Go on and enjoy the rest of the party."

She glanced away from Jack's stare. He held Lisbeth's hand and guided her to the back hall.

Amy reached for Carol Anne's purse. "I want to see those papers."

Carol Anne led her to the living room, then out the back door to the empty and blank night. Amy's senses dulled as the cold air outside became more an observation than a sensation.

Carol Anne reached into her purse and pulled out the crumpled, torn papers. "What are these?"

"The telegrams."

"These are not telegrams."

"They're the messages, the words that were *supposed* to be on the telegrams," Amy said.

"How do you know that?"

"Look at them."

"How did they end up here tonight?" Carol Anne waved them in front of Amy's face.

"I don't know. I have no idea."

"Okay, okay. Let's think." Carol Anne paced the lawn. "Eliza the Out-of-It shows up early at the party. She wanders aimlessly, drinking herself into some Gumby/Barbie-doll state until Nick shows up. Then she comes alive, like she's been waiting for someone to push her ON button. She grabs these papers from his back pocket and throws them at you."

Despite the pain growing inside her chest, Amy laughed. "Okay. So she knew he had them."

"She wanted to see if he would show up with them. But why did he have them? I thought he told you he sent these telegrams."

"When I saw him . . . at the school—"

"You saw him again?"

Amy groaned. "Yes. He stopped by the school. I didn't do anything wrong. I just saw him."

"God, why him? Why now? Go ahead . . . what did he say when you saw him?"

"He said he wanted to track down the lawyer, find out if and how he ever sent the telegrams. He wanted to know what happened to them. I told him it didn't matter. That they weren't sent, or if they were, they weren't received—end of story."

"Do you think he didn't believe that you didn't get them?"

"No, I don't think that was it at all. I think he just *had* to know what happened to them."

"Well, he found out, obviously. But why would a lawyer keep these notes for so long?"

"Maybe they were in his file. You know, the law file." Rational thought began to infuse her and she sensed the iced air. "I'm freezing."

Carol Anne looked up at the sky, as if the constellations could answer her question.

"He had them. Nick had them. A lawyer would *not* still have these," Carol Anne said.

"No . . . that makes no sense."

"Nothing about Nick Lowry makes sense."

"He didn't have them. It drove him crazy that he didn't know what happened to them. He didn't have them."

"Well, where—"

And simultaneously the conclusion dawned on them.

"Eliza."

"His wife."

Amy reached for the notes. "She hid them. Eliza had them. Hell, *kept* them."

"That's a little weird," Carol Anne said.

"She's a little weird."

"He came here to show you these and prove to you—"

"That he wrote them."

"That you should still be together." Carol Anne wrapped her arm around Amy's shoulders.

"Oh, God."

"Amy, you have *got* to stay away from him. He's dangerous. He believes that you're still his . . . that he's been cheated out of you."

"He was."

"Wake up, Amy. This is your life. You weren't cheated out of anything. So you had a few bad months or a bad year wondering what happened to him. Now you know. Put it to bed." Carol Anne laughed. "Bad choice of words."

Amy didn't laugh. Panic began its ascent from a quiver in her lower limbs to the bottom of her throat. She reached her hand to the space on her neck that Nick said he longed to touch, and emptied onto the grass all of the appetizers, champagne and white wine that she had somehow managed to shove in her mouth during the chaos of the party. The inevitability of Nick, of their bond, rose within her and overwhelmed her. Wracking heaves came again and again, until there was nothing left inside her but a desperate need to be warm and to sleep.

Carol Anne held Amy's hair behind her head, clucking, "It's okay, it's okay." She used the same words and tone of voice Amy utilized when her own children were sick.

"No, it's not. I need those people out of my house. I need to go to bed." Amy leaned on Carol Anne, sobbed.

"It's okay, it's okay," crooned Carol Anne, lost for a smart-ass comment for the first time since Amy had known her.

"No, it's *not* okay." Amy bent, heaved again, and this time ruined her silver silk dress. "It's not okay at all."

After Carol Anne tucked Amy into bed, ushered out the remaining guests and brought Amy a cup of hot lemon tea, she kissed her friend on the cheek and whispered while Phil cleaned up the parlor. "Call me in the morning. Where did you put those notes? Give them to me."

"They're safe. Hidden. I haven't even read them all yet."

"Just go to sleep, Amy. Get some sleep. It'll all seem so . . . stupid in the morning."

"I will. Thanks for taking care of me. Do you think anyone noticed I never came back to the party?"

"Anyone who's here this late—it's one thirty in the morning—wouldn't notice if you were swinging from the chandelier."

"Is Phil okay?"

"Of course he is. Cleaning up, humming to himself, locking up. But Joe is waiting for me. Gotta run. We missed his office party. He's a little peeved. I'm having a hard time explaining why. Guess I'll have to make up for it when I get home, you know?" Carol Anne winked and pulled the covers up to Amy's chin. "Let it go, Ame."

Amy closed her eyes and nodded. She desperately wanted to be alone and she only had a few minutes before Phil would come into the room and fuss over her. He was still mad about Revvy and Mr. Stevenson and she was not up for a discussion about it.

"G'night." Carol Anne closed the bedroom door.

Amy lay motionless and held her breath until the front door scraped shut. She sat up. There was no way she'd be able to sleep until she read the notes . . . the unsent pleas for her to come . . . to him. She would read them, then destroy them and move on. Enough was enough. She could not allow Nick to come into her home and toss her emotions around like a dog with a rag toy. Didn't he know this was her house? Her party? Her family? Didn't he have at least that much respect?

She tiptoed into the bathroom and listened for Phil's telltale footsteps on the warped pine floors. She locked the door, unsure if the lock even worked, as she'd never once, since the day they moved in, locked the bathroom. She pulled on the door; it was locked.

Her silver dress lay crumpled on the tile floor. She sighed; Phil would have a heart attack if he knew how much the dress had cost—the dress she'd just ruined by puking crab puffs and champagne all over it.

She opened the cabinet door under the sink and reached in the dark past the unused bottles of shampoo, conditioner and mud masks, then inside a tampon box, to a crinkle of paper. The papers felt fragile, broken in her hand, and she pulled them gently from the box she'd stuffed them into while in a panic—wanting to put them in the last place Phil would ever look. She shuffled into the commode closet, closed the door, slammed the toilet lid down, then sat on it. She opened the papers and pieced them together like an ancient puzzle.

She ordered the notes according to the dates on the top left corners, then began to read. She recognized his handwriting with a jolt of electric memory through her body— the slant of his lines, the straight-out stick of the K. Then and—God help her, now—even his handwriting was too strong, too . . . much. A single written note sent her slack.

Her acid-filled stomach growled as she leaned back on the tank of the commode. How romantic, reading his twenty-five-year-old notes on a toilet.

Amy,

Have been in accident. Am okay. Arrested. Please come. Contact below lawyer for information.

Nick

No information was attached and she assumed Eliza was supposed to have added how and where to contact him. She read the note again, then again. She attempted to feel, discern, what she would have felt then, in her dorm room, empty and howling inside, wondering where he was. Would this note have comforted her, panicked her? Sent her to Costa Rica? He gave no information about why he was arrested.

Knowing now what she didn't understand then, she couldn't find her past and genuine response. It was all too far away, too remote—something vaguely seen on the horizon—and the more she tried to focus on the feeling, the more it faded, disappearing into the thin line between water and sky.

She pieced together the second note and read.

Amy,

Please come. Am innocent. Need your help. Call below lawyer.

                                                              Nick

A rising emotion that needed a name beyond sorrow overcame her. He'd needed her. He'd wanted her to come, begged her—*Please come.* The pain she felt when he didn't return must have been nothing compared to what he felt when he believed she'd read these words and failed to respond. She wanted to comfort him, tell him she would have run, not walked, to the nearest airport. She wanted to heal a wound long since scarred over.

She groaned and remembered staring out the window of her home, telling her mother she was sick, too sick to come down to dinner—again. She had been desperate for someone, anyone to call and tell her where Nick was, why he hadn't returned to her. She hadn't given up and, dear God, neither had he.

The third paper was ripped diagonally, but it didn't matter as there were only five words on it.

Amy,

I love you.

Nick

The date was six weeks from the first telegram, and if she remembered time correctly, a year before he was released, eleven months before she became engaged to Phil.

For the second time that night she sobbed. Even when he thought she didn't come, when he believed the worst of her, he'd written of his love.

In her need to survive the agony of abandonment, she had deserted her love for Nick. Her concern about these telegrams should have been buried when she said the words "I do" to Phil; guilt flooded her mouth with leftover acid from the Christmas champagne.

Loud knocks came from beyond the commode stall, from the other side of the bathroom door.

"Amy . . . are you okay?" Phil's voice sounded muffled, underwater.

She stood and opened the commode door, called out, "I'm fine. I'll be right out."

She shuffled to the sink, washed her face, brushed the guilt from her mouth with toothpaste. Then she shoved the letters back into the tampon box—safe. She wondered dully whether the guilt she felt was from not being there for Nick—for abandoning something she would never have left behind—or from her betrayal, meager as she conceived it at that moment, of Phil. She was too tired—too damn tired—to figure it out now.

She opened the bathroom door and almost knocked Phil over.

"Babe, you okay?"

"I think the crab puffs were . . . bad or something. I never want another crab puff again in my life. Ever." She moaned and fell into bed. "Are Jack and Molly okay?"

"Yes. Molly is sound asleep on top of the bed in her clothes. All that coat-hanging wore her out, I guess."

"That or the champagne I saw her sneak."

Phil laughed. "She wasn't the only one."

"What do you mean?"

"I mean you . . ."

"It wasn't the champagne."

It wasn't the champagne. It was Nick Lowry—how do you like that?

"Okay, hon."

"How's Jack . . . Lisbeth?"

"We got her all set up in the guest room. She'll drive home in the morning."

"Hopefully before I get up."

"Not a lot of love lost between you two."

Amy didn't answer, rolled over.

Phil reached over and rubbed the top of her forehead. "Well, it was a great party except for your buddy Rebel spouting his Greenpeace agenda to my boss."

"His name is Revvy and it wasn't a Greenpeace agenda. It was . . . God, I do not want to talk about this again."

"Oh, so now you don't want to talk about it." He laughed; she didn't think he was funny. "It's all you've wanted to talk about for months."

"Phil, drop it, okay? All you care about is what your boss thinks of you."

"Uncalled for. And not true. And Revvy. What kind of name is that anyway?"

"His name, I guess."

"Okay, Amy. Get some sleep."

"I will." She closed her eyes and prayed for the blessed absence of consciousness, knowing it would be a long, long time in coming as the approaching dilemma of right and wrong, of inevitability and destiny intertwined.

What was right? What vows were made? She shoved the questions away, along with the burden of comprehending the agony she'd caused Nick, the grief she could cause Phil. She couldn't look directly at any of this mess and she used the telegrams as a solar eclipse—blocking out what she knew was there, but couldn't yet see or feel.

PART III

The only joy to be trusted is the joy on the far side of a broken heart.

—Alfred North Whitehead

Chapter Twenty-five

The commode closet seemed to be where Amy spent most of her free time these days. Pitiful, but it was the only place where she could sit and reread Nick's notes. The days were endless without borders on her feelings. Christmas had passed and Molly had started school, but SCAD didn't start until mid-January. Amy sat and read—attempting to find what haunted her. An unfulfilled longing gnawed at her and she wanted something from these notes, or they were preparing her for something. She felt that if she just read them over and over she'd discover what it was. Only reading the notes brought her close to understanding the emptiness she felt. At the same time the notes conveyed a nauseating pain.

There was a certain sense of destiny within the messages. She hadn't brought Nick back to her present life, and whatever came next wouldn't be her choice either—it would come of its own volition.

Christmas had, paradoxically, been one of the most peaceful and quiet they'd ever had as a family. She thought it due to her own stillness, which she used as a survival mechanism. Her usual hubbub—running around, fixing, re-fixing, cooking, cleaning, wrapping—had decreased in both intensity and volume. She felt as she had right before the children were born—a conserving of energy, a with-drawing into her own body that allowed only the most nec-essary activities outside herself.

She sent Phil to his office party alone. Their unresolved disagreements over both the identity of the Oystertip buyer and her guest list at the open house ran beneath the sur-face like a sharp-edged danger they didn't go near. Talking about any of it would only lead to what she really felt and she could not voice her emotions, much less explain them. Evasion of discord seemed to be in the best interest of their family.

She had ordered the remainder of the Christmas gifts on the Internet and skipped the school arts alliance party and the neighborhood block party. She kept listening to the same Christmas CDs she'd installed for the Christmas party; the thought of picking new ones, changing them, pushing the tray back in, exhausted her. She felt she was sleep-walking until life brought to her the next link in this chain of events.

She believed her lethargy existed in her own private bubble, in her own commonplace world—that no one no-ticed her slipping fortitude, her sense of an impending des-tiny over which she had no control. Yet her son came close to detecting her confused state of mind when he and Lis-beth broke up a few days after Christmas.

For the thousandth time Amy sang "Winter Wonderland." The kids were both home, usually sleeping till noon, eating at odd hours, and she was never sure whether she was cleaning up breakfast or lunch. She'd already put away all the laundry.

The phone rang and she moved toward the living room, searched for the portable that never seemed to reside in its cradle when Jack was home. "Where is the phone?" she called from the kitchen, swinging the door open.

Jack and Lisbeth sat on the couch, holding hands, gazing at each other. Lisbeth was crying—again. Amy rolled her eyes just in time for Lisbeth to turn and see her. This opened the water works once more.

"You okay, darling?" Amy thought she'd better ask.

"No, your son just broke up with me. I know it's because you told him to."

Jack held his hand up to his mother—a warning not to speak. But Amy felt free-floating, able to say anything within her own warped time and space. It didn't really matter what she did or said—circumstances just played out the way they wanted to, didn't they?

"Jack?" Amy asked. She looked at the side of Lisbeth's face, seeing Nick's defiant chin.

"I'm not breaking up with her." He touched Lisbeth's arm. "We're not breaking up."

"I call seeing other people breaking up." Lisbeth spoke clearly, considering the effort it took to cry so hard.

"I don't," Jack said, and motioned for his mother to leave the room. She tried to move her feet, but couldn't.

"Now why would you two break up?" Amy waved her hand around in the air.

"Mom. Please." Jack looked up, opened his eyes wide.

Lisbeth wiped at her face.

Amy plowed on. "Really, hon. Why would you break up when there's no reason to? Why would you leave each other, when no one has left or gone away or done . . . anything? It's not like you're in love with someone else . . . or moving."

Lisbeth released Jack's hand, turned to Amy. "What?"

Jack stood and pulled Lisbeth from the couch. "Let's go."

Lisbeth opened her mouth, shut it and turned. Jack grasped her hand and they walked to the French doors to the backyard, obviously to continue their discussion without Amy. Then Lisbeth stopped, turned again. "Why did you ever break up with anyone you said you loved?"

"What?" Amy asked.

"You . . . Why did you ever break up with anyone?"

"I don't think I ever did."

"You broke up with my daddy."

"No . . . no, I didn't."

Lisbeth came toward her. "Yes, you did. Mother told me you did. Now you want Jack to do the same to me. But Jack loves me."

"Stop. Now." Jack headed toward both of them.

"I did not break up with your daddy. He went . . . away."

"Stop!" Jack yelled and Amy saw the word in capital letters, slanted, lopsided.

She hadn't heard her son shout at her since he stood in his crib, shaking the bars and wailing for a bottle.

Amy backed away from Jack into the kitchen. What had she just said, done? The kitchen door shut and she sat down on a bar stool and dropped her face in her hands as she listened to the opening and shutting of the back door, then the swish of the swinging kitchen door.

She looked up. Jack stared at her.

"I'm sorry I shouted at you, Mom."

"That was completely disrespectful."

"I'm sorry. But what were you talking about?"

"I was just answering her."

"Mom." He hesitated, looked out the kitchen window. "Did you really used to date her dad . . . seriously date?"

"Yes."

"Have you talked to him? Kept up with him all these years?"

So that was what her son was worried about—whether she'd kept in contact with an old boyfriend for twenty-five years.

"No. If you wanted to know, you should've asked."

"Lisbeth thinks that you—"

"I said goodbye to him twenty-five years ago and didn't see him again until the day you brought Lisbeth to meet us."

"Really?"

"Really."

"Okay." Jack turned to leave the room.

"Where is she?"

"Waiting for me in the car. Mom?"

"Yes?"

"Please don't ever do that again. That was so embarrassing."

"I just wanted—"

Jack walked toward her, hugged her. "You just don't seem like yourself lately."

"I know."

Her son walked out the side door to the driveway, where his car waited with the sobbing Lisbeth. Amy ambled aimlessly through the house, then finally to her sunroom, where she sank onto her desk chair. She still waited, not knowing what she waited for; she was impatient, frustrated. She opened the top-left drawer, as she had a thousand times since the Christmas party, and lifted the scrap of pink paper from below the phone bills. Surely she needed to talk to Nick after reading the unsent telegrams; he must also want and need to talk to her.

She opened the slip of paper and stared at the phone

number. She'd memorized it by now, but she still gazed at the numbers scribbled in his handwriting. She reached for the phone, placing her hand on the receiver and tapping her finger on the curved handset.

The weather the past two weeks had been incredibly cold, the sky filled with ice-cube clouds frozen over a town shaded beneath its gray shadow. The unusual cold without snow had left the town and all her friends in a quiet mood; most people were hiding in their homes. Even when she ventured out, the streets appeared like part of an empty movie set: cars parked at the curb, empty planters on front porches, vacant Adirondack chairs on lawns, rusted bikes tipped against garages. She remembered the days when this weather would have kept her inside the house with the kids, playing Candyland a thousand times, watching videos and making chocolate-chip cookies.

Now she slid into the gray days wondering what lay on the other side. She was amazed as the kids moved in and out of the house, as Phil drove to work and came home and she cooked and smiled and even—on a few occasions— made love before drifting off into a sleep that was never really sleep, but clouded images that carried her in and out of consciousness.

The phone rang, shook beneath her finger. She flung her hand in the air as if the phone were white-hot, burning— as if it knew what she had been about to dial on its numbered face.

She rubbed her temples and let it ring three times before picking up. The background static of a car phone came before the voice and her heart rolled in the hope that it might be him, calling her at home. Maybe there was good news about the Trust or maybe he just wanted to talk.

"Hello, my dearest hibernating friend. I'm on my way

over and I didn't want to embarrass you and catch you in bed, or worse—up, but in your pajamas."

"Carol Anne, aren't you the thoughtful one? I am not in my pajamas and I've been up since five a.m."

"Well, I'm in your driveway, so let me in."

She looked out the window and there was Carol Anne pulling into the driveway, waving out the driver's-side window.

Amy hung up the phone without saying goodbye and walked to the front door; each step she took required an immense amount of concentration and the thumps on the hardwood floor sounded like *tired, tired, tired.*

She opened the front door and walked out onto the enclosed porch, once again amazed at how cold it was. Frigid enough for icicles, if there was any moisture, to hang from her front porch instead of the faux icicles of Christmas lights that Phil had still not taken down, complaining it was too frickin' cold to climb on the roof—outside, he couldn't even feel his fingers.

She looked out the window to the driveway, but didn't see Carol Anne, who came up behind her, startled her. "The back door was open."

"Don't scare me like that," Amy said. "Jack must've left it unlocked. He just left with Lisbeth."

"I don't mean unlocked. I mean open." Carol Anne unbuttoned her coat, then laid it over the bottom of the banister.

"He was a little preoccupied—in the middle of breaking up with Lisbeth."

"Good."

Amy walked back into the sunroom, ignoring Carol Anne's comment. Carol Anne followed, flopped down on the chaise longue and laced her fingers behind her head.

"Oh, yes, I'd love some hot tea."

"What?" Amy squinted.

"I know you meant to offer me some hot tea . . . so I just said yes."

"Actually that sounds wonderful. You stay all comfortable right there—in my chair. I'll be right back."

Amy stood in the kitchen waiting for the kettle to whistle and stared out at her empty bird feeder. She hadn't filled it since Christmas. What had she done since Christmas? Waited for the inevitability of whatever lay on the horizon that she could not yet see.

The phone screamed in unison with the tea kettle and she jumped, then shifted back and forth between the wall phone and the stove, not knowing which one to tend to first. She picked up the phone, hearing the same static sound as a few minutes ago.

"Hello."

"Amy . . ."

"Nick."

"I can't hear you."

"Hold on. . . hold on. It's the kettle."

She tucked the portable phone under her chin and reached over, pulled the kettle from the stove, then poured boiling water into the two prepared mugs on the sideboard. She lifted the phone back to her ear. Here it was: the beginning or maybe the end of what she'd been waiting for. She still didn't know.

"Nick, hello." She tried to sound casual as she reached into the refrigerator, pulled out a carton of milk—just a drop in Carol Anne's tea.

"Did I catch you at a bad time?"

"No . . . well, yes. Carol Anne's here to visit and I was just making a cup of tea, and—"

"I swear, that woman is the bane of my existence."

"Stop."

"Is Lisbeth there?"

"No, she and Jack left about twenty minutes ago. I don't know where they were going. They didn't say. But they definitely did not look happy."

She closed her eyes to hear his response, to hear his deep voice—so deep she felt it vibrate below her belly button.

"Okay . . . maybe they're on the way to my house."

"Are you home?"

"No . . . no. I'm in my truck. I had some business. . . ."

"Oh. Well, if you called to find her, you might want to try her cell phone. Neither one of them ever removes the things from their bodies. I believe they put them on before they put on their underwear."

He laughed. She smiled at the sound, squirted some honey in her tea, then twirled it around with a silver baby spoon she'd found at an antique shop with her maiden initials etched on the handle.

"Well, I guess I could say I was only calling looking for Lisbeth, but you'd see right through that, wouldn't you?" He sighed; she exhaled with him. "I called to hear your voice."

"No news on Oystertip?"

"Not yet."

"I haven't seen you since the Christmas party." So much garbage lay stagnant below what she just said that she could almost smell its stench.

"Yes, eighteen days ago." He paused. "Did you read them?"

"Yes. I read them."

"Do you still have them?"

"Yes."

"And?"

The truth that flowed now brought new truth with it. She

whispered—the only way she could say it. "It breaks my heart . . . that I wasn't there for you."

"You didn't know. Amy, Eliza had them. She hid them, told the lawyer she called your dorm, called your home and mailed those telegrams."

"I . . . thought so."

"I'm so damn sorry about all this—that it was my wife who kept us—"

"It doesn't change what happened."

"No, it doesn't. But can it change anything else?"

Carol Anne's voice echoed down the hall in unison with the sound of her boots hitting the pine floors. "Amy, what in the living tea bags are you doing—drying your own leaves?"

The kitchen door swung open and Amy turned her back on her friend and spoke into the phone. "Listen, I gotta go. But you might try their cell phones. Do you need Jack's number?"

"You just give Carol Anne a great big hug for me. We'll talk . . . later."

"Okay, bye now." She reached for her cheery voice and pushed the OFF button, hung the phone back up on the hook.

Amy turned to Carol Anne, held out her mug.

"Here ya go, just as you like it."

"Who was important enough to leave me waiting?"

"Nick was looking for Lisbeth."

"Yeah, right."

"He was."

"Nothing about telegrams, or love, or begging you to see him."

"Nothing about any of the above."

"Bullshit. Double bullshit."

"He asked if I read them. I said I did. End of conversation."

"It's not the end of anything. I just know it."

"He was looking for his daughter. She and Jack are in some huge fight—breaking up." Amy walked to the bar stool, sat down. "Jack said she was needy. I heard him talking to his sister about it, too. Said she was real demanding, clingy."

"Wonder where she got that from?"

"What is that supposed to mean?"

"Nothing. But it's probably a very good thing that they're breaking up."

Amy gazed off at a lone chickadee staring through the window at her, accusing her of not filling the bird feeder when food was scarce in the cold weather.

"Yeah, but there's no real reason for them to break up. I don't know why they'd break up when no one's leaving or cheating or dating someone else or . . . whatever."

"Or going to Costa Rica?" Carol Anne punched her lightly on the shoulder.

"Exactly."

"This is Jack and Lisbeth, not you and Nick."

"I know that."

"You think that if Nick hadn't gone to Costa Rica you would've never broken up, that you would've married him, had little Nickies, lived happily ever after?"

Amy looked at her best friend, then around her own kitchen. "I don't know." She leaned against the counter and lowered her voice. "Don't you think some things were, or are, just meant to be—that there's nothing you can do about it? If something's going to happen, it's going to happen, no matter who tries to stop it or even start it?"

"No, I don't think that and neither do you. You didn't get him arrested, you didn't hide the telegrams and you didn't start any of this."

"I know, I know. That's my point. There's nothing I can do about it. Nothing."

"I don't understand, Ame. I don't know what you're saying. Since when have you been so fatalistic? What about choice?"

"There are some things we have no choice about." Amy sighed. There was a relief in just saying this, in knowing it.

"But there are some things we do have a choice about," Carol Anne said.

"Doesn't seem to me like there are very many of those these days."

Carol Anne groaned. "Amy, you don't need to know what would've happened. It didn't happen."

"Do you have to be so God blessed perfect? Don't you ever, even a little, wonder what would have happened if you'd married Bill or Zach? Or what was his name, Darwin?"

"Of course I wonder, only wonder. For about two and a half seconds max."

"But you broke up with every single one of them. You chose to . . . move on."

"So did you."

"No . . . I was . . ."

"When you fell in love with Phil, you chose. Yes, you did."

"It's different. Totally different. I *do not* want to talk about this anymore. At all. I wish Jack had never brought home that weepy girlfriend of his. I wish I hadn't gone to that tailgate party. I wish I could take a nap."

"Go ahead."

"I can't. I can't sleep."

"Oh, Ame." Carol Anne came over, set her mug of tea on the counter and hugged Amy close while she let silent tears roll down her face.

"He wasn't worth crying over then, and he's not now." Carol Anne wiped at Amy's face. "Let this go."

"I'm trying."

"Well, I actually came over to talk about me. But that's all shot to hell now."

Amy wiped her face. "Something wrong?"

"No . . . I just quit my job yesterday. Just up and walked out on Farley."

"Yeehaw! It's about time. Come in the living room, sit down, tell me all about it so you can cheer me up. This is the best news I've heard in three months."

They sat down on the couch and Amy hugged Carol Anne, spilling warm tea on her sweater. "I am so proud of you."

"Thank you. I have a very fine line to walk now. My clients want to come with me, but they can't. I might not have work for a year, but I'll be able to breathe."

"When you do the right thing like this, it always works out. Always. Remember when I had no idea how I would buy this home, or work at SCAD an hour and a half away, and it all just fell into place? Even though Phil hates when I spend the night there—he complains about it, tries to get me to change it every semester. He doesn't understand how important it is to me. But when it matters that much . . . it all works out."

"I know. I feel like I've lost a hundred pounds—or if we're going to be literal in the case of Mr. Farley, three hundred pounds. I finally told Joe we weren't getting a Christmas bonus and I kinda broke down. He told me to do what I needed to do."

"So . . . you left. Wow. You knew exactly what to do."

"Amy." She leaned closer. "Hear me—that is because I knew exactly what was bothering me. I didn't blame something else, or pretend I loved something I didn't."

"What do you mean?"

"I faced the real problem."

Amy looked away; some echo of truth rested in what Carol Anne was saying, but Amy couldn't or didn't want to find it. Time slipped past them and the sun descended to the rhododendron bushes in the backyard, the tips lit like miniature green torches. Amy leaned back against the couch cushions, forgetting about telegrams, Jack and Lisbeth, and the dull longing burrowed in her chest; she was thankful for the bushes Phil had planted in the backyard, for her best friend, for her cushy couches.

Amy reached for Carol Anne's hand. "Can I say it again? I am so proud of you."

"Yes, you can. You know, Amy—you'll get mad at me for saying this, but you have to find out what's really bothering you—not just look at the old stuff to . . . I don't know—feel better."

Amy closed her eyes and hugged her friend goodbye. Carol Anne had attempted to impart some truth, but there was no way anyone could understand the tug-of-war her heart and mind played all day. Wise words, quotes and her friend's metaphors weren't going to solve this pain and she didn't know what would.

After Carol Anne's car puffed white smoke down the driveway, Amy grabbed her winter parka off the back of the kitchen chair, then walked outside to watch the sun set behind her dormant rose garden. She sagged into a lawn chair and stared at the sky, admired the overblown and shrouded sun behind the yellow and pink striated clouds. She watched and let her mind wander, once again, to the past invading the present.

A loud bang caused her to jump; Phil walked into the backyard. "What're you doing out here in the dark?"

"Watching the sun set."

"Babe, the sun set half an hour ago. Get inside. You're gonna freeze."

She glanced up at the ink black sky: no moon, no stars, no setting sun. How had she not noticed when she was watching the entire time? How could she have missed the final sinking of the sun, or the shudders of her life? She'd been watching, but obviously not carefully enough.

Chapter Twenty-six

Nick slid down in the chair, hoped the dark, greasy-haired boy in front of him was tall enough to hide his own too-long hair from Amy's sight. The classroom was shaped like an amphitheater, rising from a podium in curved rows of blue padded spring-back chairs overlooking a chalkboard wall. A musty smell, like an old gym locker mixed with chalk dust, filled the room. The floor was sticky under Nick's feet, where another student must have spilled some caffeine-laden drink, trying to stay awake during class. The name "Megan" was carved in crooked lettering on the wooden flip-down desk, which pulled up from the side of the chair like a meal tray on an airplane.

He wanted to sit in on Amy's class and listen to her teach, hear her voice, watch her body move across the room. The girl next to him wore a black turtleneck sweater, baring an inch of her tummy above her too low-cut jeans; she looked at him, wrinkled her nose. He smiled at the girl, hopefully letting her know he was completely harmless before she raised her hand and asked Mrs. Reynolds who the old geezer sitting next to her was.

Dim and dusty light illuminated the podium more than the room itself. He hoped the low light would assist him in his mission of obscurity.

Amy entered the room, making him feel warm, safe. She wore a pair of brown corduroy pants with high-heeled boots and a tan sweater with fringe at the sleeves. Her hair fell loose over her shoulders, but when she turned around to pull down another chalkboard, he saw she had tried to attach a tortoiseshell barrette in the waves. She looked like just another student, not a forty-something-year-old teacher with two grown kids. She plopped her books down on the podium and smiled at the class.

"How was break?" she asked in the general direction of the slouched and rustling students who were opening their notebooks, searching for pencils, girls opening and closing their purses.

"Fine," "Great," "Too short," "Cold."

It sounded like they all answered twice as the various replies echoed off the brick walls.

Amy squinted against the faint light. "Steve . . ." She motioned to a student sitting by the far wall. "Will you turn on the auditorium lights? I hate when I can't see everyone."

"Sure, Mrs. Reynolds." A tall blond boy stood and sauntered toward the light switch. Nick slouched further down in his seat.

Amy turned to the chalkboard. "Let's start with the syllabus for the semester." She began to pass out a pile of papers. "We'll begin with the Greek-revival period and how it made its way into the architecture of Lowcountry South Carolina."

She wrote "Greek Revival" on the board and turned to the class. "Melody, you were in my last class. Do you remember where we left off during this period?"

"I think it was with an eggnog on the back porch of the historic Calhoun Hall."

Amy laughed. "Great memory. Do you remember exactly what we were learning on the back porch of Calhoun Hall?"

"That the Greek-revival period dominated American architecture during the period between 1818 and 1850?"

Amy bowed. "Ah, my mission in teaching something, anything, has not been for naught."

The class laughed. Nick laughed—too loudly. Amy's head snapped up and she squinted to the top of the auditorium just as Steve turned on the lights. Her face fell.

Nick flicked his fingers in a tiny, hopefully inconspicuous wave.

Amy frowned, continued to talk about plans for the semester in a quiet voice, tucking her hair behind her ears, glancing up and down, left and right, but never at him. Students turned and looked at him every few minutes as if to ask, "What have you done to our fun teacher?"

Finally, after the students had scribbled across pages and Amy's nervous movements ceased, she announced, "Okay, let's end early today. We have our first field trip tomorrow—an early morning. Meet at the front steps of Prentiss Hall with a full list of the four styles of neoclassical architecture."

She snapped her book shut, waved a dismissive hand at the class. Nick stayed in his seat, gazed at her until the last student slammed the wooden door shut.

She looked up at him and didn't speak.

"Hi, Ame."

"You ruined my class."

"I did not. It was a great class."

"What are you doing here?"

"I wanted to see you teach. And I have a surprise for you."

"Okay, you saw me teach. Now what is the surprise? Did we get the Heritage Trust?"

"No, nothing on that yet. But I think you'll love this surprise just as much."

"What is it?"

"You'll have to wait. By the way, you look great."

She sighed. "So do you. You need a haircut."

He laughed, ran a hand through his hair. "I know. You're a beautiful teacher. It's a gift."

"I'm trying to let them see how much . . . how interesting it is, without it being just another subject to pass."

"Well, it seems to be working." He touched her arm. "How was your break?"

"Cold, and except for the trauma of Jack and Lisbeth's breakup, quiet."

"They broke up?"

"You didn't know?"

He didn't know and didn't care. He wanted to push Amy up against the black chalkboard, and when he was done with her find chalk dust on her brown corduroys, her tan sweater.

"Yes, they had quite the traumatic event. Please tell me Eliza told you something about it," she said.

"Nothing. I haven't been home much over the holiday break. A big job in—"

Amy smiled. "Sorry you missed it."

"I came to take you away for the afternoon, the evening."

"Nick, you know I can't do that. No."

"Amy, you have to. Trust me on this—you'll be glad you said yes." He stepped closer and lifted her chin so she was forced to look at him.

She jerked away from him; he followed her, then she turned to face him.

"Where do you want to go?" Her shoulders slumped in surrender.

"I'll show you. You'll love it."

"Okay . . . okay. Let me drop off my papers and books at the dorm."

Amy's face in the warped mirror over the wooden dresser was flushed, her eyes wide. It was just the cold, she rationalized, not the anticipation of Nick's surprise. She looked away from the obvious excitement in her face to the rectangular room standing out in bas-relief—a reverse Polaroid of the dorm room she'd lived in when Nick hadn't come back for her. Sheer pink curtains, stained with salmon-colored streaks in the pattern of a rising sun, attempted to brighten the room. A metal desk squatted under the window with a black metal chair whose peeling paint revealed a bright blue undercoat.

Once in a while she would come back to the dorm to find a burned candle, an open book or piece of clothing and the odd thought "Who has been in my room?" would pass through her mind. Then she'd remind herself the room was nothing but a place to crash one night a week.

How odd. How many times had she stood in a dorm room that didn't look much different than this—except with her own 1970s paraphernalia covering the walls—brushing her hair and wondering what she and Nick would do that night? Without the items that defined family and home surrounding her, she believed that this was just another evening with Nick, just another dorm room. Yet it was a different dorm room, and Nick was waiting for her—which is all he'd ever done . . . wait for her.

Now there really was nothing left to think about, was there? She just needed to watch it all unfold. Letting go of any control over the situation felt good, a relief warming her middle.

She grabbed her purse and headed down the concrete stairs to the foyer where Nick stood waiting, just as he had a hundred other times. She smiled at the desk attendant who, for the first time all day, actually sat at her post.

"Mrs. Reynolds . . . you need to sign in your guest."

"We're leaving. Thank you, Melissa."

He'd startled her in class, his voice echoing below her consciousness before she saw his face above the students. When she'd seen him, she'd understood she was the only one who really knew him, who could fill all those wide, empty spaces inside him.

Nick turned and flashed his "You'll forgive me for leaving" grin at the cute girl, who waved goodbye to him. He opened the door and Amy walked through, brushed up against his arm; her skin prickled beneath her coat and sweater.

His pickup truck was parked next to her SUV; a low-lying birch shed its leaves on their car roofs, on the curb and bricked street. The freezing temperatures of the past weeks had risen, but not by much. She shivered and pulled her coat closer. Nick wrapped his arms around her and walked her to the passenger side of his truck.

"I wish we could just take a walk," she said.

"Too cold, and we can't walk where we're going."

He opened the door of his truck. She climbed up on the running board, sat down in the passenger seat. He slammed the door and for the brief moment it took him to walk to the other side, she was alone in the truck. It smelled of pine, of soil, of outdoor life. Blobs of sap stained the carpet. The console held a cell phone, a few discarded beer bottle caps, jagged at the edges, and a pencil with a chewed eraser end. The cab was actually quite clean compared to the Camaro he'd had in college. She took a deep breath as he opened the driver's-side door, jumped in.

He turned and smiled at her—his smile, his beautiful smile, was all for her. All the unsolved disputes with Phil, all the echoing problems paled now. The only difference between this smile and the one she remembered from years ago was the slight crinkling beside his eyes, the wider chin. His eyes seemed to give off the same static electricity as her sweater.

She turned from him. "Where are we going?"

"It's a surprise. You'll love it."

She believed him.

He maneuvered the truck out of the parking spot, then turned right at the end of the road. She relaxed as the heater pumped pine-fragrant warmth into the cab. She leaned against the back of the seat, closed her eyes. *Still waiting.* And although she still wasn't sure what she waited for, it wouldn't be much longer.

The truck swerved, her head popped up. "What . . . what was that?"

He grimaced. "Sorry. You looked so beautiful there, your head back on the seat . . . I almost missed a stop sign. Sorry."

She rolled her eyes.

He laughed and turned back to stare out the windshield. "You are unbelievably beautiful."

"Nick . . . thank you." She looked out the side window. They left the Savannah city limits and headed for the beach road. Shadows from overhanging live oaks offered a canopy below the sky and a shield from the outside world, and she felt like the lane was a world unto itself, with its own heartbeat. The truck emerged on the other side to crisp, ironed lawns.

He eventually stopped the truck on the side of a gravel road, put it in PARK. She opened her window and leaned her head out on the windowsill and sighed. "The marina. Where are we going?"

"Reese lent me his boat—the big trawler with the inside cab. We're headed to Oystertip."

"Nick, it's freezing. We can't go out there . . . we don't have—"

"We have everything we need." He pointed to the bed of the truck, where parkas, hats, cameras and what looked like camping equipment were piled high.

She meant to ask what it was all for, what was going on—but this was where they'd been headed all along, wasn't it?

"And," he said, reaching in his pocket and pulling out a key, "we can get in the house."

"What?"

"A friend of a friend convinced the owners that he wanted to rid the house of any architectural artifacts—to prove the house is worth nothing."

"I'm not sure I want to know who your friends are."

"It doesn't matter. But I have the key and you can get inside."

All else—the cold, the boat, the coming night—seemed irrelevant.

She opened the truck door. "Okay, what're we waiting for?" *No more waiting.* The thought was warm and drowsy in the crevices of her mind, her body.

Nick laughed—a sweet sound. Moths flapped against the headlights of the truck; waves whispered against the dock.

The hum of the motor filled the boat as they huddled inside the cab. Waves slapped against the hull. Her heart slapped against her chest.

Nick anchored the trawler off the edge of the island, then lowered a small Boston Whaler Tender from the back. The island now seemed to beg to be left alone— not to be anyone else's personal haven beyond the wildlife already living there, as the afternoon light mellowed the once-inhabited playground of a rich indigo merchant.

They snuggled up in the Tender as Nick ran it aground on the beach. They bundled up in coats and hats, then he threw a hiking backpack and a large parcel of down over his shoulders and waved his hand to come on.

"I feel like a marshmallow," Amy said.

Nick poked her arm. "Yeah, it's a little big for you, but it'll keep you warm." He reached down and held up a broken shell. "Time brought us back here, Amy."

"What?"

"Remember? The shell."

"Yes." Her voice was thick despite the cold. Yes, the other beach, the other shell, making love on scorched sand . . .

He handed her the shell, placed it in her palm. He pulled her to him and she fell against the soft down of his coat, of him. He pressed the shell into her hand and the memory invaded as a flood beginning in her legs, then finally reaching the recesses of conscious memory. She lifted her face to him—only memory and body in control now.

His mouth found hers and he kissed her, slow, easy, as if making sure her mouth remembered his. Not only did her mouth remember, but also her arms and hands. She reached behind his neck and pulled his kiss deeper. There was nothing else to be done but this. He released her and she leaned into him, swallowed the words she wanted to say: "Keep holding on, just keep holding me."

"Follow me." His voice was soft, commanding and she had no choice but to follow him across the frost-concealed, pinecone-covered forest floor. Her senses became amplified— the bark dangling from a tree, a spiderweb defined by water droplets, the pure smell of torn wood, the dents in the earth from her own weight, the cracking of twigs under Nick's feet. So this was what it meant to live in the moment, absorbing nothing but what was before her—giving in to the inexorable, to destiny.

They emerged from the brush and Nick wrapped his arm around her shoulders. The house rose in front of them and the cold air surrounded it in an invitational welcome. She sensed a flood of something she couldn't label, something that rose—no—washed over her, something from a long, long time ago. Something having to do with yearning and desire and . . . purpose. That was it: purpose.

She stepped onto the front porch, then turned and held out her hand. "Key?"

He laughed and walked toward the door, slipped the backpack and bloated bundle from his shoulders. He yanked a key from his back pocket, shoved it into a rusted keyhole, shook it, maneuvered the key in then out until the door popped open, chips of paint fluttering down like angel wings. Nick bowed and swept his arm toward the open door.

"You seem very pleased with yourself," she said.

"I am." He held out his hand. "I made you smile. I am more than pleased with myself."

"Yes, you have made me smile."

She stepped into the foyer. Nick flicked on a large flashlight and its scattered beam mixed with the dusty interior.

The house smelled of must and age——it almost seemed to live and breathe.

Amy grabbed the flashlight and pointed it to the floor. She took a deep breath and grabbed Nick's arm. "The floor is Purbeck stone."

"Okay."

"It's from an evolutionary era, quarried from the Isle of Purbeck in England." She waved the flashlight over the floor, then up the curved staircase to the second floor.

She groaned. "How am I going to see the entire house with a flashlight? The windows are all boarded up."

"I have megaflashlights . . . trust me."

Trust me. The words echoed off something inside her, but she couldn't search now for what it was. He wrapped his arms around her, and this time when he kissed her, he did it with the urgency she remembered. Her hands slid to the back of his head; his hands wrapped in her hair, stroked the side of her neck. Her legs gave way beneath her and only he held her up. He kissed her until only the house and Nick existed in her world.

He placed both hands on her cheeks and leaned away from her. He looked down at her and his eyes were full, wet. "My God, Amy. I do love you."

But he didn't need to say it, he never had. She knew it, felt it, tasted it.

He grabbed her hand and held another large flashlight out in front of him and led her through the back hall into the wide, deep dining room. He moved the flashlight slowly around the room——pausing whenever she exclaimed with joy or astonishment at a particular molding or architectural detail. He ran his finger around her palm as she talked and walked. Her words danced in rhythm with the motions of his fingers and hand on hers.

They moved from room to room, entering some alternate world where she was permitted to see everything she had ever wanted in a house, in a restoration project—everything she taught about and loved—and Nick was part of everything she loved. She ran his hand over the rare papier-mâché wallpaper—gilded in some places—in the dining room, over the carved marble mantle in the parlor, over the rocaille scrolls on a mahogany staircase.

She took pictures with the camera and flash Nick provided. After every other room in the house had been photographed, touched and commented on, she entered the living room with a low, guttural sound of joy.

Nick released her hand and she grabbed for it. "Wait," he said. "I want you to see this room with more light." He opened a back window and kicked out the board. The sun sifted through the bubbled floor-to-ceiling glass windows like wavering pieces of scattered flame.

He threw his bundle on the floor, unrolled two down sleeping bags, shook them out as he dropped them to the floor.

"What're you doing?"

"Thought we might need something to sit on." He plopped down on the floor.

She pointed the flashlight where thick dirt covered the wide hand-planed heart-of-pine floors, crisscrossed with the small tracks of unknown animals she dared not think about. Dust motes rose and danced in shafts of lengthening light. She wandered around the room, touching, feeling and explaining the architecture as if her class stood with them.

She turned to Nick. He sat on a blue sleeping bag, gazing at her.

"Stop staring at me . . . ." A rush of heat filled her body.

He reached his hand out for her and she took it; he pulled her down to the covered floor.

"I want to hear something . . . I want you to tell me what you've been thinking all these weeks since you read the telegrams." He lifted her chin so she faced him. His touch was still gentle, the same whispered caress it had always been. "Do you wake up in the middle of the night and wonder how this could've happened to us—how we could have been separated like that? Do you try to get through the day, and it seems a million years long?"

Amy shivered with the truth. "Yes." Only "yes" resided within her. It was all up to him now—to end the waiting that was twenty-five years long, yet felt now like only a minute.

"I have something for you." He reached into his backpack, pulled out a silver box, plain, no wrapping, with the words SYLVIA'S ANTIQUE PARLOR stamped in bold black letters on the top.

Warmth overcame her now—a comfort of certainty and the rightness of unalterable destiny. She lifted the top of the box and fumbled with the tissue.

"I looked everywhere I could think of, every jewelry store, every antique shop. This was the closest I could find," he said.

She lifted a necklace off the cotton square on the bottom of the box and held up a small diamond cross pendant dangling off a silver chain. He held the flashlight up to the necklace; the diamonds glinted amid the sparkling, twirling dust. She dropped the necklace to the ground.

"Nick . . ." She fumbled, reached her hands out to the dirt-coated floor to pick it up.

He lifted up the necklace, then pulled her close.

"Please let me put it on," he said.

"I bought the last one for myself—no one gave it to me."

"Well, now I am giving this one to you."

She faced him now, her legs askew, not knowing where to rest her hands. Her right one covered her neck. "Oh . . ." She began to cry. Now he would replace the lost necklace, the missing pieces of her heart, the desperate, unfinished longing for him she'd thought long buried.

Nick brought the necklace around her throat, then hooked it. His fingers traced across her skin and she remembered all of it now—where he would touch, where she would. Of course she would—there was no other way.

"It's perfect. It falls exactly right. . . . It fits." His words ran under her skin—a warm river carrying her.

Of course it does. Of course you do. "My old one was just silver . . . no diamonds." Her body leaned forward.

"Well, now you have diamonds and platinum."

He reached to touch the cross; his fingers grazed her neck, ran over her collarbone to unzip the front of her coat. Her legs knew where to go and they wrapped around Nick's as he drew her closer. Her arms fell free when he pushed off the coat, which landed in another dance of dust. She didn't look away from his eyes; they were on fire with the sun, the copper indistinguishable from the light flashing off the underside of the magnolia leaves outside. Murmured light allowed the suspension of time, and she was twenty-one years old again, promises and vows intact.

She found the feel of his skin, the understanding of his touch. He knew her, what she wanted, who she was and what she loved. He knew all of her and still wanted her.

She leaned in as his mouth found hers, and he kissed her until the sandpaper of his chin shifted down her neck to the crevice where the cross lay. He slid his hands under her sweater, lifted it over her head. Her limbs were like water, fluid with his movements. It had always been like this, always would be—and she wanted him so badly, wanted to be fully understood. She tasted the inside of his mouth—this was where she'd once been and should never have left. She shivered and he pulled the other down sleeping bag over them as a blanket.

He ran his mouth down the side of her neck and she arched her body toward him, laced her fingers in his hair.

"I remembered that. God, I was hoping I'd remembered it right. The way you bend, your fingers in my hair. Amy, I want it all back—all of it." He grabbed at her, pulled her against him.

She came to him. Here they could have everything they had lost, could unearth the love buried in the memory of touch—skin to skin, arms circling flesh and eliminating any barrier. They moved as one body removing each other's clothes.

He slid down and kissed her abdomen. She moved her hand down, suddenly shy—her stomach, so different from what he'd known, years and children having changed her. He pushed her hand away, buried his mouth in the softness there, then lifted his head and looked at her. "I wish they'd been our children." He wrapped his hands around her body.

She groaned and all reality other than him and what was meant to be vanished. How could they have been denied this intimacy, this perfect knowledge of each other?

Nick mumbled in the darkness, whispered into her flesh, "My Amy, my beloved. My Amy."

"So this, this is what was out . . . there," she said, her voice raw and deep.

"Where?" He ran his finger over her lip. She bit down on it lightly.

"This was somewhere out there . . . waiting."

"Yes." He moved his finger inside her mouth, then ran it down her chin and around her neck, down her back. "I need to touch every part of you I've missed. Here." He touched the back of her knee. She squirmed and pulled closer. "And here." He shifted down and traced the outline of her anklebone. "And here." He ran his hand up her leg to the inside of her thigh. She groaned. "Even here." He ran his forefinger around the curve of her ear.

"This could take a while," she murmured.

"God, I hope so." He kissed her so gently; she lifted her head to taste more of him. "This is what my dreams are all about, all I've ever wanted." He turned her on her back and rose above her and she heard him and she believed him.

"Finally, Amy. Finally." His words were desperate and deep and her body rose to meet him, and then completely join him, in a slow choreography of bodies rediscovering a forsaken but not forgotten dance of being one.

Tangled together she felt their release spread like fire, felt the peace of completion like a benediction. She curled up next to him and traced his face with her finger. He shifted beside her.

"Don't move," she said, suddenly afraid that if he pulled his body from her she would once again live in the netherworld of longing and wanting where this intimacy was just beyond her reach. He began to move inside her again and she cried out.

He touched her face. "Am I hurting you?"

"No, no." She grabbed on to him, pulled him closer, desperate to escape the ache of him gone to a place where she couldn't find him. He kissed her again and again, keeping his lips to hers even as he spoke.

"Dear God, Amy. I have never loved anyone but you."

She tried to distinguish her hand, her leg or arm from his—her want and longing from his—but they were wrapped too tightly to separate.

"If only there was a word stronger than love, stronger than desire. I wish I could find it—find a way to tell you everything you are to me." He closed his eyes.

"Nick . . ." She arched her back, surrendered all of herself to him. She had words stronger than love, larger than desire; they were in her body, in her flesh and bones, and at last she'd found them.

Chapter Twenty-seven

She shivered, freezing. She reached down for the Irish quilt on her bed and felt her bare leg and a slippery piece of material. She opened her eyes to a filtered and fogged light. Damn, Phil had forgotten to turn the bathroom light off. She moved to stand and go to the bathroom but fumbled, landed on hard, cold wood.

Memory flooded in with the icy realization of where she was and why. She lifted her hand to her neck, grabbed the diamond cross in a flash of awareness: Oystertip, the house, Nick.

The languid memory of his touch washed over her; the pure lovemaking they had once again found in each other still throbbed through her.

"Nick," she murmured. His face was soft in the early-morning light—a mix of moon and predawn sun coming in the one window where he had kicked out the plywood the night before, a lifetime ago. Morning approached—she had a class, she had a job, she had a family.

A family: *Phil, Molly, Jack.* Their pure belief in her sent her to her knees; she bent to the ground with the full

knowledge of what she'd done. She fumbled for the flashlight that she remembered had fallen to the side of the
sleeping bag. She groaned, found her hand on a hard object and lifted it: Nick's shoe. She dropped it and searched
again for the flashlight. She found it, grasped it like a life-
line and flicked it on. The room lit up like a tank of water.

She was dizzy. She pulled her crumpled sweater from
under Nick, covered him up with the sleeping bag and his
flannel shirt. She took extreme care not to wake him as she
found her corduroys where they'd been flung on the
wooden floor. She turned the flashlight off, moving with a
panic-flooded mind, a bilious taste of guilt filling her
mouth. So this is what it feels like to be an adulterer—a
filthy adulterer who'd momentarily found freedom in rationalizations. She couldn't catch her breath in the underwater feeling of guilt, she dressed as quietly as possible.

Where exactly was she? What time was it? She grabbed
Nick's donated coat and staggered to one side of the living
room. She had to leave here, leave what she'd done. It
couldn't have happened. Amy Reynolds wouldn't have
made love to another man. She slid the coat over her shoulder, remembering Nick's hands slipping it off, feeling his
hands all over her body. She stumbled to the front door; it
was locked. She began to sob and trip through the house,
looking for a way out, any way out. Then she remembered
the window he'd pried open. She flung herself over the
windowsill and fell into the spiked bushes outside.

She'd never been so cold, so empty, as though no blood
ran through her veins. *I didn't do this. I didn't do this.* She
began to half-run, half-stumble toward the boat on the
beach, to escape from Nick, from herself.

She fell onto the sand, searching in her mass of whirling
thoughts for a solid resting place, for a decision. She

jumped into the grounded Tender. Its tip was buried in the sand as its hind end bobbed in the waves. Her hand shook violently as she held the flashlight over the ignition to find the keys. None.

She leaned over the back of the boat, lifted the rear seat to see if he'd hidden them in the empty well. She shook with fear and cold, and the flashlight fell from her hand, plopped into the sea with a lone splash.

"No!" she cried out and dipped her hand in the icy water, grabbing at only liquid as she searched for the key. Desperation and panic mixed with the freezing air and sea. She found nothing inside herself of courage or sustenance as she stumbled back onto the sand. She was a coward—only cowards ran away. She wrapped her arms around her middle, attempted to find a way out, a solution, and found she was unable to command anything of herself but shame.

She grabbed the chain Nick had given her. It snapped, gave way and she threw the chain and cross—evidence of her sin—to the sands she'd wanted to save, to the island whose salvation she had convinced herself was a decent reason to bring them back together.

She looked up to the black bowl of sky and spied the full moon—bloated and high above her, half-hidden behind a cloud-distended sky. This time she found the moon she thought she'd lost, and she swore that amid the owl's call and the frog's marsh-song, she heard it mocking her with its obvious resplendent presence, saying, "I've always been here." And now she followed it.

The clouds separated to impart the full light of the moon, and she never looked away as she followed. She vaguely sensed the brush of cordgrass, the sinking squish of mud and then the hard crack of shells. She ignored the cold, the harsh path, and the fear kept at bay by the light that led her through thick underbrush. She followed the moon until a cloud diluted its beacon and allowed her to stop, rest—just for one minute.

Piercing morning sunlight sliced through Nick's eyelids and he rolled onto his side, not wanting to wake up and face another day without Amy.

Amy.

He shot straight up, fell to his side in the tangle of sleeping bag, confused, clothes half on. He glanced around the room as quickly as he could with his eyes still bleary, his thoughts sluggish. She was gone. He stumbled to his feet. Where was she? How the hell had he slept through her getting up? He hadn't slept soundly in almost thirty years, and he had to pick now, with Amy sprawled across his body. And yet he knew why he had finally, blessedly fallen into this sleep—because she'd been there, across him, on him.

He groaned, tripped as he tried to pull on his jeans, fell onto the floor, sending a searing pain through his hip. "Damn, damn."

He yanked on his shirt and sneakers and began to call her name. He looked down—her clothes and boots were gone; the other flashlight was gone. He yanked on his coat and moaned.

He shouldn't have allowed them both to fall asleep. He had been prepared for her flash of shame and guilt when the light came in. He'd prepared what to say—but now she was gone.

He fished in his pocket and found the boat keys. He jumped out the open window and screamed her name. He glanced around like a skilled hunter, checking the ground, spying broken frozen grass. He followed the footsteps to the beach, but then they led back toward the marsh, away from the maritime forest and the house. Oh, God, not the marsh.

Dread flooded him; his toes were numb, his hands quivering more from fear than cold. The moon was still descending even as the sun rose. Nick pulled his coat sleeve back from his wrist: five thirty a.m. She could have been wandering for hours.

He followed her dented footsteps until he reached the soft ground of the marsh where her tracks were camouflaged in the thick grasses. There was nothing else to track.

"Amy!" he screamed.

Only the crickets and owl answered his call.

He jogged back to the boat to find his cell phone, staring at it even as he understood what he must do with Amy lost in the marsh of a barrier island, a maze of dead ends and false exits inhabited by cottonmouth snakes and alligators. Red wolves lived in the thicker parts of the forest, and if she headed the other way—toward the sea—the oyster beds were like razors, sharks played in the shallow surf, and more alligators roamed the tidal stream emptying into the sea.

He punched 911 and closed his eyes on his own fear and tears, feeling as if he were in one of his slow-motion dreams where he could not run, could not correctly dial the phone.

The phone rang and rang; the echoing sound rubbed his nerves raw until the operator answered and he told her there was a woman lost on Oystertip Island and to send the Coast Guard.

He found he remembered the Hail Mary from his childhood, and he uttered this prayer over and over. On his hundredth or maybe thousandth one, sirens blared across the beach; boats pulled up and disgorged men in uniforms, walkie-talkies squawking from their belts.

Sporadically and in broken sentences, Nick told the uniformed men which way he believed Amy had gone. Questions and answers came like gunshots in the flashing lights of the boat, in the beacons they carried.

"How long has she been gone?"

"I don't know. It could have been hours."

"You're trespassing."

"I know."

"Was she drunk?"

"No."

"Is she your wife?"

"No, she's Phil's wife."

"Do we need to call her family?"

Nick rattled off Amy's home phone number, which he'd long ago memorized. He began to follow the men with the radios and medical kits through the woods.

A hand grabbed his arm. "Sir, you cannot go with them. You're already trespassing. I can't let you go."

Nick swiped the Coast Guard officer's hand off his arm. "You can arrest me, but I'm going. I lost her . . ." Nick choked on a sob. "Let me find her. Now."

The Coast Guard officer released him. "Okay, man. But I didn't tell you to go."

Nick pushed his way through the woods, calling Amy's name, this time not reaching for a prayer but for the remembered feel of Amy in a sleeping bag next to him.

Chapter Twenty-eight

Something glacial and piercing ran through her forearm. Amy grabbed at it, cried out, tried to lift her hand against an unknown weight. Her eyes popped open and disorientation spread through her with the pain. The room was bright—too bright. She squinted to see the shapes and bulk of what appeared to be a metal room. Industrial mauve curtains hung in pleated folds. A metal pole stood next to her bed, dripping fluid into her arm through an IV with an amber tube. A pink plastic pitcher stood sweating puddles on a metal bedside table.

She groaned as she tried to lift her head, find a focus point. Where was she? It looked like a hospital. The oversized door at the end of the room swung open and Phil walked in, blowing into a Styrofoam cup. He didn't look up at her. She groaned again, unable to find her voice inside the nebulous and scattered pain of a closed throat.

He looked up, smiled. "Welcome back." But his eyes did not match his smile. His mouth was tight, tired looking.

"Where am I?" she tried to ask, but a grotesque croak came from her throat.

"Don't try to talk yet." Phil placed his cup on the bed-side table, sat next to her and clasped her hand. "You're in Darby Memorial. You've been asleep, or out of it at least, for a full day now. You had hypothermia, a broken rib and some pretty bad cuts. You're gonna be okay."

He sounded robotic. Her dulled senses could not ab-sorb the information as it came. She stared at him; there was something else wrong, something else. She searched in her fogged mind, lifted her hand, set it back down. *Hy-pothermia.* She closed her eyes; her eyelids were like thick cardboard and she didn't have the strength to keep them open.

Phil rubbed the top of her hand. "Yes, go back to sleep."

She shook her head no, but kept her eyes closed and searched the abyss of fear hissing at her center. What was it? Cold, she was so cold. Scared. Further back, further—before the cold and fear.

A sleeping bag, dark blue. Dust and scattered light. Legs and arms and hands and mouths. A diamond cross strewn on sand under a full moon.

The memory thrust itself to the tip of her consciousness. Her eyes flew open and she stared at Phil, at her husband. The set, tired look on his face expressed betrayal: her betrayal.

An animalistic groan came from below the roiling shame. She closed her eyes and could not look at his face again. The shame was worse than the physical pain and she scurried like a rat to a deep, dark place. She couldn't come back. She couldn't rise to the bright light, to Phil, to de-ception. Molly's words echoed across her consciousness—*It's not in her . . . to do.*

She reached for the quilt of rationalization and excuses she'd sewn for herself over the past few months; she needed it now to cover her guilt. She'd fashioned it stitch by stitch: *They were different, they had never really broken their vows, they were cheated out of their life together, she was taken for granted, she needed him, there was a purpose.* Yet all she found now was an infested, decayed quilt: useless and rotten. She was freezing cold—and empty.

She shivered. Phil's hand covered hers; he called the nurse for another blanket and she began to weep.

He leaned over her. "What hurts, Amy?"

"Everything. Oh, God, everything," she said, her eyes still closed. The hospital door scraped; the weight of a blanket fell on her body. Didn't they know they could drop a thousand blankets on her, and she would still be freezing, deadly freezing?

Phil whispered, "I think she may need some more pain meds."

A high-pitched Georgia accent answered him. "It's not time yet. Another hour."

Phil sighed. "Thank you."

She opened her eyes, looked at her husband and said the first and the last thing—the only thing—she could find within herself, "I'm sorry." The words came out in a whisper.

Phil's eyes filled with tears. He squeezed her hand, did not answer. But she wasn't looking for an answer—she wasn't seeking absolution. There couldn't be any, she knew.

She closed her eyes again, unable to tolerate his pain, her own too great for comprehension. She allowed the darkness to envelop her again and she slipped into its cold and blank tunnel.

The pain eddied and flowed as doctors, nurses and visitors came and went from the room. Amy brought her frayed and shattered self to the surface for the sake of her family: Molly wanting to play gin rummy, Jack needing to tell her about his chemistry test, and Phil's hand on hers, always his hand.

She was lucky, said the doctor, who looked young enough to go to school with Jack. One fragmented piece at a time, her family told the story of the night she was lost on Oystertip Island. These broken pieces of information formed a border to a puzzle as her memory filled in the middle details. They told her she had somehow wandered into the marsh, the endless maze of dead-end trails and high grass. The search team had found her curled and shivering on an oyster bed at the edge of the sea. It had been seven in the morning when they finally found her, unconscious with a body temperature of 90.2 degrees. She now understood where the deep cuts and piercing pain on her left side were from—even a thick coat of down was no match for the slicing razors of broken and halved oyster shells.

In the whispered voice of the defeated, Phil told her that when Nick awoke at five in the morning and found her gone, he'd called for help. If he hadn't called, she would have lain unconscious as the tide, pulled unusually high by the full moon, rolled in at nine forty that morning. She wasn't angry with Nick for this call. He'd saved her life. It wasn't his fault. It was hers, only hers.

The police did not understand why she'd wandered into the marsh. They'd come to the hospital asking endless questions about whether she'd taken medication, whether she was drunk. She couldn't tell them she believed she'd found the moon and was meant to follow it.

She assumed Jack and Molly didn't know all the details. They somehow believed she'd gone to the house for preservation purposes and become disoriented on the property in the night.

Carol Anne held her hand. She didn't lecture Amy about

searching for change the wrong way; she didn't give advice or deliver sarcastic comments. She gave only love.

The OWP members came and stood over her also. If she could have moved, if she'd any strength to run, she would have. At least Phil and Carol Anne stared down at her knowing the truth, but these four students stared down at her with undeserved admiration. They believed she and Nick had broken into the house in search of further proof of the home's historic value, evidence to save it. They thought her courageous and worthy.

Phil left the room when they came. Revvy sat on the green plastic-covered chair next to her bed.

"You know Nick was arrested."

Norah punched him on the shoulder. "I don't think she needs to hear all this right now."

"No, tell me," Amy said. She needed to know every evil thing her sin had sown.

"Well, we pooled our money for his bail and now he's kind of disappeared."

Amy scooted up on her pillows, winced at the pain shooting down her left side. "What do you mean, disappeared?"

"Well, I think he's camping out on the island," Revvy said. "But if they find out, they'll arrest him again. He's kind of freaked out about what happened to you. He blames himself—said he turned around for one minute and you were gone."

"It wasn't his fault. It was all mine." Tears filled her eyes.

Norah leaned down and grabbed Amy's hand. "We'll let you rest now. We'll take care of everything. Nick still had the camera. The photos you took are being analyzed by the historical society."

Amy nodded. They left believing in her brave and commendable effort to save Oystertip.

*   *   *

Though it seemed a lifetime, a constant battle, for only three days she faded in and out of consciousness before the experts told her all was now medically well; she was ready to go home. Little did they know about the sickness in her soul.

Phil arrived at the hospital with a pair of jeans and a black cashmere sweater; he knew these were her favorites. She sat on the bed and turned from him, slowly attempting to dress herself, slipping the underwear on below her open-in-the-back hospital gown. As she lifted her arms to put on her bra, she remembered the discarded white lace on the dusty floor of a crumbling home, and tried to stay her tears.

Phil reached for her. "Here, let me. The doc said your ribs would hurt for a while." He pulled the bra down over her back, hooked it in place.

She wept harder, the tears ripping past the pain of her ribs, into the deeper place of suffering.

Phil crawled up on the bed, turned her around. "Here, I'll slip your sweater over your head."

"No."

She wanted to explain that she did not deserve this, that he should not be here loving her, helping her, pulling clothing over her stained body. His quick turn from her told her he took it as a rejection. She sought the strength to tell him she wanted his help, needed his touch, but did not deserve it. Yet all she found was the same bottomless, whirling cold.

She slid her feet into her jeans and stood to pull them up. The pants gaped an inch away from her stomach. She turned to Phil; he was gone. The nurse stood in his place.

She set a chart on the bedside table. "Your husband went to get the car, sign your discharge papers. It'll be about an hour."

"Thank you." Amy fell back on the bed, leaned her head on the pillow with her feet still on the floor, and closed her eyes. She wanted Phil back in the room.

The door swished shut as the nurse left. The door clicked again and Amy felt the prickle of someone staring at her. She opened her eyes.

Eliza stood in the doorway, her hands stuffed into the pockets of her long black coat. "Looks like you're going home."

"Yes." Amy's voice cracked.

"I wanted . . . I was going to stop by sooner, but . . ."

Amy held up her hand. Shame made her want to crawl under the bed, pull her head into her sweater. She could not look at this woman. The skin below Eliza's eyes was dark, surely stained from a broken heart. *My fault. My fault.* Amy heard the drumming mantra in her head.

Eliza walked into the room, stood next to the bed. "I know you don't want to see me, but there are a couple things I want to say . . . a couple things you should know."

"No, Eliza. It's not that I don't want to see you. I can't. I don't know what to say. I don't know what to . . . I'm sorry."

"Will you listen to me? If I talk, will you just promise to listen?"

"Yes." Whatever this betrayed woman asked, she would supply: repentance through acquiescence.

Eliza sat, not removing her coat, on the same chair Phil had been sitting in for the past three days. She took a deep breath as if she were about to jump from a high-dive. "I've always known that Nick still loved you, so most of this is my fault. As you probably know by now, I didn't mail those telegrams twenty-five years ago. I don't know what made me believe this betrayal would never come back to haunt me, that I could . . . force Nick to love me through such lies—and still have a good marriage. But I did. I thought I was doing the right thing."

Amy sat up, swung her feet to the ground.

Eliza wept, but neither her body nor her voice betrayed the tears falling down her face; Amy wondered if Eliza was even aware of them.

"I believed, still do, that I love Nick better than anyone else can. That I love him more than he has ever been loved. I saw no other option but to save him, for me. Not to save him for any other life, but for one with me. So I used everything I had. I knew that the accident happened in order to bring us together and sending those telegrams would have ruined that. You would have come, I know."

Amy didn't answer.

"Amy, you think you know the whole story—I'm the bad one, the evil one who kept Nick from you. There's more to the story than he told you. I was in the truck when the accident happened. We all were, all seven of us."

"I know. She was drunk," Amy said. She didn't want to hear this story again—the story of the drunken woman who wandered into the road as Nick swerved and hit her, killing her.

"Yes, she was. And this saved his life—saved us. Amy, Nick was also drunk."

"What?"

"I made sure the police didn't test him. I told them he was the only sober one and that's why he was driving. I told them he didn't even . . . drink."

"Oh, God."

"We were all out celebrating our final night. We couldn't wait to get home. Nick couldn't wait to get home to *you*. I spent the entire three months trying to prove to him that

we—he and I—were right for each other, but I don't think
he even noticed that I was there. *Amy this, Amy that*. Until
finally, you never answered the telegrams. Then, until three
months ago, I never had to listen to *Amy this* and *Amy that*
again."

"I'm . . . sorry."

"No, I didn't come here for your apology. I came to tell
you the whole story so you would know the truth. If you
make decisions on half-truths, they aren't real decisions, are
they? I found that out the hard way. Nick decided to be
with me, love me, only after he thought you were gone. But
he based that decision on a half-truth . . . well, not even
half. And look where I am now. Amy, I saved him. I did.
He would still be in that jail for vehicular homicide. He
would still be there."

"You hid the truth for him."

"Yes. I made a bigger deal out of his injuries . . . steering the police away from the fact that he was . . . slammed.
Luckily for him, his leg was fractured, his ribs broken, and
while they were busy making sure those injuries weren't
life-threatening, while they were getting X-rays and trying
to save the other woman's life, I made sure they knew he
was sober, the good guy, the designated driver."

"Everyone else knew, though."

"We all swore our silence. The school and Mr. Rivera all
thought the best option was to tell anyone who asked that
he and I had decided to stay . . . to work for the preserve.
It was our last class credit anyway . . . so we both graduated. Nick graduated in jail."

Eliza stood, then sat again. "Did he tell you he was
drunk that night? Or did he just tell you the other woman
was?"

Amy closed her eyes. "No, he just said that you saved

him by bringing in a lawyer from the States who was able to work with the lawyer in Costa Rica and track down this woman's companion that night."

"She was leaving a house belonging to a man she should not have been with. It took a long time to get a confession from the man who was with her. It ruined his life, too. His wife and children left him and moved to Brazil. The whole thing was horrible, so horrible."

"You did this to save Nick?"

"Yes." Eliza stood and looked down at Amy. "Do you know where he is?"

"No."

"He came home the morning you got lost, told me what happened, and left. I haven't seen him since."

"No . . . I have no idea."

"You will. He'll come to you. When he does, tell him—"

"No." Amy held up her hand.

"I don't blame you, Amy."

"I do."

And she did. She blamed herself and the stain spread wider, longer, deeper as Eliza walked out the door.

The bedroom at home looked empty, although it wasn't. The sleigh bed she and Phil had bought together in Charleston was still there, made up with the faded-flower Irish quilt and tossed pillows. The bench, clean laundry piled on it, sat in the same spot against the wall. The book she'd left a million lives ago still lay on the bedside table.

Phil carried her bag into the room. She stopped in the doorway. All of his familiar belongings that had once made her feel secure were gone: no tray of coins and pens on the dresser, no suit coat over the chair. She swung around; his bedside table was empty, dusted clean. Abandonment and panic rode on a trail of muscles beginning in her hands, and numbness spread through her body.

Phil looked up from the bed where he was unpacking her hospital suitcase in small, neat piles.

"You left." She walked into the room and leaned against the dresser as the isolation, the separation, weakened her.

"What?" He looked up.

"Your stuff . . . it's gone. You left."

"No, I just moved into the guest room. I thought you might want me to . . . leave the room. I wanted to give you some time to rest."

She shook her head. "No. I don't want you to . . . sleep in there. I will. If you want to be away from me, I'll sleep in there. I can't have you leave . . . our bedroom." She folded her hands over her face as the enormity of what she'd done, long looming on the horizon and avoided in the thrumming machinery of the hospital, approached with immense weight.

"No, Amy. I'll stay in there for now."

She sat on the side of the bed next to him and held up her hand. "Can we talk?" She didn't know what she was going to say, she just had to say or do something.

"When you're ready."

"I'm ready." She dropped her hand.

He looked at her and shook his head. "No, you're not."

She choked on the coming tears. "I'm so sorry. I can't explain it. I don't know what happened. I didn't know where I was, who I was. I don't know how to tell you. . . . I don't know how to make it up. I don't know . . ." The old feeling—the one from her life before she was an adulteress—the feeling that she had to rush out the words, finish quickly or he wouldn't hear her, overwhelmed her.

Phil turned away from her and started to leave the room.

She wanted to scream, *Listen to me. Just listen to me.* But she didn't. She couldn't say it before—and didn't deserve to say it now.

He turned back to her. She didn't recognize his set, hard face.

"Listen, Amy. I told the kids and anyone who asked that you went to Oystertip for research, got confused and lost, then headed the wrong way in the marsh."

"Why? Why did you protect me like that?" She dropped her head back down.

"I wasn't protecting you. The truth is yours to tell if you want."

"You were protecting me."

"I was protecting me . . . the kids."

"Same thing."

He sighed. "Amy, the doc said you still need a lot of rest. I'll take Molly to tennis this afternoon. Go back to bed. I'll be in to check on you."

"I don't want to go to bed."

"Then read, rest. I have to go to work. I have to . . . leave."

"Of course you do." She sank into herself, leaned back on the pillows. Anger prodded her for recognition, but it was his turn to be angry—she had nothing to rage at; he was the offended one.

He left the room without kissing her, without touching her. She lay down on top of the unpacked pile of clothes and sleep crawled upon her. Phil had never, ever walked out of their bedroom without kissing her. Then again, she'd never run off and slept with an ex-lover.

She made an effort to piece together how she had arrived here; one step forward, back two, over one and here she was. She could only see betrayal in the looking back, not the stepping ahead; in the forward movement she had seen nothing but her own reasons.

She still couldn't believe she'd done it—the memory of it nothing more or less than the memory of other times with Nick, twenty-five years ago. The night on the island hid in shadow—in the same gauzelike, fragmented pictures as the memories of college: separate from her, part of her.

The phone screamed from across the room, across the shadows behind her eyelids. She sat up too fast, sending a shock wave of pain down her left side where the worst of the cuts were still raw. Oddly, the pain felt good. At least she felt it, knew she deserved it. For eighteen years she'd watched the way the late-afternoon light fell on the bed, on the pillows and on the scratched wooden floors; the amber light was the sign of evening. How long had she been asleep?

She reached for the phone, groaned as her sweater pulled a bandage loose. "Hello?"

"Mom? Did I wake you up?"

Jack's voice flowed across the line and instead of relief, she experienced a new and surging flood of guilt. "Hi, hon. No, I'm awake. Totally."

Jack laughed. "Don't lie, Mom."

Don't lie. Don't lie.

"Okay, so you woke me. But I'm glad to hear your voice. What's up?"

"I'm in between classes, but I wanted to check on you. Dad said he took you home today."

"I'm great. More important, how are you?"

"How in the world did you end up in the middle of the marsh? You're smarter than that."

Don't lie. Don't lie.

"I just got confused . . . very confused and lost."

"Okay . . ."

"So how are you?"

"Good. I hate my freakin' chemistry class. Lisbeth and I are totally over——she's dating some Sigma Nu geek."

"She's already dating someone else? I thought she was so heartbroken she couldn't eat, couldn't sleep, would wait until she was shriveled and old for you to come back to her."

Jack laughed, and for a moment she forgot her own pain as she submerged herself in her son's good humor. "That's what she said . . . dying, you know, just dying. But she found someone to relieve the pain, I guess."

"Well, that's not true love. You can't just . . . fall in love with someone else that quick—if it's real."

"That's exactly what I said."

"That's what . . ."

That's what Nick did, just fell in love with someone else. That's what I did.

The realization was so complete she almost spoke it out loud.

"I can't wait to see you this weekend. Study hard. I'll see you Friday night."

"Okay, Mom. Get some rest."

"I will."

"I love you, Mom."

Would he, if he knew what I had done?

"I love you too, Jack baby."

Chapter Twenty-nine

She was prolonging her illness, willingly settling into the mind-numbing darkness of sleep. But the looming guilt was more than she could bear. Phil avoided her; he left whatever room he was in whenever she entered it. Communication consisted of exchanges of facts and needed information.

A week passed in an aberrant mix of days and nights, but she allowed sleep to confuse her. Then she stared at the empty pillow next to her at five thirty Friday morning and figured it out: she'd work her way out of this hole, prove her worth. She rose from the bed, showered, ripped the bandages off her side and ignored the pain. No use in complaining about it; time to fix all this. Time to fix it.

She dressed in her pearl gray wool slacks with the matching blazer over a black V-neck sweater. She slid on gray suede pumps and walked to the kitchen to cook omelets, biscuits and sausage, squeeze fresh orange juice. She set the breakfast table with the fine china, brought out the real silver and cloth napkins—no eating at the breakfast bar in a hurry, no quick half-toasted bagels for Molly and Phil. She would labor her way out of this crisis and *make* Phil listen to her. She would prove her value and stamina; prove . . . she loved them. There was no other way for Phil to know, since she couldn't tell him; he wouldn't believe her.

Molly stumbled into the kitchen at six thirty, rubbing her eyes, pulling at the tank top of her pajamas.

"Mom, what are you doing? I don't have to get up for like another half hour and you are banging away down here, and you're all . . . dressed up. Did I miss something?"

"No, hon." She kissed Molly on the side of her mouth. "I just wanted to get up and cook you and Dad a special breakfast. I feel so much better . . . and I missed getting up with you."

"Wow. This is a lot of food." Molly looked around the kitchen, waved her hand over the table. "Is someone else coming or something?"

"No, it's for you and Dad."

"Jeez, I can barely choke down a Pop-Tart in the morning."

"Not this morning. We're all going to sit down and enjoy each other, enjoy breakfast. Then, starting today, I am going to clean out every single closet in the house—get our lives in order."

"Don't you dare touch my closet. No way."

"Hiding something, Molly?"

"No, I just have everything the way I like it. The last time you cleaned out my room, you threw away all the good stuff and kept all the stupid baby stuff. I never did find my bird's nest."

"It smelled."

"Just stay out of my room."

"No promises."

"I'm getting a lock and keeping the only key. Lucky Jack, you can't get into his dorm room."

"Go get ready for school. I'll wake Dad up for breakfast."

She dropped the last omelet on a vintage transfer-ware platter and placed it under the heating lamp. It felt good to use the dishes she usually saved for special occasions. She would begin her redemption right here, right now, and not stop until she had earned it.

She climbed the stairs, her high heels clicking on the hardwood, to the guest room door. She turned the handle; it was locked. She knocked gently.

"Yes?" His voice called from the bedroom, like an echo from far away.

"I cooked breakfast . . . I want you to come down to breakfast." Amy used a voice she hoped sounded normal, maybe even cheery.

Phil opened the door, his hair sticking up on one side, dark circles under his eyes, the impact of her betrayal on his face. Tears welled up in her eyes.

"I made . . . made breakfast."

He rubbed his cheeks. "I'm really not hungry. I have an early staff meeting."

"Can't you eat just a little? Sit down with me and Molly?"

"The staff meeting *is* a breakfast, Amy. You know—every Friday morning."

"Oh, yeah. Why do you have to be there so early today? Usually you don't have to go until seven or so—you have time to sit with us for a second."

"No, I have to lead the meeting. I have to be there early, and I'm already running late." He shuffled toward the guest bathroom. Her heart fell to the pit of her stomach in one long lurch as he entered a bathroom meant only for those who were transient. He turned his back on her and anything she had to say.

"You have to head up the meeting?" She wanted to hang

on for one more minute, talk him into staying—maybe even listening.

"Yes. I got a promotion last week—head of the division."

"Oh, Phil." She leaned toward him, instinct taking over; she reached to hug him. He stood with stiff arms, then patted her on the back.

"Congratulations. You didn't tell me. You—"

"I didn't want to disturb you."

"Okay. I'll cook us a huge celebratory dinner tonight. What do you want? Steak, shrimp, tenderloin? I'll whip up your favorite buttermilk pie. Jack's coming home tonight for the weekend. We'll have a big family dinner."

"I'm taking Jack camping tonight . . . I promised him."

"Well, then we'll all go. Family camping. We haven't done that in . . . years."

"No, Ame. I'm taking Jack. Listen, I have to shower. I'm late. Really . . . I'll talk to you after work today."

She went back to the kitchen and slumped in a pine ladder-back chair and listened to the whistle of the guest bathroom shower, to the opening and shutting of closets and doors. She knew the sound of each pipe, each creak of floor.

Molly bounced into the kitchen, grabbed a biscuit and kissed her on the head. "Bye, Mom. I'm going home with Cindy after school, spending the night. I'll call from her house. Love ya."

Amy smiled, nodded—nothing left to say. She pushed an omelet around the plate with her fork.

Phil shuffled into the kitchen and looked around, never at his wife. "Oh, Amy."

"Go on. I know you're late."

She didn't look up—her humiliation greater now than her need to see his face as he left the house. The door clicked shut and she stared out the kitchen window and noticed, again, the empty bird feeder. She rose from the chair, opened the storage closet, then yanked out a bag of bird seed, walked into the backyard, her heels spiking into the ground. She pulled down the bird feeder and filled it to the top, not caring about her suede pumps now coated with soil.

A cardinal perched on the top branch of the birch tree above looked down at her.

"I know, I know. I'm sorry. But here you go. I'm here now. I won't forget again."

She walked back into the kitchen, dumped the entire breakfast in the garbage disposal and cleaned the remnants of the uneaten feast. She stood back, surveyed her clean kitchen. "Okay," she said out loud. "We'll start with the linen closet."

Although she kept the house in almost pristine condition, she loved artifacts and mementos, so her closets and drawers overflowed with paraphernalia she thought she just might need one day, things she couldn't bear to throw away: old clothes, antique linens, papers, knickknacks and crafts.

The clothes and towels, the closet essentials of their lives, poured out from the hidden places and landed on the floor and on tables; she sorted them as if their family's collective life depended on how she organized them. If she was so messed up—surely she could fix this—at least this.

She was so intent on her work that the OWP group told her they rang the bell four times before she entered the foyer. She smiled at them when she opened the front door—poised and ready with the self she woke up with, the new self who would force redemption.

Norah, Revvy and Reese stared at her. They all opened their mouths as if to speak, but only stared.

"What?" She looked at them, tilted her head.

"Your clothes," Norah said and laughed.

She looked down; she was covered with dust, streaks of dirt smeared across her black sweater, and she had on only one shoe. "Oh, I've been cleaning out closets." She laughed, a coarse sound. "Come in, come in. What are y'all doing here?"

Norah held up a box. "We brought you dinner. We thought you were still—you know—confined to bed."

"You cooked me dinner?" Guilt rose.

Reese stepped up and touched the box. "Well, not exactly cooked. You wouldn't want that. But we did pitch in for it—all vegetarian, of course. Hope ya don't mind."

"No. No. You are so . . . sweet. Come on in. I have to warn you that it is a huge mess. Just step over the piles. I can't believe you drove all this way to bring me dinner."

"Mrs. Reynolds, are you sure you're supposed to be up like this?" asked Norah.

"Oh, yes."

They all looked at one another.

"Really," she said.

They followed her to the kitchen. "Sit, sit," she said and gestured toward the bar stools. "Hey, where's Brenton?"

"He couldn't bear to come with us."

"Why—can't stand to burn all that fossil fuel?"

"No—he didn't want to see your face when we told you about the island."

Instead of them sitting on a bar stool, she did—already defeated before the end of the conversation. Of course there would be bad news. Did she believe anything good could come of her actions?

"Go ahead, tell me."

"Well, it seems that we don't have enough evidence to get a Heritage Trust and they were a bit miffed by the fact that Nick broke into the house and illegally collected evidence."

"He didn't break into the house. He had a key. And"— she sighed—"it was both of us, not just Nick."

"Well, he told them you had no idea he was doing anything illegal—that it was all him."

"He protected me. Everybody's protecting me." She wanted to lie down on the kitchen floor and curl in on herself; she deserved nothing of the sort.

"Even if he had the key, I guess he got it—illegally. Not that we blame him—he was only trying to help," Revvy said.

"Have you talked to him?" she asked in a hoarse whisper, wanting and not wanting to know.

Norah took her hand. "No—he showed up for his hearing, so we didn't lose our bail money, and then he disappeared again. All the judge gave him was some community service, which he already does—land preservation on the barrier islands. He didn't want to talk to us—he waved, then left. Even his wife doesn't know where he is."

"I'm so, so sorry about all this. I really am," she said.

"Oh, Mrs. Reynolds, there's no reason to be sorry—you did all you could, and having Nick help us could have saved it," Revvy said.

"But it didn't."

"Well, I'm partly to blame. I lent him the boat and I knew what he was doing," Reese said.

"Did you get in any trouble?" She looked up at him.

"Nah, he protected me, too. Said he borrowed the boat from a friend without permission."

"I wish I could do something to fix this." She wished she could *do* something to fix everything. "Has the sale gone through?"

Norah sighed and leaned up against the kitchen counter. "Tomorrow they're going to close the deal. At least we'll find out who the buyer is."

"I wasn't much help, was I? Couldn't even find out who the buyer was."

"Oh, yes, yes, you were a huge help." Norah hugged her for the first time. "The gilded wallpaper and the Purbeck stone almost swayed them—I guess they're really valuable. But they said we used illegal means and there just wasn't enough evidence to warrant the amount of money it'd cost to buy the island."

"I'm sorry."

Revvy thumped her on the back—she considered this a hug. "Stop saying that. You did as much or more than we did. It just didn't work and that sucks."

"Yes, it does," she agreed.

The OWP walked out as a somber group and promised to contact her if they needed anything else in their efforts to protect the ACE basin. She opened the boxed dinner and smiled at the vegetarian lasagna, the whole-wheat bread and the largest chocolate chip cookies she'd ever seen. She picked up a cookie and took a huge bite, sat down on the bar stool and ate alone—feeling there was so much lost in all this mess, so much.

The kitchen side door shuddered open, caught on a pile of towels and stopped. Jack poked his head in the crack. "Hey, Mom?" He kicked the door open, spreading the neat pile of towels across the floor.

"Hey, bucko. Don't mess up my piles."

"What is all this?"

"I'm cleaning the house—the entire house."

"In a suit and high heels?"

"Don't mix those piles up. They're divided into 'give away,' 'sell,' and 'keep.' "

"Are you sure you're supposed to be up doing all this?"

"I feel great . . . fine. I'm going to fix everything."

"Okay . . ." Jack tilted his head.

"I have a month's leave of absence from work. I'm going to—"

"Where's Dad? Is he home from work yet?"

"Did you know he got a promotion?"

"Yeah, he told me last week."

She picked up the towels Jack had scattered and began to fold them. "Oh."

"Is he home or not?"

"No . . . not yet. I haven't heard from him all day." She turned away from Jack, from his eyes. The sound of the garage door opening and closing on its rusted track vibrated through the kitchen.

"Well, there he is now." She stood, smiled and smoothed the front of her black sweater. "Oh, my, I'm all wrinkled."

Jack laughed. "Gee, I wonder why." He swept his hand over the piles scattered across the kitchen floor, the kitchen table shoved against the wall.

"Tell your dad I'll be right out." She scurried toward the bedroom to change into something clean and ironed. The deep voices of her husband and son echoed across the house. She stared at her closet, at the pile of laundry. She pulled out a red sweater; it was wrinkled. She yanked a blue silk shirt from a hanger, but there was a crease right down the front. Finally she found a smooth brown cashmere sweater, tugged it over her head, and emerged from the closet.

She entered the hall; her smile fell before it fully crossed her face. The empty sound of the house told her; they were gone, had left without saying goodbye. She walked unsteadily into the kitchen, loneliness now settling deeper than she'd ever known.

She opened the door to the garage and stared at the empty space where Phil's car had been parked ten minutes before. He must have already been packed, ready to go. A slimy patch of oil shone under the fluorescent garage light.

"Well, then." She went into the kitchen, fished around under the sink and pulled out a bottle of Lysol, paper towels and a scouring pad. She walked back into the garage, squatted in the empty parking spot and scrubbed at the oil spot until clean gray concrete came through. She stood, smiled.

"Okay, fixed."

She dumped the cleaning supplies under the sink, stood in the pile-strewn kitchen. "Well, then. I guess I just need to iron all those wrinkled clothes now."

She walked through the house on her heels, into her closet to pluck down every single shirt she owned—then piled them according to color, material and texture. She grabbed the ironing board from behind the belt rack, then plugged in the iron—a wedding present that hadn't been used as often as the fine china. Her motto had been "If it needs ironing, it goes to the dry cleaners." But not now; now she would do everything correctly.

She began to iron one shirt at a time, beginning with white and moving to colors—bright to dark.

Chapter Thirty

"**I** told her."

"What?" Nick started at the sound of his wife's voice. He'd watched the house, assumed he'd correctly timed his visit to retrieve more clothes. Eliza was supposed to be at Alex's and Max's wrestling match. He turned from his dust-coated backpack lying on the Oriental carpet. He just needed clean underwear, clean shirts.

"I went to the hospital and told her."

"Told who what?"

"Amy—that you were drunk the night you ran over that woman. You left that part out, didn't you? You wanted her to believe you were the victim of some horrible twist of fate that took her away from you."

Nick stood, grabbed some clean shirts from a drawer. "No, I don't believe that, Eliza. I believe you took her away from me with your manipulative lies."

"If you want to hate me, if you want to believe that, you can convince yourself of it—but you know it's not completely true."

"Not completely true?" Nick spit in his anger, kicked a

wicker hamper across the floor. "Not all the way true? You lied to me for twenty-five years, let me believe she—"

"Say her name, say her name," Eliza whispered.

"Amy. Amy. You let me believe Amy didn't answer my telegrams, that you were the only one there for me. That you were the one who . . ." He turned to his backpack and shoved clothing into it.

"I *was* the one who was there for you. You lied to me, too."

"How?" He slammed his backpack onto the floor.

"I believed you were over her, that you loved me. That you . . . were here with us, with our family. But you weren't. The whole time you were waiting, wondering about her."

Nick leaned down and grabbed his bag, threw it over his shoulder.

"Where are you going?" Eliza asked.

"I don't know."

"What if I . . . what if the kids have to get ahold of you?"

"I have my cell phone."

"I've tried that."

"Leave a message. I'll get it."

"Nick . . . please. Can't we talk?"

"Not now. No." He walked past his wife, down the hall, then stood in the foyer. His two sons' wrestling duffel bags sat beside the front door. He reached down, touched the bags. He'd missed four wrestling meets since all this started; he'd never missed anything for his sons. He blamed this on Eliza—her lies. He kicked the front door open, walked to his pickup truck.

He was frantic with the need to know if Amy was okay, to find out why she'd left him in the middle of the night.

He alternated between believing she'd told her family she loved him and believing she hated him, hated what he'd become to her.

He shoved a hand in his pocket, fingered the necklace he'd found on the beach while looking for her. He wanted to hand it back to her, see her, hear her.

In the week and a half since the night with Amy, he'd been camping out on Oystertip. He was taking a chance, but getting caught trespassing paled in comparison to his need to be alone in the last place he'd been with Amy. He'd been paddling a kayak back and forth and he'd planted his tent in the thick brush, where passersby wouldn't find him unless they knew to look for him.

Amy had come home from the hospital; he'd called the nurses' desk so many times that they knew his name and always told him how she was, when she left. He'd driven past her house five, maybe six times now in the past week, but couldn't tell if anyone had been home. He would go today—give it one more try before heading back to Oystertip—an island he'd believed would bring her back to him.

When he'd first seen the island, he had become convinced their mutual work would save it, and that all his wishes, hell, his prayers, had been answered. Fate had finally intervened; she also had to see it. And for the briefest time she had seen it. He just had to make her see and know their destiny again.

Lost in his thoughts, he found he was already in Darby, driving past the house he had memorized: the gingerbread trim on the front porch, the frozen ferns in the front planters, the curtain pulled further open on the right window than the left, the front-porch light that remained on all the time.

The garage was open, empty save for Amy's SUV. Nick looked at the truck's clock: ten fifteen in the morning. It was time.

He pulled the truck up to the curb and parked, opened the driver's-side door, then shut it with a soft push. He didn't want to make a single noise to startle her, to make her scurry to the far corners of the house where he couldn't reach her. He walked to the front porch and stood for a minute, breathing in, out. He lifted his hand and knocked.

No sound came from the house: no footsteps, no muffled music wafting through the front door's glass side panels. He took a deep breath, knocked again, more forcefully this time.

"I'm coming . . . coming." Amy opened the door, pushing something aside with her foot. She glanced up. Only silence dropped from her open mouth.

"Say something. Anything," Nick said.

"What . . . what are you doing here?" She glanced outside, motioned for him to come in, then shut the door behind him. "You can't . . . come here. I thought you were my neighbor bringing dinner. They've all organized dinners. How humiliating is that?"

He reached out to touch her; she backed away from him.

She held up her hand to stop him. "Yes, sir. The entire town believes that I got lost in the woods trying to save our precious earth. They believe this because it's what Phil told them. So they come by with dinners and flowers and books and . . . sympathy. I want to scream at them, tell them I don't deserve their dinners . . . that I can't eat their food, because I have a rock where my stomach used to be. . . ."

"Amy." He took a step forward, reached for her.

"Why are you here?"

"I have to know exactly what happened to you. I've been sick with worry. I have to know."

"All that knowing—all that wondering . . . wanting to know why you left, why you never came back, why you still loved me. Knowing. *Damn* knowing." She bowed her head.

Nick moved toward her again. If he could just touch her. . . . He whispered, scared that she might disappear. "It's more than just knowing."

"Well, now I *know*, don't I? Yep, found out what I really am." She looked up at him. "You know, I really, truly thought I was a great person. Good wife, good mother—all of it—the whole package."

"You are."

She held up her hand again. "Let me finish. You are so . . . overwhelming, and I have so much trouble separating your feelings from my own. So you have to listen to mine. To me. And I'm still confused about this part—about how something that used to be so good and right could dredge up the most terrible part of me, expose all the rotten pieces of me. Look at me—I never even thanked you for saving my life."

"That's it. All the good and right things about us—"

"Nick, stop."

"Okay, okay." He loved her; he would grant her whatever she asked of him.

She held her palms upward, as if showing him something she'd hidden in her hands. "You've always been . . . too much. Too much of everything. And I remembered that, and the feeling and the knowing, and I got lost. So lost. And I'm trying to find my way back, find out who I really am, because I am definitely not as good as I thought."

She turned away from him and kicked a pile of clothes

from the bottom of the stairs, sat on the bottom step, and dropped her face into her hands.

"So lost," she mumbled into her palms.

He sat next to her, placed his hand on her knee. "I'm here. You're not lost."

"Yes, I am." She looked up.

Weakness and nausea enveloped Nick as he saw she was gone from him. "No, you're not. Us, how we were together, that is not lost—that is found," he said.

"How . . . how can it be? How can that be . . . right?"

"Because we're supposed to be together."

"That is a worn-out excuse for what we did."

He touched her face. "Don't you still . . . want this?"

"No."

"Yes, you do. I know you do."

"This time you're wrong."

"I can't be. I felt you. I know."

"It's almost like—I don't know how to explain this—but it's almost as if in fulfilling all that . . . want, I killed it. And there's something else. . . ."

"What is it?"

She looked up and for an instant her face was alive again, full—and he thought it was for him, of him, until she spoke.

"You lied," she said.

"What? Not to you."

"Yes, to me. You didn't tell me you were . . . drunk . . . the night you ran over that woman. That Eliza protected you."

"I was not drunk. I'd been drinking, yes. But I was perfectly capable of driving. That woman walked out in front of the car—drunk as hell. I didn't hit her because I was drunk or driving crazy. She walked out. In front. Of. My. Truck. I did not lie to you."

He panicked, desperate; Amy saw something in him that was *not* wholly true: that he was a drunk who ran over and killed a woman, that he was a killer because of a bottle of tequila. A long time ago it was what he'd believed of himself too . . . back when Amy didn't answer the telegrams, when his life had spiraled down to the echoing loneliness of knowing he was responsible for where he was—jail—and why.

"Amy, I did not—*did not*—run over her because I was drunk. Shit, I spent a year in jail for it . . . and she was the one staggering across the road. Yes, I killed her. I ran over her. I drove the truck. I spent a year in jail, thinking you deserted me because of it. You don't think I've had enough guilt over that? Enough pain? You want me to relive it—go back to Costa Rica and tell her family, tell the police that I had a little celebratory tequila before driving six students home?"

"No, I don't want that. No. I wanted to know everything. God, I just wanted to know everything, and you left that part out. It's all just so terrible . . . so sad."

"Would it have made a difference in your feelings? If it had, it would have been exactly what I thought then, anyway. Just coming full circle twenty-five years later."

"No, I don't think it would've made a difference in how I feel. . . . Oh, my God, what have I done? Nothing is what I thought . . . *I'm* not what I thought."

"Yes, you are . . ."

"No. No." Her body shook as she wept.

He touched her hair. "Please don't cry, Amy. Please. It breaks my heart in a thousand places. I came to make sure you're okay . . . to tell you I'm here, that I still love you. It was not just a random night in a deserted house to me. . . . You've owned my heart since you fell through the doorway at that fraternity party."

She looked up and he saw her face broken in as many places as his heart. He grabbed her shoulders and pulled her to him; she leaned away.

"Nick, go home to your family."

"I can't."

"The OWP is looking for you. You can't just disappear—they bailed you out of jail. God, because of me you had to go to jail again. Eliza is looking for you."

"I wish you were looking for me. I've been camping out on Oystertip—"

"You'll get arrested again. Go home."

"No, I won't. I can't go home."

"Are you staying in that cold, empty house?"

"No, I'm camping out in the woods. Directly underneath a magnificent osprey nest. And every minute I want you there."

"If you love me—if you really love me—you'll leave right now and let me find my own way out . . . of this lost place. I can't find it with you. . . ."

He reached into his pocket for the necklace: his last hope. "I brought this back to you."

He held it out to her, his hand uncurled, open.

She stood, backed into the far wall, tripped. "No." She grabbed on to the hall table.

"It's yours."

She walked toward the front door, opened it. "You have to leave. I can't . . ."

He trudged to the front door, his feet heavy with the burden of leaving. "It's under there. Under all this pain is what you know and feel for us."

She didn't answer, but held the door open.

"Say something," he said.

"Goodbye, Nick. I'm sorry for all this . . . I am. I'm sorry

I brought us to this place. I'm sorry you went back to jail. I'm sorry we lost the island. I'm sorry I was not stronger, wiser."

He held out his hand one more time, the pendant dangling between his fingers. "Please take this."

"I can't. I can't."

He released the chain and it slithered to the hall floor. "I'll be waiting for you. I always have been and I will now."

She shut the door; the locks clicked against the door, against his heart.

"What are you doing? What is all . . . this?

Amy sat on top of Jack's old jeans, shirts and unmatched socks, her head buried in her knees. She hadn't moved from the foyer floor since Nick had left. She placed her chin on top of her knees and looked up at Phil.

"Amy, are you okay? What are you doing?" He gestured toward the piles. "What is all this?"

She stared at him.

"Get up."

She stood and faced him. There was so much she needed to say to him—so many words of apology and remorse that she didn't know where to begin. It seemed there were years of words stored below the unheard ones—the silence of being ignored—and she just didn't know what to tell him first, everything she'd ever wanted to say jumbled together in a screaming crowd.

"Will you please move back in our room? Please?" Pleading came first and tears formed when she had thought she had no more.

"No . . . you aren't ready."

"Stop saying that. Stop saying it's me." She stood and grabbed Phil's arm. "That's not what I meant to say. I just want you to . . . hear me."

"Hear you?"

She sighed and shuddered. "Yes."

"Go ahead, Amy. Go ahead." He turned and his face was set, his teeth rubbing back and forth as his jawline tensed from one side to the other.

There he was—ready to listen, and when she opened her mouth nothing came out.

"What is it?" he asked.

And she resorted to ingrained habit—letting him take care of everything. "What can I do? I just can't stand this."

Phil leaned down suddenly and picked up a neatly stacked pile of clothes, then another, and flung them across the foyer. Clothes scattered on the floor, on the steps, the entrance of the parlor.

He looked at her. "What can you do?" He reached down into a box of discarded books and grabbed a Stephen King hardcover, heaved it across the foyer. He bent to pick up another book as the first one slammed into the mirror over the hall table. Glass shards flew onto the floor, onto the table, across Jack's old clothes.

He turned to her, held a large dictionary above his head. "There is nothing, nothing you can *do*. You already did it."

He reached his arm behind him like a pitcher ready to release a fastball, tossed the book against the steps. The binding of the dictionary popped and pages fluttered to the floor.

She stared at the pieces of shattered mirror, broken pieces of her home on the floor: shattered and broken family. Rage washed over his face, his body; the waves of it reached her and she covered her face with her hands.

"Stop. Just listen to me. *Just listen to me*." She spoke the words she'd wanted to say a thousand times, a million times, and like stagnant water released from a cracked dam, the phrases came pouring out. "I'm sorry. I got lost . . . lonely and I didn't mean to do this. God, I am so sorry and alone. I just wanted someone to listen, to understand . . . to—I don't know. And there he was. There he was—all listening and helping and understanding, and I got lost in it, in the past. It's not an excuse—I just want you to hear it. It has nothing to do with how much I love you—or Molly and Jack."

"Bullshit." It was the first time he'd ever cursed at her. "It has everything to do with how much you love us. How . . . how in the hell could you do this to us? To them . . . to me?"

She was desperate to have him understand what even she did not. "I never told you about Nick."

"Why not?" He kicked the base of the stairs.

"It was a terrible memory . . ."

"I would've listened."

"I was . . . scared to tell you. Too much time had passed and it didn't seem important to . . . us." She looked away as she began to speak of Nick to her husband for the first time. "I dated him in college—for years. Then he went on a preservation trip."

"To Costa Rica."

"Yes. And he never came back and I never knew why. That was twenty-five years ago—and it was awful. I dropped out of school that semester."

"When we started dating."

"Yes."

"Where was he?"

Amy told her husband the story—Eliza's version, and how Eliza saved but also deceived Nick.

Phil leaned against the hall table as if the story had drained him of his remaining anger. "When did you find out about all this?"

"When I saw him . . . at the lake, he asked why I never came when he was in jail. Then I slowly learned the story and it all came rushing back at me. All the things I'd thought I'd forgotten or stored away came back."

"You love him."

"I did." She'd already lost everything and now only truth remained. "But I *love* you. I do. I got caught in some whirlwind, something . . . lost from the past. I'm more than sorry, but I can't find another word. I don't know how many times I can say it, but however many times there are, I will. I didn't mean to. I didn't plan to . . . I promise. I was feeling so ignored and . . . extraneous and there he was—there was everything I'd thought I lost a long, long time ago."

"Ignored? You felt ignored? Give me a break. Don't I take care of everything? *Everything?*"

"Listen to me. This is not about you taking care of everything. This is not about your valor and your responsibility to the family. This is about the horrible part of me that said my behavior was justified because you didn't care about what I care about—that I felt you never listened to me or took more than the three minutes required for me to tell you the facts and schedule of the day."

He held up his hand. "I don't want to hear the details, the excuse of how you didn't plan this . . . how it just happened. It's vulgar."

"Please. Please listen." God, how many times had she asked him to listen? It was sounding pitiful to her own ears.

"Stop." He turned and kicked at another pile of clothing.

"Even now—when it is more important than ever that you listen to me—you won't. When our family and our life hinges on you listening to me—you still won't." She was screaming now. "I'm sorry. I'm sorry. I didn't plan on this and it is more than I can even understand of myself and—"

A flash of silver gleamed from under the pile he'd just kicked. Her stomach lurched up, forward: the discarded necklace.

Phil leaned down and picked it up. "What is this?"

"He was here today . . . came today." She had nothing left in her but the truth.

"Son of a bitch." He turned to her, the necklace dangling between his fingers. "Some guy from your past comes sauntering in like a beer-drinking frat boy, all cool and tall and suave, and you forget everything. Me, Molly, Jack."

"It wasn't like that. I thought he left . . . and then I found out—"

"I don't give a shit. I don't care what you did or did not know. You allowed him to come in here and destroy us."

Destroy us. She heard the words and fought against them.

"I made him leave. I told him to leave and never come back. He didn't destroy us. I made him go . . . told him I loved *you.*"

Phil looked down at the necklace in his hand and held it out. And for the second time that day, she refused to take it.

Phil dropped it on the hall table and turned away.

She shuddered. "Don't go. . . ."

"I'll go pick up Molly from tennis, bring her home for dinner." He walked away from her.

"Phil."

He stopped. "What?"

"What can I do? What can I do to prove to you . . . ?"

"Nothing. There is nothing you can do."

And the words were so hopeless, so full of uncompromising authority; she slumped back onto the clothes, empty. If there was nothing she could *do* . . . what then?

Chapter Thirty-one

The emotional elements of the family became more than Amy could face, so she lost herself in the material aspects of their life. Closets, organization, facts—these became her primary concern. She sat on the foyer floor, folding the last strewn pile from Phil's and her fight three days before—she had been dodging the evidence from the afternoon her husband told her there was nothing she could do. Although she'd immediately cleaned up the broken mirror, she'd been avoiding the rest of the mess in the foyer: the scattered books, the clothes and the necklace. Now she would pack them away. She lifted the necklace from the table and held it up to the light, then opened the drawer to the hall table and stuffed it into the dark.

The front door opened with the slam of the drawer. She turned to see Carol Anne standing in the threshold, stepping over a pile of clothes and waving the *Darby Chronicle* in her face. "Look, look at this." Amy was not in the mood to read the local gossip of who had won the track meet, or how the fund-raising for the new flower bed in front of the courthouse was going. She turned away from Carol Anne. "I've got so much to do here."

"Take a break, come here. You'll work yourself to death and nothing will be solved." She walked into Amy's office, she sat on the edge of the flowered chaise and patted the seat next to her. "Sit."

Amy did. Carol Anne handed her the paper, and Amy looked down at the front page: DARBY WOMAN SACRIFICES TO SAVE DOOMED ISLAND. Amy looked up. "What is this?"

"Read it."

The story told of how she'd been working to save the small island and house from development, and then how she'd gone to the island with a group called the Oystertip Wilderness Protectors and become lost in the maze of marsh while collecting samples to prove the property should be saved. A chart listed the attributes and species of the island.

She looked up at Carol Anne. "I can't read any more of these lies."

"They're not all lies. You did try hard to save it. Keep reading."

The article revealed that the sale had closed that week and the island was now lost to the development of a personal home and playground for a local descendant of a Darby founder—Mr. Farley, a hometown man.

She gasped and looked up at Carol Anne. "Farley?"

"Yes. Do you believe it?"

"God, yes, I do. No wonder he hates me. I thought it was because you were my friend."

The article ended by discussing how she'd been working against him without knowing who he was, how she almost lost her life, only to then lose the doomed island. She was painted as a folk hero, while Mr. Farley came across as the evil villain.

"Good Lord," Amy said.

"You should see it. There are demonstrations outside his building—hate mail pouring into the newspaper. He's a pariah."

"Carol Anne—it's not right. They believe something . . . that isn't true."

"Amy." Carol Anne touched her face, grabbed her hand. "You did everything you could to save it. It *is* right. They don't need to know everything that happened the last time you were out there. You think this town doesn't have secrets? You think everyone you see on the street or in the market doesn't have something they don't want you to know—that would kill them if you found out?"

"But that is them. This is me and they"—she waved the paper—"have me out to be some bizarre hero, while I cheated on my husband." She choked on the words and started to sob.

Carol Anne wrapped her arms around her. "How is Phil?"

"He's here, but he won't really talk to me—just once and it was a disaster. How can I blame him? Damn, he never talked anyway. How could I expect him to listen to me now?"

"Because it's important, that's why."

"What if he leaves?"

"He won't leave. He'll do what he considers the right thing."

"I don't want it to be a responsibility, for God's sake."

"He loves you. He'll stay for that, too."

"If he loved me, he'd talk about it—he'd listen to me."

"You can't expect him to change just like that—to hear what you have to say when he's hurt and pissed off and—"

"Betrayed."

"Yeah, that, too."

"What if he never listens? What if he walks around acting cold and fulfilling his responsibilities, but never—"

"He will. He loves you."

"I don't know, Carol Anne. I don't know."

Amy crumpled up the newspaper and threw it on the floor.

Carol Anne pulled her closer. "Well, you did accomplish one thing. Who in the living island would have thought it would be you and your passion for saving things that would finally turn the town of Darby against Farley?"

Amy wanted to laugh, but she couldn't find her sense of humor beneath the tears. She leaned into Carol Anne and allowed herself to be held.

Friends dropped by with dinners, believing Amy was still in bed with the lingering effects of her brave act. Amy thought that if they knew what she really suffered from—a betraying soul—they would never bring another bite. She wandered the house attempting to fill her days with more than the ache of her own sin.

The guest room appeared completely occupied by Phil—full of his belongings and smelling of him. Every morning after he left for work, she stood in the middle of the room and inhaled his scent, pushed her face into the pillow where he laid his head at night. He wasn't sleeping well, although each evening he disappeared into the room as soon as was acceptable or as soon as Molly escaped to her own room. The telltale signs of fatigue lay on his face like a road map.

SCAD hired a substitute teacher for the remainder of the semester, leaving Amy to wander her house during the day, cook meals that brought them all to the table at night—

although both Molly and Phil scattered to the far corners of their own world as soon as the dishes were done.

She received calls from Norah, Brenton, Revvy and Reese, all congratulating her on her role as the champion of ill-fated Oysterip Island. Molly had brought home the newspaper and waved it around the kitchen like a flag of victory.

But the island was still lost to development, Nick was lost in his own anguish and she had lost everything positive she'd once believed about herself. Phil was lost to her and she could see nothing good in any of it.

She sat at the kitchen table, staring at her mug of cold tea—the one she'd made an hour ago and not yet drunk a sip of—and she thought of the stashed telegrams in the tampon box. She hadn't touched or read the notes since coming home from the hospital; it was time to take them out, discard them. They didn't belong in her home or in her life.

They were crumpled pieces of paper that represented so much more than just a bad Christmas party, a "could-have-been" with an old boyfriend. The telegrams now symbolized the possibility of an entirely different life—one not lived, but one that somehow existed nonetheless: a life with Nick. If all the dark places inside of her had risen to be exposed and destroyed, so must these papers.

Anger swelled, ballooning in her belly, and then sinking into her with an added weight. She ran down the hall into her bathroom, leaned down to the cabinet. She dropped to her knees and threw open the cabinet door hard enough to bang against the wall, dent the plaster. She threw the shampoo bottles, old hairbrushes and unused curling iron onto the tile floor.

She ripped the yellowed papers from the tampon box and held them up to the light: the damned telegrams. How in the hell could three small pieces of paper change destinies, destroy families? She scrunched the papers into a ball. She kicked the cabinet shut, stomped out of the bathroom, back through her home to the kitchen.

She opened the pantry door, then pulled out Phil's barbecue lighter. She sat down at the kitchen table, plopped the papers next to her tea mug. She smoothed the papers before she read them one last time.

Not once since Nick had returned to her life had she tried to imagine what it would have been like if she'd received these messages twenty-five years ago. She'd only focused on feeling what she'd felt then, in college, letting herself be surrounded by the stored blood and muscle memories of Nick.

Now she attempted to reimagine her life from the day she would have received the first telegram. She tried to picture herself flying to Costa Rica, attempting to save Nick, to release him from jail. What would it have been like if she had been unable to free him? What if even now he was still in jail for vehicular homicide?

And what of Jack and Molly? They would not exist. Phil would not love her. *No.* It was impossible to imagine a different life built from one pivotal moment, from one fork in the road.

She reread the first telegram and allowed one last imagining of what Nick felt when she did not respond. She lifted the paper, raised Phil's lighter and flicked it on, touched it to the corner of the paper. The note lit quickly as if it was more than ready to combust. She allowed the ashes to fall to the kitchen table, and as the flames reached the edges of her fingers, she dropped the remains into her mug, where the ashes floated to the top of the cold liquid.

She lifted the second telegram and it burst into flames as

she lit the paper; then she dropped its remnants on top of the other. She lifted the last note—the one that declared his love for her even as he believed she had deserted him. She read that final message: *Amy, I love you, Nick*, as the flames licked each word, as they were consumed into an irrevocable fire. The paper curled, and then disintegrated, matching the ashes of her life.

She stood and walked to the sink, poured the liquid into the garbage disposal. She turned the faucet on and the ashes and tea floated down the drain. She rubbed her hands across her jeans and felt oddly cleansed, as if she'd just taken Communion.

She walked up the stairs to the hall; two closets stood sentinel at either end, the only ones left to be cleaned out. She opened the scratched wooden door to the one next to Molly's room. Carved into the wood with Daddy's pocketknife was MOLLY, slanted and crooked, from the summer she was five years old and first learned to spell her name, then wrote it on everything. Amy ran her finger over the letters. She had plopped Molly in an hour of time-out, lectured the wide-eyed girl about having respect for the house, about defacing the handmade door.

She desperately wished she could hold her five-year-old again. A deep longing for *then,* when none of this had happened, when she hadn't wandered lost into the land of wanting to know about Nick, overwhelmed her. She lifted a pile of Molly's old Cinderella sheets, buried her face in them, and fought back tears. She opened her eyes and automatically sorted the towels and sheets—knowing instinctively which ones to keep or discard.

She emptied everything out of the closet except for the boxes and shoes. In the back corner, underneath a boot box, she spied a pink silk jewelry box she'd given Molly for her tenth birthday. She yanked it from the bottom of the closet and lifted it to her face, rubbed the worn silk across her cheek. She remembered that when you raised the top, a small, rail-thin ballerina would pirouette in endless circles on one toe. Once upon a time, the ballerina would dance around and around while Molly organized her ten-year-old's jewelry, hid her favorites under the pink flannel false bottom.

Molly had been so excited to have her own jewelry box, but she'd been even more excited about her first piece of jewelry: a small silver cross she'd found in the bottom of her mother's jewelry box.

Amy took a quick breath.

She'd given it to Molly. She hadn't lost it.

She pulled at the false bottom, yanked the square out with a cloud of dust as a fake pearl flew from the side of the box. She scooted out to the light and stared into the cushion of cotton on the bottom. There it was: her necklace, her cross. What she thought she'd lost was still there.

She picked up the chain and held it to the light. A sudden discernment came with a wave of nausea, a flash of silver: what she'd been looking for all along was not Nick, not what they'd had, but the part of her that was once with him, the pieces of herself that she'd sequestered when he'd left her. She hadn't lost Nick, she hadn't lost her small silver cross—she'd given them away.

I lost . . . me.

The thought was as clear as the silver cross dangling from her fingers. She stood and ran down the stairs, looked up at the clock: six in the evening. Phil would be home soon.

She sat at the kitchen table, the old necklace held lightly between her fingers, and waited.

*   *   *

Phil walked in the side door from the garage, looked at her. She stood and went to him. The sides of his eyes were crinkled, his head tilted in question. She held up her hand, held up the cross and threw her arms around her husband's neck.

"It was me . . . me I lost. It wasn't anything else. It was never him."

Phil pulled away from her. "What?"

She took a deep breath. Of all the things he should hear—he had to hear this. "There is a part of me that I still have . . . the part I thought I lost is still here." She held up her necklace. "The part of me that doesn't love just for safety, but loves the way I once loved him—recklessly, with all of me—the part of me that loves you and Molly and Jack—is still here. It's not Nick I love. He just made me remember . . . it's not him at all."

Phil crossed his arms as a shield across his chest and backed further away. "We were safe . . . just safe . . . ?"

"No, Phil, that is not it. *I* was trying to be safe, afraid that if I loved with all of me, I'd get hurt, abandoned again. I know I'm not making any sense, and you still may not be able to hear it, but of all things—I need you to understand how much I love you and Molly and Jack."

He closed his eyes and turned away. "Go ahead. I'm listening. I don't understand what you're saying, but go ahead."

"I got lost. I thought that part of me was gone and that I needed to get it from somewhere . . . else. And now I know. I was out *there* looking for what is already *here* in me, with me."

"Lost—where Amy, where?" He slammed the counter with his fist. "In the marsh, in the woods, in him, in what, for God's sake?"

"I don't know how to explain it. I got lost in remembering that *other* Amy, the one who loved like that. And I thought it was him. . . you know? That it was all wrapped up in him—but it was in me . . . still in me. I never lost it or even gave it to him—"

"You think it's that simple? You find an old necklace . . . tell me you got lost, just old memories . . . that it's that simple and the explanation will cure everything?"

"No . . . God, no. I don't think it's simple at all. I'm trying to explain. I'm standing here, humiliated, ashamed, knowing you'll never believe in me the same way, that I'll never think the same of myself. I'm standing here knowing all the terrible parts of me are showing and I'm so scared that you'll never love me again. I'm trying to find my way back to something I don't deserve—that I know I don't deserve—and I'm asking you to see . . . to listen. I'm trying to show you why and how I got lost. To ask you to forgive me."

The front door slammed and Molly's footsteps pounded up the stairs on the other side of the house. Phil looked at Amy, whispered, "What you did . . . It can never be the same."

"I know. Don't you think I know that? It couldn't be the same, because if the bad stuff—if what I did—doesn't matter, then the good stuff doesn't matter, either. And it all matters, it all counts—all of it. I chose you—then and now—and I choose you and it all counts: you, Jack, Molly, me—we all matter."

Phil turned away from her and leaned against the counter; his shoulders sagged. She touched his back. He turned to her. "I don't know. I just don't know."

She nodded and touched his cheek.

Molly ambled into the kitchen. "Mom, what in the world did you do in the hall upstairs?"

Amy went to Molly and hugged her. "I found your Cinderella sheets."

Molly laughed. "Oh, great. I'll just pack them for college now."

Amy held up her hand. "Look what else I found. It was in your old pink jewelry box."

"Your necklace that you gave me—that's what you were looking for?"

"Yes. Yes, I guess I was."

Nick slammed the front door, then walked into the living room. Eliza was bent over a sewing machine, hemming Alex's school-uniform khakis. She didn't look up.

"Eliza," he said loudly.

She didn't respond.

"Eliza." He slammed his hand on the sewing machine, knocked the pants to the floor.

She looked up at him. "What is it, Nick?"

"I haven't been home in three weeks and that's all you have to say?"

"I don't know what else to say." Tears filled her eyes.

Sorrow washed over him; the pain he'd caused was evident everywhere he turned—his own shattered heart, Eliza's anguish, Amy's broken spirit. He didn't know if he could look at any more of the havoc his desire had wreaked. He asked what he'd come to find out—it seemed vital to resolving the situation.

"Eliza, why do you love me?"

"I always have."

"That is not what I asked."

She threw the khakis on the couch and stood. "Why do I need to answer that? You left—why do I need to answer that question?"

"I need to know."

"I don't know, Nick. I love your strength. I love your eyes. I love . . . Why are you making me say this? It hurts."

He grabbed her shoulders. "I want to know why. If you think I'm so terrible—a killer . . ."

"I never, ever said that."

"You've said it without saying it. Tell me out loud, then—do you think I would have missed that woman if I hadn't been drinking?"

"I don't know."

"Answer me. Do you think I would've killed her if I'd been sober?" He squeezed her shoulders, each word a staccato beat.

She lifted her hand and pushed his hands off her shoulders. "No. I don't think you would've hit her if you'd been . . . sober."

"So you think I killed her because of my drinking? That the other six of you who also drank the shots of tequila that night weren't responsible at all?"

"That is not what you asked. I protected you because of that. So did they. You asked a question. I answered it. I don't have anything left to give. And I need you to leave. I don't want you here if you don't want to be here. Go to her. Leave."

She turned away from him and sat back down at the sewing machine.

"Nick, why do *you* love *me?*" she asked without looking up.

"What?"

She kept her face down. "Only fair—you asked me. Why do you love me?"

He backed away. He had no answer at all.

She stood and grabbed his arm. "You want to know

why? I'll tell you why. Because I love you—completely. You only loved me for the way I loved you. You never really loved me back. You only loved what I did for you— how *I* loved *you*."

The bitter taste of truth rose in the back of his throat; he was ashamed, humiliated that Eliza had to be the one to tell him this truth. He had never been able to accurately define his feelings, but even he had not recognized this fact. His love was built on the fragile basis of how she loved him. He turned away from her.

"When you found out that I hid the telegrams, you believed I screwed up, and the last of your love for me disintegrated. Do you know how exhausting it's been all these years, trying so damn hard not to screw up so that you'd keep on loving me?" She choked on a sob. "Go, Nick. Now."

Her footsteps echoed up the stairs as she walked away. "Eliza." Her words wrapped around his throat and sorrow rose.

"Go, Nick."

He turned away from his wife, walked to the front door of his house and kicked the baseboard as the smells and sights of his home assaulted him with blinding force.

He walked out the front door, across the lawn to the driveway, and climbed into his pickup truck. He sat for a long time, head back against the headrest. Eliza had told the truth, and it was humiliating, distasteful. He could rationalize his yearning for Amy, but Eliza's declaration of how little he actually loved her, how poorly he'd loved, mortified him.

Now he knew what his wife had said when she'd first discovered Amy Reynolds was Amy Malone, the words she'd mumbled as she'd walked into the bathroom. He heard them now as plainly as if she spoke them into the window of his truck. *Now we'll pay for what we've done.*

And he was paying now, wasn't he? For killing a woman, for never truly loving his wife, for loving another man's wife.

Eliza was paying for her manipulation and lies.

Amy paid for all of them with her wounded spirit and shattered family.

Guilt consumed him, and he bent over with the force of it. The two things he'd avoided most of his life—how he loved and blood guilt—now sat in the cab with him as unwanted guests; he turned to them, acknowledged them.

Chapter Thirty-two

A push of Amy's feet kept the porch swing floating back and forth with the wind on a balmy Saturday afternoon. Jack and Molly were home and their hollers and footsteps sounded out the open upstairs window in a muffled song of family. The air was warm and clean after a two-day rain. Phil had opened all the windows as spring teased them with its late arrival. The daffodils he and Molly had planted last year poked their heads out, opening their petals to the sun.

She closed her eyes and listened to the sounds of her family, to the pleasant dissonance of the various birdcalls. Hope—that was what she felt. Spring represented hope. The undercurrent of sorrow beneath her breast would be a constant reminder of what she'd done, of how she'd almost discarded her soul in a search that ended on her front porch. Yet spring and hope both existed.

Carol Anne's car pulled up to the curb. She jumped out and waved at Amy, then leaned into the backseat and pulled out a pile of papers.

She climbed the steps to the porch and sat down next

to Amy, dropped her parcel on the porch. "I need your help."

"You got it. What do you need?"

"Okay, here's the deal. A client just hired me to do her new home—"

"How? You didn't go back to Farley, did you?"

"Nope—it's a brand-new customer. Never used Farley—he can't go after me. And—get this—this client was referred to me by one of Farley's clients. Oh, if he only knew . . ." She looked up to the sky. "Anyway—it's the Picker house on Fourth."

"The old neoclassical building on the corner?"

Carol Anne smiled and stomped her foot. "You got it, darlin'."

"What a coup. That is awesome! I told you it would work out—I told you." Tears filled Amy's eyes. "What do you need from me?"

"Well, it's more than a little favor—they want to restore it to its original look. And I can't really help them without my best friend."

"The entire house?"

"Yes, and I promised them it would be authentic right down to the last banister."

"Yes, yes, I'll help. What, are you kidding?"

"Okay, that took a lot of convincing."

"You know how much I love doing this. It'll be perfect. You'll make sure it looks good and I'll make sure it's accurate."

"Exactly."

Amy hugged her, then reached down for the papers. She opened the first folder and sighed at a picture of the front entryway. "This needs wrought iron."

"Oh, this is gonna be fun," Carol Anne said as a truck rumbled by. "Who is that?" She pointed to a dark blue van pulling up to the curb.

"Darby Youth Foundation. I'm donating all those boxes in the hall."

Amy stood to wave at the large man who jumped down from the driver's seat. She winced as the bruised rib on her left side sent out a searing pain, reminding her that all wounds take time to heal. She had to give Phil time. And she would.

There was, as he said, nothing she could *do.*

The man from the van stepped up to the porch. "Hello there. I'm Mr. Adams from the Darby Youth Foundation to pick up your donations."

She opened the front door and swept her hand across the boxes in the hall. "All this is yours."

"All these? You want me to take all these?" He leaned against a porch pillar.

"Yes. The whole shebang."

"Looks like you're moving."

"No, just cleaning out stuff I don't need anymore."

The man hitched his fingers into the straps of his overalls. "Okay, then. This'll take me a while."

"I'll help you." Amy picked up a box.

Carol Anne grabbed another box. "I'll help, too. Let's get this stuff out of here."

Molly and Jack came down the stairs. Jack threw a bag over his shoulder and moved toward the van.

Those who loved her still surrounded her, she realized. She was humbled.

"Yeah," Molly said. "Whatever it takes to get Mom to quit going through all my stuff. This is it, right, Mom?"

"Whatever, Molly." Amy laughed, walked toward the van with her box.

When the entire load filled the back of the van, Mr. Adams, wiping his sweating neck with a bandanna, asked, "We done now?"

"I think so," Amy said. "Would you like something cold to drink?"

"Yes, ma'am, I would. A nice glass of ice water would be great."

She walked into the house, kissed her children, hugged Carol Anne, and thanked them for helping. "I'll be right back."

She grabbed a glass of ice water from the kitchen, then walked through the front hall to Mr. Adams. She glanced at the hall table with an empty space above it where a mirror used to hang. She cringed at the memory of Phil hurling the book into the mirror, of the diamond cross dangling from his fingers.

She opened the top drawer of the table and stared at the necklace she had hastily thrown there. She lifted the chain and pendant, and then closed her fist around them. It was time, past time to give it away; she opened the front door and handed the water to Mr. Adams.

He chugged the water and handed the glass back to her. "I'm sure the Foundation appreciates all these donations. Thank you, ma'am."

"There's one more thing I want to give away."

She opened her fist and reached her hand out to Mr. Adams. "Here, take this, too."

"Diamonds?"

"Yes. Please take it."

"Are you sure you want to give that away? Really sure?"

"Very sure."

"Well, thank you. . . . Have a beautiful day." Mr. Adams plucked the necklace from her fingers and walked down the front steps toward his truck.

She turned back to the house. Phil stared at her through the screen door; he'd watched her give away the necklace. She hadn't even heard him come home. He wiped his face with his hand and turned away. She didn't call his name, didn't reach for him, as there were times when he couldn't face her desperate need for forgiveness and reconciliation.

Carol Anne came out, hugged Amy goodbye. Amy sat back down on the swing and closed her eyes until the lowering sun slid behind the house and she shivered. She walked into the house to climb the stairs to her bedroom and grab a sweater.

She stopped short at the bedroom doorway: Phil's things. His blessed and scattered things: his ashtray with coins, pen and gum wrappers on the dresser, his comb on the highboy, his dirty shirt in the laundry pile, his book open with reading glasses hanging crooked on the bedside table.

She sat on the edge of the bed and touched his book and glasses. A rustling noise came from the bathroom and she glanced up; Phil leaned against the door frame, stared at her.

She lifted his glasses. "Your stuff."

"Yes."

"Thank you, Phil." She started to cry, reach out her hand for him. But he didn't move and her fingers found only air. She closed her hand into a fist and dropped it onto her lap.

"You know—if you wanted me to listen, there were better ways to tell me than running off with Nick Lowry."

"I tried."

"You didn't think I cared. You didn't think I heard you."

"Yes—but that's no excuse."

"You know, I've done everything I can to take care of you—to prove I love you. Why didn't you just tell me?"

"I don't know. That's what I'm telling you now—it was something horrible of me—not you. I was afraid to tell you I felt ignored or extraneous, and I was scared to talk about how seeing Nick made me feel. It was horrible, and I wanted to be who you wanted me to be. And yes, I was afraid you wouldn't hear me anyway."

"You could have tried."

"I know." She dropped her face in her hands. "I know. I'm a coward."

"No, you're not that at all."

For a second she expected his touch. Yet it did not come.

"These"—he swept his hand across the room—"are just my things."

She nodded.

"I'm here for all of us—for the family."

"You aren't . . . here for me?" she asked.

"Yes and no. I love you." He exhaled a shaky breath. "I want . . . this. All of this. But these are just things. I'm still not sure how much of me is here yet."

She nodded again, bereft of any more explanations or arguments. She closed her eyes and listened to his familiar footsteps on the uneven pine floors as he walked out of their bedroom. When he was gone, she stood and walked to the dresser, ran her hands across his pocket change and pens, and wept.

Chapter Thirty-three

Nick threw the trawler's rope to Revvy on the dock and smiled. "Man, I don't remember the last time I felt this good."

"I don't know how. Damn, you haven't slept since we started this company six months ago. I don't know what you're runnin' on—but I wish I had some."

"Lost time, buddy, lost time. And you don't want any of that."

Revvy wrapped the rope around the cleat and looked up. "No, thank you. I'll just keep the time I've got."

Nick stood and stretched his back, leaned into the wind. "I smell rain."

Revvy lifted his head. "Yeah, it's in the air. Not many tourists want to head to the islands in the rain."

"Good. We can catch up on the research project." Nick jumped onto the dock. "I'm out of here."

"Where you headed? Wanna grab some dinner?"

Nick smiled; he'd worn this same goofy grin since the day he and Revvy had hung up the pine etched sign LOWRY LOWCOUNTRY and underneath in smaller letters: RESEARCH, ED-

UCATION AND WILDLIFE PRESERVATION. Even after he knew what to do, it still had taken months to get the business running and the lab set up.

"No, man, I'm headed back to the lab—wanna check on the dropwort experiment."

"Take a break, Nick."

"Not now, Rev. Not now."

Nick understood what waited for him if he stopped and took a breath—the abyss he'd fallen into the first time he saw Amy again. He knew what he needed to do, what he wanted to do now—even if he couldn't do it with the woman he most loved. His misspent life was not Eliza's fault or Amy's—it was his.

He jumped into the cab of the pickup truck and headed for the dirt and shell driveway behind the tin-roofed lab he and Revvy had bought with every bit of money he'd saved. He'd made sure to set aside enough money for his boys and Lisbeth, for alimony and child support. He planned on spending as much time as possible with his kids.

Eliza—well, he couldn't fix her pain. He couldn't love her the way she deserved—for who she was and not for what she did. She said she'd wait, and he'd held her and told her not to, but she had insisted she would. It wasn't hard between them—but then again, it never had been hard, only empty.

The hectic pace at which he now operated was a making up for lost time—doing everything he'd meant to do. Only he was to blame. It was he—not Eliza—who needed to pay for his sins. Thinking of all his missed chances and might-have-beens did him no good when he should be thinking about his new company, reconciling with his children.

The pit in his gut reminded him that he'd forgotten to

eat again. He pulled into the first place he saw: Heaven's Deli. They had the sloppiest, most tender oyster sandwiches in town.

He was still in his truck when the front door of the deli swung open and a woman walked out alone, carrying a sack and swinging it next to her leg. She had on a pair of jeans and a white button-down shirt. A familiar ache of loss washed over him.

Amy.

A black cord hung around her neck with a single shell from Oystertip—a token of appreciation from the OWP. Norah had made one for each of them. His larger shell necklace was in the glove compartment right now.

"Oh, Amy." He groaned as he gripped the steering wheel.

He could run after her again, feel the longing rush through him, but it would paralyze him. He would talk to her, see her, feel her; then he would wander through the maze of what he loved and needed but couldn't have.

He shook his head, rubbed his eyes. She wasn't everything he loved and needed, no matter how she overshadowed the rest. He couldn't get lost now—not just for Amy, but for himself.

He closed his eyes and leaned his forehead against the steering wheel. Would the ache ever leave? Would he ever be able to breathe correctly when he saw her? To not weigh every action with her against the past and then the future?

He lifted his head and she was gone. He looked behind him as she pulled out from her parking space. He wanted to share with her what he'd discovered about himself in the days he'd spent alone on Oystertip Island—that he was ashamed he'd never really loved his wife for who she was, and that Eliza had to be the one to tell him this. He wanted to tell Amy how one morning, in the soft, filtered light drifting through the live oak above him, he'd understood that even if he couldn't be with the woman he was meant for, at least he could be the man he was meant to be. He'd have to keep these revelations to himself for now.

But he hadn't kept the dropwort plant and bald eagle's nest he found on Oystertip to himself—he'd taken proof of both to the Heritage Program in one last desperate attempt to redeem his mistakes by saving the island.

He grabbed his shell necklace from the glove compartment, clasped it tight in his fist, let the rough edges rub against his hand. He allowed the memory of Amy in the deserted house to wash over him one more time, glanced at the shell before placing it back in the glove compartment. He took a deep breath and jumped from the truck to grab an oyster sandwich, then headed to his lab to check on his research.

For him, there were no second chances—only second choices.

Epilogue

Amy stood on the back porch of the Summerhill Home with her class behind her, their pencils scratching with the sound of dry leaves underfoot as they sketched the columns of the back porch. She stared out to the backyard gardens of the antebellum home, and as often happened in quieter moments of beauty, the memory of Nick washed over her. Over the past year and a half only time had forged whatever good could have come from what had happened with him.

She'd been right about Oystertip—it must have called to Nick from its lush depths because while camping in his self-imposed isolation he'd found a dropwort—an endangered flowering plant—and a bald eagle's nest. Both these discoveries were the final proof needed for a Heritage Trust from the Department of Natural Resources. After the article in the *Darby Chronicle* had come out, donations flagged for Oystertip had come pouring in. The land was now designated as a Heritage Preserve, and the Trust had purchased it from Mr. Farley.

Amy's love for preservation now had an outlet as she

and Carol Anne worked together on historic homes, their clientele rising in both number and stature. They were doing what they loved—together; their energy poured where it was wanted and needed. The flow of clients increased every day, and Carol Anne was hiring more employees. Her clients signed waivers stating they came to her of their own free will and she didn't take them from Mr. Farley, who lost most of his clients from the negative publicity over his plans to develop Oystertip. He was still ranting to whoever would listen about the evil ways of Carol Anne and Amy; he seemed to be tolerated in Darby as an amusing attraction.

Jack was dating a darling blonde from a family Amy had never heard of. The day Molly graduated with honors and obtained a full tennis scholarship to Saxton University was one in an increasing number of days when Amy knew she understood her place in the world.

She was still attempting to speak her truth to Phil, and her heartbeat had begun to return to the reliable rhythm she once knew—a scar over the softer places of regret, remorse and shame. Phil's hard-won attempts at caring and listening were endearing, and at times amusing.

She didn't blame Phil for what happened between them—even in her worst moments she knew it was a weakness within her—but the pain allowed them to talk about what they thought was missing in their marriage and life, and what they could do about it because they loved each other—then and now.

It was a long, circular journey that on her best days—like today—she was sure she could make, and on her worst, she was scared she wouldn't be able to finish.

Although there were moments when she wanted to know how Nick was, if he was all right, she hadn't contacted him. She did see the advertisement for Lowry Low-country in the SCAD newspaper with an explanation of the research and education he provided, and she'd smiled. At least he was doing what he always said he would.

Life's rhythms had returned both at work and at home; she was content in this comfort. As her students worked on their sketches, she leaned against a peeling pillar of the Summerhill Home and stared at five men clustered around a fading live oak, apparently evaluating its ability to withstand another day—or century.

The late-morning sun poured, distilled, through a wrought-iron fence surrounding the yard, illuminating the dark bulk of a man bent over the base of the tree. The other men watched him pull back a layer of moss to expose a root, run his hand across it. The scene contained a sharp, cut-glass quality and this time she understood the preternatural clarity: the honed edges of the leaves, the waves of light seen in flowing air, the punctuated outline of the man's body—clarity that came with her body's recognition of Nick.

Nick stood and, as if she'd called his name, turned and looked directly at her. She half-lifted her hand under what felt like an unnatural weight in the air. Nick moved toward her as if she'd crooked her finger and motioned for him. Maybe she had.

He reached the bottom step of the porch and looked up at her; his hair was a thousand different colors in the sun. She walked down three concrete steps to the soft ground to join him. She lifted a hand to shield her eyes from the sun and walked away from her class. He followed her until they stopped at the iron fence. She turned and stood underneath the shadow of a magnolia tree to face him.

He reached his hand out, brushed the tips of her hair as

if touching the outline of a painting, or just the frame; she didn't move.

"Amy."

"Hello, Nick." Her voice was too loud, or maybe too soft.

"How are you?"

She waved toward the tree. "Trying to save . . . that tree?"

"Yeah, the garden has . . ." He looked off to the group of men, then back at her. "Amy, how are you?"

"Oh, Nick, how are *you*?"

"I'm fine. Busy. A lot of work."

"I saw . . . you started your own company. Research—" She started to cry and squeezed back the tears.

"Yep, with Revvy."

She wanted to cry so badly, to reach for him and sob into his flannel shirt. "I'm proud of you."

"Don't be."

"I am. Are you still in Garvey?"

"No. I moved out. I'm in Savannah now—a studio apartment overlooking the river. You'd love it."

She wanted to groan, but didn't. "Are you okay? You and Eliza?" Her hand fluttered in the air.

He looked away. "No."

This time she did groan. "My fault. God, I'm so sorry."

"No." His hand lifted as if he would touch her; then he dropped it. "Never your fault. It's all mine. Everything's mine."

"If I hadn't—"

He placed an index finger on her lips. "Shh. No."

She was dizzy. "Your kids."

"Well, Lisbeth is involved with school and not speaking to me . . . but I hope, every day, for it to get better. I keep on tryin'. I see the boys as much as I did when I lived at home. They stay with me on the weekends and"—he lifted her chin with his finger to make her look up at him—"and I miss you."

"Oh . . . oh."

"I've wanted to tell you so many things—like how I'd always blamed you, then Eliza, and now . . . well, now I just blame myself. I'm the only reason we're not together." He was whispering now. "I used it all as an excuse not to do what I wanted, needed to do. But, Amy, knowing all this doesn't stop the love."

She covered her face with both hands.

"The hell of it is that, of all the parts of you that I love, one of them is your devotion for your family. And that same quality in you is what keeps you from me. But I need to know that you're gonna be okay . . . that you *are* okay."

She looked down to the leaf-strewn ground, shifted her feet. "It's been so hard."

"What we were—no, what we have, doesn't that ever just come . . . crashing in?"

"Yes . . . once in a while, in a wave or a flash, and I try to let it pass and continue on my way . . . home."

"For me, nothing about us passes."

"Don't say that. I can't . . . fix that."

"I know you can't."

She reached out her hand to him, then pulled it away. "I have to . . ." She motioned toward her class.

"I know."

"Please be okay," she said.

"I'm trying." He placed his fist over his chest. "You live here, Amy."

She began to turn away, then looked back at him,

hugged him. He folded her in his arms and grasped the back of her neck.

"God, I love you, Amy."

She touched his cheek, turned, then walked toward her students. She placed her hand over the space between her breast and stomach: the resting place of Nick and all he seemed to occupy within her, and told herself that he was the sand pattern left by the wave, not the wave itself.

She turned to look at him one more time, backlit against the sun. But he was gone—only a shiver of disturbed air remained.

LOSING *the* MOON

Patti Callahan Henry

This Conversation Guide is intended to enrich the
individual reading experience, as well as encourage us
to explore these topics together—because books,
and life, are meant for sharing.

A CONVERSATION WITH PATTI CALLAHAN HENRY

Q. What inspired you to write this novel?

A. I wanted to portray the multiplicity of ways in which desire affects even the most settled life—how desire can reveal to people who they really are, and shine a light on aspects of their character that they have been ignoring. As often happens when a writer tackles a vague idea, I began to ask, "What if?" What if your son or daughter began to date your first love's son or daughter? What if there were unresolved issues that echoed during the years when you and your first love didn't see each other?

The endless complications and multifaceted dimensions of love and desire fascinate me—the promises these feelings prompt us to make. I have been married for thirteen years and dated my husband for four years before getting married. The richer connection that grows in a stable marriage is often different from the relationship one has with a first love. I didn't begin to date my husband until after college, so he was not my first "boyfriend," and although my husband is nothing like either Phil or Nick in *Losing the Moon*, I wanted to portray two entirely different types of love: first love, with its intense emotions; and marital love, with its subtler, potentially deeper rewards.

Q. Losing the Moon is your first novel. Can you tell us something about how you became a writer, and what led to this publication?

A. My first novel—actually a memoir—was called "My Life" and was never published. I wrote it when I was twelve years old. Although I've been writing ever since then, professionally I pursued a medical career. I am a nurse with a master's degree in pediatrics.

Four years ago, I finally understood that writing is all I've ever really wanted to do. When I knew I had no choice—that writing was a necessary part of who I was—I pursued it as seriously as I did my master's degree. It became essential that I take classes, read books on writing, and actually write every day.

Writing and selling this novel required an incredible belief in myself, along with persistence, courage, faith, serendipity, and a willingness to study the craft of writing. The catalyst for each step of the journey was the decision—the commitment to write. For more on my writing and publication history, visit www.patticallahanhenry.com.

Q. The setting of Losing the Moon, *Georgia's Lowcountry, plays an important role in shaping the story and its characters. Why did you decide to set the novel there, and what about that part of the country particularly inspired you?*

A. The moss-draped Lowcountry is where my heart truly resides, where I feel the most alive—as if I can hear the earth's heartbeat. I believe people have a landscape or geography that speaks most clearly to their spirit. I grew up spending summers on the craggy coast of Cape Cod and maybe that's where the sea and marsh began their call to me.

I consider the Lowcountry setting to be as essential a

character in the novel as the people who occupy it. I chose the Lowcountry for Amy and Nick because it is seductive—lush, overgrown, frivolous, passionate, mystical, and dangerous, just like Nick and Amy's relationship. My intention was to use the setting both to bring them together and to echo their dilemma.

Q. The idea of a former lover who reenters a woman's life in her middle years seems to have enormous appeal to women. Judging from your own experiences, and those of your friends and family, why do you think that is?

A. A woman's middle years seem to be a time for reevaluating life. How did I get here? Do I want to be here? Have I made the right decisions? This is when questions rise to the surface, when the exhaustion of raising young children may have worn off and women revisit their life goals. Memories of a past love, and the feelings associated with it, may also return when times are hard or when life seems emptier than one expected—one may then imagine the "road not taken."

Often (not always, by any means), memories of a first love carry a strong sense of possibility and passion. Memories of these feelings—the pungent, almost innocent and intense emotions of first love—seem easier, simpler than the complicated emotions involved in committed or broken relationships. Of course this is just an illusion, but first love seems to carry a certain longing and reminds some women of a time when love wasn't so much an act of will, but of pure, raw sensation.

Q. At the beginning of the book you quote a passage from C. S. Lewis's The Screwtape Letters. *Why did you choose that particular sentence? How does it relate to the book, and what personal meaning does it have for you?*

A. C. S. Lewis (1898–1963), a scholar and teacher at both Oxford and Cambridge Universities who is best known for his Narnia Chronicles for children, was an atheist for most of his early life, but he converted to Christianity in 1931.

A talented debater and writer, Lewis published many works on a wide variety of topics—but the subjects that most interest me, especially as a writer, revolve around his exploration of human longing and the search for meaning. His writing has inspired me since I read *The Lion, the Witch, and the Wardrobe* as a child. *The Screwtape Letters* offers profound insights into human nature.

The quote I chose echoes the theme of Amy and Nick's story. When the novel opens, both of them have become deadened to their feelings about their lives, marriages, and goals. First, they need to *feel* again. Seeing each other is the catalyst that raises "them to a level of awareness where mortal sin [becomes] possible." But the sin is only possible—they must choose whether or not to act on the temptation. I believe it is most often a person, and the emotion that person evokes, that raises another person's awareness.

Amy and Nick have become "passively responsive" to their lives, marriages, and circumstances. They've quietly accepted the way things are. Seeing each other, remembering what they felt for each other, and what they meant to do and be in life marks a new beginning and a major dilemma for them.

Q. Losing the Moon is told in the third person, using "she" and "he," from Amy's and Nick's points of view. Yet as a reader, I feel as if I am right inside their heads, almost as if the book were told from the first-person "I" point of view. Can you tell us why you chose to use third person, which sometimes creates more distance between the character and the reader, and how you keep the reader so in touch with Amy's and Nick's thoughts and emotions?

A. I originally wrote this story in the first person, from Amy's point of view, until I realized how strong Nick's story and motivations were. When he stepped (or, rather, strode) onto the page, I understood the story must also be told from his point of view. The novel then moved into the third person in the next draft. There went my original idea that I just had to write the novel once, and it would be ready for publication!

The third-person point of view can create some distance, but in this case I worked hard to not just narrate the events but also to convey Nick's and Amy's unique emotional *perspectives*. Amy's "voice" as well as her perspective is completely different from Nick's voice and his perspective on the same events.

Memory and desire are the key ingredients in this story. The reader must be able to feel Amy's and Nick's longing and understand their reasoning to become fully engaged in the story. I wrote each scene asking what each felt—what the particular place, action, interaction meant to them.

Q. You're a wife and the mother of three small children. How do you manage your hectic schedule and still find time to write?

A. Ah, the bottom line is that I don't *find* the time—I *make* the time. Right now I am typing downstairs early in the morning while my three children are asleep upstairs. I have about fifteen minutes before I must wake them for school.

Although writing has always been a constant desire, the commitment came to me four years ago. We tend to fill our lives with so much "to do" that we forget "to be." And part of writing involves allowing the "being." I had to reassess my commitments and obligations, then let go of certain activities to allow room to write. But I felt I had no choice— the writing was too important.

Most days I rise before the sun to write. I also carve out specific times during the day. I believe this is very hard for all writers—especially when they are unpublished. Making and committing time is difficult in the blazing glare of the critical world with its demand to know exactly what you are doing with your time.

I've made a commitment that I believe in and I do it even when I don't feel like it. That said . . . achieving balance is a battle I win some days and lose many days. But writing is a joy and a journey. When I get it all just right, I'll let you know.

Q. What did you hope to achieve in writing this novel? What did you want to convey most strongly to readers? Do you feel you succeeded?

A. I hoped to write a story that would accomplish several things: touch the heart, maybe inspire a few people to consider what they most long for, and finally, to entertain and spark some interesting discussion.

I attempted to show that we all have places or people in our lives that—if only for a moment—make us feel like the people we were always meant to be. Often people abandon their dreams until someone or something comes along and awakens them. Then the question becomes—can the person, place or thing that awakened our desire satisfy it, or are they only a reminder of what we really want, who we really are? Each person will have his own answer to this question. I only give you, the reader, Nick's and Amy's answers.

Only you, the reader, can tell me if I've succeeded in all I set out to do when I wrote *Losing the Moon.*

Q. What writers are particular favorites of yours and how have they inspired you? What are you working on now?

A. As I mentioned before, my avid reading began in childhood with C. S. Lewis and *The Lion, the Witch, and the Wardrobe* and E. B. White's *Charlotte's Web*. As a teenager, I read Margaret Mitchell's *Gone with the Wind*. Madeline L'Engle, Anne Lamott, and Julia Cameron have deeply influenced my view of the art of writing. These days, I adore the wit and wisdom of Deborah Smith and Dorothea Benton Frank. I admire the imagery of Elizabeth Berg and Anita Shreve.

The lyrical prose, deep emotion, and excellent craftsmanship of novels by Anne Rivers Siddons and Pat Conroy amaze me. These writers somehow know how to take the deeper places of hurt and transform them into poetry. I don't believe there is anything they've published that I haven't read. That Deborah Smith has compared my work to theirs leaves me speechless.

Beyond that, I'm now deep into writing my second novel and am saving for another time lots of wonderful work by writers I greatly admire.

QUESTIONS FOR DISCUSSION

1. Seeing Nick again produces a strong reaction in Amy—a heightened awareness of her physical surroundings, a rush of memories, conflicting feelings of attraction and wariness. Why do you think her response is so immediate and intense? Have you ever encountered someone from your past and responded similarly?

2. Meeting each other again reminds both Amy and Nick of the young people of passion and promise that they were long ago, and makes them aware of the compromises and accommodations they've made in their marriages and in their lives. Discuss how each character is different now from what s/he was in college, and list some of the dreams they've given up or modified. Is "giving up" a natural and inevitable part of life? What dreams have you abandoned? What accommodations have you made?

3. What role do you think desire plays in bringing Nick and Amy together again? Both of them feel abandoned—how much does that unresolved abandonment play into the desire they now feel for each other? Have you ever been abandoned, rejected, or betrayed by someone, and yet continue to feel strongly drawn to him or her?

4. The rebirth of desire comes to Amy as her children are growing up and beginning to leave home. Does that have

any influence on her new relationship with Nick? Is Amy more vulnerable at this time of life, or could their affair have happened at any time?

5. As the novel progresses, Amy comes to believe that the universe is bringing her and Nick together—through their children, their mutual interest in Oystertip Island, and all the circumstances of their lives. Is this just a way for Amy to excuse her behavior with Nick? Or do you agree that some larger force is at work to unite them, and if so, why?

6. What does it mean when Amy says she has "lost the moon," and how does she find it again?

7. Discuss the roles of Eliza and Phil in the novel. Do you like them and sympathize with them? Do you feel you know them by the end? How do they change during the novel and what new understanding do they gain?

8. Do you like the way the book ends? Did Amy make the right choice? How do you see Amy's and Nick's futures unfolding?

9. Part III is prefaced with a quote by Alfred North Whitehead: "The only joy to be trusted is the joy found on the far side of a broken heart." What does this mean? How do you think it applies to Amy and Nick? Does your own experience support or contradict this statement?

10. Do you have a former lover or spouse with whom you've lost touch? How do you think you would react if you saw her/him? Are there things you wish you could say now that you didn't say then? Is there a small part of you that is still bitter or regretful because s/he got away?